ALASKA'S FIRY

Cheryle Coapstick

／

Acknowledgments

This novel was inspired by stories I heard from my Mother and Papa Bill. The photograph of Firy and Anna Marie used on the cover was taken in the late 1930s.

Bodie Thoene: your texts and phone calls encouraged me to keep going. Your friendship is treasured.

Kay Frey, Jo Hamilton, and Maureen Harlan: your suggestions gave me direction.

Denise Phillips: from the beginning, you declared I was a writer, even when I remained unconvinced.

Toni Enos: your statements of "That's Alaska" meant more than you know.

Vicki Karlsson: your vigilance on comma patrol was invaluable.

Patty Huey: you refined me as a writer.

Linda, Ron, Patty, Jesse, and Olivia, members of the Pond and Parchment Writers Guild: you gave honest and helpful critiques that were needed.

Sam O'Neal, editor: your insights gave the story a richness and the characters a depth that was needed.

Andy Towler, designer, formatter, and all-around tech person: your grace and patience walking me through the process calmed me. Your design of the cover is perfect.

My deepest gratitude is for my Lord Jesus: The Shepherd who carries His broken lambs. Redeemer. Sustainer. Healer. King.

PROLOGUE

Aleksandrovsk, Russian America
The Mid-1800s

Most women in the village declined to accompany their men in winter. Not so Matrona Balashoff. Salty sea air, clear skies, and cold waters made her shiver with anticipation. This year, the hunger in her belly added to it.

It had been a harsh winter, and game was scarce. They had eaten all the dried salmon and muktuk. Father Munin said the trading vessels from Mother Russia would come soon. No one believed him.

Many of the young men had traveled deep into the Kenai several weeks ago. They followed the deer and the elk. They had not returned, and a second hunting party left the village five days ago. They also had not returned.

Three babies had already died. Lack of food dried up their mother's milk. Matrona feared for the children and agreed with the few villagers who said they must take the thirty-foot oomiak into dark waters. The time was not right for salmon or halibut, but maybe they could find a lone seal or whale.

Winter had not given up its possession of the sea. The wind was unpredictable. Dangerous. Yet, most of the elders felt it also dangerous to let their bellies remain empty.

Matrona watched her husband, Gregorii, and her father, Vasilli, as they rubbed an extra layer of whale oil over the seams of the oomiak. Vasilli set his oil aside and began to climb into the sealskin boat. Gregorii took him by the arm and led the old man to

Babushka, his aged wife. Vasilli muttered and moved toward the oomiak once again. His wife held him back.

Gregorii climbed in, but none of the remaining young men followed him. The villagers watched as the Chief and Priest walked away, heads down, shoulders slumped. The Chief would not sanction the hunt, and the Priest would not bless the boat. One by one, the men of the village left until only women and children remained.

There were eleven elders with Gregorii in the oomiak. It wasn't enough. Matrona raised her brows and caught her husband's eye, then looked into the face of her two-week-old daughter. She handed the baby to her own mother and said, "Stay with Babushka. Mama's going hunting."

She pushed her father away when he would take her place in the oomiak. Vasilli glared as he heard the village women murmur.

"Bad enough she named the baby after herself," one said, "Now she hunts in winter, tempting fate."

"It's one thing to hunt with the men when the weather is good, and you have no children..."

"She is no mother!"

"Ignorant."

"Stupid."

"Enough!" Babushka growled, "You will take care of your attitude toward my daughter and little Matrona, or you will no longer have Babushka to deliver your young and take care of you during your time."

Matrona settled herself in the oomiak as the elders launched the boat. She took the paddle, then lifted her head and put a hand to her chest as a terrible pain shot through her heart. She half rose and pictured herself and the baby at home safe and warm under many furs.

Matrona's milk was gone, but Babushka had a small stash of tinned milk from the Russians if a mother died giving birth and no wet-nurse could be found. Matrona, confident her baby would live, at least for a while, waved to her parents. They raised their hands but did not smile.

The elders decided to sail to Seal Island and return by nightfall. Matrona smiled to herself. These days, the sun's attempts to climb above the skyline failed. They hunted in near darkness.

They caught nothing, so paddled to the ocean side of Seal Island. Hunger hindered their progress. Matrona's and Gregorii's labored breathing and heaving chests gave witness to strong ocean currents and the lack of men to paddle the large oomiak.

Unseen, the storm leaped out of the darkness and pushed them out to sea for a day and a night. The wind smashed the rain into their eyes and blinded them. Two of the elders let go of their paddles to cover their faces.

First one, then another pointed to the failing seams of the seal skin boat. Cupping their hands, they tried to give the water back to the sea. Waves pounded and washed over the ill-fated vessel.

The rain stopped, and the wind died, but the gray arctic fog remained. If the land was near, they did not see it. They could see nothing beyond the faces of those in the oomiak. Gregorii barely made out his wife's features as the weak sun slid through the clouds and dropped into the dark water.

Matrona crawled the length of the oomiak. Exhausted from battling the storm, she curled up next to her husband. He let her sleep. During the night, the fog lifted, and by starlight, he watched the elders, one by one, shed their parkas and slip over the side of the water-drenched boat. Death had come for them, but they chose the time.

Gregorii didn't know if he felt anger or admiration for these old men. He looked away from their silent acceptance that their lives had ended. He prayed Bozhe would find a way to spare him and his wife.

The stars glittered across the now calm sea—no sign of land. Matrona stirred and stretched. The water in the oomiak had soaked through her mukluks and leggings. She shivered. She saw the heap of empty parkas. By starlight, she looked deep into Gregorii's eyes and fought the pain in her chest.

"Pooshkay," he said.

"Yes, my love, it will be what it will be." She thought of all the Russian words he had taught her but would not live to teach their daughter.

"Perhaps it is fitting. We take our life from the sea. The herring, the salmon, the halibut."

"The walrus, the sea lion, the whale."

"Crab."

"Seal."

"Clams."

"And your favorite, sea celery."

They smiled at each other as they listed all that the sea gave. Now they would give back.

Matrona rested her head on Gregorii's shoulder and looked at the Big Bear. She wondered what the women would think when the oomiak did not return. How long would they wait before they blamed her? When would they turn their disdain toward little Matrona?

She shook her head and gave a slight smile. Babushka would pack up in the middle of the night and leave the village if they disrespected little Matrona, and the women knew it.

The oomiak's seams strained and tore apart. They held each other as the frigid sea soaked through their clothing. Numbness crept up Matrona's body. It told her that soon they would be unable to hold each other.

It had been a good life. Did the number of days matter as long as they included salmon and berries? A good man? A child?

Tears froze on her cheeks as she thought of the daughter who would never know her. *Perhaps the fact that I've given her my name will show her my love.* Babushka would tell the little one stories of her mother and father.

"Bozhe is here," Gregorii whispered.

When he told her about the God who lived in a land of strong sunshine and no snow, she asked, "Like summers on the Kenai?"

He had laughed but was unable to explain. Father Munin, who had come with the Russian-American Fur Trading Company, taught about Bozhe and His Great Son. Matrona knew He waited in the sky, beyond the Big Bear in a land of eternal summer.

The Aurora Borealis danced across the night. Its ethereal light prodded her to ask Bozhe to show her the future. She saw rainbows, bright and shiny. Two men stood before this wall of color. One young and handsome, strong and vigorous. The other old, stooped, frail.

"Father, you are the most successful merchant in Kaluga, and you taught me to love Bozhe and do what is right."

Matrona saw the older man's face fall and heard him sigh. He sank onto a bench in front of the rainbow. "What will you do?" he asked his son.

"Russian-America has a great need for lay priests. I will travel with the fur company and speak of Bozhe to our people. I will learn the language of the natives and tell them also."

The old man reached for his son. His heart cracked as he realized he would not see him again. Filled with tears, he took a deep breath and said, "Very well, but you will allow me to finance your journey."

The older man gestured to the bolts of silk, filling the shelves from floor to ceiling. "This is your inheritance. Go and make the Oskolkoff family proud, my son."

The scene changed, and Matrona saw her daughter, grown and running down a beach. Not Aleksandrovsk, but part of the Kenai for sure. The young man from the vision caught her and twirled her around. "Gregorii, put me down! You're stumbling over the children."

Matrona, despite her frozen face and chattering teeth, laughed. Gregorii! His name was Gregorii! *Thank you, Bozhe. They will know us.*

She saw the sun bright on the children's faces, and in the midst of them, she could see descending generations of Balashoffs, Oskolkoffs, and Demidoffs. And in the future, Glaphira Oskolkoff, a girl called Firy.

Their spirits soared as Bozhe took them to a land without snow or darkness.

La Conner, Washington — Present Day

Emma Lee Stanton tucked her keys into her purse and tossed it along with her jacket on the living room chair. "I'm here, Mom."

"I'm in Grandma's office."

"I've got two hours before the kids get home. Where do you want me to start?"

"I've pulled her financials from the desk. You can go through them and her personal papers, too. I'll attack the bookshelves. The realtors will be here first thing in the morning." Sharon pushed her hair away from her face.

Emma Lee sat at the desk and pulled open the drawers. "Mom, do you think Grandma is happy at the care center?"

"I hope so. I feel so guilty for putting her there."

"What else could you have done?"

Her mother turned back to pulling books from the shelves without answering. Emma Lee frowned, then pulled a faded photograph from the chaos scattered across the desk. "Mom, who's the toddler?"

Her mother took the photo but didn't answer.

"Mom?"

"Your grandmother looks about twelve, so the little girl must be her baby sister. I think her name was Anna Marie."

"I thought Aunt Betty was her only sister."

"It's in the past. Leave it alone."

Emma Lee's eyes widened. She opened her mouth to argue, but her mother had turned back to the bookshelves. Another pile of books slammed into the discard box.

Emma Lee tucked the photograph into her back pocket and emptied the desk drawers. She sorted through her grandmother's paperwork, unsure of what to keep and what to discard. She pulled a stack of letters from the back of the bottom drawer.

"Mom, did you know a Miss Ruth? Funny, there's no last name."

"Never heard of her."

"Gramma kept these letters for more than half a century. They must be important."

"Dusty old things. Toss them."

"I don't think so."

Emma Lee saw her mother's lips tighten. Maybe cleaning out Gramma's house was too much for her. "Have you been here all day? I'll put the coffee on."

Her mother leaned against the bookcase and sighed.

"Have you eaten, Mom? You look tired."

"I just want to be finished." Sharon pushed the hair out of her face. "Too many memories."

Emma Lee set the stack of letters aside. She'd read them tonight.

The dining room decor straight out of the 1940s echoed the music of that era. An aide wheeled Gramma to the table. "Tea?"

Emma Lee nodded and commented on the room's furnishings. The aide said, "Our research shows clients' memories are enhanced by surroundings and music from their past. Listen, your grandmother is humming along to Glenn Miller."

"Looks like she wants to get up and dance."

"Most mornings, if she's up to it, we take a little stroll around the courtyard. Her legs are weak, and her balance is unsteady, but I guide her, and the wheelchair is always near-by."

Emma Lee smiled her thanks and placed the packet of letters on the table. Gramma took them and held them close to her heart. "Miss Ruth, have you come for tea?"

Emma Lee frowned, "Gramma, it's me."

The aide set two mugs of hot tea on the table and whispered, "If you can, dear, play along."

"Won't that confuse her even more?"

"I've been working with Alzheimer's patients for twenty years. I don't care if they talk about what happened yesterday, fifty years ago, or somewhere in between. I've learned they're more content if we're with them, whatever time they're inhabiting."

Emma Lee nodded and patted her grandmother's arm. "Yes, Firy, Miss Ruth has come to tea."

"Excuse me," interrupted the aide, "We've been saying 'firey.' No wonder she didn't answer."

"When it's printed, it looks like it should be said that way."

"She sometimes seems fearful, poor thing, so 'feary' is appropriate." The middle-aged aide reached over and patted Firy's shoulder, "She's one of my favorites."

"Mine, too," Emma Lee didn't like the idea that her grandmother was often fearful, but who wouldn't be in a place like this, a disease like that?

Firy seemed unaware of their conversation as she counted out sugar cubes and said, "Let's drink it the Russian way."

Emma Lee watched her grandmother place a sugar cube between her teeth and sip the tea through it. She'd never seen this before, but she followed suit and wondered what else she didn't know about this woman.

Emma Lee placed her hand on the bundle of letters. "Tell me about Indiantown."

"I was six when we left Indiantown, and I wanted it to rain. I remember I wanted it to rain."

Emma Lee leaned back in the chair, closed her eyes, and let the words form pictures in her mind.

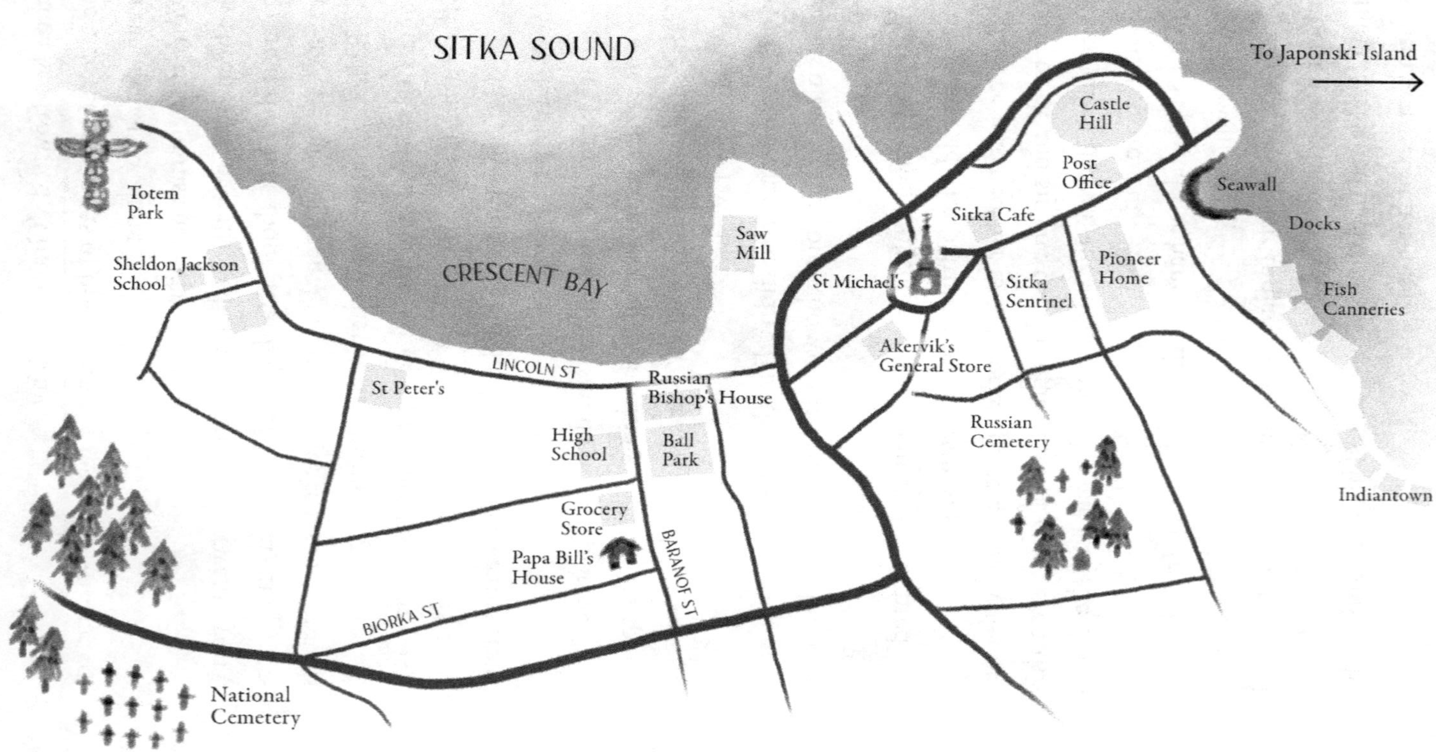
Map of Sitka
1930s-40s
SITKA SOUND
To Japonski Island
Totem Park
Sheldon Jackson School
CRESCENT BAY
Saw Mill
Castle Hill
Post Office
Seawall
Docks
Sitka Cafe
St Michael's
Pioneer Home
Sitka Sentinel
Fish Canneries
LINCOLN ST
St Peter's
Russian Bishop's House
Akervik's General Store
Russian Cemetery
High School
Ball Park
Grocery Store
Papa Bill's House
BARANOF ST
BIORKA ST
Indiantown
National Cemetery

ONE

Sitka, Alaska 1932

Firy Oskolkoff pulled the stained salt sack curtain away from the window, even as her little sister, Elizaveta, tried to snuggle. Firy turned away and wished she had her own bed, rather than this too small cot.

The sun, yellow and round like one of Mama's lemon drops, painted the houses and sheds of Indiantown. It shouldn't be shining on a day like today. She let the makeshift curtain fall back and pulled the covers over her head.

"Firy," Mama said.

Firy's face scrunched, and she blew out the breath she'd been holding. Oh, how she hated that name. When first starting to talk, little Elizaveta tried to pronounce the Russian "Glaphira" but said "feary" instead. Soon everyone called her that, and she complained to Mama.

"I tell you often to love Bozhe and do what's right, but let your name be a reminder of something else you will need in this life."

"What, Mama?"

"Sometimes, you will need to be fierce. Firy sounds like fierce."

"Fierce?"

"Strong and brave."

Firy needed that reminder today because they were getting a new papa.

She had frowned when she first heard, but Mama said, "Don't be sad," and rocked her as if she were a baby.

Firy punched the pillow and buried her face. She pictured the faces of the four papas she could remember and forced herself to lie still. She mustn't disturb Elizaveta, and she hoped Mama wouldn't see her anxiety.

In the beginning, some papas acted friendly, but it didn't last. Then Firy dragged her younger sister behind couches or under kitchen tables to hide. She cupped her hands over Elizaveta's ears and whispered, "Close your eyes and pretend we're gathering shells at Sandy Beach."

Firy pushed herself further under the covers and remembered how her older brother Henry, armed with his slingshot, often marched toward the papas and yelled, "You leave my mama alone!" She could still see him getting smacked across the face or shoved across the room.

She squeezed her hands into fists and slammed her eyelids shut as memory after memory crawled into bed with her.

When the papas found her alone, they warned, "It's our secret. Be nice and don't tell." Firy pushed those memories deep into her soul until they lay dormant.

Mama had put up with a lot from the papas, but if she saw them turn on Henry, Firy, or Elizaveta, she smiled her pretend smile. The one that meant, *You don't know what I am thinking.*

When the papas went to work or fell asleep from too much to drink, Mama led her children away.

If the fish were running, Mama walked them to the edge of Sitka, beyond the docks and canneries to the area known as Indian-town. The canneries ran twenty-four hours a day, seven days a week during the fishing season. Mama usually found work even though she hated the noise and smell. After a ten or twelve-hour shift at the conveyor belt where hundreds of fish rolled by and were grabbed and gutted by Mama, she shuffled home exhausted, ears ringing from the loud clanking machines. Wet. Cold. Hands frozen. Fingers stiff from hours of gripping the sharp knife. Bits of blood and scales stuck to her clothing.

Firy always ran to hug her, but Elizaveta held her nose and said, "Fishy Mama, you stink." Henry appeared when called for supper, and he wouldn't hug anyone, ever.

Behind Petrov Bravebird's was a storage shed for his fishing gear. He put two cots and a small table in it and made it available whenever Mama appeared in Indiantown. For a portion of her wages, they not only had use of the shed but ate all their meals with the Bravebird family.

Firy begged to live next to them forever, but Mama said, "We must learn to live the white way. Even the Alaska Native Brotherhood says we must become totally civilized and completely assimilated to obtain full citizenship."

Firy didn't know what all those big words meant. Just the same, she'd rather have a fishy mama with no papa.

When the fishing season ended, and the canneries shut down, Petrov Bravebird said they could stay and pay later, but Mama refused. When Firy wailed, Mama whispered, "Bozhe, forgive me, I cannot be in debt."

Firy patted Mama's cheek, and her arms circled Mama's neck. "Okay, okay." If Mama didn't want debt, it must be bad.

Joey Bravebird and his five brothers lived their whole lives in the same big house. Most of the homes in Indiantown were large, two-storied structures. Unpainted, the cedar planks weathered to a silver-grey. Several families of the same clan shared each dwelling.

Crowded. Noisy. Happy. Firy couldn't imagine. Still, Joey's mama had died, and his papa left, but his grandparents seemed nice.

Firy and her brother and sister fell into the Bravebirds' routine. Joey's grandmother fed them. His grandfather told them stories of the Tlingit and Haida and some about Mama's people, the Yupik. Firy liked to listen to Mr. Bravebird's stories. She thought he might be a nice man but knew most weren't—especially papas.

She rolled over and pulled the thumb from Elizaveta's mouth.

"Get up, girls," Mama shook the covers. "Time to go."

Elizaveta, with her dark hair and eyes, was the image of their mother. She crawled over Firy and held her arms up. Mama scooped her up, looked over Elizaveta's head, and spoke to Firy. "The way of the native people is lost. We must become a part of the white world. Come, put your things in this bag."

Mama threw the covers back and handed Firy a salt sack. All the cannery workers were allowed to take the empty bags, and Mama had stocked up. Mama packed the Beautiful Corner and great-great-grandfather's samovar.

"Hurry, children. Papa Bill is here."

Firy hid behind Mama and only peeked at the new papa. Tall, eyes creased with laugh lines, or maybe they were just wrinkles, the man leaning against the wagon seemed familiar to Firy, or perhaps it was the horse she had seen before.

Mama laughed as she lifted Elizaveta and Firy into the new papa's wagon. Henry aimed his slingshot at the horse's rump, caught Mama's eye, and put the weapon in his pocket. He scrambled in by himself.

Firy, sandwiched between Henry, a year older than she, and Elizaveta, a year younger, crouched between the salt sacks and squeezed her eyes shut. Henry and Elizaveta shared their mother's dark skin and eyes. Why couldn't she?

Firy's skin was several shades lighter, and her hair was wavy and brown instead of straight and black. The kids in Indiantown either ignored her or taunted her and called her 'white Indian.' They knew she didn't belong. When Petrov Bravebird heard them, he took a stick and chased them. Firy never looked to see what happened when he caught them.

Now this lean, but well-muscled, sandy-haired stranger named Bill was taking them away from Indiantown to somewhere else where she wouldn't belong.

Joey and two of his little brothers ran alongside the wagon with their slingshots. A large pebble hit the new papa.

"Scram, you filthy siwashes." Bill's face, weathered by Alaska's harsh climate, scowled. He flicked the reins, and the wagon lurched forward.

"Bill!" Mama's voice was shocked.

He turned toward her. "How you can stand to live in Indiantown among those—"

"You know I'm Creole, Bill," Mama answered. "Russian AND native."

His muscles bulged as his grip on the reins tightened. "I won't argue about this, Anna. You are Russian."

"I look native," Mama turned away and muttered, "because I am."

"You look Russian, especially when you wear your hair up. And I love your high cheekbones."

Mama frowned and did not answer.

"You understand, kids? Anybody asks, you're Russian." He didn't wait to see them respond but turned back to his wife.

"Problem solved."

"Yes, Bill."

Firy thought he sounded angry, and Mama sounded sad, but she saw him reach over and take hold of Mama's hand. Still, his mean, hateful word echoed in her mind, and his mad face stabbed her heart. She lifted her head and stuck her tongue out at this papa's back, glad he and Mama did not see.

The storm slammed out of the sky like a cast-iron skillet. Hard. Black. Solid. Rain pounded the wagon. Mama shook a blanket out of a salt sack so her children could huddle under it. Elizaveta pulled it over her head. Henry declared blankets were for babies and fired his slingshot's pebbles into the wagon wheels' muddy ruts.

Mama tightened her headscarf and leaned against the new papa. Her head barely came to his shoulder, even when standing. The rain dripped from his beat-up hat, but he didn't seem to notice as he put his arm around her and pulled her close. "You are as pretty as the first time I saw you. On the beach. Middle of the night. Afraid. Remember?"

Mama smiled as the wind blew and the horse snorted.

The creak of the leather harness, the rattle of the wagon wheels, convinced Firy she had huddled here before. It was more a feeling than a memory, and she fought against it. Firy shrunk down between the salt sacks, clutched the damp blanket tight, and hated the rain she had longed for.

They rolled past the place where the Russian barracks had been. This new papa said the town was building a home for old sourdoughs there. Firy shivered and put her hands over her ears. She wouldn't listen to anything he said.

They followed Lincoln Street east of St. Michael the Archangel Russian Orthodox Church and turned onto Baranof. The horse plodded past the ballpark and stopped near the head of Biorka Street. It was only a mile and a half from Indiantown to Papa Bill's house, but it was a world away.

Unlike the two-storied structures of Indiantown, his house was painted a crisp white and had dark green shutters. A picket fence, also painted white, enclosed the big yard. A shed in the back with a stall for the horse was painted to match the house.

When Papa Bill lifted Firy out of the wagon, she looked over his head in wonder. White curtains billowed in the open windows: real curtains, rain-soaked now but even so—not blankets, burlap, or even salt sacks.

He set her and Elizaveta on the wooden sidewalk just inside the gate. "Two rooms upstairs. One's storage, the other's for you kids."

The children raced to their room. No more sleeping on couches or cots in a shack or rolled in blankets under a kitchen table. Firy stood in the doorway and stared. Elizaveta and Henry rushed past her and exclaimed over everything in the room. Firy saw a bed big enough for her and her sister, covered by a pink frilly bedspread with curtains to match. In the corner stood a dresser with four drawers. One for each of them and an extra just in case. Her fear faded, and she decided this papa was nice, good.

Henry flopped onto a quilt made of old flannel shirts. The single pine bed still smelled of the woods. "Mine! You girls better not touch it." He waved his slingshot above his head.

Ignoring him, they jumped on their pink playground, tossed pillows at each other, fell and rolled across the pink field, then jumped up to do it again.

Henry sat on the bed and watched. He gazed around the room

and fingered the small round rocks in his pocket. Whiz! Ping! A pebble smacked into the window frame, narrowly missing the glass and his sisters.

"Why did you do that?" Elizaveta cried.

"Practicing. If he's not a good papa, I'll get him. I will."

Firy jumped from the bed and smacked Henry in the face with a pillow, hard.

"Ow, that hurt."

"You ruined it, Henry. You just ruined it."

"I didn't do anything."

"Yes, you did!" How could Firy tell him she had pushed away all her doubt and fear about this new papa. The pebbles from Henry's slingshot that whizzed past her head brought new anxiety and suspicion.

He grabbed the pillow, ready to defend himself, but Firy had crawled under the covers and pulled the pink bedspread over her head. Muffled sobs escaped.

Elizaveta tiptoed over to her brother, "What did you do?"

"I don't know." He gestured to the bed then took Elizaveta's hand, "Let's go. She doesn't like anybody to see her cry."

Firy stayed under the covers until Mama called them to supper. She clomped down the stairs, hair a mess, face blotchy. Elizaveta and Henry rushed in from the backyard with cold, red cheeks and happy faces.

"There's a puppy in the backyard," Henry yelled.

"Name's Popeye." Papa Bill said.

"Is he ours?" Elizaveta asked.

"Long as you treat him right."

Firy glared at her brother and sister. How could they look so happy? They didn't know if that dog was safe or this new papa either.

Her eyes traveled around the room and widened. Up near the ceiling, Mama had hung the small triangular shelf she called the Beautiful Corner. It was anchored between the kitchen's north and east walls, about a foot below the ceiling. It held the pysanka, Mama's wooden egg, painted with icons of Mother Mary and Baby Jesus. Her old Russian candlesticks and Bible were also displayed there.

Mama said the pysanka was a symbol of new life and beginnings. Mama, always hopeful whenever she made a new beginning, didn't understand Firy's clenched teeth and held breath. For Firy, those new beginnings were often worse than the old.

Firy gazed again at the Beautiful Corner and thought of all the walls it had adorned. Some not very nice places. She frowned and hoped this life would be a good one. She scrambled to the table when she heard Papa Bill.

"Sit," he commanded as he grabbed a ladle. Mama set bowls of venison stew before them.

"Children, I have something to tell you."

Firy's head jerked up, her eyes widened, and her face paled.

Papa Bill crossed the room and put his arm around Mama as she told the children, "Bill Wall and I are married."

None of the children reacted. Firy reached for a baking powder biscuit. Her brother and sister continued to eat.

Bill frowned, "Do you know what that means?"

Elizaveta shoved a spoonful of stew into her mouth, head down. Firy looked at the new papa from the corner of her eye. Henry shook his head, no.

Mama said, "It means he's your real papa."

"It means," the new papa said as he took his place at the table, "no more moving around from place to place. This is home."

Mama placed a bowl of stew in front of Papa Bill and kissed the top of his head.

Firy nibbled at her biscuit and wondered or perhaps, worried. This papa said they would never move again. Good. He smiled at Mama all the time. Good. He hadn't smiled at her. Bad. He used a mean word. Bad. This papa put a pink bedspread on the bed and real curtains on the windows. Good.

Still, most papas were bad.

After they ate, Papa Bill took green jadeite mugs from a shelf above the wood cookstove and placed a generous portion of brown powder in each. He added milk from a tin can and hot water from the kettle. After stirring, he handed them to his new wife and children.

"On your birthdays and Christmas, I will make hot cocoa. It is a way to celebrate special times." He held up his cup and tapped the others. "This is a toast."

They tapped their mugs together again, then laughed as Elizaveta said, "Where's the toast? I don't see any toast."

Henry drained his mug, then held it out to Papa Bill. Elizaveta took dainty sips and ruined the effect by licking at her cocoa mustache. Firy stared at the hot cocoa, hands clenched in her lap.

"Try it, Firy," Mama said.

Firy took the tiniest taste, followed her brother's example by draining the cup, and wanted more.

Papa Bill's eyes twinkled. He refilled her mug and turned to his wife, "I predict our Firy will love hot cocoa forever."

Mama padded up the stairs and tiptoed into the children's room. Henry, asleep in his pine bed, still clutched his slingshot. She tugged it from his grip and tucked it under the pillow. She pulled Elizaveta's thumb from her mouth and sighed when the little girl rolled over, and the errant thumb promptly found its way back home.

Mama sat on the edge of the bed, "You okay, our Firy?"

"Our Firy?"

"Papa Bill called you that. It means he wants to be a real papa, a good papa."

Firy shuddered, leaned against the pillows, and pulled the covers up to her chin. "Will he find you jobs, and will we have to stay with him by ourselves?"

Mama didn't answer for a long time. Firy lifted her head and saw tears pool in Mama's eyes. She batted at her own, sorry she had spoken.

Mama pulled her close. "Papa Bill works every day at the sawmill. I'll stay here and take care of the house and garden."

Firy felt something melt within her. "You won't leave us alone with him, ever?"

"My sweet girl, is there anything you want to tell me ... about any of the papas?"

Something buried deep within Firy stirred. Memories meandered, then meshed, then formed themselves into images that hovered behind her eyes. She squeezed her lids so tight her face hurt. The memories with their foul scent crawled along her skin, seeking, probing, penetrating. Firy held her breath and tried to force the evil back into the deep. She could not lift her head.

"No, Mama."

Mama sighed as she tucked her daughter in and kissed her good night. "Poor little one, only six years old...."

"Almost seven," yawned Firy.

"Not for a while yet." Mama tried to smile and failed. "It makes me sad to think of all that's happened ... all my fault. I love you."

"Me, too."

Mama stood in the doorway while Firy settled, then turned and went downstairs. Firy heard her whisper, "Oh, Bozhe, sometimes it feels like love is not enough.

TWO

Most days, Firy looked out the window and watched the tide ebb and flow. She paid attention to readin', writin', and 'rithmetic when Miss Swearinger grabbed her by the hair and pulled, lifting Firy to her toes. The teacher, cumbersome and bulky, was as strong as a she-bear and just as ugly. Some of the kids thought she looked more like a walrus, with long teeth that resembled tusks. All agreed she was as unpredictable as any of Alaska's predators and just as strong, even if she was old and grey.

Firy gritted her teeth and blocked out the teacher's angry words. Miss Swearinger's hands never lost their grip, even when her spittle sprayed Firy's face.

Whenever Miss Swearinger's breath gave out, she wheezed and shuffled to her desk and pulled chocolate out of the bottom drawer. Her cheeks bulged as she stuffed them with a confection most of her students had never tasted.

Firy slumped into her seat, silent and stoic. Harsh words and spit were a small price to pay for the luxury of looking out the window all day.

Miss Swearinger couldn't move her since the school board decreed students sit in strict alphabetical order. Firy, glad Papa Bill made her use his last name, enjoyed staring at the bay with its variety of seabirds.

Stupid, dumb, white school. Why couldn't she go to the Sheldon Jackson School for Natives like Henry? Why did she have to go to school at all? She turned toward the window once more.

Grey gulls and black ravens, seeking food, reminded Firy's stomach it was almost lunchtime. She sneaked a peek at the big clock on the wall. Nine more marks until both hands reached the twelve. She patted her belly and told it to settle down.

The bay drew her gaze again. Fishers went to sea, miners to the mountains, and loggers into the forests. Cannery and sawmill workers, shopkeepers, and boat builders stayed in town. The natives and Creoles hiked deep into the woods to hunt deer and brown bear. The native women gathered berries, wild onions, sea celery, and ferns. But the fourteen white students here were prisoners in the Russian Bishop's House.

Firy sighed and looked at the clock again. Four marks until Miss Swearinger reached for the bell on the corner of her desk.

Whoever decided to hold classes in the Russian Bishop's house lacked wisdom. Built by the Russians more than a hundred years ago, the house had double walls insulated with tons of sand from the nearby beach and double-paned windows, making it one of Sitka's warmest buildings.

All the mothers in Sitka knew schools should not be across the street from beaches. Too many of those mamas questioned their children after school. "Where are your shoes and socks?"

"I left them on the beach."

"What happened to your books?"

"The tide came in, washed them away."

In the winter, they saw wet pantlegs and frozen fingers. "I told you to stay out of the water."

"We were trying to get a starfish."

"Look at your hands. They're turning blue."

"My gloves floated away."

This past week Sitka's mamas praised the Lord. The Tlingits were building a traditional seventy-foot cedar canoe and had taken control of the beach at Crescent Bay. Miss Swearinger confined her students to the Bishop's yard during recess. No students of hers were going to mingle with the local native clans. The children prayed for release, and ancient Father Alexi was the answer to their prayers.

Flanked by several young lay priests, he opened the door to the classroom and beckoned the teacher to join him in the hallway.

Miss Swearinger frowned and turned the page of her lesson book. The black-robed, stern-eyed priest thumped his staff on the wooden floor. At the sound, heads jerked to see the teacher's response. She bent over a stack of papers and picked up a red pencil. Heads swung toward the priest.

Thump. Thump. Eyes flashed, and he banged the staff again. Its beaten gold overlay glistened under the crystal lamps hung from the ceiling.

Miss Swearinger jabbed the pencil into a mason jar and stood. The frown never left her face as she crossed the room. She glared at the children and hissed, "Quiet!" then closed the door as she stepped into the hallway.

Even with their ears pressed against the door, they heard nothing except the staff thudding. Once. Twice. Three times. They scampered back to their places as hinges squeaked, and a subdued Miss Swearinger returned to her desk, frown intact.

Father Alexi came to the front of the classroom, "While some neither recognize the cultural significance nor the historical importance of certain local events, I do."

The grind of the pencil sharpener claimed their attention. He glared at the teacher and lifted his staff. Before it hit the floor, she let go of the hand crank, and unsharpened pencils fell from her other hand. They clattered and rolled across the floor.

Miss Swearinger's red face and pulled down eyebrows told the boys and girls she was about to explode. They held a collective breath. Would she erupt in front of the Father? They waited, fear in their eyes but also gleeful anticipation.

The priest ignored her and continued. "The school board has decided to let you witness the blessing of Raven and Eagle's canoe. These two moieties have come together, and it will be an educational and cultural experience for you."

Their applause was cut off by the teacher's mottled face and burning eyes and by the Father's raised eyebrows. He cleared his throat and gave each of the fourteen students a long look.

"Observe in silence. Show respect. Native ways are not our ways, and often," he cleared his throat again, glanced at the young priests with him, gripped his staff more firmly, and continued, "not the best ways."

Father Alexi's words drifted away as he gazed out the window at the clans' wild dancing around the cedar canoe. He sighed and thumped his golden staff. "Come, children."

Their eyes widened, and they looked toward Miss Swearinger, expecting an objection. None came.

Books closed. Papers rustled. Feet shuffled. Father Alexi pointed his staff at the students. "The fathers and I will escort you to the beach. Stay together and remember, no talking."

Last in line, Firy looked over her shoulder then wished she

hadn't. Miss Swearinger, eyes scrunched up, pounded the desk. "I'm a teacher. He has no right, even if the school's in his house." She ground her teeth, "Going to see heathen Indians and their stupid canoe. They'll pay. All of them."

Firy shuddered and remembered the day Papa Bill enrolled her in this school. Firy dreaded each step that brought them closer to the Bishop's house. The Bishop lived upstairs with Spode china the Russians had imported from England. Priceless icons and tapestries from Russia adorned his private chapel. It was even said he had a golden samovar and teacups. Firy wondered if she would ever see such precious things. The main floor's reception rooms housed the school.

Today Father Alexi, freed from his priestly garb, looked to Firy like a grandpa man. Grey hair and beard, long and flowing, masked the sternness usually seen in his face. He rose from his knees and met them by the gate.

"Your flowers are looking good, Father."

"Thank you. Can I help you?"

"No, sir, just going to register our Firy for school."

"Anna agrees?"

"Her idea, Father."

Father Alexi's eyebrows almost left his face. A long look passed between the two men, and then the priest opened the gate. He placed his hands on Firy's head and murmured a blessing, but she didn't look at him or say amen. Father Alexi sighed and followed them into the building. He gave Papa Bill another long look then went to his quarters on the second floor.

"I'll have no native children in my classroom." Miss Swearinger sniffed.

Firy looked at the floor. Papa Bill jerked Firy's head up and growled at the teacher, "Look at her. She's white."

"But, I'm..." Firy wanted to protest, but the look on Papa Bill's face stopped the words. She trembled and kept her eyes on the floor.

Miss Swearinger pulled a hanky from the sleeve of her blouse and blew her nose, "Her skin is light, I'll grant that, but I heard your wife is a—."

"Be careful what you say." Papa Bill's voice whispered as he took a step closer and towered over her.

She backed up against the desk. "Are you threatening me?"

"Certainly not." Papa Bill said with the pretend smile Firy knew he learned from Mama. "I'm simply telling you I'm related to half the school board, and I convinced them to my way of thinking. You're new to Alaska, a cheechako."

Firy tried to hide behind Papa Bill as Miss Swearinger said, "You guarantee she's white? She's your daughter?"

Firy's fingers hurt as Papa Bill squeezed her hand tight and said, "Her name is Firy Wall."

Firy's heart pounded faster than Petrov Bravebird's drum during Tlingit ceremonies. She knew Papa Bill didn't exactly tell the truth. Papa Bill wasn't her real father, and Mama was Russian and native all mixed together.

The sound of Miss Swearinger's voice and the wrinkled anger on her face made Firy think the teacher knew it, too. Firy ducked her head again and held her breath.

Several thumps on the floor above them turned Miss Swearinger's eyes toward the ceiling. Her shoulders slumped, and she stuffed the snotty hanky back under her sleeve and snarled. "See you don't cause me any trouble."

Firy peaked around Papa Bill and nodded but knew being in the classroom would be trouble enough.

As they left, Firy asked Papa, "What was that noisy thumping?"

Papa's eye's twinkled, but all he said was, "I think you have an ally."

Firy trudged along beside him. She didn't know what an ally was and didn't ask.

The very next day, when Firy entered the schoolroom, Miss Swearinger grabbed her. The teacher's claw-like hand clamped Firy's shoulder, "Children, this is our new student."

She wrote Firy's name on the chalkboard. "Funny name. F-u-r-y sounds like furious or some furry animal.

"My name is F-i-r-y."

"Don't contradict me." The claw tightened, and Firy winced. The students looked everywhere except toward the front of the room.

"Be careful around this girl. Furious."

Miss Swearinger gave her a shove, and Firy stumbled to her seat. Tears clung to her lashes, but she didn't acknowledge them. The teacher said she was furious, but Mama said fierce. Poor Firy didn't know the difference.

Low tide. Dry sand. Warm sun. Raven and Eagle swarmed over their cedar creation. Eagle motifs would be etched into one side of the canoe and Raven on the other. The elders sat in the dugout, and Father Alexi pronounced the blessings.

Firy glanced at the townspeople hovering nearby. She saw Ade Bunderson, who had married Mama's sister, Ollyanna. Mike Evans, who owned the Sitka Café. His wife, Agrafena, was also a native. Firy couldn't understand why some people hated the natives, and others married them. It didn't make any sense. She shook her head and refused to think about it.

Young Jake Steiner and that old Russian, Ivan Mishkin, rounded out the group. Thankfully, Papa Bill had a day shift at the sawmill. School or no school, he wouldn't want her here.

Old Man Budnikov brought his pushcart and sold coffee and sandwiches as if this were a baseball game. She heard the men from the café complain and condemn Budnikov for charging them double what they would have paid at the café.

Ivan Mishkin glanced at Mike. "You let him make us pay more?

"It's a free country, Ivan." Mike shrugged, gulped his coffee, and held out his mug for more. "This is Budnikov's business. He can charge what he wants, nothing to do with me."

"Here you go, Mike. For you. Is good? Yes? Like café, no?" Budnikov filled Mike's mug to the brim.

Ivan spat out his coffee. "Mud."

Jake Steiner, the youngest man to ever pilot a shore boat, threw a couple of driftwood sticks. Popeye and several town dogs chased them. "Ivan, old man, enjoy the sunshine. Watch the natives."

"Better I watch dog." Ivan kicked at the stick Popeye dropped at the old Russian's feet.

Firy gave a low whistle to fetch Popeye, then paid attention to Petrov Bravebird and Father Alexi. She kept one ear tuned to the men of the café. They had been interfering in her life ever since Papa Bill married Mama. At least they didn't mind that Mama was native. The café was one of several places in town that welcomed natives, as well as whites, even the Asians that worked in the canneries were welcome.

"Better I stop at café," Ivan moaned.

"You could have filled a thermos at home," Ade said.

"Olga say coffee and talk waste of time. She not know men decide important things."

"Important things? Like what?" Ade said.

"Like where natives get log. Government land, I think."

"I saw a federal agent out here earlier." Jake said, "He and Petrov Bravebird were going at it."

Firy looked toward the native elder who gave no sign he had heard, although the men did not bother to lower their voices.

"The agent waved his arms and yelled, but I didn't see Petrov respond," Ade said.

"Better when Russia have Sitka."

"Don't get started, Ivan. We don't want any lectures today." Jake said and winked at the others.

"You have no respect for elder."

Jake laughed, "As the youngest member of your café pals, I certainly respect the fact that you married a woman twenty or so years younger than yourself and have five beautiful daughters."

"I hope I have that much stamina when I reach your age," Ade, nearing forty, said.

Ivan shook his head, "You Swede, not have stamina of Russian."

Ade grinned and shook his head. He scratched at his blond stubble and refused to be baited.

Ivan bought another cup of coffee, muttering the whole time about cheating Russians. Budnikov had to pry the coins out of Ivan's clenched fist. Ivan endured Budnikov's tongue lashing, then turned his back and muttered, "Mud."

Budnikov snatched the nearly full mug and dumped the coffee on the sand. Ivan fisted his hands and took a step toward the coffee seller.

"Hey, boys," Sam Mitchell, Sr., editor of Sitka's weekly newspaper, called, striding in their direction. "What do you think about all this?"

"My opinion is fact of matter..." Ivan began.

"It's definitely not," Mike said.

Ivan scowled, but Firy laughed. Not too many people were interested in Ivan's opinions, although he liked to voice them.

Sam, his shabby suit coat and unruly longish hair both flapped in the breeze, said. "I have quotes from the Alaska Native Brotherhood, the Federal Bureau of Indian Affairs and Land Management, and the Tlingit elders. Now I need quotes from the townspeople."

"What does the Brotherhood say?" Jake rubbed his upper lip and wished he had an old-growth mustache like Ivan or even a pencil-thin one like the newspaper editor.

"They're against building the canoe." Sam sighed, "They say to show the US government the natives are ready to receive citizenship, they must give up all the old ways."

"Is good." Ivan slapped his knee.

"So, Ivan..." Sam replied, "are you ready to give up your Russian holidays, customs, and food, even the Russian language?"

Ivan bristled, "Is different."

"What about Miss Ruth?" Ade asked the editor.

"She agreed with Petrov Bravebird and some of the elders that it isn't necessary to abandon your heritage to pledge allegiance to America."

"Where she is?" Ivan asked.

"Some fancy doings at one of the churches," Sam replied,

"but she was here last week when they floated that log down from the Tongass."

"Government land!" Ivan yelled.

"It's off the record." Sam shook his head then rubbed his hand over his hair. "Everybody knows that's where it came from, but nobody will say so." Disgust dripped from his features. "You won't see that detail in the paper."

"Back to your question, Sam," Ade said, "I think it's good to remember some of the old ways, and it doesn't matter to me if they got that cedar on federal land. Too much government interference anyway."

"Law is law!" Ivan hollered and slammed his fist on his knee.

Jake finished his coffee and laid his hand on Ivan's arm, "You are the most law-abiding man I know."

"Yes. True."

"When it suits you." Jake finished and rubbed his nearly non-existent mustache again.

The others laughed, and Ivan scowled. Budnikov refilled Jake's mug for free and glared at Ivan, "Hunting and fishing law not for Ivan, yes? I think you go into Tongass, no? Take Sitka spruce to build boat. Is true, yes?"

Ivan stood and raised his fists again. Budnikov slipped behind the bulky editor and muttered what sounded like prayers. The two bandy-legged old men could have been twins, short, thick around the middle, and utterly convinced, he alone was the only true Russian left in Sitka.

Sam winked at the others, licked the tip of his pencil, put the point to his notebook, and said, "Shoot, Ivan."

Ivan glared and muttered about evil Russians he would like

to shoot.

"Ivan, I do want your opinion." the editor said.

Budnikov, still behind Sam, breathed easier when Ivan began to pontificate.

When Ivan finally drew a breath, Jake said, "What do you think, Sam?"

"You'll see my story in the Sentinel."

"That won't even give me a clue about what you think," the young man snorted.

The editor chuckled as he stuffed his notepad into his pocket, "That's as it should be, boys. If you want personal opinions, skewed perspectives, and facts that have been washed, rinsed, and hung out to dry, pick up a copy of the Anchorage Daily News, the Alaskan, or even the Seattle Times. If you want the facts of a story told from all sides, read The Sentinel."

The others nodded and turned their attention back to the beach. Prayers said. Dances done. The townspeople drifted back to their daily activities as Budnikov collected empty coffee cups, packed up his pushcart, and left.

Firy's heart pounded as she slipped away from her white schoolmates. Henry, among the native kids from the Sheldon Jackson school, gave no indication he noticed her.

A look over her shoulder told her Uncle Ade saw. He gave her the A-Okay sign. He put his finger to his lips, letting her know he'd keep her secret, then turned toward his café cronies. "Let's go. The tide at Halibut Point is right for clamming."

"I've got to pilot a shore boat this afternoon. I'll catch you next time."

"When are you going to get a real job, Jake? It takes two and a half minutes to cross to Japonski."

"Yeah, but I do it every fifteen minutes."

"Show over," Ivan yelled. "Chowder for supper."

Ade laughed and corralled the men away from the beach. None had noticed Firy.

The copper-skinned native children and Firy gathered around Petrov Bravebird. "Eagle here and Raven over there. Watch as the elder demonstrates how to use the Salish carving tool. Listen as I explain the meaning of each symbol."

Firy, last in Raven's line, stared at her shoes. She wiped her palms on her thighs and clenched her fists. She inched closer and swallowed around the lump in her throat. "Please, please, please."

As the child ahead of her finished, she took a step forward. Heart thudding, palms damp with sweat, eyes on the sand, she held out her hand for the tool.

"You are white," the elder said and turned his back.

Henry took a few steps toward his sister. Her eyes pleaded with him to defend her, but he turned away when his native friends pulled on his arm.

Firy dropped her hand, and shame climbed up her throat like bile. Petrov Bravebird frowned. The lines in his face showed wisdom as well as age. "Firy, you are not Haida."

His voice carried, and Firy knew everyone heard. Shame grew

as she folded into herself.

"You are not Tsimshian."

She lowered her head and closed her eyes.

"This day, I declare you Tlingit," the Raven elder said.

Firy raised a hopeful face to Petrov Bravebird, but behind him, she saw the other natives' frowning faces. Some had turned their backs, although none dared object. Firy's hope shriveled.

"Although your mother is Yupik from the Kenai, I declared her Raven years ago. As her daughter, you are also."

The diminutive Bravebird placed his hand on her head in silent blessing, then gave her the carving tool. Firy, heart pounding like a Haida drum, ignored the hostile eyes of the master carver and cut her mark into the giant cedar.

A small smile reached her eyes. Dare she believe? Firy knew Papa Bill wouldn't like it. Mama was proud to be Creole but said she must learn to live in the white world. Mama seemed to think a person had to be one or the other.

Firy dug at the sand with her foot. Love Bozhe and do what's right. Native? White? Nobody seemed to think it possible to be both. Not Mama, not Papa Bill, not most of the people in Sitka. Firy kicked at the sand again.

THREE

Mama handed Henry his lunch sack, kissed him on the cheek, and pushed him out the door. Once outside, he spat in his palm and rubbed at his face. Looking back, he said, "Hurry up, Elizaveta. You always make me late. Dumb little first-grader."

"Am not. I'm smart. You're just a dumb boy." the girl said as she shrugged into her sweater and jumped down the stairs.

Firy glared after them. Just because her skin and eyes were light, she had to endure Miss Swearinger. Although, if she were honest, she would admit the Indian school had longer hours, more rules, and homework, even for day students like her brother and sister. Still.

Mama turned green, clutched her stomach, and raced to the bathroom. "Go to school, Firy."

The sound of her retching made Firy think she might turn green and retch too. She followed her mother. "Are you okay?"

Mama leaned against the sink and washed her mouth, "Just a tummy-ache."

"It's that baby in there that's doing it."

"It's alright, dear."

"No, it's not. I hate that baby."

Mama hugged Firy, "When you see your little brother or sister for the first time, you are going to fall in love. But now you need to go to school."

"I did first grade already, and the second one, too. I don't need to go anymore."

Mama laughed. "You have so many more years of schooling ahead. Don't waste them."

"I want to stay with you."

Mama ran a comb through Firy's hair and tugged when she hit a snag.

"Oww! why can't I have straight black hair and eyes like you and Elizaveta?"

"I love your wavy brown hair." Mama laid the comb aside and tied Firy's hair back with Papa's big red bandana. "My father was Russian. I loved his curly brown hair and pale blue eyes, a handsome man. You are much like him." Mama squeezed Firy's shoulder, "Your eyes are darker, like ripe blueberries. Be proud of who you are."

"But Mama, the whites say I'm too native. The natives say I'm too white. I don't belong." Firy wanted to ask if her skin was light because her real father was white, but the words wouldn't come.

Mama got on her knees and looked her daughter in the eye. "You belong to Bozhe, and you belong to yourself. Always."

Firy chewed on her lip. "But Mama, I, that is..."

"It's true you must learn to live as a white in the white world, but do not let anyone shame you."

Firy nodded but knew that was impossible. She was neither the one nor the other.

Mama handed her a lunch sack. "Papa Bill worked hard to get the school board to look the other way. Go."

"What are they looking at?"

"Never mind." Mama gently forced her to the door.

Firy dragged herself to the Russian Bishop's house. She thought of how helpful she could be if only Mama would let her stay home.

❦

The end of October arrived, and Mama's screams pierced the pre-dawn peace of the house. Firy met Papa in the hallway. "Last night's storm knocked out the telephone lines. Get dressed and fetch Ollyanna and Babushka."

Papa shooed a sleepy Elizaveta down the street to the Checkinov sisters, "Pound on the door until they wake up," he told her.

Henry had been gone all weekend to a Boy Scout camp out. Hopefully, everything would be over by the time he returned.

Bill checked on his wife, whose pains were closer now. He rubbed his sweaty palms on his pants.

"It's okay, Bill. I've done this before." Her face clenched, and she stifled a scream.

"I haven't." He reached for his cigarettes then pulled his hand from his pocket, empty, "What should I do?"

Anna, between contractions, managed a smile, "I think you've done your part already."

"I mean it, Anna. How can I help you?"

"Boil some water and sterilize a pair of scissors and a piece of string."

"String?"

"Just do it." She gasped as another contraction reached its peak.

He was back too soon. "What else?"

"Put some blankets in the oven to warm."

He returned in a minute seeking another job.

"Where's Ollyanna? I need my sister."

"She's on her way, I think." Bill shoved his balled fists into his pockets. His labored breathing echoed his wife's. Anna's moan morphed into a low growl, then a piercing scream. He wiped the sweat from his brow, "How long is this going to take?"

"Rub my back."

He helped her roll onto her side and rubbed the small of her back.

"Come on, Bill. Put some muscle into it."

"I don't want to hurt you."

"Don't worry about that. Oh, I want to push."

"You can't. I'm here all by myself. I mean, maybe you should wait for your sister."

"I don't know if I can."

"I'm not ready, Anna. Please."

"You're not ready. I'm sorry the baby didn't consult you."

He took her hand and gulped, "I didn't mean anything, Anna. It's just-"

"What?"

"It rips me apart inside to see you in pain. I should never have let you get pregnant."

She laughed and then held her belly as another pain began to rise through her. "It's a little late to be thinking about that."

"I'm afraid. For you." He rubbed his palm over his eyes, most of the fear was for himself, but he couldn't admit it. "I need to do something. Help you."

"There's nothing for you to do." Her voice gentled.

He paced the room, sat down, paced again, looked out the window, reached for his smokes, threw them across the room, and growled, "I need to help you, Anna. Let me help you."

Anna, panting like Popeye after a hard run, snapped at her husband, "Make a pot of coffee."

"Are you sure you should be drinking coffee at a time like this?" He barely asked the question when she screamed again, longer this time.

"Go to the café. Tell Agrefena the baby's coming, and you need coffee. Stay there until I send for you."

His face told her he thought it a brilliant idea, but he took her hand and said, "I won't leave you."

The front door opened, and Ollyanna yelled, "I heard someone's having a baby."

Bill rushed past her without a word. He didn't even stop to grab his jacket.

"Where's Papa going?" Firy asked as she ran up the sidewalk.

"Doesn't matter. Where's Babushka?" Ollyanna said.

"Joey said a baby's being born in Indiantown. On the beach."

"Do you mean breach?" Aunt Ollyanna shook her head, "Let's wash our hands and help your Mama."

Mama screamed, but her Aunt just said, "Bring that stool and sit near the head of the bed. Hold her hand. Talk to her."

"Do I have to?" Firy's panicked voice rose, but Mama didn't notice.

"Firy, you're nine years old. Your mama needs you. Just keep your eyes on her face and talk or sing, okay?"

Every pain Mama felt pierced Firy's heart, and she hated that baby even more.

Mama tried to hold them in, but her moans became wails. Firy's eyes, wild and panicked, latched onto Mama's.

"It's alright," Mama said.

"No, it's not."

Mama panted and grimaced as another contraction gripped her. It passed, and she said, "If it's a boy, I want to name him after

Bill. He's been so good to us."

"If it's a girl, she'll be Anna, after you," Firy said.

"Wouldn't you rather call her Shirley? I know how you love her movies."

There was only one Shirley Temple. This wretched baby was not going to take her name, and that's all there was to it. If there was any hope that Firy would ever accept this baby, "It has to be Anna." She squeezed Mama's hands to confirm her words.

"We'll ask Papa Bill."

The hours passed like a slow tide in winter. Mid-afternoon, Babushka arrived, feet dragging and face frowning.

"The breach?" Ollyanna asked.

Babushka shook her head.

"The mother?"

Another slight shake, then Babushka turned to Mama and held up a mason jar. "Devil's Claw. Fresh batch." She smeared the salve all over Mama's belly and back.

Mama took a deep breath and let it out slowly. "I can't believe the whites think Devil's Claw is invasive and useless. Such a lovely bushy plant."

"They chop it down," Aunt Ollyanna said.

"But we make medicine."

The salve penetrated deep into Mama's cramping muscles. "Thank you, Babushka."

The old Indian woman grunted and examined Mama, "It's time to push. You won't thank me for that."

For the next three hours, Mama squeezed Firy's hand. Firy bit her lip to keep from screaming along with Mama. She stared at Mama's belly and knew the creature within was to blame for everything.

"One more, Anna, just one more push," Babushka said.

"Firy, get the scissors and string." Aunt Ollyanna ordered.

The front door slammed, sleeping bag and knapsack fell to the floor. Henry yelled, "Where is everybody? Where's supper?"

"Mama's having a baby."

"What? Right now?" The boy backed up a step.

"She's been trying to all day. Screaming, too."

"Screaming?"

"It hurts a lot, you dumb boy."

Henry ignored his sister. "What are the scissors for?"

"I don't know."

"Are they going to cut Mama open to get the baby?"

"I don't think so." But Firy didn't sound too sure.

"It's a girl!" Aunt Ollyanna poked her head out of the bedroom doorway, "Bring the scissors and string."

Aunt Ollyanna did something with the scissors that Firy couldn't see, rubbed the baby with salt, wrapped her in a blanket, and held her out to Firy.

Firy shook her head and backed up a step. She looked at Mama, who smiled and said, "It's your little sister, take her. Come sit beside me."

Firy took the baby, who didn't weigh anything at all. The baby's soft light eyes looked into Firy's, and something stirred in the girl's heart.

Henry tiptoed after his sister. "Looks like a lizard."

Firy clutched the baby tight and turned on her brother, "You shut up, Henry. She's beautiful. Her name is Anna, and she's mine."

Just like Mama said, Firy had taken one look at the new baby and fallen in love.

❦

Forks stopped their journey midway between plate and mouth as Bill Wall's stepson busted into the café. "Papa Bill, it's a girl. Mama says you can come home now."

Bill blushed as the dark-skinned boy called him papa, then shrugged the guilt away. He blushed again when forks dropped, and the diners at the Sitka Café applauded his accomplishment.

Agrefena said, "Supper is on the house, Bill."

Ivan held up his hand, fingers spread wide, "Five girl."

Agrefena set his plate down, none too gently, "Full price for you."

Henry tugged on Bill's shirt, "Papa Bill, she looks like a lizard."

"Here we go," Bill muttered.

"So, Bill, you spawned a lizard?" Jake said.

"Must take after your side of the family, eh, Bill?" Ade said, "Certainly not Anna's."

"Always knew you were a cold-blooded reptile," Mike chuckled.

Bill glared at his stepson, who grinned along with the others, although Bill could see Henry's confusion. "You ever see a lizard, boy?"

"No lizard on island," Ivan said.

"In my schoolbooks, Papa Bill. Ugly things."

"So, Bill, you're the father of an ugly thing." Jake laughed, and the others joined him.

"I have a box of cigars at the house, fellas." Bill put his watch cap on and threw his napkin at Jake, "None for you, I'm afraid. Ugly thing, humph."

Jake grinned and slapped Bill on the back, "I'm sure there hasn't been a prettier girl born on this island in the last hundred years."

Bill raised his eyebrows.

"I mean since before the Russians," Jake said.

"Okay. Two cigars for you." Bill followed Henry out of the café.

"Russian girl more beautiful," Ivan said, but nobody paid any attention to him.

FOUR

It was not a happy New Year. The baby, born just over two months ago, was healthy, but mama had not left her bed. She had little energy and no milk.

Every morning, Firy heated tinned condensed milk and water. A few drops on her wrist told her when the temperature was just right.

Mama liked to watch Firy feed the baby. "You're such a good big sister."

Firy's eyes sparkled, "It's like having my very own baby doll. I like her name too."

Mama touched the baby's cheek, "I chose Marie for her middle name because it sounds pretty."

"Shall we use both names?"

"Anna Marie? I like that," Mama said.

Aunt Ollyanna sent to Ninilchik for her and Mama's niece, Masha Demidoff. "She'll earn her keep by cleaning and cooking when she's not attending high school at Sheldon Jackson. Even when you get up and out of bed, you'll be weak. She's needed."

"And she'll take care of the baby," Bill said.

Mama shook her head, "Our Firy will look after Anna Marie."

"She's just nine."

"She's a good little mother already, and she'll still be here when Masha finishes school and goes back home."

Ollyanna said, "I've set a chowder on the back of the stove. It's time for me to get home and feed my own brood."

Bill walked his sister-in-law to the door. "I don't know why she's still so unwell. Doc says the childbed fever and infection are gone."

Ollyanna's eyes looked like dried seaweed. She laid her hand on Bill's arm. "Did he tell you the rest?"

Bill stood mute.

"Cancer."

"Why didn't he say?"

"Anna didn't want you to know." Ollyanna bit her lip, "Maybe I shouldn't have said anything."

Bill stumbled to a kitchen chair and put his face in his hands. He looked to his sister-in-law and mumbled his thanks, then shook his head and said, "I've been threatening the Doc for not finding a medicine strong enough for her pain, but I had no idea," Bill took a step toward her, then stopped. His eyes pleaded, "How long?"

"A year, maybe two. It depends on how fast the cancer grows. My poor sister." Ollyanna's voice broke.

"My wife."

Bill and Ollyanna held each other without words. In a moment, she pulled away and gathered her things. "I'm so sorry, Bill. You are the best thing that ever happened to her."

He felt the heat rush to his face and said, "It's the other way around."

When Ollyanna left, Bill bit his lip until it bled. Otherwise, he would have howled like an arctic wolf. He felt like ripping the door off its hinges but grabbed the doorframe instead and doubled over. His breathing too rapid, his heartbeat too fast, he stumbled into the bedroom.

Anna looked at his face. "You know."

He pressed his cheek to hers, and their tears mingled.

"Doc says maybe the cancer will go into remission. I might get stronger, even get up and around."

"We'll do whatever it takes to make you well."

"I might not get well, Bill."

"We're going to fight this." He smoothed the hair back from her face.

"I'll do my best, but you must promise me something."

"Anything. You know how much I love you."

"Take care of my children."

"Of course. They're my children, too."

"I don't want them going to the orphanage."

He inched onto the bed and drew her close, "I'll adopt them now. Make it legal."

"You're a good man, Bill Wall."

Masha, a fifteen-year-old freshman at Sheldon Jackson School for natives, inserted herself into the household swiftly and silently. Much to Firy's irritation, Masha had the same black eyes and hair as Henry and Elizaveta. They all looked native like Mama. Firy was stuck in the middle, not as white as Papa Bill but not as dark as the others. It wasn't fair. Masha even had mama's high Russian cheekbones and eyebrows as dramatic as raven's wings.

Whenever Masha picked up Anna Marie, Firy said, "That's my sister, not yours."

"She has light skin like you," Masha said, rubbing the baby's forearm.

That almost made Firy feel better, and she said, "I guess you can hold her, just a little."

The days turned into weeks and the weeks, months. The household settled into a sad routine. Anna, weak and lethargic, tried to do a few chores or sit at the dinner table. Most days, she was unsuccessful. Her dark skin sallowed, and her beautiful doe eyes lost their sparkle. Her always slender frame became skeletal, and when she traveled from the bed to the kitchen table or the living room rocker, she had to hold onto the furniture or to Papa Bill.

When he wasn't in school or playing ball, Henry offered to do all the outside chores, anything to keep him away from seeing his sick mother. Elizaveta clung to Masha and wouldn't go near Mama. This made Firy mad, but Mama told her everyone had to cope in their own way, and Firy mustn't blame them.

Mama hoped Firy would remember how she used to look.

Every day, Firy said, "You're still pretty to me, Mama."

Nightly, Bill frowned at the newspaper's articles about the depression. He had lost his job at the mill, but Mr. Robertson, president of the school board, offered him work cleaning the grammar school. Every day Firy changed from school clothes to play clothes and trudged back to help.

"Why can't Masha help you?" she asked Papa one evening. "I need to stay with Anna Marie and Mama."

"Masha has enough to do, cleaning and cooking."

"What about Henry and Elizaveta?"

"You know how your sister putters and never finishes. Henry helps Gram, and you're to start helping out there. I need him to spend more time fishing and clamming. Gotta eat."

Firy knew she was the better fisherman and clammer, but Papa's tone let her know she could not change his mind.

Miss Swearinger graded papers after school. "Wipe those windowsills, again. They're still dirty."

"Yes, ma'am."

"You did a terrible job with that broom. Sweep again."

"Yes, ma'am."

Sometimes Miss Swearinger tossed things toward her wastebasket and missed. "Pick that up, will you, Firy, dear?" The words echoed with false sweetness, and her eyes radiated a perverse delight.

Miss Swearinger missed on purpose. Firy knew that. But she replied, "Yes, ma'am."

Miss Swearinger's attitude carried over to the classroom, "Children, I am happy to announce we have our very own janitor, the only good job for an India..." She let the word hang in the air, "Never mind, but if you drop a piece of paper, Firy will pick it up. Come in with muddy boots, and Firy will clean them. If you see any dirt anywhere, let her know."

School, which Firy had previously tolerated, became torture. Fortunately, most of the kids hated the teacher as much as she did. Their stares of pity shamed Firy, and she turned her head to the window and the calming waters of Sitka Sound.

Firy had finished cleaning the school earlier than usual and raced home. She stood in the doorway and watched Mama with Anna Marie while the rain slithered down the windowpane and cocooned them in time and place. Firy put her hand over her heart. Mama looked more like herself today. Everything was going to be okay.

"Look at how Anna Marie smiles at you and reaches for you. You are such a good little mama. I know Anna Marie will always have you."

"And you, Mama. She'll always have you."

"No matter what happens, I know you will take care of her."

Firy's lip quivered, and her stomach started to spasm. She turned away and forced the fear from her face.

"Bring her," Mama patted the bed. "You, me, and our baby, let's all nap together."

Firy snuggled next to her mother and baby sister. She tried to breathe easy, but Mama's words lingered. She watched Mama and Anna Marie as they slept and wondered what would happen and when.

FIVE

When Mama first got sick, Papa hung a chenille bedspread near the wood cookstove. Behind it, he shoved an old dresser and the brass bed he had bought when he and Mama married. During the day, he tied it back so Mama could see them. When she rested or slept, he let it hang like a drape. It was a signal for everyone to be still.

He kept the fire stoked and said it didn't matter if they sweated, as long as Mama kept warm. Even the dog panted all the time. Other than a few trips outside to do his business, Popeye kept vigil under Mama's bed.

Firy ignored the chenille curtain, climbed on the bed, and tried not to disturb Mama. "You've been in bed forever."

The thin woman groaned, opened her eyes, and said, "How's our Firy?"

Firy swallowed the lump in her throat. "I'm okay, but why don't you get better? It's been over a year."

A canine whine echoed Firy's question. Mama winced, "Have the newspapers come?"

Firy snatched the papers from the kitchen table where they lay next to Papa's dirty breakfast dishes. She scrambled back on the bed, forgetting to be careful. Mama gasped, and Firy raised her hand to pat Mama's cheek but froze in mid-air. She didn't want to hurt her again.

They had always shared the funnies: Betty Boop, Felix the Cat, and Little Orphan Annie. Today Mama let the papers scatter across the bed. She closed her eyes, and her cheeks lost color.

A tear crawled down Firy's cheek, and she batted it away. "It's okay, Mama, I'll do the voices. You rest."

Papa pulled back the chenille, cheeks unshaven, and eyes wet with tears, "Pick up the papers, girl, and get off the bed. The Fathers are here." He turned and left as abruptly as he had come.

Poor Papa, I bet the Fathers woke him up. He took care of Anna Marie during the day, then cleaned the school while Masha babysat. On weekends and some nights, he picked up odd jobs to stay ahead of the bills for Mama's medicine. When they couldn't get it, the doctor said to give Mama whiskey until she didn't feel any pain.

Firy remembered when whiskey was against the law and Uncle Ade hid bottles of it in the hold of his fishing boat. Bottles that his friends had smuggled into Alaska from Canada.

Firy liked it better when Mama had real medicine. It didn't smell bad or make Mama confused and cranky.

Cousin Masha had taken Henry and Elizaveta to the Saturday matinee a little while ago, the new Shirley Temple movie. Now that the Fathers were here, Firy wished she had gone.

She stacked the papers on the dresser and dove under the bed as Father Alexi pushed the chenille aside and stepped into the makeshift bedroom. He greeted Mama in Russian.

Firy pushed Papa's suitcase out of her way and cradled Popeye in her arms. She could only pick out a word or two. Russian school had stopped when Mama got sick.

She heard a match flare, and soon the sticky, sweet incense became thick in the room as Father Alexi swung his silver censer over Mama's bed. The prayers droned on, and Firy buried her face in Popeye's fur.

After the final amen, she turned her head and stared at four black boots peeking out of long dark robes. They looked alike, these men in black. Full beards, high headpieces, large crosses on heavy gold chains, and wire-rimmed glasses. Did all priests have bad eyes or only the Russian ones?

The black boots turned, and Firy pushed Popeye away, stretched her cramped legs, and rolled over. She stared into a young Father's face. He had crouched down and peeked under the bed!

"Ah, Glaphira, there you are," he said as if she sat in Mama's rocker. "It's good to see you taking such good care of your Mama. I am Father Mikhail, Father Alexi's new assistant."

"They call me Firy," she looked past him but did not see Father Alexi. The young priest reached for her hand, pulled her out, and winked, "Let us get rid of these dust rabbits. Your Mama would be distressed to see you so."

"I know," she whispered, brushing at her clothes, glad it was not Father Alexi who saw the dust rabbits. She glanced and saw Mama had her eyes closed, then laughed out loud when Mama whispered, "Bunnies."

"Yes, bunnies," Firy repeated.

Father Mikhail made the sign of the cross over Mama and shook Firy's hand as if she were a grown-up. "I must hurry to catch Father Alexi. Can't disturb his schedule, you know."

The girl watched him leave. Cheerful. Friendly. She wondered why he was a priest.

Later Firy ladled soup into a mug and brought it to Mama. "I don't think the Fathers' prayers are any good."

"Hush, child. It's not for you to say what will become of their prayers."

"But Mama, you're getting sicker."

"Bozhe might have another plan for me. Promise me that no matter what happens, you will always love Him."

"Alright, Mama, because you say so." Behind her back, where Mama couldn't see, Firy crossed her fingers.

Mama motioned her closer. "Next time you are at the church, ask to see the tapestry on the south wall."

"I've seen it, Mama. Saints Peter and Paul and the Holy Mary. It's pretty."

"I did some repair work on it with a thin gold thread. On the back, it's all knots and tangles. On the front, you see the glory of Bozhe. Life often looks tangled and knotted, but we will be on the other side when we get to heaven. Do you understand?"

"Sure, Mama," said the girl looking down at her too small, well-worn shoes, "But I want you to stay on this side of the picture. Tapestry, I mean."

Mama tried to hug her but didn't have the strength. She fell back against the pillows and whispered, "Promise me... love Bozhe. Do what's right."

Firy nodded, fighting tears and guilt. No longer did she and her siblings attend St. Michael's. It had been difficult even when Mama took them. Standing for the three-hour services wearied them, and they often sank to the floor. Mama portioned out lemon drops as they leaned against her.

They peeked around her legs and waited for Father Alexi to notice and glare at Mama. He could do it without losing a single word of his sermon. To Firy, his eyes seemed to scream, "How dare you let your children disrespect the church and me?" Mama simply reached for more lemon drops.

Nowadays, Papa sent them to St Peter's by the Sea, Episcopal Church that he had attended as a boy. Across the street from Crescent Bay, the church led Firy and her siblings to discard their shoes and socks and make their way to Sunday School through wet sand and cold surf.

Firy loved the missionary ladies, especially Miss Ruth, who sat on the floor with them, handed out graham crackers, and told Bible stories. She spoke English, not Russian. Best of all, the Father, who traveled between all the Episcopal churches in Southeast Alaska, presided over services just a few times a year.

The guilt of not going to St. Michael's or its Russian classes after regular school gripped Firy's stomach. She looked at Mama, pale, shiny with sweat, almost asleep. The need to rid herself of the pain in her belly was too great.

"Mama?"

"I know, darlin'. Did you think you could go to St. Peter's without Father Alexi knowing? I told him you had my blessing."

"I don't go to Russian class either. After school, I come straight home."

Mama's eyes misted, but she smiled, "I'm glad you want to be with me."

Several days later, Firy wedged herself between the dresser and the wall. She crouched as low as possible and watched as the neighbor ladies took care of Mama. Aunt Ollyanna called Masha out of the kitchen. "You're old enough to help."

Masha stood in the doorway until Aunt Ollyanna gestured toward the dresser. Masha picked up the brush and comb and looked at her cousin huddled on the floor. Firy saw teardrops dancing on the end of Masha's lashes. Firy hated the look of pity she saw behind those drops.

Masha didn't speak as Firy turned her head away and pulled up her knees. She didn't want anyone to see Mama like this. She wanted to slap the women's hands away as they removed Mama's nightgown and bathed her still body. Firy hid her eyes, and that feeling hit her in the stomach again. The one that attacked when things went terribly wrong.

The women talked about food for the funeral and which of Mama's two dresses they should use for her burial. They decided on the yellow rose print because Mama loved it when the flowers budded and the sun stayed longer.

Aunt Ollyanna shared her memories. "Do you remember when she..."

Vavara Checkinov sniffed back her tears and chimed in, "I will never forget the time she..."

A couple of the older ladies talked about Mama as a young girl. Firy tried to picture that. Would Mama like her? Firy decided she and little girl mama would have been best friends. For a while, she pictured them finding shells on Sandy Beach or watching the fishing boats, but she couldn't keep the image in her mind. The women's chatter interfered, and Firy wished they would go away and leave Mama alone.

She took a deep breath and let it out slowly. Aunt Ollyanna looked her way. Her eyes widened, but she gave a slight nod and turned back to braiding Mama's long hair. When they finished, she called the men from the front room. Firy hid her eyes and dragged her sleeve across her nose when they carried Mama's body to the kitchen table.

The men moved all the chairs except one to the front room. The mourner's chair, next to Mama, would be occupied until they buried her after the funeral tomorrow evening. Tradition demanded it.

Papa settled himself and reached for Mama's hand. Henry said he would run away if they forced him into that chair. Elizaveta cried. Papa closed his eyes and sighed. Firy laid her hand on papa's shoulder. "I'll do it, Papa. I'll take my turn and Henry's and Elizaveta's too." Firy wasn't sure if he heard her, but Masha said it was okay.

Aunt Ollyanna put her arm around Masha and whispered. Masha shook her head, and Ollyanna gave her a little shove. Firy saw her cousin look at the Beautiful Corner. Mama always said it was like having a small altar in the house, a reminder that Bozhe was watching.

Firy covered her mouth as Masha stood on the kitchen stool, took the pysanka, laid it on Mama's chest, and then placed Mama's hand over it.

Aunt Ollyanna whispered to Firy. "Glaphira, I think it is fitting for the egg to go to heaven. When you look at the Beautiful Corner and do not see the sacred pysanka, look with your heart and see your mama beginning a new life in heaven. She will present the pysanka to Bozhe to give to His Great Son."

Firy stood mute, unable to breathe past the hardness in her throat. She did not understand how putting Mama and the egg in the ground would send them both to heaven.

Papa had made a pine coffin and leaned it against the back porch. The men would put Mama in it tomorrow night, and the family would lead the procession from their home through town to the Russian cemetery, on the hill, high above Indiantown. Men would carry the coffin above their heads with family and mourners following.

At three in the morning, Masha stoked the woodstove, then woke Firy, "It's toasty in the kitchen, but you can bring a blanket, and there is a pot of cocoa on the back burner."

Cocoa was for special occasions. This occasion was horrible, and she would remember forever, but it was no celebration. Firy would not drink the cocoa. Maybe she would never drink it again.

The moon, shining through the kitchen windows, cast fearful shadows across Mama's cold, pale face. It was Mama. Firy knew that. But at the same time, it wasn't, and she knew that too.

Masha spoke around her yawn. "I would stay if Aunt Ollyanna didn't have so much for me to do tomorrow."

Firy saw shadows under her cousin's sad and worried eyes. "It's okay, go to bed."

"Are you sure?" Masha gave her a long hug.

Firy nodded. She didn't sit until she heard the stairs squeak. Even though the stove burned with good Sitka spruce, Firy shivered for reasons her little girl's mind could not articulate.

She had spent most of the day under this very table. People came and went, paying their respects. Sometimes, she leaned her head against Papa's knee as he sat in the mourner's chair. Mid-afternoon, the door flew open, and Father Alexi entered with an entourage of young priests. No one spoke. Women and children moved out of his way; men nodded.

He made the sign of the cross over Mama's body and lit his censer. When the house reeked with the acrid scent of his prayers, he left. The young priests scampered after him like a flock of young ravens.

Firy crawled out from under the table and stuck her tongue out at Father Alexi's back, then threw her hands over her mouth. Whew! Papa didn't notice, and the other mourners had resumed their conversations or were making their way to the samovar for more tea.

Miss Ruth saw and beckoned. Firy felt sinful as she crossed the room, so kept her eyes on the diamond pattern of the faded linoleum. The tall, slender missionary lady almost looked like the Russian priests. She wore a long black dress that covered her from neck to ankle. All that was missing was the high headpiece. Instead, Miss Ruth's white hair was piled into a bun on the top of her head. She had wire-rimmed glasses like the priests. But goodness, she had real American cowboy boots on her feet.

Firy took Miss Ruth's outstretched hand and let the old woman lead her out of the back door. Their eyes did not meet. They sat on a log in the back yard facing away from the coffin.

"How are you, dear?"

The girl shook her head.

Miss Ruth pulled Firy onto her lap. "It's okay if you cry."

Firy shook her head again.

Miss Ruth gently rocked her back and forth. "Tell me about your Mama."

"Sick."

"And there was no money to go off-island for treatment? Juneau? Seattle?"

Firy shook her head.

"What did your Mama like to do?"

"Sing, read the funny papers, go to church."

"And what did she say about church?"

"Respect Father Alexi even if he's mad."

Miss Ruth frowned and held her tighter. "Is that why you stuck your tongue out at him?"

The little girl squirmed. "Mama didn't say he was mad exactly, but he looks that way."

"Hmmm." Miss Ruth hugged her tighter.

"She wants me to do what's right, love Bozhe."

"Your Mama was wise. You must always love God."

They sat together for a long time. Silent tears fell from Firy's eyes, which she ignored. Miss Ruth reached into the deep pocket of her black skirt and pulled out a small bag. How did she know about lemon drops? Firy looked at her in wonder while letting the drop melt in her mouth.

The clouds covered the sun, and Miss Ruth said she had to go. Firy had been pretending the lap she sat on was Mama's. Miss Ruth must have known because she gave Firy an extra hug. "Always remember, Firy, Bozhe loves you. If you sit still and breathe as slowly and quietly as you can, you will feel His arms around you."

Firy sat on the log for a long time.

The moon crawled across the sky; the fire in the stove burned low. Firy wondered if she should add another log but didn't want to leave Mama. She bit her lip. Not true. She wanted to be in bed with the covers pulled over her head. Sitting alone with her mother's cold body and the noises of the night made her shake.

The clouds in front of the moon darkened Mama's face. An owl flew past the window, and Firy jumped. Popeye whimpered. He pushed his nose into her knee. Even though her heart pounded and her hands shook, she rubbed his ears. She longed for the comfort she would find under the table with him but remained rooted in the mourner's chair.

She saw the pysanka in Mama's hands. The flat images of Mother Mary and Baby Jesus stared at her. Perhaps if she put the egg back where it belonged, things would go back to the way they were. She reached, but her fingers closed above it as the placid Mary gazed at her.

Firy wondered if Mama lived in heaven with Baby Jesus now. Aunt Ollyanna said so. Others said Mama slept, but that wasn't true because she wouldn't wake up. The more Firy thought about it, the less sense it made.

She wanted the sun to chase away the darkness. She wanted it to be the day before yesterday when Mama was alive. No, she wanted it to be when Mama wasn't sick at all. Firy's eyes emptied until she had no tears. Whether Mama slept until grownup Jesus came to wake her up or drank cocoa at heaven's table with Baby Jesus, Firy hoped it would be okay.

"I want to love you, Bozhe." She almost felt His arms around her.

SIX

Firy grabbed the strap, pulled it across her shoulder, and jammed it into the buckle of her overalls. She jerked the sweater off the hook and yanked it on. Her breath came in short, staccato bursts as she stomped to the shed and grabbed that sorry excuse for a bicycle. Bad enough, she had to share it with her siblings. Not fair. She did most of the work. By rights, it should be hers alone.

As she pedaled the mile to the post office, her thoughts bounced around her head like tires off the rocks of the unpaved road. Stupid, old woman! Why can't she live in town like a regular person? We have electricity now and indoor plumbing. It's not like we live in the old west.

She supposed the north had more of an effect on them than their westerly-ness if that was even a word. *Don't start with me!* she barked at that part of her brain that always distracted her with random thoughts. *She's a stubborn old woman, and we're the ones who suffer for it.*

Every Friday, she and Henry took turns caring for Papa Bill's grandmother. Why couldn't Masha do it so Firy could stay with Anna Marie?

She leaned the bike against the flag pole in front of the post office. It took longer to get Great-Gram's mail than expected. It seemed everyone in line had something to offer in that awkward way well-meaning adults have when they don't know what to say. Firy bit her lip and looked away.

She endured their sympathetic comments as the line crawled

toward the postmaster. Firy clutched the cloth bag deep in her pocket and imagined grinding and gnashing its contents. But no, she'd save the last three of Mama's lemon drops for when she was desperate, not gosh-awful mad.

Instead, she fished around in that same pocket for the piece of Double Bubble gum she earned last Sunday for saying her Bible verse. The gum snapped and popped as she chewed fast and furious. The line snailed forward.

Why couldn't she be like Johnny the Bear Boy with snot running down his nose and food stains all over his shirt? Nobody expected a polite answer from him. Most people didn't even talk to him. Today Firy would have gladly traded places with the old Tlingit known as Johnny the Bear Boy.

She scowled as Father Alexi nodded regally to those in line. He gave an extra nod to Firy as he assumed a place at the head of the line. Mama said there were reasons the priest seemed remote and aloof. Grown-up reasons, and Firy must respect him anyway. Firy was glad Mama never knew she didn't like the old priest, no matter how close to Bozhe he was.

Finally, her turn. She blew a bubble, and it popped over her face.

Mr. Jack laughed, his face reddened, and he stuttered, "Sorry about your, sorry, that is, you be careful now," He held a week's worth of mail for the old woman. "You're on that rickety old bike, ain't ya?"

She knew it was rickety. He didn't have to say it out loud for everyone to hear. "Careful crossin' that creek," he said. "It's a favorite place for the bears to catch salmon."

Firy grabbed the mail without answering.

Father Mikhail swept the steps at St. Michael's. He motioned to Firy. "How are you?"

She stopped pedaling, her knuckles white on the handlebars. "Fine."

"It is not possible with your mama not long in the ground."

Firy tore her eyes away. The kindness in the young priest's face made her swallow, she opened her mouth, but no words came. He laid his hand on her shoulder, "I pray for you every night, child, and again when I wake up in the morning."

"How can you be so nice when Father Alexi is so, so..."

"Reserved?"

"... mad all the time."

"Ah, Firy, Father Alexi is like you."

"Is not." Firy blushed. She mustn't argue with a priest.

He leaned her bike against the church and motioned her to sit on the steps. "It is not generally known, but Father Alexi escaped from Russia some fifteen years ago."

"Escaped?"

"There were battles between the Tzar and those who wanted to take the government away from him." The priest shrugged. "When the Bolsheviks murdered the Tzar and all his family, Father Alexi fled across Russia—always hiding. Always hungry. It took him over a year to reach the Siberian coast. His wife, their sons, and their sons' children were all lost at sea. Only Father Alexi survived. He pushed the sadness and grief away and let the anger come. Is that not what you do?"

Firy looked away and tried to imagine Father Alexi with a family. They had all drowned in front of him. She shivered and turned away.

"It is a lot easier to feel anger than grief. Is that not so our Firy?"

Firy looked into the priest's face, gentle like the icons in the church. She felt warm in his presence and didn't want to move. Reluctantly, she got to her feet, "I have to go. Can't be late to Great-Grams."

"Go with Bozhe, dear one."

With no line at the grocery store, Firy bought Great-Gram's sugar and bacon quickly. No coffee in stock. Firy put the scant groceries and this week's copy of the Sentinel in the wooden box Papa had attached to the back fender. She pedaled parallel to Crescent Bay all the way to St. Peter's.

She blinked the sun's reflection out of her eyes and looked toward the church. She thought about Miss Ruth's large flannel-graph board and cutout figures of Bible people like Daniel and his lion, Joseph and his coat, and David and his slingshot. They stuck to the board until Miss Ruth moved them or took them down. Fancy.

Thinking about Miss Ruth put her in a slightly better mood that lasted until she came to Totem Park. Firy tried to out-pedal her thoughts. They put Mama in the ground three months ago, that's all. She could feel the anger and something else creeping toward her heart as she dragged her arm across her face. She refused to let her tears come. Father Alexi was right. Mad didn't hurt as much.

She pedaled faster. Look at the ducks on the water, the eagles, or the clouds, anywhere but the fierce totems. Firy pedaled as fast as she could with her eyes straight ahead. She muttered the mantra, "They are not looking at me."

The stern and forbidding multi-faced totems lined the lane for the next half mile before the trees thinned, and she approached a shallow creek that flowed into Indian River.

She got off her bike and listened, head swiveled to the north, then the south: no bears, no black-tailed deer, no beaver. The water barely came up to the bike's chains, but it froze her toes. The numbness crept past her ankles, and the icy water pulled all feeling from her feet. She shivered and pictured her feelings freezing, not only the ones from Mama's death but the ones about the bad papas, too.

Her teeth clicked against each other, and she snapped her lips together to stop their chatter. Her body trembled and ached as she pushed the bike to the edge of the creek. Her legs didn't want to move as she heaved the bike up the bank.

She wished Great-Gram had died instead of Mama. Firy imagined the funeral procession, Mama beside her and Great-Gram in the pine coffin. But wait, Great-Gram was from the United States and couldn't be buried in the Russian Cemetery.

The wicked picture faded, and Firy grabbed great gulps of air. Mama would be ashamed to know Firy wished for such things.

She let the bike fall on the meadow's sweetgrass and plunged back into the water. She walked upstream until she found an eddy with a small whirlpool. Firy shoved her head under the water and asked Mama or Bozhe or somebody to numb her heart and wash away such evil thoughts.

Fresh from snow-topped Mount Verstovia, the icy water soon replaced the numbness with burning pain. Firy kept her head under until she was dizzy for air.

She stumbled, then stood. Her hair fell across her face, and water dripped down between her shoulder blades. She wrung out her hair, retrieved the bike, and continued to the homestead taking glaciers of grief with her—a block of ice deep in her soul.

She made a mental list of the day's chores: fill the buckets with creek water and empty them into the barrel outside the cabin door, chop the kindling, weed the garden, and since it's the last Friday of the month, wipe down the outhouse and kill a chicken.

Firy hated dead chicken Fridays. Build a fire outside, hang the large kettle over it, and hope the water boiled by the time the chicken was killed and bled. Dunking the lifeless chicken in boiling water to loosen its feathers produced a nasty smell. She'd just as soon skin the chicken, but Great-Gram wouldn't hear of it. "Why girl, chicken fried in its own fat or even bear grease makes its skin tasty and oh, so crispy."

Firy hoped chickens went to heaven, and forgiveness for chicken murderers, a possibility. She hugged and petted the condemned bird. Her final good-byes took two minutes or ten, depending on how long it took resolve to overcome guilt.

When it did, she slid her hand up the chicken's neck, grasped it tight, and swung her arm full circle. If the neck bones didn't break, she would have to do it again, fast and furious. The combination of breaking the chicken's neck and suffocating it with her tight grip made her want to throw up.

Then she clipped its head off with rusty tin snips and let the blood drain into a bucket. She buried the head, feathers, blood, and innards deep so it wouldn't attract unwanted critters.

Firy blew out her breath and banished dead chicken thoughts as Great-Gram's cabin came into view.

The rocker's slight movement and creak told her Great-Gram was awake, even though the old woman's eyes were closed and her head tilted back. In her nineties, she still put on the morning coffee, gathered the eggs, and weeded the garden, after a fashion.

Firy balanced on both pedals and coasted into the yard. "Great-Gram."

The old woman's eyes flew open, and she rose stiffly from the rocker, talking a mile a minute, "How are you, girl? And the family? You stayin' out of trouble? Where's my mail? Did that steamship bring my coffee? What's going on in town? You hungry? I'm all for a tasty, fried chicken dinner myself!"

Firy felt her face fall, and the older woman noticed. "But what I have a real hankerin' for, if you don't mind, is a big bowl of clam chowder. I was down to the beach just after dawn and got a nice mess of clams. You go milk that nanny goat, girl, and dig up some spuds and onions. We'll have a fine chowder."

Firy, relieved for the chickens and herself, said. "Sure, Great-Gram."

Sometimes Firy wondered if Great-Gram knew her name. For as long as she could remember, Great-Gram called her "girl." Firy shrugged and went to find the nanny. After that, the day went as expected, except no chicken murder. Nice. Still, the outhouse waited, as nasty as chicken death.

"Yoo-hoo, girl, come up on the porch. That's enough for today."

"But Great-Gram, the outhouse!"

"Come, sit a while before you have to go home, come on now."

Firy obeyed and hustled up to the porch. Papa Bill was all about obedience, so it wouldn't be her fault if the outhouse remained unscrubbed.

Great-Gram brewed a pot of tea, complained about the Alaska Steamship Company's inefficiencies and their disregard for the island's coffee drinkers.

Great-Gram held out a cookie bigger than her hand, "I saved this for you, girl. 'Course it's a bit stale, but if you dunk it in your tea, it will soften."

Firy took the cookie and dunked it in the tea.

"Sometimes, girl, life is as hard and stale as this cookie with no sweet tea to fix it."

Firy felt Great-Gram's eyes on her, soft and sad, almost as if she could feel Firy's resentment.

"Thank you for coming when you could be having fun with your chums." The old woman said.

Firy chomped down on the tough cookie. Fun with my chums. Ha! "Great-Gram, why don't you move into town? Everything would be easier."

Great-Gram laughed. "What would I do in town? I have my chickens, nanny, and billy, the creek for water, the beach for clams and lichens, my garden, such as it is these days, and my great grands to come and see me."

"But Great-Gram..."

The old woman slapped her knee and rocked back and forth. "Girl, it is much easier than when I first arrived. How long has it been now..." her words trailed off as she counted the decades, "why, it's been over sixty years. Look in the corner. That genuine Singer sewing machine came from San Francisco, like me. And that old cookstove? Do you know how long I had to cook over an open fire in the yard?"

Firy shrugged. It didn't sound like Great-Gram cared about town at all.

"I know precisely how much kindling to put in to fry my eggs or what size log to bake my biscuits. If it got any easier, I wouldn't know what to do with myself. It was different back in the early days." She wiped her eyes with the corner of her apron.

"Was it hard, Great-Gram?"

"Your Papa, I know he's your step-Papa, but he can be a real one if you let him."

Firy dropped her head.

"Hmm." Great-Gram continued, "Your Papa's grandfather left the states sometime in the middle of the 1800s. He said good-bye to North Dakota, saddled up his horse, took his rifle and dog, and headed west. How he ended up on this island in southeast Alaska was something he never mentioned. I know he headed down to Texas, then the Californy goldfields, and on to the Yukon."

Great-Gram shuffled to the camel-back trunk in the corner. She rummaged through it. "I still have his pride and joy. See this here, walnut-sized gold nugget."

Firy had seen the nugget and heard the story many times. She didn't comment, and Great Gram continued.

"He built this cabin, but I guess he spent one too many winters alone. So, he takes himself down to San Fran to his cousin's place. And what do you think was waiting for him?"

"You, Great-Gram? Was it you?"

"Now, don't be getting ahead of yourself, girl. This is my story. Life in the east wasn't so good with the war and all. The Confederates had killed my intended, and I resigned myself to being a spinster. Then, Pastor and Mrs. Pastor," She scratched her head, "I can't remember their names, asked me to come west and care for their children. I tell you, those young' uns wore me out. I think Mrs. Pastor slept all the way across the country."

"But Great-Gram, what about meeting Great-Gramps and falling in love and everything?"

Great-Gram brushed away a tear. "There was no falling, only necessity and practicality. Your Great-Gramps seemed like a

God-fearing man, and I wanted a family, children. His cousin, an elder in the church, introduced us and suggested we marry."

"You were brave, great-Gram."

"The day after the wedding, we boarded a schooner and headed north. As for your Great Grandfather, he wasn't so bad. Life is hard, but you can find bits of good in it if someone cares for you, and I think that man loved me." Her voice faded, and she stared at the sky.

"Tell me about the time you took a bath in the big washtub while Great-Gramps checked his trap line, and you heard knocking and got scared, but it turned out to be a black-tailed deer on the front porch eating your geraniums."

They both laughed, then Great-Gram said, "That's a story for another time. See how low the sun is. I'll walk with you to the creek."

Firy gathered eggs and goodies from the garden while Great-Gram got ready to accompany her. The girl pushed her bike to accommodate the old woman's slower pace.

Great-Gram carried what looked like a relic from WWI. When they reached the creek, she raised it to her shoulder and fired. The recoil nearly knocked her down. "That ought to scare away any critters that might be about."

Great-Gram patted Firy's cheek and looked deep into her eyes. "You're a good girl, our Firy. An awful good girl."

Firy got on her bike and crossed the creek. *I guess I'm glad she's not dead. But what about Mama?* She put her head down and pedaled faster.

SEVEN

Miss Ruth timed her early morning walk to intercept Bill Wall coming off the night shift at the sawmill. School was out for the summer, and he was back working at the mill. She would have four short blocks to convince him. "Morning. Can I walk with you, Bill?"

He shrugged.

"I'm worried about our Firy."

He didn't answer.

"She won't allow herself to feel her grief."

"Don't blame her."

Miss Ruth laid her hand on his arm, "I know this past year has been hard for all of you."

He wouldn't meet her eyes.

She took a breath. "She's still hiding behind a wall of anger."

Bill turned up Baranof Street. Miss Ruth trudged after him. Firy might be hiding behind her anger, but at least she felt something. "Bill?"

He looked at her with empty eyes.

"We must do something about our Firy."

"Nothing to do."

She gentled her voice. "For the past year, Masha and Elizaveta have shared their sorrow with me. We've talked and wept together. Even Henry, tough little guy that he is, has cried in my arms, more than once."

Bill looked away. "Not manly."

"Yes, it is, Bill Wall. It's very manly."

Color crept into Bill's face, and Miss Ruth realized he hadn't meant to speak aloud. She ignored his embarrassment. "I know your grief is still deep and fresh even after these many months. It's difficult for you to get through the day, much less help the kids."

He shuffled from one foot to the other and looked at Miss Ruth for the first time. "They'll have to figure it out. I can't do anything for them."

Miss Ruth's lips tightened, but she kept her voice calm. "I know, and everyone but our Firy is trying to sort things out."

Bill pulled his handkerchief from his back pocket and wiped his face.

"I want to take her away."

His head jerked up.

"For the summer. Port Alexander."

"She's needed here. Masha does the cooking and cleaning, but Anna Marie clings to our Firy."

"I can't reach her here, and I don't think it's wise to let her anger fester."

"All summer?" His shoulders slumped, and Miss Ruth knew she'd won.

"I've asked Ollyanna to look in more often, and the sisters from the See House will help."

"But all summer?"

"It will probably take that long. I have a plan."

"Seems you always have a plan. I don't know that our Firy will leave Anna Marie." The sweat beaded his brow.

"Ade is taking me to Port Alexander next week. I'll tell our Firy I need her help with Vacation Bible School and Sunday School.

There's a girl in Port Alexander that needs her, and I think Franella Feddersen will be good for our Firy.

"You can't help everybody." His shoulders sagged

"Please, Bill, I can help these two girls. I know I can. I'll even take our Firy to the women's sewing circles with me."

"She won't like that, rather be outside."

"There are specific womanly skills she needs to learn."

"I won't force her to go, and now's not the time for those womanly things."

"It's precisely the time." Miss Ruth stopped herself from stamping her foot, "Do I have your permission, Bill?"

The taciturn man gave a slight nod as they turned the corner onto Biorka Street. Bill's house was just beyond the corner. He opened the front gate. Anna Marie waved from the window.

Miss Ruth waved back. "Smile, Bill. Even if you don't mean it, your little girl needs you. They all need you."

Miss Ruth stood by the gate as the door closed behind Bill. He picked up the toddler and nuzzled her cheek, but he did not smile.

Miss Ruth didn't, either. *Oh, Anna, I'm doing my best for your sweet family, but it's going to take some time.*

"Franella Feddersen, have you got yourself up that tree again?"

"No, ma'am." She pictured herself in the chicken coop, gathering eggs.

"Did you sneak a book up there with you?"

"No, ma'am," she thrust the picture book under the bib of her overalls.

"The strident voice carried through the neighborhood, "Are those berry buckets full?"

"Yes, ma'am." She saw them full of huckleberries, or maybe she'd picked sweet nagoon berries.

"Come here. Now." Her mother flapped her apron and stamped her foot. Franella dropped out of the tree, the picture book and empty buckets fell at her feet.

"Child, the Good Book says, 'Let your yes be yes and your no be no.'"

"Huh?"

"I declare, girl, you wouldn't know the truth if it up and slapped you in the face."

Franella cupped her cheeks with her hands and wondered how it would feel to be slapped by the truth.

Mama tugged on her daughter's braid, re-tying the ribbon. "Get that wild look out of your eyes. The truth won't really slap you."

"No, ma'am. I mean, yes, ma'am."

"Take these buckets and don't come back until they're full." Franella opened her mouth to protest. Her mother pulled a cookie from her apron pocket and slipped it between her daughter's lips. "No more, yes ma'aming and no ma'aming me, or we'll never get the pies made."

The girl groaned. Mama stamped her foot again. "Don't groan and complain like the Israelites did in the desert. It brought the wrath of God."

Franella tried to picture that. She knew God sent the Bible people manna bread and quail birds to eat. Maybe wrath was a dessert. Wrath cake. Probably better than manna bread.

The mother shoved her daughter through the gate, looked up,

and questioned the Almighty. "I declare, Lord, I don't know why You saddled me with that girl. Uff da, she ain't a bad child, just off somewhere in her own head. It don't get the chores done."

Franella lumbered across Port Alexander's meadows, then sat on an upturned bucket and played the other like a drum. The warm sun enticed her, and soon, she lay next to the thimbleberry bushes and went to sleep. When she awoke, she wondered why she was there. She didn't even like thimbleberries. Nagoons, now those were berries.

"Franella," her father called from the back door, "come to supper."

She arrived with a berry-stained face and one bucket half full. Her mother ladled fish chowder into a bowl, knowing she would have to find the missing bucket in the morning and finish the berry picking.

"Tomorrow, we bake pie," she set the bowl on the table. "Come. Eat."

"Aww..."

"You must learn. You will bake a pie. Tomorrow at supper, you will present it to Miss Ruth."

Franella jumped out of her chair. Over went the bowl of chowder. She threw out her arms. "She's coming? Hooray!" The glass of milk crashed to the floor. "Sorry, Mama. Sorry, Papa."

Papa looked toward heaven then spoke in his soft voice, "Get mop and rag. Clean up this mess." He patted his wife's hand, "It's okay, Britta, messes can be cleaned." To his daughter, he said, " Miss Ruth will be in Port Alexander all summer."

"All summer?" The mop stabbed her father in the eye as Franella turned and squealed in delight.

Gunnar Feddersen rubbed his eyes and saw his tired wife reach for a biscuit. She slathered it with butter and jam. Sometimes biscuits and jam were all that got them through the day. Pies. Cakes. Doughnuts. He pictured all the sweet things they liked to eat in the wake of their daughter's many mishaps. "Pass the biscuits, Britta."

The next morning the gangly, freckle-faced Franella finished her oatmeal and asked permission to meet Miss Ruth at the dock. They didn't know what hour she would arrive, but Franella wanted to be there anyway. She grabbed her biscuit, and the jam toppled to the floor as she raced out the door, strawberry-blond pigtails flying.

Britta sighed and wiped up the mess. Gunnar lit his pipe. "Did you tell the girl Miss Ruth is bringing her a friend?"

Britta shook her head and let the dishes clatter into the sink. "I don't know if I can have an Indian in my house."

"Miss Ruth says she is Creole, Russian as well as native."

"Yah, sure," Britta shuddered, "everyone knows they're still heathenish and dirty, uncivilized."

"Britta, anyone Miss Ruth brings into our home, you will welcome. Be kind."

Britta frowned and wiped the table.

"Our Franella has no friends. We do this for her, eh, Britta?"

She grabbed the broom. Her husband took it from her and forced her to meet his eyes. "People are people. Do you remember how you felt when my mother would not accept you, my little Danish..."?

"Because I wasn't Norwegian..."

"So, look at this girl who is also not Norwegian, and remember how you felt."

"But Gunnar, a native."

"God loves all people, is it not so?"

Britta nodded, but as Gunnar left the house, she muttered, "You betcha, but some He loves more than others. How He can care about those dirty...?"

Britta attacked her already clean house with a dust cloth and a broom. As she swept her immaculate floors, she thought about how she would like to sweep her daughter in a different direction. No matter how hard she pushed or pulled, her daughter did not fit. Now, Miss Ruth was bringing someone who also would not fit. Not in this town, not in this house.

Before noon, Britta's racing thoughts settled into a plan. Not a good one, to be sure, but a strategy nonetheless. She stripped off her apron and grabbed her pocketbook. Like a seiner who carefully sets out his net to capture a particular species of salmon, Britta set out by innuendo and rumor to do the same.

First, she stopped at the Lutheran Women's Society for the Propagation of the Gospel. Then she spoke to the president of the Women's Auxiliary of the Sons of Norway. Next, she visited members of the Port Alexander Ladies' Sewing Circle. Of course, she swore them all to secrecy.

By the time Britta reached home, everyone in the bustling fishing village knew Miss Ruth was bringing a full-blooded Russian to spend the summer with Franella Feddersen. Britta cautioned them not to treat Firy Oskolkoff like the aristocrat she was, the great-great-granddaughter of Princess Maria Maksoutoff, the wife of the last Russian governor of Alaska. After all, Alaska had been part of America for over sixty years, and royalty was of no consequence.

When she met the young girl, she had to stop herself from curtsying. Firy's light skin and blueberry eyes convinced Britta the rumors she had spread were true.

The eighty-five miles down the coast of Baranof Island from Sitka to Port Alexander were covered with variegated green forests. Miss Ruth inhaled salty air under a cornflower sky and breathed a prayer for the summer. There was much in her heart for two young girls, one who had lost her mother and one who might as well have.

Firy huddled in the cabin and listened.

"Tell me, Uncle Ade, is this the third Olly-B or the fourth?" Miss Ruth pushed back the gray strands that escaped their confining braid then patted the name painted on the life ring.

He slapped his work gloves against his thighs and ignored her question. "I get tickled every time you call me uncle. Why you must be..." He gulped and stopped.

"Many years older." Her crow's feet highlighted the sparkle her eyes caught from the sun.

"Sorry, not polite to mention a woman's age."

"To our Firy and Anna Marie, it's always Uncle Ade this and Uncle Ade that. I got used to thinking of you that way."

"I'm honored."

"You can call me Auntie Ruthie."

Ade busied himself with the wheel, checked his navigation chart, flicked the radio switch, anything to cover his embarrassment. "I don't think I could call you anything but Miss Ruth, but I think of you like family."

"And we are. Uncle." She gave him a playful swat on the arm.

Firy threw herself face down on the bunk. She pressed her face into the pillow. It would serve them right if she couldn't breathe and suffocated to death. It wasn't fair. Miss Ruth had no right to take her away from home. It didn't matter that some girl, whose name she couldn't remember, needed her. It didn't matter that Firy had agreed to come. How did that happen, anyway? Miss Ruth said it was the right thing to do. How could leaving Anna Marie for the whole summer be right? What would Mama think?

Firy kicked against the bulkhead and threw the pillow across the room but refused to cry. *I'll show them.* She pounded her fists on the bunk and thought of every nasty word she had ever heard. She thought about saying them out loud. Serve them right if she did.

She blew her nose and stuffed the hanky into her jean pocket, looked through the porthole, then scampered onto the deck as Uncle Ade cut the engine.

Port Alexander looked bigger than Sitka. How could that be? Uncle Ade said most of the fishermen and their families only stayed for the season, then went back to their real homes, most in Alaska, but some as far away as Washington State.

The harbor swarmed with boats coming and going. Supplies arrived for Anderson's Bakery, Finn's General Store, Torvalds's Tavern and Bathhouse, and the several nearby canneries. During the spawning season, businesses flourished as the population increased more than tenfold, sometimes up to several thousand.

Uncle Ade's boat carried Miss Ruth's supplies for the summer. Minimal clothing. Adequate foodstuffs. Abundant Sunday School materials. She even had a box of what she called fripperies for the

Ladies' Sewing Circle.

The docks flooded with townsfolk who came to welcome the fishing fleet and pick up mail and supplies. A skinny girl, all arms and legs, ran up and down the pier, pigtails flying. She waved and screeched, "Miss Ruth, did you bring them?"

Miss Ruth waved from the bow. "I brought you the biggest hug in Alaska. Just wait till I get ashore."

"What else?"

"I brought you a friend."

Firy hunched behind Miss Ruth. Franella frowned, standing on one foot, then the other. "Nobody wants me for a friend. I'd rather have the picture books."

Firy tugged on the edge of Miss Ruth's jacket. "Now, can I go home?"

"You have a job to do this summer, my girl."

"She doesn't want me for a friend, and I don't like her either." When Miss Ruth wasn't looking, Firy stuck out her tongue. But Franella had turned and waved to the mailman two boats over and didn't see.

Miss Ruth knelt and held Firy's hands. "I need you to help me with Franella."

"I can't do anything, don't want to," Firy growled and wished Miss Ruth didn't see the sad, mad within her.

"It's the right thing to do, Firy."

"What's the matter with her?"

Miss Ruth lifted the last box of books and looked at Franella, who leaned over and scraped at the barnacles on the pilings. "I say nothing, but the people in Port Alexander say everything is wrong with her."

"Is it nothing or everything?" Firy put her hand on her head.

It started to hurt.

"They say I'm addled," she yelled to Firy. Franella had heard bits of the conversation.

"What?"

"Addlepated. Most people say I'm half-witted, but Miss Ruth says I'm not, so I must be a full wit."

"I never heard of anybody being full-witted."

"Pelican."

"What?" Firy looked around.

"Gone now. You like pelicans? Beds, blue coverlets."

"What?"

"You and Miss Ruth, staying with us. They like fish, you know, all kinds."

"Who? What?" Firy scratched her head.

"The pelicans, silly, what did you think I was talking about?"

"Grab a box, girls." Uncle Ade ordered. He stacked Miss Ruth's boxes and Firy's salt sack in the cart Franella Feddersen had brought. "Lead the way."

Franella Feddersen chattered to Miss Ruth since Firy refused to talk. Firy turned away and kicked at a rock in the road. Why must she stay with this strange girl who wouldn't shut up? How could it be the right thing to do when little Anna Marie was still in Sitka, and Firy was down the coast at the end of Baranof Island.

EIGHT

"Firy. Heart's like a sunflower. Bent over. Droopy."

"Is not..."

"I see it."

"Do not." Firy put her hands over her heart just in case.

"Mama's a teakettle. Boils. Steams. Stopper blows when I don't answer."

Firy rubbed her chest, glad Franella's attention had moved on. "Do you know the answers?"

"Sometimes. See them on her face."

Firy shook her head. "I never met anybody like you, Frannie."

"Frannie?"

"I think it sounds prettier than Franella."

"Yah, you betcha. Best friends."

"Uh, okay." Firy felt sorry for Franella, who had no siblings and whose mother was nothing like Firy's mama.

"Mama doesn't know how I got into the family." Franella bit her lip to stop its quiver.

Firy looked away. "What picture do you have of your Papa?"

Franella Feddersen laughed, "Tabby cat. Asleep in front of the fireplace."

Firy tucked her hair behind her ear and picked up a stick. "I wish I could see pictures like you do."

"Secret. Twelve years old. Two years older than you. Can't read. Just picture books." She dug at the sand with her barefoot.

Firy had outgrown her fondness for reading when Uncle Ade

taught her to fish. Boats rather than books called to her. Still, whenever she wanted, she could pick up a book and read. This must be the job Miss Ruth had for her. "I'll teach you."

"Teachers here and in Wrangell and Seattle said no. Hopeless."

"The words are made of little letters."

"I know that. Don't remember their names."

"You don't have to. You can put pictures of the sounds in your head."

"Don't know what sounds look like."

Firy put her hands on her hips and stamped her foot. "Frannie! Miss Ruth said I'm stuck here all summer to do a job, and that job is you. Now lay down on the sand."

The low tide had left the sand damp, but Franella Feddersen obeyed. Firy picked up a stick and drew a line the length of the girl's body.

"Squirrels..."

"What?"

"Squirrels in the clouds searching. Nuts."

Firy gripped her stick tighter and sighed; this was going to be a long summer. Oh, how she wished she was back in Sitka. She pushed the image of Anna Marie out of her heart. Don't think. Don't feel. Concentrate on this girl. Do what's right even if it doesn't feel right. "Close your eyes."

"Doesn't matter. Still see them."

"You tell those squirrels to go back to their tree clouds, then pull the curtains over your eyes, so you don't see anything until I tell you. Now stretch out your right hand, try to reach that kelp." Firy drew another line, pulled Franella to her feet, and pointed. "See, that's almost you."

"What?"

"The long up-and-down line is your body. The half-line across the top is your arm."

Firy handed a wary Franella the stick. "Poke the sand where your bellybutton would be and draw a short line across to the right."

Again, the older girl did as Firy instructed, barely seeing the squirrels in the tree clouds.

Firy made the F sound. "Hear that? That is the sound of F-F-F-F Franella Feddersen."

Franella Feddersen made the sound again and again as she drew F's up and down the beach. "Franella Feddersen. F-F-Friend. Firy. F-F-F."

"That's right," Firy yelled.

The beach became their classroom. The sand, their paper. Sticks, their pencils. Franella Feddersen worked hard, but the pictures of the letters wouldn't stay in her head.

"I quit."

"Frannie, look at me. You are the smartest girl I know."

"Can't sit still. Don't pay attention."

"You are going to learn to read if it kills me. Now, let me think." Firy snapped her fingers. "It's because your brain's too full. It spills over and runs through your body and gets your muscles riled up." Firy sat on a log and stared at the glistening sun, silver on the water. "Miss Ruth says when we have a problem, we can ask Bozhe. He knows everything."

"Did He tell you why your mama died?"

Hands on her hips, Firy Oskolkoff Wall looked Franella Feddersen in the eye and growled, "Don't talk about my Mama. Ever."

Franella held her hands behind her back to stop their shaking.

She rocked toe to heel and took a shallow breath. "Sorry."

"Shut up."

Franella cried. Seeing her body shake, Firy, although still mad, came close and patted her shoulder. "Sorry. But know this, Frannie, you're going to learn to read this summer."

"What if it does?"

"Does what?"

"Kill you!"

Firy waved Franella away and watched her run up and down the beach doing somersaults and cartwheels.

"Better now." Franella lay in the sand above the tide line and made a sand angel. "Cloud squirrels. Go away." She pounded her fist on her head. "Ready."

"That's it, Frannie. You're a genius!"

"What?"

"You have to keep moving. Do jumping jacks or somersaults or wave your arms. Do something before and after your lesson."

Franella Feddersen laughed out loud, picked up the writing stick, and waved it above her head. "In the middle, too."

"That's the secret."

"With squirrels."

NINE

The summer dragged on. Firy's heart was home in Sitka with Anna Marie, part of it anyway. Most of it was in heaven with Mama. At least, that's where Firy wanted it to be.

Every few days, Firy had to escape from Franella and Miss Ruth. She walked the beaches or sat on the dock and gazed north toward home. Thinking of Mama's death last year hurt too much, but Firy couldn't help it. And Anna Marie? Firy watched the outgoing fishing boats and wished she could hide among the nets or crab pots until she was back in Sitka. Would this dreadful summer never end?

Today there was another sewing party with all the ladies of Port Alexander. Torture. Firy would rather gut fish or dig for clams. Anything. Being trapped inside while the women either questioned her or fawned over her was awful. Firy felt her stomach cramp and her heart race just thinking about it. Never mind, just a few more weeks, and she could go home. She vowed she would never leave Sitka again.

"Ouch." Week after week, Firy sat among these Scandinavian housewives and often stabbed her fingers and stained the salt sack fabric with blood. "Let's go outside, Frannie."

Franella concentrated on the huck embroidering she was learning.

"Frannie?" Firy whispered louder.

Several ladies of the sewing circle looked up, then put their heads together.

"You would think a princess would be more, more..."

"Accomplished?" one said.

"Regal?" another said.

"Yes," whispered another, "or at least not so, I don't know, wild-looking."

"I think she looks like a princess, exotic."

"I'm beginning to wonder..." another said.

"Maybe some Yupik or Tlingit?"

"But her eyes are so blue."

"And her skin is lighter than the natives."

"But darker than ours."

"Uff da, maybe there's a touch of Russian, but only a touch."

"I still think she looks royal."

Britta bustled in with coffee and pastries, heard fragments of the conversations, and banished both girls to the yard. Speculation ceased when Miss Ruth opened her box of fripperies. The yards of colorful ribbon, lace, rick-rack, and embroidery floss eliminated all thoughts of Firy's heritage.

Once outside, Franella continued to embroider.

"How can you stay so still, Frannie? You're so different from when I first came."

The girl looked up and whispered, "Letters with needle and thread. In and out. Up and down. Fingers always moving. Calm inside. No squirrels."

Miss Ruth leaned out of the open window. "Bring me the white coverlet from the clothesline, please."

Miss Ruth spread the coverlet so the women could admire the

white on white embroidery.

"Yes, it is pretty," Britta said. "It took me three weeks to finish the design my Franella drew for me."

"But what is it?" Miss Ruth asked.

Britta wrinkled her brow, "Wiggles and swirls."

Miss Ruth laughed and held up the coverlet, "You are right, of course, but if you look closer, you will see..."

"Psst. Miss Ruth," Franella motioned from the doorway and drew the older woman outside. "Mama can't read. Doesn't know I hid words in the coverlet."

Miss Ruth hugged Franella. "I am so proud of you. You've worked so hard this summer."

"Thank you for the notebook. Favorite words. Pictures too."

"I noticed the aprons, smocks, and pillowcases you've made these past three months all have words embroidered on them."

"Favorites. Firy helped. With spelling, not sewing."

"And the names of God embroidered on the coverlet?"

"Copied them from your Sunday School paper. Then wiggles. Swirls."

"Please tell your mama what you've done. I think it would make her happy."

Franella put her hands on her hips, looked heavenward, and used her mother's strident voice. "You couldn't bless me with a dozen children, like all my friends. You only give one and such a one! She is like no one else, doncha know? What to do with her?" Franella dropped her arms and sniffed.

Miss Ruth hugged the young girl. "You know your mama loves you."

"I wish you were my mama."

"Why do you say that?"

"Heavy."

Miss Ruth raised her eyebrows. "What do you mean?"

"Mama wails when I do wrong. Shows me off when I do right. Too heavy, you know?"

"The Lord has chosen you to be Britta's child. You're twelve now, so I'm going to talk with you woman to woman."

They sat on the grass in the back yard. Franella straightened her skirt and folded her legs under her. The girl looked into Miss Ruth's eyes and heard her whisper, "My mama died the day I was born."

Franella sniffed, hiccupped, and leaned against Miss Ruth's shoulder. She heard the thump of the older woman's heart.

"I was raised by my grandpa and his sister. Like your mama, she excelled at cooking, cleaning, canning, and sewing."

Franella's face scrunched up. She waited for Miss Ruth to tell her she needed to excel also.

"It is important to do all those things and do them well. Some women give their lives to this because God has called them. Others, He calls to a different path."

"Mama doesn't know."

"Aunt Ellie didn't know either. She didn't understand me here..." Miss Ruth tapped her heart and then her temple. "Or here."

Franella sighed and wished again that Miss Ruth was her mama.

"I remember she wanted me to bake the best piecrust in the territory."

"Did you?"

Miss Ruth threw her head back and laughed, "No, and I haven't made a pie for nearly fifty years."

"Long time. You're so old!"

Miss Ruth reached into the pocket of her long black skirt. "Have a lemon drop, and let me tell you about the women the Lord brought into my life to give me what my aunt couldn't."

Franella settled in the grass. She saw Firy peeking around the corner of the house but did not motion her over.

"Their names were Maureen, Iolana, and Sister Agnes."

The picture in Franella's head of a young Miss Ruth and the women who filled up the lonely places captured her attention and focused her. She remained still.

Miss Ruth finished and said, "You just wait, Franella. Learn all you can from your mama, and the Lord will bring others into your life to teach you the rest."

"Like you, Miss Ruth." Franella squeezed the old woman in a desperate hug.

"I think your mama could use some help serving the coffee and pie."

"I will be the best server in the territory." The screen door banged behind her. Miss Ruth prayed Franella would not drop the pie or slosh the coffee.

Firy tiptoed around the corner of the house, then ran into the older woman's open arms. Miss Ruth cleared her throat, handed Firy a lemon drop, and began again. "My mother died the day I was born...

At the end of the fishing season, most families prepared to leave. They shared goodbyes and promises to keep in touch. The finish of the salmon season in Port Alexander mirrored its beginning.

"Firy. Miss you."

"Yeah, me too." Firy watched the horizon and didn't hear the longing in the other girl's voice. The Olly-B should be here soon. Home. Family. Anna Marie. She feared her little sister wouldn't remember her.

"Write me?"

"Sure."

"Look at me." Franella blew her nose and rubbed her eyes. "Never had a friend. Lonely." She scrubbed her eyes again with the now soggy handkerchief.

Firy did look, perhaps for the first time that summer. "Frannie, I wish you had sisters or a cousin to live with you or even a brother."

The Olly-B slid to the dock, and Uncle Ade threw Firy the mooring rope.

"Firy?" Franella watched as Firy wrapped and tied the rope, "Don't forget me. Write to me."

"Okay."

"Promise?"

Firy put her hand on her hip and, in her best Scandinavian voice, said, "Yah, sure, you betcha."

Uncle Ade loaded the bags and boxes as Miss Ruth said her goodbyes. The women of Port Alexander hugged her and then turned to Firy.

"Pleasure to make your acquaintance," one bobbed her head.

"So nice to have you here for the summer," another attempted a curtsy.

"So sweet of you to befriend that addlepated Franella Feddersen."

"Thank you for coming, your Maj... that is, farewell your

High...that is, goodbye."

Gunnar shook Firy's hand, and Britta enveloped her in a suffocating embrace, "I knew you were royal from the first moment I saw you. Come back anytime, little princess." Firy's stiff posture relaxed once the pleasantries were over, and the hugs and handshakes ceased.

Miss Ruth gave Franella one last hug and a large bag of lemon drops. She boarded the Olly-B.

"How did the summer go?" Uncle Ade talked around the pipe clamped in his mouth.

"Our Firy was good for Franella. She taught her to read. Calmed her some."

"But was Franella Feddersen good for our Firy?" Uncle Ade frowned.

Miss Ruth shoved her hands in her pockets. In one, she fingered the ever-present bag of lemon drops. In the other, she crumpled her handkerchief. "I don't know, Ade. I had so much hope for Firy this summer. She helped Franella, but only because it was the right thing to do."

"Didn't they get along?"

"They did, and Franella loved Firy, but I don't think Firy opened her heart. This summer was a minor distraction for our Firy rather than a major healing. The Lord says not to be anxious about anything, but I can't help myself. I worry about our Firy."

"So do Ollyanna and I. We've tried talking to her, and Bill, too. He's another one that can't seem to get over his grief." Ade pulled off his watch cap, scratched his head, and replaced it. "That's not exactly what I mean. Anna's death is not something they can get over, but you have to go on living." He wiped his eyes and gazed out to sea. "They just have to find a way."

Miss Ruth stood beside him and stared at the horizon as he did. "Dear Ade, I know exactly what you mean. All we can do is be here in case they need us."

Ade squinted against the sun, "Trouble is, they do need us. They just don't know it. And I, for one, don't know what to do about it."

Miss Ruth sighed, "Me either. I just have to keep praying."

He turned and shouted, "Time to shove off."

TEN

The yellow flowers Mama loved inched through the dirt by the front porch. Some even peeked through the wooden slats of the sidewalk near the front gate. They came when the snow melted, and the rains began. Mama always said they were Bozhe's promise of spring. For as long as Firy could remember, the yellow flowers signaled Johnny the Bear Boy's return.

Nobody knew how he survived the winters. Some sourdoughs said he hunkered down in an abandoned cabin on Mount Verstovia, and others said he stayed in a cave with a hibernating she-bear. Old-timers insisted he lived in an abandoned fisherman's shack beyond Halibut Point. Everyone had an opinion, but nobody cared enough to find out.

Like everyone else, Firy breathed a sigh of relief when Johnny left in the fall and one of annoyance when he returned in the spring. No one welcomed Johnny the Bear Boy. No invitations to supper. No, 'We've missed you, Johnny. Sit. Have a cup of coffee.'

Once, Firy asked Mama who took care of him and why did he come and go as he did? Mama sighed and looked to heaven. "Bozhe has ways of caring for his broken lambs, Firy."

As she hung another of Papa's long johns on the line, Firy heard her whisper, "Oh, Bozhe, there is so much more I would like to do."

"Do what, Mama?"

"What's right."

Doing the right thing for Johnny, the Bear Boy eluded Firy, and truth be told, she didn't care. Johnny would be along soon. She dug at the dirt with the toe of her shoe and decided not to talk to him. She kicked the soil next to the flowers.

Mama had welcomed spring by pressing the first yellow blossoms between the pages of her Bible and getting the washtub out of the shed for Johnny. She'd set the tub on the back porch, fill it with hot water, and wait. How Mama knew what day he would appear and how he knew what day she readied the washtub was a mystery.

Johnny liked to play with the wooden boats Papa whittled from cedar scraps and the floating soap Mama added to the warm water. The first few springs, he leaned over the tub and pushed the boats back and forth. Then Mama convinced him to sit on the rocker and put his feet in the water. Johnny hummed with pleasure when Mama washed his feet. Firy never knew how Mama convinced Johnny to sit in the tub. Everyone said Mama had created a monster in long johns.

Now, who would encourage Johnny the Bear Boy to have his spring bath? Who would cut his hair or shave his beard? Johnny would look like the monster everyone thought he was. People would forget Mama's wise words, "He's a little boy trapped in a big man's body. Be kind. He is one of Bozhe's special lambs."

On her way to Mr. Akervik's store that Saturday, Firy saw Johnny the Bear Boy in the middle of the road. The Jensen twins and Sven Anderson pelted him with rocks. They called him names and made remarks about the twigs matted in his gray hair and the snot in his beard.

Almost without thinking, Firy picked up a rock. It bounced off his arm. He turned and looked. She got a bigger stone and let it fly. It hit him in the shoulder. She pictured Johnny the Bear Boy dead in the ground instead of Mama. Big, dumb native.

Encouraged by her participation, the twins took their slingshots out of their back pockets and grabbed handfuls of pebbles. Johnny winced whenever the twins' aim was accurate.

"I quit," Sven yelled and ran off.

Firy's arm ached, and she dropped her rock when she saw tears running out of Johnny's eyes and into his beard. He fumbled in his pocket.

"Uh oh," the twins yelled, "he's got a gun!"

They took off. Firy's feet wouldn't move.

Johnny held out a yellow pressed flower. "Mama?"

Blinded by tears, Firy ran. She pictured Mama in heaven, weeping for Johnny the Bear Boy, and saw the hand of Bozhe wipe away Mama's tears. Firy scrubbed her face with her fists, "Who will wipe mine?"

Firy heard Mama's words, "Always love Bozhe, Glaphira, and do what is right."

"I don't know how."

"Yes, child, you do."

Mama's image faded, and Firy ran through the house to the shed. "Henry, help me get this old washtub down. I can't reach it."

"Can't, got to finish chopping the kindling before Papa gets home."

"I need it for Johnny the Bear Boy."

"Are you nuts?"

"Please, you know it would make Mama happy."

"It won't make me happy." The boy grumbled, but he got the tub and dragged it to the back porch. "Don't ask me to do anything else. And I won't be here when that crazy old Indian is, you hear me?"

Firy ignored him and arranged towels around the tub, and unwrapped a new bar of the floating soap. She and Masha set pots of water to boil on the stove. Masha agreed Firy was doing a good thing. "I'll keep Anna Marie in the bedroom when Johnny's here. She's little, and he might scare her."

Firy barely heard her as she forced herself to open Mama's cedar chest and take out the last quilt Mama had ever made. She held it to her face. In her heart, she heard a faint, "Well done."

"No, Mama. It's too much."

"The quilt is a thing, Firy. Life and love are more important."

This time Firy welcomed the tears. Their sweetness enveloped her. She hung the quilt over the railing and went to find Johnny the Bear Boy.

ELEVEN

A bleak Christmas! What kind of a word was bleak, anyway? Horrible, low down, dirty, and rotten awful! Papa Bill already told the kids not to expect any gifts. When asked why he blamed it on the Depression, Masha said it was Papa Bill who was depressed.

Before Mama got sick, Papa Bill helped with homework and played ball in the backyard. He sang and danced around the kitchen, first with Mama and then with her and Elizaveta. Henry danced with Popeye.

Christmas! Her thoughts circled back to Papa. All he did was work, listen to the radio, and smoke cigarettes. Then he dragged himself to bed, and the next day did it all over again. He seldom went to the café anymore.

Papa also avoided his workshop. There'd be no cedar boxes to hold small treasures. No wooden bowls for pine cones and holly. No carved horses to add to Henry's collection. No wooden blocks for Anna Marie. Papa acted like he didn't care about Christmas or them.

Firy made a new rag doll for Anna Marie and thought about giving Henry her two Nancy Drew books, even though he liked the Hardy Boys. For Masha, Elizaveta, and Papa, she had no ideas.

She felt as empty as the old suitcase under the bed. Once, Firy asked Mama why Papa kept it since he never traveled. "It's packed with hope and love." After Mama died, Firy dragged it out and looked inside. Empty.

She pushed those thoughts away as she approached Mr. Akervik's general store. She always thought about how nice he was to

Mama and how she had laughed and talked with him. Sometimes, he winked at her and put extra things in her bag.

Firy had heard other grown-ups say things about it, but not in a friendly way. Was it because Mama was native and Mr. Akervik was white or something else, something wicked?

Still, Mr. Akervik had always been kind to Mama, and now he was extra nice to Firy. Why did the grown-ups smirk and talk about Mama and Mr. Akervik? Why did they have to add mean things about Mama? Still, there was one thing they said that Firy hoped was real. Someday she would ask Mr. Akervik about it.

Native women sat on the sidewalk and displayed sealskin gloves, mukluks, and woven cedar hats. They leaned against the storefront and gnawed pieces of sealskin. Their constant chewing turned it to the softest leather, but the women's teeth had worn down to mere nubs over the years. Slobber ran down their chins, but Firy plastered a smile on her face and said, "Excuse me."

They looked at her with twinkled eyes as they chewed. Firy tried to step between them, but they blocked her way, laughed, and jabbered in Tlingit. Mr. Akervik heard them and brandished his broom. "Get away from here, you siwashes. Sell your filthy Indian crap somewhere else."

Firy looked at the storekeeper. "She's here, isn't she, Mr. Akervik?"

He lowered his broom. "Look for yourself, girl."

Firy closed her eyes and turned to the window. When she popped them open, there she was, glorious, amid the fishing gear, hunting rifles, kettles, boots, and Evening in Paris perfume.

Mr. Akervik beamed. "Yes sir, that is one genuine, blond-haired, blue-eyed, Shirley Temple doll from Hollywood, America. As far as I know, she is the only one in all of Southeast Alaska."

Firy pressed her hands hard against the window and leaned close to the glass, "Oh my goodness! Oh, my goodness!"

Mr. Akervik looked up and down the street then whispered, "You may hold her for a minute, but you mustn't tell."

Glorious, heavenly day! Firy's heart swelled as she held the doll close. All too soon, Mr. Akervik took Shirley and put her back. "You come to visit as long as she is here."

Firy, brutally reminded of the for-sale tag dangling from Shirley's wrist, remembered her manners. She thanked Mr. Akervik and headed toward the docks.

Twice a week, Firy and her friends met at the Alaska Steamship Company's dock and watched the stevedores offload the cargo. Almost everything came into Sitka by ship. Old Man Budnikov appeared right on schedule to receive the movie reels from Hollywood. The captain gave them to Sven Anderson's papa, the dock foreman.

Firy and the others craned their necks, hoping for a peek. Budnikov, nobody called him mister, carried his precious box through town two times a week. He ignored their pleas to reveal even one of the upcoming titles.

Once, Arkady Restov, a young dockhand, broke into the captain's quarters and read the manifest. The kids cheered when he whispered the titles. When Budnikov found out, he swore he'd close the theater. Rumors flew through town about how his wife made him see reason. No movies, no tickets. No tickets, no money. Simple.

Budnikov banned Arkady for six months. The more experienced dock hands laughed at him for getting caught, the captain docked his pay and threatened to fire him. Arkady's six-month sentence ended today.

Vivien Livo nudged Firy, "I can get Arkady to do it again." A couple of years older than the rest of them, Vivian, displaying budding female wiles, sashayed up to Arkady, and whispered in his ear.

He pushed her away and yelled in Russian. Firy didn't understand anything except the swear words and wondered how she knew them. Mama never swore, and Papa swore in English.

The Jensen twins asked Vivian if she wanted them to beat up Arkady. She turned away and wiped her eyes.

Elizaveta, the youngest of the group, took Vivian's arm. "Come on, Viv, he's a stupid old boy! Let's go to the movie house. We can ask Budnikov to put the posters out early."

"He won't," Vivian said.

They reached the corner, and Firy whispered to Viv, "If Budnikov's wife's there, she'll whisper the titles to you. Tell her I said you're trustworthy."

Viv nodded, still teary-eyed and red-faced.

"Are you coming, Firy?" Elizaveta asked.

"No, I have some errands to do for Papa." It was the tiniest of lies, and Firy didn't feel guilty.

Every day and sometimes twice a day, Firy visited the store and laid her face on the glass. When the store was empty, Mr. Akervik invited her in. Oh, those precious moments cheek to cheek and heart to heart with Shirley Temple!

Like her, Shirley had no mama or papa, but still, she sang and danced. There was always a happy ending. Firy sailed on the Good Ship Lollipop, visited Rebecca at Sunnybrook Farm, danced on stage with Little Miss Broadway, lived in a lighthouse with Star and Captain January, and flew with Bright Eyes. There were animal crackers in her soup. Life was good.

But all too soon, Shirley went back in the window, and Firy returned to housework and homework, garden chores and cleaning the school, fishing and hunting with Uncle Ade, cooking with Masha, and helping Great-Gram. Dreariness and drudgery.

She tried not to listen when others talked about the precious doll. Shirley Temple caused more debates and arguments among Sitka's girls than anything Firy could remember. When Mr. Akervik couldn't stop these explosive conversations from taking place in his store, he put a SOLD sign on the doll. When girls of a certain age wailed and moaned, Mr. Akervik got his broom and swept them toward the door.

When Firy saw the sign, she couldn't breathe. Mr. Akervik patted her on the head. "It's okay. You come the same as always until Christmas Eve. Yes?"

She looked into the storekeeper's face, ready to say no. "All right."

The Christmas Eve service at St. Peters was a family affair, and each child received an orange and a gift, usually a pair of sox and a small toy. The Wall family tramped home through the snow. Masha and Elizaveta sang Jingle Bells and stomped their feet.

Unbidden, Firy saw Henry slip a chocolate bar into Masha's coat pocket and Elizaveta's too. He turned to Firy, and his face colored. She smiled at him, and he pressed a Hershey bar into her hand, "Christmas."

"But I don't have anything for you."

"Doesn't matter." He bit his lip and looked away.

"You can have my Nancy Drew's."

"Nah, too girly."

"Merry Christmas, Henry." Firy wondered where he had gotten the money for the chocolate. Was he a thief? She hated herself for thinking that but then remembered he had shoveled snow, chopped kindling, and stacked wood for the neighbors for weeks. Few had money to pay him, but maybe the Checkinov sisters gave him the candy bars. They had an enormous love for sweets and always seemed to have the money to buy them.

Papa Bill carried Anna Marie. Her grey eyes peeked over his shoulder. Henry broke off a piece of chocolate and placed it in the toddler's mouth. She drooled chocolate down her chin and onto Papa's jacket collar, but he didn't notice.

A block from home, Firy told Papa she had a Christmas errand.

"Hurry and get your Christmas business done. It's getting late."

Without Shirley Temple, the window had lost its glory. Mr. Akervik opened the door, "Merry Christmas! Everyone is gone, but I waited for you." He hung the closed sign on the door.

She pulled the homemade card from her pocket. "Merry Christmas, Mr. Akervik."

Firy shuffled from one foot to the other while Mr. Akervik read the card. She moved toward the door.

"Wait, Firy," he said. "For you."

She expected a candy cane like he gave all the kids. Instead, he held a large paper bag. Firy's heart thumped. She peeked in — beautiful blond curls.

"For me?"

He beamed but said nothing. Firy's heart pounded so loud she didn't know why he couldn't hear it. She couldn't stop herself. She closed her eyes tight, hung her head, and whispered, "Mr. Akervik, are you my father?"

The silence drummed in Firy's ears and beat in rhythm with her heart. She slowly opened one eye and looked. Mr. Akervik's face had become as pale as arctic snow, then red as the Alaska King crab she'd eaten for dinner.

He fumbled for his broom and swept the dustless floor. He did not raise his head. "No." His voice cracked like ice in spring. "You go home now, girl."

Firy wondered if she should have been so bold. She felt terrible. Or maybe it was his answer that caused such sadness. "I'm sorry, Mr. Akervik."

As the door closed behind her, Firy heard him sigh and whisper, "You have a Merry Christmas, Glaphira Larissa Oskolkoff Wall."

Firy stumbled half a block toward home before she realized he knew her middle name. Did all the storekeepers know the middle names of all the kids in Sitka? No, they did not. The knowledge hit her like one of Henry's icy snowballs. Fathers always know their daughters' middle names. That's just a fact.

Firy's heart swelled and swirled like the Aurora Borealis above her. The moon and stars reflected off the snow and gave a silver brightness to the neighborhood. The glory of the Borealis looked like Bozhe's angels come to sing to Baby Jesus.

She pushed open the gate and carefully set the paper bag down at the corner of the back porch. She fell back on the snow and made an angel. "That's for you, Mama," she whispered, "For you and Mr. Akervik."

She slipped into the house and went directly to her room. She sat on the bed and talked to Shirley. "You know he's my real papa, don't you, Shirley. I wonder why Mama didn't marry him."

Shirley's blue eyes looked into her own. Firy hugged her. "I think you're right, Shirley, his mean sister, Old Pinch Nose, wouldn't let him. That's so sad. I'm Mr. Akervik's secret, and you have to be mine. If Papa Bill sees you, he'll feel bad. He'll know Mr. Akervik's my real papa."

She put Shirley under the bed. Popeye came and lay next to her, and she put her arm around the mongrel mutt. "It's not right, is it, Popeye?"

The dog whined and licked her face. "That's an excellent idea. Stay here and guard Shirley. I'll be right back."

When she returned, Firy had Papa's suitcase. Discarding the paper bag, she lay the doll inside. She drew a picture of the night sky and wrote down all the things she felt about this night and Mr. Akervik, too.

After Christmas, nobody claimed ownership of Shirley Temple. There were speculations and theories but no facts. When asked who purchased the doll, Mr. Akervik said storekeeper-customer privilege prevented him from telling.

And so, the Shirley Temple doll disappeared from Sitka forever, and so did Firy's desire to talk to Mr. Akervik. On her trips to the post office or the market, she crossed the street to avoid his store. When Papa Bill sent her there to make a purchase, she tried to go when his sister was behind the counter. Firy still believed he was her father, but how could she be near him when he wouldn't say so. He must love her; he gave her the doll. He just didn't love her enough or Mama either. Confusing. Sad. Firy crossed her heart and promised herself she wouldn't think about it anymore. Maybe then it wouldn't hurt so much. That was the right thing to do, wasn't it?

TWELVE

They called it the Depression. It had already lasted most of Firy's childhood. Sometimes she thought it would go on forever. The gloom, the hopelessness, the poverty. The weeks and months merged into years, and nothing changed. Nothing except Anna Marie. She was a skinny little thing, but smart, already in the second grade. With her blond hair and skin lighter than Firy's, she didn't look native at all. Firy hoped this would make the girl's life easier, although Anna Marie repeatedly begged for stories about when Mama was young and lived in a native village on the Kenai.

Anna Marie often tried to sneak into Sheldon Jackson school. When either Henry or Elizaveta caught her, they ran her back to the Russian Bishop's house. The three older siblings agreed Bill mustn't know how much Anna Marie wanted to go to the native school. Firy didn't blame her one bit and wished she had dared to sneak away from Miss Swearinger.

Just yesterday, Anna Marie came into Firy's room and closed the door. "Firy, I did a bad thing."

Firy put down her nail file, "What, Dodo?"

"I don't want to tell you."

"Why not?"

"Because I might have to do it again."

Firy patted Anna Marie's shoulder and laughed, "Now you definitely have to tell me."

"Okay, but you can't tell, especially Papa, and I'm going to keep my eyes closed the whole time."

Firy hid her smile, "It sounds serious."

Anna Marie climbed onto Firy's bed, leaned back on the pillows, and closed her eyes. "Today in school Miss Swearinger jerked me out of my seat. She grabbed my hair and pulled and pulled. It made me so mad I wanted to slap or kick her."

Firy remembered how Miss Swearinger delighted in this particular punishment. Firy always stood silent, stoic, refusing to react. "You didn't, did you?"

Anna Marie opened one eye, "Do you think I'm dumb? I knew that would land me in big trouble."

"But you did do something. Tell me."

"I screamed my head off, as loud as I could. Even after she stopped pulling, I screamed and screamed. Father Alexi and two of his helper priests came in. The Father talked to Miss Swearinger, and one of his helpers took over the class. The other took me to the hallway to calm me down."

"It looks like you're okay now, so it's best to forget the whole thing. Try not to draw any attention to yourself in class. We'll just hope it doesn't happen again."

"It won't. I made sure of that."

"Oh, Dodo, what did you do?"

"When everyone was at recess, I marched back into the classroom. Father Alexi was across the hall. I wanted him to hear, so I talked real loud."

Firy clutched her middle as memories of Miss Swearinger poured acid into her stomach. "What did you say to her?"

"I told her if she ever tried to pull my hair or slap me or talk ugly to me ever again, I would scream and yell and holler, and I wouldn't stop until Father Alexi came, and Stormy Durrand

and even Miss Ruth. I told her she was a mean old lady, and she would never hurt me again. I told her nobody was ever going to hurt me. Then I said every nasty Russian word I knew. That's the bad thing."

Firy hugged her little sister and said. "I'm proud of you, Anna Marie. I wish I were as brave as you."

"I swore in Tlingit, too."

"Just this once, I think you were justified, but don't do it again. Mama never liked swearing."

"Papa swears all the time. I put my hands over my ears."

Anna Marie's homework last week was to ask two people about the Depression. Papa Bill said even though they were a year into the 1940s, everyone was still depressed because of a big, dusty bowl down in America. No matter how much Papa explained, Anna Marie didn't understand how things that far away could affect the people here. Firy just said it meant nobody had any money, and most didn't have jobs either. Everybody was poor, and lots of people were hungry.

School had just let out for the summer, and Papa returned to his job at the mill. Then when lumber prices dropped and the mill closed, he went hunting and fishing. Masha said it wasn't the right time, and if he got caught, they would haul him off to jail and send them to the Russian Orthodox Orphanage.

Anna Marie shuddered, "Couldn't you take care of us?"

"I could, Dodo, but they wouldn't let me."

"But you're all grown up, out of school even."

"But I'm native. They wouldn't think I was good enough, at least not for you."

Anna Marie wasn't sure who *they* were but knew she wouldn't like them. She shook her head and told herself to concentrate on the job at hand.

Anna Marie finished her Saturday chores and told Papa she had an important errand. Her heart pounded as she stood outside of the Sitka Sentinel. The clacks and clangs of the linotype boomed out the doors.

Editor, Sam Mitchell, scowled across his desk at Anna Marie's cousin, nine-year-old Yelena Bunderson, who stood on tiptoe and talked furiously at him. Yelena yelled over her shoulder. "Go away!"

Anna Marie scurried over and stood next to her cousin. "But it was my idea."

Yelena elbowed her, cheeks flaming, "Keep quiet, Dodo."

Margaret Mary called from her perch at the linotype, "Don't call your little friend names. She's not a dodo."

Editor Mitchell waved away her concern, "It's all right, Margaret Mary, everybody calls Anna Marie Dodo. Don't they, sweetie?"

Imagine that! The editor of the Sitka Sentinel knew her nickname. "Yes, sir, everybody in town likes me, and they'll buy a paper from me."

"Will not."

"Will too."

Back and forth, the cousins bickered until old man Mitchell rubbed his temples, suddenly glad Sam, Jr. was an only child. "Enough!" He sighed and said, "I'll give each of you fifteen papers a week. You can both be newsboys, er, newsgirls."

They beamed. "Yes, sir."

Yelena saluted, then turned and stuck her tongue out at Anna Marie, who ignored her.

"We run the press on Fridays. Margaret Mary will show you how to catch the papers as they fly off that big black machine over there." He looked at their eager but oh, so young faces. "You think you can do that? You have to catch one, fold it, and get ready for the next one."

"We can. We're fast." Anna Marie was eying the metal monster. Yelena nodded.

"Okay then, scram. Come back Friday at three o'clock." He watched them as he reached for the battered coffee pot on a hot plate in the windowsill. They ran down Lincoln Street until they came to St. Michaels, Anna Marie went right, and Yelena left.

Anna Marie hugged this delicious secret to herself. A working woman, making real money. She would give it all to Papa, or maybe she would stop at Wellerton's drugstore and buy a piece of penny candy for herself and her sisters. Henry too.

Sam rubbed his hand over his thinning hair; he must be nuts. Margaret Mary looked his way. He slid his eyes toward her without making contact. "Looks like a dang Cheshire cat."

"What, boss?" She asked, eyes crinkling.

"Nothing," he yelled. "And I don't want to hear another word about it."

"Yes, boss."

"You take care of those kids. I don't want to talk to them again."

"Why's that, boss?"

"I know Bill Wall's girl, smart as a whip. Next thing you know, she'll bring me little stories and get all teary-eyed if I don't print them. She probably thinks she'll have my job one day."

"Yes, boss." Margaret Mary loaded the linotype as Sam slammed the coffee pot onto its perch, stuck the tattered derby on his head, and slunk off to the Sitka Café.

"What a fool," he whispered to himself, "the country's not out of the depression, and I give thirty papers away. Give? Yes, give." He knew he wouldn't demand his cut from the little urchins.

A light rain fell on Friday, and Anna Marie hurried through her chores then played with Popeye—Papa chopped wood in the backyard.

"Bye, Papa, I'm off to meet Yelena," she called as she pulled on her thin sweater.

"You know our Firy likes you to be here when she gets home from Gram's."

"I know, but Yelena and I have a meeting."

"With who?"

"Can't tell you."

"Come, give me a hug before you go." He sat on the stump he had been using as a chopping block and held out his arms.

She avoided the ax leaning against the stump as she threw her arms around his neck and squeezed. "Papa, Henry is a boy, and I know he doesn't like it, but why don't you ever hug Elizaveta or our Firy?"

He rested his chin on the top of her head. He blinked several times and said, "They don't like hugs."

"Yes, they do. I hug them all the time. Well, not Henry." She pulled away and searched his face.

Teardrops hovered on the end of his lashes, and he sniffed. Even when his two step-daughters were young, they ran whenever he tried to hug them. They cringed when he patted them on the shoulder or the top of their heads. He remembered how he used to dance around the kitchen with his dear Anna before she became ill.

At her insistence, both Elizaveta and Firy danced with him. After many months Elizaveta relaxed and even giggled when he pretended to stumble and told her she would have to lead. Firy remained stoic and stiff. He saw a pleading in her eyes but didn't know if she wanted him to stop or keep dancing until she could enjoy it. His sweaty palms and hers was always a good excuse to quit.

"Papa, why do you think they don't like hugs?"

Anna Marie's question brought him back to the present. He sniffed again, stood her up, and reached for his ax. "You give them extra hugs, Dodo, and tell them they're from me."

"Okay, but now I'm late. Yelena is waiting." She patted Popeye, blew her father a kiss, and ran down the dirt road.

He called after her, "When the cannery's five o'clock whistle blows, you head for home. Don't be late for supper." Bill set another piece of wood on the stump, lifted the ax with arms as weary as his heart, and swung.

"She's like her mother. Isn't she Popeye?"

The dog wagged his tail and continued to gnaw his bone. Bill wiped his eyes and remembered his wife's last moments of life.

"Don't forget... Don't forget...Do..." Anna gasped and breathed her last.

He had stifled his moans and picked up his baby daughter. She clasped chubby little arms around his neck. "Doh...doh..."

Firy bit her lip and leaned against Papa Bill. "What do you think Mama tried to say?"

"Sounded like, don't forget I love you."

Firy, eyes wet and itchy, whispered, "Don't forget to love Bozhe and do what's right.'"

She took Anna Marie from Papa's arms, nuzzled the baby, and whispered. "I'll always remind you to love Bozhe and do what's right."

"Dodo," chirped Anna Marie.

"Yes, you're our little Dodo."

Not a day went by that Bill didn't miss his Anna. What did he know about mothering? All he could do was put food in their bellies and clothes on their backs. He sighed and went back to his chopping even as his tears mixed with the drizzle.

Anna Marie caught up with Yelena near Akervik's general store.

"What do you think?" Her cousin spun around.

"You look like a giant dandelion."

Yelena stamped her foot. "A beautiful dandelion."

"Sure, but how?"

Yelena, dressed from head to toe in yellow, opened a small umbrella, also yellow, and pointed to the store.

Anna Marie's eyes grew wide, "Mr. Akervik? But you don't have any money."

"Mr. Akervik's sick today. I bought these from his sister."

"Old Pinch Nose?"

"I looked at the hat and wished I had money to buy it. But guess what? Old Pinch Nose, I mean Miss Akervik, was so nice."

Anna Marie thought Mr. Akervik got the family's goodness, and his sister got the misery. Whenever displeased, which was most of the time, Miss Akervik closed her eyes, pinched the bridge of her nose, and sniffed.

"I can't believe it. How did you pay for it?" Anna Marie frowned.

"I didn't."

"Old Pinch Nose wouldn't give you the boots and everything else. I know she wouldn't."

"I told her I worked for Mr. Mitchell and got paid every week. She said to come by and give her my money," she stuck out her foot to admire her shiny new rubber boots that matched the yellow slicker. "She said I'd look like sunshine if I bought the whole outfit. So, I did."

"But Yelena, we were going to help our families."

"Miss Akervik told me if I looked bright and cheery, people would be happy to buy my papers."

Anna Marie had to admit her cousin looked pretty. And expensive. "How much did all that cost?"

Yelena shrugged then twirled her umbrella. "Miss Akervik said to bring her my money every week for the next ten months."

Anna Marie stared at her cousin, who looked like Shirley Temple on the posters outside Budnikov's. Almost of their own volition, Anna Marie's feet turned toward the store. Rain dripped from her nose and landed on her soggy shoes, the worn soles stuffed with cardboard. She looked at the yellow boots in the window and pictured them on her own feet.

"Come on, Dodo. We don't want to be late," Yelena said.

Relieved at the urgency in her cousin's voice, Anna Marie ran from temptation. Maybe she wasn't as pretty and bright as Yelena, but she'd be richer.

Margaret Mary gushed over Yelena, and Anna Marie swallowed the lump in her throat as she squeezed the rain out of her hair. But didn't take her shoes off to squeeze the water out of her socks. It wouldn't be polite.

The newswoman showed them how to catch the paper as it came off the press, fold it in half, then again, and stack it in a wooden crate at their feet. They were to alternate as the papers flew at them.

Yelena refused to take off her raingear, and its bulkiness slowed her down. The newspapers came fast and furious. Anna Marie pushed her cousin aside and did all the catching, folding, and stacking. Yelena sat on the floor and played with the buckles on her slicker.

After what seemed like forever, the noisy press stopped, but Anna Marie's ears still heard it. She caught the last paper with weary arms and sank to the floor.

Margaret Mary then showed them how to roll their papers and stuff them into canvas shoulder bags. When full, she slipped them over the girls' heads. "There, now you are official newsgirls. See, on the side of the bag, it says, Sitka Sentinel."

"Let's go." Anna Marie opened the door.

"I'll go this way, Dodo, to the stores and the hotel. You go to the canneries and Indiantown."

"But..." Annoyed with her cousin for taking the busy part of town, Anna Marie did some quick calculations and changed her mind. "Okay." The Pioneer Home was in her territory.

Anna Marie wandered through the sitting room and saw an old-timer with milky white eyes. She asked him if he wanted to buy a paper, but he said he had cataracts and couldn't see. An elderly logger next to him who had been blinded in an accident years ago said, "Don't forget me. I can't see neither."

A miner in a large overstuffed chair said, "I can see, but I ain't never learned to read. Little girl, can you tell us what's in the newspaper?"

Anna Marie sighed. There'd be no money in reading to these old-timers. Nevertheless, she took a newspaper out of her canvas bag and spread it on the low coffee table in front of her. She sat among the old men and described the pictures.

Anna Marie didn't remember when Firy taught her to read. It seemed like she always knew. When a word stumped her, she spelled out the letters, and the men told her how to pronounce it. In the end, they applauded, gave her their pennies and a peppermint.

At the door, the head nurse said, "You're Bill Wall's girl, aren't you? Anna Marie?"

"Yes, ma'am."

The nurse eyed her canvas bag, "How many papers do you have left?"

"Fifteen."

"You come here every week and read the newspaper like you did today, and I'll buy all of them."

"For real?" Anna Marie squealed. "Thank you, nurse..." She looked at her name tag, "Nurse Maddie."

Clutching the empty bag, she rushed out the door then slowed to a stop. The rain had disappeared. She sat on a wet bench near the front door and didn't feel her dungarees absorb the water. She leaned back and talked to the clouds tumbling out to sea. "I'd better keep this deal to myself. I can't let Yelena find out Nurse Maddie's buying all my papers. I wonder if Mr. Mitchell will give me more."

She laughed out loud, grabbed her empty news bag, and ran to the Sentinel. *I'm going to be rich.* She pictured herself in bright yellow galoshes.

Memory Care Center — Present Day

Fierce winds rattled cold rain against the windows. The sun dropped below the heavy cloud cover. It blazed for a few moments then sank into the sea at the horizon's edge. That's life in the Pacific Northwest, gray and wet all day with glorious sunsets at night.

"I didn't realize it was so late." Emma Lee gathered her things.

"I suppose it is. I live in the gloaming."

The unfamiliar word stopped Emma Lee. She sat down again and reached for her grandmother's hand. "What do you mean, Gramma?"

Firy sat silently for a moment, but her eyes showed awareness. She recited:

"Oh gloaming, thou hast richly shed
Sadness over me.
As thy pale mantle thou hast spread
Alike o'er land and sea.
And while I've wandered forth alone
In thy sweet tranquil hour
I've soared in thought to worlds unknown
Through thy enchanting power."

"That's beautiful, Gramma, but what does it mean?"

"I learned that in school... one of the Scottish poets, not Robbie Burns. Who was it?" Firy wrinkled her nose, trying to think.

"That's okay. I can Google it."

"You ask that Google everything. How do you know it's telling the truth?"

Emma Lee laughed. "I never thought of that. All right then, you tell me about it." As she held up her phone, she said, "Google says Robert Gemmel wrote that poem."

Firy settled back in her chair. "In Alaska, I watched as daylight faded, but night had not filled the sky with diamonds. My soul yearned..." Firy shrugged her shoulders, lost in thought, "Soon, I will walk through the gloaming and into the forest.

"And what does that mean?" Emma Lee asked.

After the old woman explained, Emma Lee scooted her plastic chair close and put her arm around her grandmother, "Don't talk like that. I don't want you to die, walk into the forest."

"Nonsense." Firy sniffed. "I'm not aware of myself half the time, and my mind, well, I don't know where it goes. It's frightening. I don't know why I'm still here."

Emma Lee swallowed the lump in her throat, not once, but twice, and said, "You've lived a whole life I know nothing about, and it has made you who you are. Maybe you're still here so you can share that life with me."

Firy leaned back and closed her tired eyes. Nevertheless, she took a breath, straightened her shoulders, and said, "Come when you can, and I will try to remember."

Emma Lee tried to smile as her grandmother patted her cheek. The light in Gramma's eyes faded, and she was gone, at least for now. She held her grandmother's hand and waited.

Firy's thoughts traveled from present hours to the distant past. So many pictures flashed through her mind. Awareness dawned. "Next time, I'll tell you about the war."

Silverware clattered and clanked as the aides brought dinner. Emma Lee turned up her nose at the pale mashed potatoes, rubbery green beans, and something that resembled Salisbury steak.

"Don't worry, dear, when you get old, your taste buds do, too," Firy chuckled. "But I wouldn't mind some of Agrafena's fry bread."

"How about a hamburger? I'll come tomorrow and bring us lunch."

"Can we have hot cocoa? I bet I could still taste that."

Emma Lee laughed out loud. Her mother, Firy's daughter, had carried on the family tradition and only allowed hot cocoa on special occasions. They celebrated sunshine and rain, laundry and Thursday, getting a cold, walking the dog, just about everything.

"Tomorrow's a special occasion, so we must have hot cocoa."

"What are we celebrating?"

"Don't you know? You're showing me Alaska's Firy."

Firy clapped her hands and sang the 'Humpback Salmon' song.

As Emma Lee drove home, she decided she'd Google how to make Indian fry bread. It wouldn't taste anything like Agrafena's, but Gramma would love her for trying.

THIRTEEN

Firy left the post office and stood at the sea wall that protected the village from the waters of Sitka Sound. Her heart, colored black as the many ravens looking for crumbs on the sidewalk, felt as cold as the seawater. With hands stuffed into the pockets of her navy jacket, Firy fingered the small bag of candy. She wished she was little when lemon drops seemed to fix everything.

Low hanging, murky clouds, and fog accompanied the incoming tide. Today's weather seemed to suggest the coming evil.

Who told her about 'The Day that Would Live in Infamy'? One of her teachers? Not likely: even though fifteen and a freshman in high school, the teachers still thought of their students as children. Perhaps Papa brought the news home from work. She knew she hadn't heard about the attack on the radio.

Papa kept the small Philco radio next to his rocking chair. It proudly sat on one of Aunt Ollyanna's crocheted doilies. He read the paper and listened to Big Band music every night after dinner while Firy and her siblings finished their chores and did their homework.

Firy turned her face into the wind. It didn't matter when or where she heard the news. It only mattered that it was true. She looked across the narrow channel to that scrap of an island. Nearly a hundred and fifty years ago, some Japanese sailors had been shipwrecked there, so the Russians called it Japonski. Firy shivered. Japan Island in the middle of Sitka Sound.

The Navy had been on Japonski since the early 1900s, but

only as a coaling station to refuel its steamships. In 1937 they established a seaplane base and began construction for a full naval air station. When the Japanese attacked Pearl Harbor, Alaskans became nervous. What if Japan turned their eyes northward? The facility on Japonski Island was the only established military installation in Alaska and barely operational. NAS Sitka was meant for the territory's defense, but it was also a prime target.

Firy gazed at the horizon. Beyond the Aleutians, Japan. Terrifying. Just the other day, she heard Papa and Mr. Anderson arguing. Papa Bill said three thousand miles from Japan to the Aleutians was much too close.

Firy wondered what war would look like here in the north. Yesterday, Elizaveta found two Japanese floats. Those glass balls had torn free from their fishing nets. If they made their way here, so could the Japanese Navy. What could Firy do to protect her sisters?

Fear crawled up her throat, and she looked for a way of escape. She felt like screaming but clamped her lips until she tasted blood, preferable to letting even an echo pass her lips.

Firy saw fish scows offloading their catch. Don't the waters of Japan have enough fish for its people? Maybe it's the timber. Perhaps it's the coal and gold still in the mountains. What if it's the land itself?

She doubled over, unable to breathe. *Oh, Bozhe, take my mind and put it someplace else.* The cannery's whistle blew, and Firy looked across the sea wall and watched as workers opened lunch pails or lit up their smokes. Some sagged to the dock for a few minutes of rest.

Captain Frank's boat slid into its mooring and blocked Firy's view of the cannery's dock. He waved and disappeared below deck, emerging with a beautiful silver salmon. She shook her head, no.

The Captain shrugged and tossed the fish back into the icy hold.

Firy remembered a time when Captain Frank's offer meant a hearty dinner. Back when Firy was young, and Mama was a northern Pied Piper. During the height of the fishing season, Mama started at the National Cemetery and arranged a little parade. Instead of playing a pipe, she banged a dishpan with a large wooden spoon. She collected kids of all ages as she wound through the neighborhood on her way to the docks.

They came with buckets, pails, and large pots. Most of the boys picked up sticks along the way and turned their buckets into drums. Mama raised her wooden spoon and directed them as if they were the most exceptional marching band. She taught them to sing, "I like humpback salmon, good ole humpback salmon, caught by the Sitka fisherman."

The mothers in the neighborhood watched while they hung clothes on the line or swept their wooden walks, grateful for Anna Wall's parade results, but annoyed their children were under the direction of a Creole. Anna knew most resented her marriage to a white man but never acknowledged their animosity.

The little parade turned the corner. "Mama, mean ole Mrs. Anderson is staring at us."

Mama turned and waved, but the curtain fell back. "Try to be kind. You don't know what kind of life she's had."

"Sven says she's the meanest mother in Alaska."

Mama held up her spoon, and the parade halted. She dropped to her knees before Firy. "I do not want you to think unkind thoughts about anyone. Understand?"

Even as she nodded, Firy wondered what was happening in the Anderson's unpainted, faded, cedar-shingled house.

The boy heard the salmon song before seeing his mother pull back the kitchen curtain and peek out. "Sven, bucket."

He threw down his Lincoln Logs in disgust. His stomach churned as it always did when his mother got that tone. "Aww, Ma."

"Hurry, join parade."

"You know Pa doesn't want me on the docks, especially Conway's."

"Conway may own dock, but Papa is boss."

"I know, and he says I should stay away."

She shrugged her shoulders and frowned at him, "So, hide behind Jensen twins."

"What if he sees me?"

"Do not let Papa see. He knows you are better than those-," She let the curtain fall back, "little beggars." She clamped her lips tight, pulled a wooden spoon from the crock, and beat the contents of a large bowl.

Sven held his stomach with both hands. He would not win this argument, "Okay, Ma."

She turned and shook the spoon in his direction, "I want King crab or halibut cheeks. You hear? No herring. No salmon. I am sick of salmon."

He watched the drips from the spoon splat onto the floor, glad she hadn't noticed. "But why make me go to the docks when Papa doesn't like it?"

His mother jabbed him in the chest with the wooden spoon. Whatever she stirred now stuck to his shirt. "I tell you why. Everything costs too much. These fishers, if they are stupid enough to give, I am smart enough to take. You see?"

He hung his head and told his stomach to stop churning. "Yes, Ma."

Firy saw Sven grab the bucket by his back door. He picked up a stick and pretended to bang and sing as he joined the parade. Mrs. Anderson yelled out the window. "No salmon. Crab or cheeks. You mind me."

They rounded the corner, and Mama held up her spoon and halted the parade. She motioned to Sven. He dropped his stick and dragged his feet.

"Sven, you and Henry are going to be my rear guard."

"What's that?"

"I need you to follow behind us, keep us in sight and watch for stragglers. Meet us at the docks."

Sven's head jerked up, "You mean we don't have to march with the little kids and the girls?"

"Or sing?" Henry said.

"No, give our Firy your buckets, and off you go."

The boys slapped each other on the back and ran to the end of the line and beyond.

"Why did you do that, Mama?"

"Did you see how free and joyful they looked? Whenever we do a kindness, it makes Bozhe happy."

Firy vowed to be extra kind to Sven for the rest of her life.

"Henry, too?" Mama said.

Firy knew that would be a lot harder but promised to try.

Mama's parade marched down Lincoln Street, past the Russian Church, the Pioneer Home, and right up to the docks' edge. Mama turned her band into a choir that sang all the verses of the Humpback Salmon song, and then they sang Sitka, Gem of the Western Ocean.

The captains applauded. And the kids took their bows as Mama had taught them. She pulled off her pink scarf, shook her dark hair, and blew kisses to the captains. Her red lips glistened in the sun.

Mama always joked with the skippers as she arranged the children in a single line, shortest to tallest. She reminded them to be respectful, thankful, and to mind their manners. The skippers, generous with their catch, mostly when the fishing was good, teased the children.

Firy shivered as the wind picked up in Sitka Sound. The briny air tickled her nose. Remembering reminded her that Mama was no longer here. Even thinking about the good times hurt. Firy leaned against the sea wall. Tears threatened as she pictured how the little band struggled when Mama got sick. It fell apart when she died.

Just then, the shrill sound of the cannery's whistle jerked Firy's attention away from the past, and Mama's face faded. Firy watched as the younger siblings of those who had marched with Mama stood in ragged clothes and held out their buckets. Grimly, the fisherman filled them. Firy doubted they even knew the words to "Humpback Salmon."

She breathed in salty, fishy air and saw Captain Frank attempt to sing. He tried to dance and joke — all for naught. The kids did not smile. Those not white, ashamed of their heritage, kept their heads down.

Charity had become a grudging responsibility. Pity from the fisherman. Shame from the children. A stink stronger than fish.

She swallowed the lump in her throat and dragged her jacket sleeve across her nose as she sniffed. She gazed once more over the water toward Japan.

FOURTEEN

As Firy tossed her books into her locker and slammed the door, Marie bumped into her and unwrapped a piece of bubble gum. "Vivian's in the girls' bathroom putting on her makeup."

"We all know Viv is a Lana Turner look-alike. Why does she have to pile on the make-up?"

"Who knows, but I'd kill for her long blond hair."

"Your thick brown curls are just as nice."

"Not with my chubby face." Marie wrinkled her nose and blew another bubble.

Firy rolled her eyes. "Where's Mardel? I haven't seen her all day."

"She skipped school again to be with a sailor. Don't look so horrified. She'll be careful."

"She's too curvy for her own good."

Marie looked down at her pudgy frame. "Again, I'd kill to be so curvy."

Vivian saw the girls enter as she leaned into the mirror and wiped the lipstick smudge from her upper lip. Plaid pleated skirts, bobby sox, and saddle shoes, the girls looked like typical teenagers from anywhere, America.

Firy tapped her foot, "You look fine, Viv. We're only going to the post office."

"You know, Firy, you could be pretty if you tried. Your hair's all wild, and you need to control it. Your eyes are a pretty color but need a little shadow." She blotted her lips on a tissue. "Besides, you never know who we'll see on the way."

Marie chomped her bubblegum and blew, "That's my biggest one yet."

Vivian picked up her purse and ignored the pink mess all over Marie's pimpled face, "Maybe we'll see a cute soldier who'll want to go to the castle."

Firy pulled on her jacket. "One of these days, you girls are going to go too far. You will bring shame to your elders."

Marie stopped mid-bubble, eyes wide. Vivian, hands on her hips, lipstick forgotten, said, "Honestly, Firy, sometimes you sound so—"

"Old and boring," Marie said, unwrapping another piece of bubblegum.

"Native!" Vivian finished.

"There's a reason for that." Firy stomped out. Chest heaving, breathing hard, she punched one fist into the other. They caught up with her half a block later.

"My mom said your mama was Russian. She said Bill Wall would never marry a . . ." Vivian stopped, her face almost as red as her lipstick.

"Just because you're a mighty senior and we're lowly sophomores doesn't mean you know anything," Firy snarled.

Marie laid her hand on Firy's arm, "Don't be mad. We don't think of you as native, not very often anyway."

Vivian tossed her long blond hair and stood toe to toe with Firy and said, "We want you to have fun. Come to the castle if you're brave enough."

Firy wanted to smack the smirk off of Vivian's face. She wanted to declare she was a full-blooded Yupik, but of course, she wasn't. And even if Petrov Bravebird said she was Tlingit all those years ago, it wasn't her bloodline. Her light skin and eyes betrayed her. She put her hands on her hot cheeks, "Stop talking about who I am, what I am, and stop asking me to go to the castle!"

"Don't try to convince her, Viv. Firy's as stodgy as Ivana Mishkin. There is no way either one of them will ever go to the castle or even have a boyfriend."

"You're almost sixteen, Firy. You need a boyfriend."

"Do not."

"You don't know what you're missing." Vivian winked.

Marie's bubble popped, and she pulled the sticky mess from her face. "Ivana won't go because she's afraid of her dad."

"Mean old Russian," Vivian said.

Firy, glad the girls had stopped talking about her native heritage, pulled a red bandanna from her jacket pocket, and tied back her hair. "He's not so bad. Sometimes I sneak into the café and listen. Ivan's gruff, but he loves his daughters."

Her girlfriends stared, horrified. "You listen to those old men in that shabby old café? Wortman's drugstore with its new soda fountain is the place to go." Marie said.

"Firy, I don't understand you." Vivian pulled her brush out of her purse and shook it in Firy's face. "Let me give you some advice. I have much more experience and wisdom than you."

Firy doubted that but didn't say so, "I want to know what's happening with the war and all."

"You can get the war news from Budnikov's newsreels."

"They're weeks old."

"The Navy's radio broadcasts several hours a day. I like Frank Sinatra the best." Marie grabbed Vivian and did a little jitterbug on the sidewalk.

Vivian pulled away, "Don't be so juvenile."

Marie's face fell, and she reached into her pocket for more gum.

"They don't tell us everything, too many censors, but the men at the café seem to be in the know," Firy said.

"I, for one, don't want to know. Come on, Marie, Firy's no fun today."

Marie threw a look of apology toward Firy and then followed Vivian.

Once or twice a week since the beginning of the war, Firy ducked into the Sitka Café. The customers now included sailors, soldiers, and coast guardsmen. Firy always kept her head down and her ears closed to any greetings or whistles. Agrafena appeared as if summoned by some kind of flare or radio signal. She slapped down plates of food and cups of coffee and admonished these young soldiers to mind their manners. She'd wink at Firy on her way back to the kitchen.

Within the walls of the café, Agrefena was the supreme commander and not afraid to exercise her power. Firy had watched her banish a captain and two sergeants for making remarks about the uncivilized north and its lousy weather. The townspeople knew it was prudent to keep on Agrafena's good side if they wanted to continue to enjoy her food. The US military was learning.

For the past six months, the news and rumors she heard were often unreliable, exaggerated, seldom accurate. Today, a warm afternoon in later summer, 1942, Firy settled at a corner table and leaned close to the half-curtained partition that separated the main dining area from the back room.

The décor, such as it was, a couple of deer heads mounted on the wall, and oilcloth placemats on the varnished wooden tables were decades older than Firy. Every few years, Mike suggested putting in booths to make their customers more comfortable. Agrefena objected. He tried to spruce up the place with new paint or curtains, but Agrefena said people came for the food, not to look at the walls.

When their son landed his first king salmon, she had it stuffed and hung over the kitchen door. "It's decoration enough," she said.

Firy, like everyone else in town, was unaware of the café's lack of charm. The Sitka Café was an institution; no need to change anything.

The men at the round table settled in with their coffee and the secret ingredient. Firy leaned close and listened. Soon she grabbed her chest and tried not to groan.

"I'm telling you the Japanese have invaded the Aleutian's, Attu, and Kiska," Ade said.

"Rumors," Mike's hair seemed greyer with the news of every battle and the shadows around his eyes, darker.

"It hasn't been on the radio or in the newspapers." Jake drained his coffee mug. Jake had tried to enlist three times, but a boating accident years ago left him deaf in one ear. The men were careful not to comment.

"How you know this thing?" Ivan puffed on his cigar. His wrinkles etched deeper in his face, and his mustache seemed bushier than ever.

"Fisherman's relay. All across the gulf, the news jumped from boat to boat. Apparently, they've been there for months."

"If what you say is true, Ade, we are not in a good position. If the Japs plan to use the Aleutians as a staging area for attacks on Kodiak and the Kenai, it won't be long until they're on our side of the gulf." Jake said.

"If they take Alaska, they're in a good position to take the whole west coast." Mike set the coffee pot on the table, all thoughts of refilling everyone's cups gone.

"There has to be a counter-attack. I think some of these GIs will soon ship out," Bill said. He looked haggard, and his sandy-hair had thinned to the point of disappearing.

"We need them here to defend Sitka. With the naval air station on Japonski, the only operational military installation in Alaska, we're a prime target."

Firy closed her eyes but couldn't stop her pounding heart. She was surprised Papa Bill didn't hear and order her home. *Be fierce. Remember, Mama said your name's a reminder to be strong. Brave.*

"I suspect Japanese submarines are already on our side of the gulf," Bob Nelson, a bush pilot just in from Ketchikan, said, "At least some of my fellow pilots think they've spotted one or two."

"A fisherman near Kodiak reported seeing one," Ade said.

Firy blocked their words from her mind. She knew most men in town who were too old for the draft had volunteered for the ATG, the Alaska Territorial Guard. All across Alaska, men up to age eighty had joined. Indians, Eskimos, natives, white, it didn't make any difference. All were Alaskans, and all were welcome. In some communities, boys as young as twelve could join. The ATG offered support to the military. Reconnaissance, patrolling their towns, enforcing blackouts. Whatever was needed.

Firy knew these old men would fight to the death if the Japanese invaded Sitka. Small comfort. If the GIs shipped out, there wouldn't be that many men left in town. She stumbled out of the café.

"You okay, Firy? You look a little green." Bob Nelson caught up with her near the corner.

Firy looked into his serious hazel eyes. "When are you flying out?"

"Soon. I just had to see the guys at the café. I promised I'd stop in whenever I'm in Sitka and share the news."

"Are the Japanese really on Kiska and Attu? Are they going to attack? Did you really see a submarine?"

The color drained from Bob's face, and he turned to face her, "Where did you hear that?"

"At the café."

"I noticed you behind the curtain." Bob ran his hand over his hair and took a deep breath, "Just a bunch of old men gossiping. It makes them feel important. Nothing for you to worry about. Probably just a reflection off the water." His knuckles white, he zipped and unzipped his jacket and muttered, "See you next time."

Firy watched the tiny man leave. She always thought he could be a horse jockey like she'd read about. Bob always said it was a good thing he was small. He could fly more cargo that way.

She wiped her sweaty palms on her pants and wished she were more like Vivian and the others. They seemed to push all thoughts of the war aside to focus on cute soldiers and sailors.

Popeye whined and scratched at the back door.

"What is it, boy?" Firy held out a cookie and tried to lure

Popeye back to his rug in front of the woodstove. He continued whining. She shrugged into her jacket and thought about grabbing Papa's shotgun. A peek out the window showed her there was nothing there, but she grabbed Anna Marie's baseball bat anyway.

As Firy cracked open the door, Popeye raced through and stood at the edge of the yard growling and pawing at the bushes. A hand batted at him, and a voice whispered, "Scram, Popeye."

"Sven? Is that you?" Firy yelled into the darkness.

"Shh. Ivan just ran past. I don't want him to double back."

"Why is he after you?" Firy lowered the bat.

"He caught me up at the castle."

"You and Ivana at the castle?"

"Not her, but he must think so." Sven brushed a branch from his face, "Your dad was there, too."

"What?" Firy's shrill voice cracked the night sky.

"Shh. I was on the third floor. I thought I might spot a Japanese submarine."

"Did you?" Firy trembled and fell to her knees. She hugged Popeye and stared into Sven's eyes, "And why was Papa Bill there?"

"Naw, no sub. Bill was with a bunch of men from the café. They were crawling up both sides of the hill."

"That must've been Jake's ATG unit."

"The Alaska Territorial Guard is a joke. Bunch of old codgers couldn't defend anything. They need to let us younger guys join. Give them some real power."

"C'mon Sven. They might be older, but they're tough."

"I heard high school kids on Kodiak are allowed to join. It's not fair. Anyway, the guys had their guns drawn. And then I saw several naval skiffs reach the shore."

"Japanese?"

"American. I yelled a warning to the Jensen twins and lit out of there."

"Then what happened?"

"Ivan jumped out of the bushes and screamed he was going to beat me with his seal club and Ivana, too. I lost him a block back, laid a false trail, but he's a good tracker, even if he is an old man." Sven shuddered.

Firy ignored his fear. "Did Vivian and Marie get away?"

"Viv and Marie? At the castle?"

"They go all the time."

"Nope."

Firy chuckled to herself, so that's the way of it. Her girlfriends were all talk. *I wonder what they would say if I suddenly agreed to go with them.*

She turned her attention back to Sven. "I thought you wanted to marry Ivana. When she finds out you were at the castle with someone else..."

"Don't tell her."

"I won't, but she will find out."

Sven lowered his eyes then brightened. "I'll enlist and become a war hero, and then she'll forgive me. Ivan will have to let her marry me."

"But, you're only 17."

"Plenty of guys lied about their age. Henry did. I should have gone with him."

"Don't you dare enlist! I'm still mad at Henry. Please, Sven."

Sven pulled back and let the bushes cover him, "Go! Somebody's coming."

Firy and Popeye scrambled back to the house, but she pulled the curtains back and watched Stormy Durand and Bull come around the corner.

The bushes rustled, and the mastiff's low growl alerted Stormy as he patrolled Sitka's neighborhoods. He tossed his cigarette and drew his gun. "Come out of there."

"Can't."

"That you, Sven Anderson? What have you done now?"

"Nothing, but Ivan Mishkin thinks I've been fooling around with Ivana."

"Have you?" The Chief holstered his weapon.

"No, sir. Call off your dog, uh, please."

Ivan huffed around the corner, winded. "Chief, you see evil Sven Anderson?"

Stormy tugged Bull's collar and forced the mastiff to sit. The dog continued a low growl. "What do you mean, evil?"

"Sven at castle with my Ivana." Ivan leaned against the picket fence, breathing hard.

"What evidence do you have?"

"The ATG, that is, Jake, I mean Navy, charge up Castle Hill. We..."

Stormy held up his hand. "I don't want to know about Jake and the ATG, crazy old men trying to be soldiers. And the Navy, why can't they keep all the sailors on Japonski Island. It'd make my life a lot easier. This town, with all the soldiers and sailors, is making my job into more than I want it to be."

The bushes rustled, the dog jumped, and Sven sneezed. Ivan

grabbed Stormy's arm. "You are law. Put Sven in jail. Maybe shoot."

Stormy Durand held on to the enraged father. "I got him, Sven. Run home and stay away from the castle."

"Keep away from Ivana. I beat you, sure." Ivan squirmed and swore. He punched the air and swore again. Worn out, he sagged against the Chief. "Is not good to have girls."

"Go home, Ivan."

"But you are law, you must..."

"I'll handle it, but stay away from Sven."

"You swear on life of dog?"

Bull bared his teeth and fixed his eyes on Ivan. Stormy scratched his beloved Bull behind the ears. "I swear on the life of my dog."

Bull growled as Ivan went home, and the Chief continued patrolling the neighborhood. "Don't worry, Bull, this incident has already had more attention than it deserves."

By the time Ivan reached his front gate, he had worked himself into a rage once more. "Where is Ivana? Where girl?"

"I'm here, Papa."

"Where you been?"

His wife, Olga, answered, "Here, knitting socks for war and listening to Tommy Dorsey on station from San Francisco, America."

"Sure?" Ivan yelled, shaking his fist at his wife and daughter.

"Husband, quiet yourself. Other girls sleep." Olga went to his side and guided him to his chair by the fireplace.

"Me and boys up to Castle, maybe see Japs." He sank into his chair. His wife and daughter both gasped, their faces full of fear.

"No, no, just kids. Sven Anderson and dark-hair girl. I think it you." He glared at his oldest daughter, "I want to catch, beat with club."

Olga stamped her foot and cried, "How you think such a thing about your daughter. Up to Castle!"

Ivana burst into tears, "You chased Sven with your club!" She ran out of the room and up the stairs. "I hate you!" she threw the words over her shoulder.

"Hate me? Why she not hate Sven."

Olga explained, but Ivan stared into the flames and didn't hear. What could he tell the men at the café without looking like a fool? He pulled his socks and shoes off and held his feet toward the fire. Five daughters. *Why Bozhe not give me sons?*

On Castle Hill, Captain Barnes assembled Jake's ATG unit on the veranda. He cursed and upbraided them as only a career Navy officer could do. His verbal lashing matched the staccato stomp of his boots as he strutted up and down the vast porch. "When the spotter on Harbor mountain radioed me about the lights flickering in the castle, out of courtesy, I advised you about our mission."

"You did, Captain, but we thought..."

"I don't care what you thought. I ordered you to let the Navy handle this."

"Yes, sir, but we suspected..."

"There could have been a submarine in the harbor. The Japanese could have occupied this building. Take this hill, and you take the town. It's my job to protect this town, all of Alaska, for that matter. You know NAS Sitka is Alaska's protection against the Japanese." He sputtered to a stop, swore, and began again. "You don't know what those lights meant."

"Captain, we knew..."

"When I say stand down, that is a direct command from the United States Navy." Captain Barnes stabbed Jake in the chest with his finger. "The Navy's authority is above that of your little militia. Got that? You think because the naval air station was a mishmash of forgotten ordinance with little personnel..." He took his cap off and rubbed it across his eyes. "I've worked hard to bring that base up to current Navy standards, and we will soon be fully operational."

Jake's stiff shoulders and clenched jaw told the men they needed to act. Ade stood in front of Jake and blocked his view of the Captain. Mike pulled a flask from his back pocket and handed it to his red-faced friend. They formed a phalanx around their young leader.

Bill quietly took Jake's rifle. "Easy, Jake. It's not worth it."

Ade stepped forward and saluted, "Captain Barnes, sir, I suspect the Japanese Navy does not include giggling females, and I don't think they smoke Lucky Strikes." His boot shoved an empty cigarette package off the porch.

Suddenly, a light in the dark hall flickered. Bill Wall raised his handgun. "That's an awful dangerous light, Captain. Maybe I should shoot it."

"Belay that!" Captain Barnes yelled. He turned to two of his sailors and ordered, "Remove every light bulb in this building. Jake, you tell those kids the Castle is off-limits for the duration of the war."

"But Captain, the castle is the one place in town where the kids can..."

"I don't care. It's off-limits.'

The men of the ATG lined up, winked at Jake, then saluted Captain Barnes, "Aye, aye, Sir."

As they scrambled down the hill, Jake groused and said, "The Navy needs to stay on Japonski and let us see to the defense of the town."

"Remember fellas, the Navy's not the enemy," Mike said.

"Sure seems like it sometimes," Jake growled.

"We could have won the battle of the light bulb without any help from the United States Navy," Bill said.

"Life was easier before the Navy started throwing its weight around," Jake swore.

"Life was easier before the war," Ade said.

"If Ivan were here, he'd say life was easier when Alaska belonged to Russia," Bill added.

The men trudged down the hill, convinced there was no need for the United States Navy to interfere in their lives or their land. They could defend both, thank you very much.

FIFTEEN

"Men is..." Ivan began, "I think...maybe..." Shushed by the others, he shoveled another bite into his mouth.

Sven Anderson rushed into the café. "Mike Evans! Telegram for Mr. Mike Evans!" Mike hurried out of the kitchen, wiped his hands on his grease-spattered apron, and grabbed the telegram. He shooed the boy out of the café while he opened the folded yellow paper. He took a deep breath and let it out in a whoosh.

The diners still held theirs. As far as they knew, Mike didn't have anyone in the service, but no one knew about his life before Alaska. It was an unwritten rule in the territory; you waited for information. Mike never shared.

He fell into the chair between Jake and Ivan. "Listen: Touch and go across the gulf. Stop. On way to village. Stop. Lost big birds. Stop. Back to you after war. Stop."

They slapped each other's backs and raised their mugs.

"He must have made it to his grandparents deep in the Kenai," Jake said.

"No one knows the coast and gulf islands like uh, him," Ade said.

"Navy not catch Bob," Ivan leaped from his chair. The men at the table shushed him.

"No names, Ivan," Jake cautioned, "Never any names."

Mike brought out another round of the secret ingredient. "He must have had a friend send the telegram from Seward. He would have had to refuel. The big birds were obviously navy planes."

Jake looked across the table at Bill and asked him, "How does a little trip to the Kenai sound to you?"

"Why, Jake," drawled Bill, "you know I have no reason to leave Sitka."

"If you say so."

"I say so," Bill leaned back in his chair, "Okay, Jake, I know you are dying to tell what you think you know."

"Wait a minute! Wait!" Mike jumped up and clapped his hands. "Important meeting for Jake's ATG. The backroom is closed. Everyone, please take your breakfast to the front dining area. Very nice. View of the street. Free butterhorns and bear claws for all."

The reluctant diners picked up their plates and shuffled toward the front dining area. They grumbled and complained as Mike hurried them along. The Sitka Café's backroom had large windows overlooking the water, and most of his customers liked to watch the boats as they ate. More importantly, they wanted to eavesdrop on the round table.

Mike flapped his apron at Budnikov, who lingered.

"Ah, Mike. I can stay, yes?" the little man whined. He gazed at the now empty chair between Jake and Bill. Mike looked at Jake, who looked at Ade, who looked at Bill, who looked at Ivan, who gave a slight shake of his head. Budnikov muttered Russian curses as he stamped out.

"What'd he say?" Jake asked.

"You not want to know," Ivan said, "don't meet in dark alley. Probably Russian spy."

"Ivan, you do know America's flying planes across Alaska to supply Russia. We're allies."

"Budnikov not good Russian. I think Red."

Ade shook his head. "I never saw a guy who jumped at the

chance to make a buck.

No way is Budnikov a communist!"

"Maybe not Red. Not good Russian."

The backroom cleared, and Mike poured another round of coffee. He bowed to Jake. "You may begin."

Now that he knew Bob Nelson was safe from prosecution by the Navy, Jake could enjoy telling the story, most of which the men already knew. "It all started when a certain fisherman..." He stared across the table at Ade, "shall we say a certain fisherman out of Wrangell heard from a certain pilot from Ketchikan?"

"I definitely heard it was a fisherman from Wrangell," Ade said. The men rolled their eyes and laughed.

"Why you laugh? Who is Wrangell fisher?" Ivan said.

The men pointed to Ade.

"From Sitka, no Wrangell." A confused Ivan chewed on his mustache.

"Stop laughing, guys, or I will never get this tale told. This fisherman spotted a Japanese submarine thirty nautical miles west of Japonski." Jake cleared his throat and reminded everyone how construction at the Navy base was full speed ahead, acres of concrete poured, runways graded, and Quonset huts erected. There was still only a token force of sailors stationed there, although several army forts had been established on islands in Sitka Sound.

"Remember, Ade, when you told me about the sub, I said I didn't think the Navy could do anything and then..." The men leaned back in their chairs and drank their coffee.

"Be fair, Jake," Bill replied, "All the Navy had were two PBY's, and they were still waiting for parts from the States. Pilots too."

Jake pointed to the old Russian, "Remind me, Ivan, how your

eyes nearly bulged out. You pounded your fist on the table and demanded we fight. Bob Nelson had just landed his floatplane and come into the café. Perfect timing. Bob had a plane, and the Navy had bombs. Mike told us Bob had gone to Annapolis back in the day. They say, 'once a Marine, always a Marine, and we told Bob, once a sailor, always a sailor." Jake nodded across the table at Bill, "And you were in ordinance during the Great War."

"I was a lowly supply clerk."

None of the men at the table interrupted Jake to ask the obvious questions. How did Bill and Bob steal the bomb? Who at this table helped him? Did they bribe the Navy's supply clerk? Did Bill forge an official-looking requisition? Who was complicit in this robbery?

Jake ignored the questions he saw in the men's eyes and continued the story, "The Navy's blackout meant the buildings in town and the boats in the harbor had extinguished their lights or blacked out their windows at dusk. However, the Navy couldn't darken the moon or stars. Bill and Bob, with two accomplices, moved about in the night's light.

"My hands shook as we maneuvered that bomb onto a trolley and pushed it across the tarmac. It must have weighed five hundred pounds. We should have planned a diversion." Bill said and bowed to Jake to continue.

"They reached Bob's plane, moored on the far side of Japonski, without mishap, then removed one of the back seats and lashed the bomb to the other. They tied a rope around the plane's struts and the other end to Ade's boat. He towed Bob's plane half a mile into the Sound. This is the conversation as I remember it." Jake said.

"That's right." Bill lifted his mug for Mike to refill.

"One of our accomplices said we needed to get home before we were spotted. Curfew, you know."

"Who says what?" Ivan asked.

"I'm not going to tell you that, Ivan. Bob landed the small floatplane in a hidden cove off an unnamed island. He and Bill drank coffee and smoked cigarettes until dawn. Take it, Bill." Jake buttered his toast and ate while Bill talked.

"We approached the coordinates, and Bob started a grid search. Soon we saw the submarine's dark shape near the surface. Bob circled the target, and I climbed into the back to unfetter the bomb."

Bill didn't particularly like hearing this story, much less telling it. Even as he spoke, he remembered his time in the Great War. After being wounded, he was reassigned to supply, an easy job behind the lines. The trenches were up close and personal, dangerous. He had looked at the cold, Alaskan waters and shuddered. The men in the submarine had no chance to defend themselves.

Bill remembered how his stomach churned and the doubts that surfaced in his mind as the Cessna circled the target. But he did his duty and dispatched the enemy to their eternal destiny.

Now he lit a cigarette and motioned for Jake to describe what happened. Bill wouldn't speak of it if he could avoid it.

"The way I heard it, Bob had to circle the target twice. The latch on the door was broken, and Bill almost pitched out of the plane. Bill got behind the bomb, braced himself, and pushed with his legs. Nothing. Bill instructed Bob to go around again and bank some more, and then he hung on for dear life. The bomb pitched out of the plane. They yelled 'bombs away' at the top of their lungs. Perfect. A few seconds later, the water exploded like Old Faithful. The force of it shook the little Cessna as it sped away."

"That's right," Bill said.

"Bob fought to steady the plane from the shock waves, and Bill climbed back into the front seat and yelled for Bob to turn around and look for survivors. Bob shrugged and flew low over the debris field. He and Bill stared at each other, and their eyebrows disappeared beneath their watch caps. Mission Accomplished. A perfect hit. They had blown up a whale!"

When Jake whispered whale, the men at the table stamped their feet, slapped each other on the back, and raised their coffee cups to all who shall remain nameless, including the whale.

Captain Barnes and another officer had just finished their breakfast in the street-side dining area. They headed to the back room when they heard the ruckus. They sat at the counter and ordered more coffee.

"Is good, bomb is nameless." Ivan chuckled. The naval officers at the counter looked his way. Ivan picked up his coffee and gulped.

A red-faced Captain Barnes marched over to the table. "You know," he growled, "we have witnesses of suspicious activity on base. Ordinance is missing, a bomb, to be specific. A blue and yellow Cessna left Sitka Sound under cloudy circumstances last week. We've identified the pilot as a Bob Nelson. He will be caught, and so will his accomplices."

Captain Barnes gave the men a stern look and slapped the table. "We know men from the town were involved. Stealing from the Navy is a serious offense, especially during a war."

He looked at each man in the eye. They stared him down. He may have been Navy, but they were Alaskans. As he lowered his eyes and left the café, he said. "They're all yours, Captain Hough. It's the South Pacific for me. I'm sure the inhabitants of the south seas islands will be more cooperative and civilized."

Captain Hough motioned to Mike for a refill and pointed to the secret compartment. Mike shook his head and held out empty hands. Captain Hough motioned again. Reluctantly, Mike poured a generous portion of the ingredient for the Captain.

Captain Hough, tall and mild-mannered, carried the steaming mug to the table. He spoke slowly and softly, and the men leaned in to hear him. "It's like this, men. I wouldn't want to hear any tall tales around town that might embarrass the United States Navy. No rumors or exaggerated stories. Don't force me to take any actions that would be, uh, uncomfortable."

He finished his coffee and set his mug carefully on the table. His grey eyes steeled the men. He reached the archway between the two dining areas, turned, and gave each man a long look. "By the way, thanks for saving the US Navy from Moby Dick." He saluted, then whistled as he left.

The men leaned back in their chairs, breakfast forgotten. They didn't know if they should laugh or be afraid. True, this new captain was soft-spoken, but there was iron in his eyes.

Bill looked at his watch with red-rimmed, tired eyes, relieved that Firy had not yet arrived. He reached for his coffee and thought of all the changes since the war began. Masha married a sailor and lived with his family in California. As soon as the war began, Henry had lied about his age and enlisted. Elizaveta was about to run off with her Coastie; he could feel it and didn't know how to stop her. She cut her hair, wore makeup, skipped school. Bill rubbed his hand over his thinning hair and sighed.

That left only Anna Marie and Firy. On weekdays they met him and walked him home before going to school. Today was Firy's turn. She came in as Captain Hough left.

"Is that the new commander of the Navy base?" Firy's gaze followed Captain Hough as he left.

Bill nodded.

"I heard he's a little more reasonable than Captain Barnes. More human."

"More humane, you mean," Mike said.

"What is humane?" Ivan asked.

Jake leaned over and laughed, "It means human."

Ivan shook his head, opened his mouth, looked from Mike to Jake and back again. "Human? Humane? English, bah!"

Firy and Bill waved their goodbyes and walked home in Sitka's slight drizzle. "Anna Marie is hoping you're hungry enough for another breakfast before she goes to school."

"Did she make it herself?"

"She was stirring some rather gloopy oatmeal when I left."

"Sounds wonderful." Bill rubbed his stomach and belched. "I'm sure you'll join me."

"I'm not hungry."

"You haven't eaten for days, and it looks like you've lost weight. What's troubling you?"

"I'm fine."

"It's the war, isn't it?"

"I'm fine."

"You don't need to worry. Everything will be okay." Even to his ears, it sounded like a lie. "I wish your mother was here. She'd know how to talk to you."

Firy put her hand in his. "Papa, can I skip school today and go to the cemetery? I need Mama."

It was the first time she had ever called him papa without adding 'Bill.' He swallowed the lump in his throat. "What about Miss Ruth?"

"She's in Hoonah for two weeks. Please, I need to talk to Mama."

"Go now, but don't stay too long. School was very important to your mother." He stood on the sidewalk and watched her cross the street and run up the hill toward the Russian cemetery. He shoved his hands in his pockets and turned toward home. *Darn it, Anna, I'm doing the best I can.*

SIXTEEN

The sun glistened off the water as it always did after a good rain. Looking for scraps from the canneries running at full capacity, grey seabirds and black ravens screeched and swooped over the seiners and trawlers coming into the docks. Fishers bustled, offloading their catch. Cannery workers hustled to keep the lines running and the hoppers full.

Sitka was in the midst of an invasion. Not Russians looking for furs nor the Americans seeking gold. The invaders were not the Japanese, but the United States military. Army. Navy. Coast Guard.

Rumors flew throughout town after the Japanese occupied Attu and Kiska. The servicemen who had dribbled into Alaska by the hundreds now exploded to the thousands. The men of the Sitka Café couldn't tell where their anxiety of the Imperial Navy ended, and that of the United States military began.

"If the sailors stay on the Naval Air Base on Japonski and the soldiers on all their bases in the Sound, it shouldn't be a problem," Jake said.

"Not going to happen," Ade said, "I thank God my daughter is too young to be tempting."

Ivan sputtered into his coffee, "I protect mine." He looked in each man's eyes, and his dark, bushy mustache quivered. Ivan, usually all bluster and bravado, began to weep.

"We all will, Ivan. Not to worry."

Bill, worried about his step-daughters, squinted, "Let's consider the logistics of the situation. Sitka has about a thousand residents, right?"

"If all the fishermen are in port, miners in town, loggers out of the woods, and natives between hunting and foraging parties, then yes, about a thousand," Mike noted as he placed plates of venison and herring roe before the men.

Bill continued, "I heard the town would be hosting about 30,000 members of the military."

"I host them with Katerina." Ivan's eyes bulged.

Jake chuckled and slapped Ivan on the back, "I still don't know how you smuggled that rifle from France after the Great War."

A look of tenderness crossed Ivan's face. He leaned back and rubbed the stock of the rifle leaning against his chair. "She served me well."

"I can't believe you named her," Ade reached for the cream.

Ivan sighed and stared into his coffee. "Katerina, my love."

Jake leaned toward Ade, "Isn't his wife named Olga?"

"It is." Ade whispered back, "Don't ask."

Bill rapped his knuckles on the table. "I've thought about this a lot. It's a simple matter of supply and demand."

"My daughters, I not supply," Ivan snapped.

Bill sighed, then continued as if Ivan had not spoken. "Those two uh, floozie shacks beyond Indiantown can barely supply the needs of Sitka's uh, wayward men. There's no way 30,000 servicemen will be satisfied."

"Better they go to France or South Sea. Many loose women." Ivan mumbled as he cradled his coffee cup with big rough hands.

"The demand will be high," Jake said.

"And the supply will not increase," Ade added.

"That's a problem," Mike said. He lingered with the large enamel coffeepot and refilled half-empty cups.

"We must protect woman," Ivan said and chewed on his unlit cigar.

"Trouble is," Jake laughed, "they'd say they could defend themselves from amorous sailors and soldiers."

"You know, Bill, our Firy can outshoot you any day of the week," Ade said.

Bill rubbed the stubble on his cheek, not at all chagrined, "I'm not too proud to admit it. Still, I don't want her shooting any US military personnel."

"At least, not with bullets," Ade said.

All the heads at the table jerked in his direction.

"What you say?" Ivan asked.

"Two summers ago, I took several government agents up the Lynn Canal to Haines. They continued up through Chilkat Pass with guns that shot bears with tranquilizer pellets. Crazy."

"Do you think we could get our hands on some of that stuff?" Bill asked.

"If it's strong enough to knock out a brownie or a black bear, it might kill a man. We should make our own."

"Jake, you wise man. I go. See Doc." Ivan rubbed his palms together and slapped Jake on the back. He patted the rifle and slung it over his shoulder, and headed to Doc's office to see if the physician might donate some knockout drops or ether.

Jake stood and drained his coffee cup. "I'll stroll over to the drugstore and see what Wellerton has available. Ade, can you talk to Bravebird?"

"Sure. He knows about the island's medicinal plants. There should be something sedating."

The combination of ingredients to produce incapacitating fumes proved tricky. It took a while to create a stable formula.

A week later, the men promised Johnny the Bear Boy two large venison steaks, a chicken egg omelet, and as much fry bread as he could eat. He let the men take him halfway up Harbor Mountain. He sat on a log and ate the breakfast Agrafena had provided.

"Doesn't seem sporting, him just sitting there eating," Jake said, looking through his rifle's sight. "I don't know if I can pull the trigger."

"Pretend he's a GI who's had his way with your daughter," Ade said.

"You know I don't have a daughter."

"Your sister, then."

"She's in the lower 48."

Ivan grabbed the gun, fired, and hit Johnny in the shoulder. The pellet burst on impact. Johnny cursed and slapped at his shoulder. Ivan threw down Jake's gun and picked up Katerina, and shot again. Johnny swatted the pellets as if they were nothing more than Alaska's giant mosquitoes.

"The formula's not strong enough," Ade said.

Over the next week and a half, the men tinkered with the formula then went into the woods again.

The well-muscled Spanish mastiff picked up the scent long before his master. He eased his way through the underbrush with stealth that belied his 180 pounds. He lay at the edge of the meadow. Nose pointed toward the prey.

"Good boy. Watch the horse." The chocolate-colored dog rose to his feet and looked over in contempt as his master dismounted. His low growl said he was a warrior, not a watchdog.

"I know," the lawman patted the dog's head, "but there are wolves in these woods. Protect my horse."

Stormy Durand's jurisdiction as Sitka's Chief of Police extended through water and wood. Exactly how far had never been platted. Today, he followed a rumor halfway up Harbor Mountain.

Bam! Bam!

He swore as he un-holstered the rifle and gentled his horse. The mastiff growled and rested his massive head on his paws, eyes darting between hunter and prey. The Chief reached down and reassured the dog, "I'll whistle if I need you."

At the far end of the meadow, he saw Johnny the Bear Boy. What are those idiots from the café…?

Bam! Bam! Bam! Johnny tumbled over.

Chief Durand aimed his rifle and hollered, "Drop your guns. I don't want to shoot, but you know I will."

"Dang it, Chief, why can't you drive a pickup like the rest of us?"

Chief Durand spat tobacco juice into the fireweed, "I come barreling up that logging road, and you guys are going to hear and scatter."

"Is true."

"Shut up, Ivan," Jake said.

"The horse and I get where we're going. It looks like we got here just in time. NOW DROP THOSE GUNS!"

Ivan shivered and ducked behind six-foot-two Jake Steiner. He laid his precious Katerina on the ground. "Is only Johnny Bear Boy."

"Don't get riled up, Stormy. There is a perfectly good explanation." Jake shouted.

The Chief turned his head and sent a stream of tobacco juice three feet to the left, his walrus mustache catching a few drops. "Not when there's a dead body, there ain't."

"Nobody's dead," Ade yelled as he nudged the old Tlingit with the toe of his boot.

Johnny, the Bear Boy, moaned and sat up. He gathered the scattered pieces of fry bread and shoved them in his mouth.

Stormy made his way across the meadow, rifle still aimed at the knot of men. Jake stepped aside, and Ivan tugged on the lawman's sleeve. "There, you see..."

"Doggone it, Ivan. I nearly pulled the trigger." Stormy's eyes flashed.

Johnny scratched his chest and shoulder and moaned again.

"That's it," Bill said. "We're going to have to make it more lethal and shoot him again."

"I agree." Jake said, "he wasn't out nearly long enough."

"Now, see here..." Stormy had lowered his weapon but raised it again and aimed it at those idiots. They all talked at once, but Stormy watched Johnny. He seemed okay and didn't want to leave.

Stormy Durand scratched his head and refused to listen to any explanations as he and Bill Wall walked toward the dog and the horse. Stormy eased himself into the saddle. "Just tell me you ain't doing anything illegal, Bill."

"I'm not a lawyer, but if something happens down the road, it's better you don't know."

Stormy shoved his rifle back in its holder and frowned, "I tell you again, I don't like it, but I can't say there's a law against volunteering to be a target." He looked at Johnny, who smiled and waved.

Relief flooded Bill's face. He scratched Bull's head and said goodbye.

"See you don't kill him." Stormy flicked the reins and muttered over his shoulder, "It would make my life a whole lot easier if you louts would confine yourselves to the café."

"Sure, Chief," Bill laughed, "we can do that."

The ride down the mountain took an hour or two, and it began to rain. Stormy Durand pulled his collar up and his hat down. He moaned to the mastiff. "I tell you, being a shoe salesman in Chicago wasn't so bad. Maybe I should've stayed."

Several days later, there was another meeting of the round table. They had tripled the formula with no better results.

"I don't think we're going to succeed, fellas," Ade said.

Silently, Mike laid a few vials of a greenish liquid on the table.

"What is?" Ivan asked.

"I don't know exactly, so let's just say those government agents I told you about are protecting Sitka's women."

"They gave you that tranquilizer stuff?" Bill asked.

"I honored them with more of my secret ingredient than usual." Mike wiggled his eyebrows like Groucho Marx, and the others laughed as they pictured him appropriating the vials from tipsy government agents.

They promised Johnny the Bear Boy a week's worth of café meals if they could shoot him tomorrow.

"Mike, if you take that old Tlingit into the woods again, I promise you will sleep on the couch all week," Agrafena stomped back to the kitchen. The sounds of banging pots and pans clanged through the café.

"Fellas, I have to withhold these vials, or I'm banished."

The men grumbled, but Mike said, "If I suffer, you suffer."

They argued with him, and he pleaded with Agrefena.

"Do you want to make it two weeks?" she said.

However, the next morning the men found the vials under their napkins. Nothing was said, and they disappeared into Ade's pocket.

Target practice resumed, and the pellets exploded on impact with a satisfying green splatter. Ivan rushed to see if Johnny the Bear Boy still breathed. Almost immediately, Ivan grabbed his stomach and deposited his breakfast behind the log.

"I told you to stand back," Ade yelled, "those fumes will get you."

The men circled Johnny at a distance. They glanced at each other, frowned, and continued to watch. After forty-five minutes, Johnny the Bear Boy twitched and moaned.

Bill slapped his knee. "I think we've done it, boys. A shot to the upper chest or shoulder is all that's needed."

"Those gassy fumes dropped him in one breath," Mike laughed out loud. "I'll leave you to take care of Johnny. I've got to get back before the wife finds out I'm gone." He ran to his pickup.

"I think it would be long enough for our women to get help," Jake said.

Ade rubbed his hand over his chin. "If we can convince them to do that. They might want to finish the job themselves."

All the Sitka women were supplied with the anti-GI pellets, even those who worked at the fish canneries. It was thought bits of smelly fish guts clinging to female cannery workers would be an insufficient deterrent to desperate men far from home.

And so, life in Sitka continued. Men in uniform clogged the sidewalks. Local businessmen were thrilled. Local fathers were not. Mothers worried as their teenage daughters batted eyes at these handsome soldiers.

The military did its part by limiting weekend passes. The American Legion and the VFW organized well-chaperoned dances, baseball games, and bingo. In town, the various churches arranged social nights with board games and served homemade cookies baked by local girls and their mothers.

Most of the GIs were boys fresh from the farm or small-town America. Young. Awkward. Uncertain. These soldiers and sailors, raised by patriotic church-goers, had brought their parents' values to the north.

Still, a certain percentage of servicemen filed through the floozie shacks beyond Indiantown. Supply was not keeping up with demand.

The Checkinov sisters decided they should increase the supply. Vavara, a ticket clerk at Budnikov's, and Larissa, who took in laundry, had plenty of free time. The not so young spinsters thought this would be a marvelous way to supplement their income.

They painted their front door bright yellow to be cheerful and posted flyers around town, inviting any military personnel to their home. It took Father Alexi and his priests all weekend to tear them down, but the word was out.

❦

"Why are those soldiers lined up outside the Checkinov's house?" Anna Marie asked one evening.

"Never mind." Papa growled, "Don't talk to any GIs, and don't talk to those crazy spinsters anymore, either."

"But why?" she asked.

Bill shot Firy a look, rattled his newspaper, and hid behind it.

"Come, Dodo." Firy said, "Help me with the dishes."

"But I want to know."

"I'll tell you what I can."

That Saturday night Papa left for the mill. Firy tucked Elizaveta, who was sick, into bed, then made popcorn and, with Papa's permission, hot cocoa. Anna Marie wanted to celebrate Popeye's doggie birthday, and Papa never refused his little Dodo.

Firy stoked the woodstove and fireplace as she listened to Glenn Miller on the radio. Anna Marie and Popeye snuggled in a fort made by blankets draped over the kitchen table. Popeye panted in the enclosed space but stayed for the popcorn.

Firy hummed along to the music as she darned Papa's socks. She jabbed her finger for the second time and shoved it into her mouth before she could say a bad word.

Raucous laughter accompanied a pounding on the door. "Popeye, Down!" Firy commanded as the dog growled and pawed at the door. "Anna Marie, hold him while I see what this is about."

"No," the girl cried. "I'm staying in my fort."

Firy peeked through the curtains. Several soldiers leaned on the gate, three others sprawled on the stairs by the door of the enclosed porch, and one had broken through its arctic entrance and pounded on the living room door.

"Let me in, girly. I just got paid, and I'm ready for some fun!" The doorknob rattled, the hinges creaked, and the pounding turned to kicking. Popeye pawed at the door and barked.

Firy reached behind the radio for Papa's shotgun, loaded with the special pellets. She had never pointed a gun at a person before. Could she pull the trigger? She raised the rifle with sweaty hands and yelled at Popeye to get behind her. "Popeye! Now!" The canine growled, but he obeyed.

The door burst open, and a burly soldier fell in. He held on to the door and pulled himself upright. He stared at the girl and tried to focus his rheumy eyes. "I'm here for a good time." His words were slurred, and he hiccupped.

Firy's hands shook, and she gripped the gun tighter. "Stop right there."

The GI pulled a flask out of his back pocket but dropped it before he could take a swig. He circled himself, but couldn't locate it, then squinted at Firy, "Just here for some fun, girly."

Firy's eyes narrowed, "You're not a man. You're a monster."

"Shoot him, Firy!" Anna Marie peaked out of her blanket fort then hid again. "Hurry, Firy! Shoot him! Shoot him!"

Popeye ran toward the GI, pawed him, growled, and barked. The drunk soldier kicked at the dog, swore, and stumbled toward Firy.

"Get away, Popeye." The dog whined but retreated. The soldier advanced. She fired, then stood in disbelief as he dropped to the floor. *Bozhe, what have I done?*

Popeye sniffed and licked the prone soldier. Soon the dog lay unconscious. Anna Marie screamed, "He's kilt. You kilt him," she threw her arms around the dog.

The sound of Firy's shot, Anna Marie's screams, and Popeye's howls ricocheted through the neighborhood. The soldiers outside scattered at the sound of the shotgun's blast even as the neighbors ran toward the house. Threats were shouted at the backs of the retreating GIs.

Firy shoved Anna Marie aside, dragged Popeye to the kitchen, and opened the back door. Anna Marie followed sobbing.

Vivian and Marie hovered in the doorway, afraid to come in. Coats were thrown over their pajamas, and their hair was pinned up in rag rolls. Maire was barefoot. Ivan pushed past them, stared at the prone soldier, then bolted. "I fix."

Jake rubbed his forehead, then poked the GI with his boot. This fellow looked about half the size of Johnny the Bear Boy.

The neighbors whispered among themselves and glanced at Firy. No one asked any questions. The body on the floor told the tale. Firy gripped the arms of the old rocking chair and rocked furiously, eyes staring, seeing nothing. The shotgun lay on the floor.

Ivan returned with Miss Ruth in tow. A thick, white braid hung nearly to her waist, a long black coat hastily thrown over her flannel nightgown and cowboy boots on her feet. Miss Ruth surveyed the scene and sighed. All eyes turned to her.

"Anna Marie, put your hand on Popeye's chest. Is his heart beating?"

The girl nodded.

"Good. Ade, take the dog to the back yard where the fresh air will help revive him. Anna Marie, wrap yourself in a blanket and go with them. Vivian put on a pot of coffee. Marie, take Firy upstairs and put her to bed. I'll be along directly. I'm surprised Mardel isn't here. She lives just next door. Surely, she's heard all this commotion."

Vivian and Marie looked at each other and shrugged.

Their red faces let Miss Ruth know Mardel was up to something, and the girls knew it. Miss Ruth frowned, mumbled something about sailors in uniform, and how she must talk to that girl. "Oh, and check on Elizaveta. Hopefully, the flu has kept her unaware."

Everyone rushed to do her bidding. The men breathed a sigh of relief as Miss Ruth turned her attention to the neighbors and said, "We can't let the United States Army find out who shot one of their own, no matter how justified."

Miss Ruth put her ear on the soldier's chest. "He's still breathing. Thank you, Bozhe."

"But what to do with him..." Jake sighed.

"I believe he needs medical attention."

"Better we dump in Indian River."

"Shut up, Ivan."

"Doc's hunting on the other side of the island, won't be back for two days," Ade said.

Three pairs of masculine eyes looked at Miss Ruth.

"Take him to the infirmary at the Pioneers' home. Have the chaplain call the commander at the Mount Edgecombe base. I pray he will recover. Gentlemen, I suggest you all get on your knees."

Hearing that, the neighbors scattered. The three men reluctantly lowered themselves to the floor around the unconscious GI. They bowed their heads.

Miss Ruth prayed for this GI Joe in particular and all the others stationed in Sitka in general. After a few minutes, Ade nudged Jake, "Do what I do when Ollyanna prays. Think about fishing."

"Amen. Miss Ruth. Amen. Whistle at mill blow. Bill will come."

Ivan crossed himself several times.

"Then, amen, it is."

Jake's unit of the Alaska Territorial Guard went door to door and informed everyone about keeping the facts from the authorities and from Bill as well. No telling how he would react.

The telephone's shrill ring roused the Chief of Police. When informed of the situation by Miss Ruth, he covered the receiver of the phone and swore. Bull nudged him with a gentle growl. Stormy stopped his tirade mid-sentence and told Miss Ruth, "I'll take care of it."

He called his magistrate, Frank Calvin, "Better make the warning from the ATG official." then went back to bed.

Frank went from house to house and gave strict orders for the facts to remain unspoken for the war's duration. Sitka's residents, irritated at being awakened a second time that night, merely nodded and slammed their doors.

The soldier awoke two days later with the worst hangover in his life and a nasty welt on his chest. He remembered nothing and never drank again.

For weeks, Firy cringed every time someone winked and said, "Nice shot, Firy." Or "Atta girl." Or "You always were good with a gun, girl."

The stories spread by the half dozen drunk GIs differed in the details. It grew and morphed with each telling. The people of Sitka raised their eyebrows but did not respond. Rumors grew until there were dozens of stories and many attempted attacks.

The army and navy restricted their passes and increased their patrols. They assigned a special unit of MPs to escort the town's women to and from their jobs. Clerks, secretaries, shop girls, waitresses, and fish slimers had military escorts for the duration. No incidents were reported, and no shots were fired. But before the war's end, seventeen MPs found themselves engaged.

And the Checkinov sister's money-making enterprise?

"I don't see what all the fuss is about. I'm going back to Budnikov's." Vavara said.

"Well, I'm never taking in laundry again." Larissa winked.

SEVENTEEN

The girl in the mirror flexed her arm and formed a muscle that made her proud. Her hair, tangled and wild, she tied back with Papa's red bandanna. Firy turned from her reflection. She knew how she looked.

High Russian cheekbones, although not as distinct and dramatic as Mama's. A nose, broader and flatter than she liked, spoke of her Yupik heritage. Her skin might be a shade or two darker than Vivian's or Mardel's, but not enough for them to care. She bit her lips and pinched her cheeks to give them color. Sixteen years old today, and the one girl in her class not allowed to wear rouge or lipstick.

Mama always said she had blueberry eyes, and Franella Feddersen's mother said Firy was a Russian princess. What a joke.

She traveled the miserable road of complaints and grumbles. If she couldn't have a real party, she'd have a pity party. She turned back to the mirror, stuck her tongue out, and promised to be cheerful in her misery.

Firy knew that tonight Vivian, Marie, and Mardel planned to dance until midnight at the American Legion Hall and then eat sandwiches with the soldiers and sailors. Fun-loving Mardel loved those navy uniforms and vowed she'd go with any sailor who asked her.

The thought of the VFW hall crowded with military men excited her girlfriends, but Firy's heart pounded when she imagined the noise and smoke and strange men standing too close.

She grabbed Mama's apron from its hook by the kitchen door and startled her sister.

"Don't try to stop me." Elizaveta's hand grasped the doorknob.

"All that make-up! And you cut your hair. What will Papa Bill say?"

Betty ran her hand through her cropped hair. "I don't care what he'd say. It's my hair."

"Are you meeting someone? You're not old enough!"

"You'd be surprised what a little make-up can do. My guy thinks I'm 18."

"Elizaveta, you're just fifteen, much too young. And you're not supposed to wear make-up!"

Her sister rolled her eyes, "Call me, Betty. He says it sounds more American."

"Does he know you're Yupik, a native?"

"Doesn't matter. His great-grandmother was a Cherokee."

Firy took a deep breath and tried again, "Won't you stay? You know it's my birthday."

There was a flicker in Elizaveta's dark eyes, but she stiffened her shoulders and slammed the door on her way out. Firy scrunched the apron in her fists and choked back her tears.

The eight quarters Papa had given her clinked in her pants pocket. Papa said she could buy whatever she wanted, except no rouge or lipstick. How her sister dared to wear the forbidden make-up and where she got it was beyond her.

Firy snapped the dust rag at the mantle, knocking over one of Mama's Russian candlesticks. *Be careful, you're angry at Elizaveta and frustrated about your birthday, but it doesn't mean you can be careless.*

"Love Bozhe, and do what's right." She heard Mama's voice in her ear. Her heart responded with the whine, why is that so hard? No answer. Firy forced herself to be careful as she continued cleaning.

Papa Bill had a double shift at the mill, but even so, she felt he had abandoned her.

"Firy! Firy!" Eight-year-old Anna Marie raced around the corner with her cousin, Yelena, close behind. They looked so much alike they could have been sisters.

"Firy! Guess what? The high school boys are going to play the soldiers. Happy Birthday, Firy. Baseball, I mean. Starting right now. It's a double-header. Can we go?"

The speed and staccato rhythm of her voice matched the beating Firy gave the porch with her broom. Back and forth, she stabbed the worn wooden steps. So, her little sister was deserting her, too.

She frowned and said, "It's nearly bedtime," she saw the excitement fall off the little girl's freckled face. Firy paused and looked at their eager little faces. There was little enough entertainment in Sitka, especially for kids. Besides, it was hard to go to sleep when it stayed light so late. Firy crouched down and hugged her sister, "Yes, you can go."

Anna Marie turned, all gangly arms and legs. She never walked when she could run.

"Wait." Firy tugged on her little sister's amber ponytail. "Here, sweetheart. You can have hot dogs or popcorn. You know Budnikov will be there with his pushcart."

Their faces lit up like the Northern Lights. "Gosh, Firy. Thanks. Come on, Yelena." They ran around the corner to the town's ball field.

In spring, summer, and early fall, the crack of the bat, yell of the umpire, and cheers of the spectators pierced the evening air. Tonight, it sounded like half the town filled the bleachers. She knew somebody would keep an eye on Anna Marie. In Sitka, somebody always had their eye on you, whether you liked it or not.

"Strike One." A baseball game was not her idea of a special birthday.

"Strike Two." The little bit of hope that her birthday would be memorable faded.

"Strike Three." Fine. She'd go to the game after she filled the wood box.

The pile of kindling grew high as the strike-outs came fast and furious. The crowd cheered louder with each one. Nobody in Sitka pitched like that. Tired and a little sweaty, she left the rest of the wood for tomorrow.

She hung up Mama's old apron, pulled the bandanna out of her hair, and pulled at the tangles. She gave up and let it fall around her shoulders. She pulled on her sweater and walked on the edge around the center field. She heard the thwack of the bat.

The center fielder chased the ball across the street, nearly crashing into her. The crowd stamped their feet against the bleachers and clapped, "Bumps! Bumps!"

"Firy! Over here!" Anna Marie yelled. Aunt Ollyanna waved. Yelena sat next to her mother but looked away. Firy waved back as the runner rounded third and slid into home.

Firy hunched her shoulders and stared at the ground as everyone looked her way. She knew they focused on the home run hitter, but still. Above the crowd, she heard Anna Marie once more, "Over here, Firy!"

Several soldiers picked up the chant. "Over here, Firy, over here." One strutted up to her, "Do your part for the war effort, sweetie. Give this GI a smooch."

The home run hitter retrieved his bat and took a couple of swings at the offensive GI.

"Knock it off, Bumps."

"You knock it off," the ballplayer growled, "leave the lady alone."

The GI mumbled an apology and slunk off. Her rescuer offered his arm, which Firy ignored. He followed her over to Anna Marie, who jumped up and down and soaked in his charm. Firy retreated into herself as the crowd yelled, "Bumps!" again.

The next inning, when he stood on the mound and warmed up, Firy refused to look in his direction.

Anna Marie gushed, "Isn't he grand? He's the pitcher."

Firy didn't answer.

"He's ever so good." Anna Marie rattled on as Firy fought to regain her composure.

Anna Marie slid close to her big sister and slipped the quarters into her hand. "I told Yelena I wasn't going to spend my sister's birthday money on her. She got mad, but Aunt Ollyanna wouldn't let her go home."

Firy pocketed the coins. She saw Vivian and Marie across the bleachers, waved, and mouthed 'dance'? Vivian shrugged her shoulders and motioned to the men on the field. Firy mouthed 'Mardel'?

Marie jerked her head in the direction of town and rolled her eyes. Firy laughed. Some poor sailor must have caught Mardel's eye.

"Firy," Anna Marie whispered, "Budnikov's still here. I'm starving, even if it is your birthday."

"Let's celebrate. Tell Budnikov we want two of everything. She pressed the coins back into her sister's hands. Yelena leaned around her mother and stuck out her tongue, but Firy didn't see.

"Strike one!" Uncle Ade, tonight's umpire, yelled.

"Budnikov, it's our Firy's birthday, two of everything, extra sauerkraut." Anna Marie hollered as she made her way over to his pushcart.

"Strike two."

Firy tried to deflect birthday greetings from friends and unknown soldiers. Her face flamed.

"Don't be embarrassed." Aunt Ollyanna gave her a quick hug.

Firy nodded, embarrassed about being embarrassed. Will it never end?

"Strike three."

When Anna Marie returned, Firy buried her face in a big bag of popcorn even as the sauerkraut fell off her hot dog.

The teams exchanged places on the field. Firy, head down, wished she could have celebrated her Sweet Sixteen some other way. Anna Marie tugged on her sister's arm and brought Firy's attention back to the game.

"Come on, Bumps!" Anna Marie cried.

Bumps took a few practice swings, turned, and pointed the bat in Firy's direction, "This one's for you, birthday girl!"

Another home run! The crowd went wild. Firy wanted to throw herself into Sitka Sound. Aunt Ollyanna hugged Firy and said, "I think someone in the United States Armed Forces thinks you're pretty special."

Firy shuddered and looked at her hands, clenched in her lap. Then she peaked at the pitcher. Bumps, what a stupid name! Stupid ballplayer!

Aunt Ollyanna nudged her, "Enjoy the attention. See how cute he is. All that curly brown hair and eyes blue as the sky."

Firy bit the inside of her cheek to keep from responding to her aunt. Stupid birthday! Stupid baseball!

The first game was a no-hitter, the second, not quite. Bumps gave up two runs in the ninth, not enough for the high school boys to win. They didn't seem to mind as they swarmed the pitcher's mound.

Firy seethed and didn't know why. He probably thought he deserved all that glory. Even the high school coach patted him on the back.

Anna Marie pulled on his shirttail. Bumps leaned down to hear, then threw back his head and laughed. He gave her a big hug.

We'll see about that! He's not going to get familiar with my little sister. She plowed through the crowd that surrounded him. "Come on, Anna Marie. It's time to go home."

"Bumps is going to walk with us."

"It's a block and a half. We don't need him."

"I don't mind." Bumps said, blue eyes twinkling.

"I do." Firy snapped.

Anna Marie looked from the pitcher to her sister. "What's wrong?"

Firy softened her voice, "Nothing, Dodo."

"She's got the birthday blues," Bumps said.

"What's that?" Anna Marie asked.

"Look at her. She's almost an old lady."

Firy couldn't think of anything to say unless she used words Anna Marie shouldn't hear. Her face flamed, and she tossed her head.

"I'm teasing, Firy. You look lovely." The young GI took her hand. She snatched it back, rubbed it on her jeans, and put it in her pocket. Grinning, he turned to Anna Marie, talked about the game, and ignored Firy as she stomped home ahead of them.

"Bumps?" Anna Marie frowned up at him. "My brother Henry joined the army, but he left his catcher's mitt at home. Do you think he's okay?"

"Wherever he is in the army, there's baseball. I bet he has a new mitt by now."

"For sure?"

He nodded.

"Can you come in and have hot cocoa?" Anna Marie asked.

"No," Firy yelled.

He raised an eyebrow, and she noticed his long lashes. Lashes all her girlfriends would kill to possess. What a waste. She must have stared, and her face flamed when he said, "No?"

"I mean, Papa's not home," she said in a milder tone, "and it's not a special occasion."

"Bumps could show me how to hold a knuckleball. That's special."

Bumps squatted down to Anna Marie's level and said, "Your sister's right, little one. You shouldn't let any soldiers into your house when your Papa's not home. And the only one you should ever let in is me."

The little girl hugged Bumps around the neck. He looked up at Firy and winked, then turned back to Anna Marie, "Besides, I don't usually pitch eighteen innings. I need to ice my arm, or it will fall off."

"No!" Anna Marie squealed.

"Yes," he laughed. "Goodbye, ladies. I'll show you that knuckleball next time, Squirt."

"There isn't going to be a next time." Firy shoved her fists in her pockets, this time to stop herself from doing him bodily harm.

He gave her a long look. "Yes, our Firy," He had heard Anna Marie use the term, "there will be many next times."

Firy shoved Anna Marie inside and slammed the door in his face. His laughter lingered as he jumped down the steps to the wooden sidewalk.

"Time to get ready for bed, Dodo. By the way, what did you say to him on the pitcher's mound?"

"You mean, Bumps?"

Firy nodded but wouldn't meet her sister's eyes.

Anna Marie poked her head out of the nightgown and turned so Firy could button it down the back. "I told him he had the bluest eyes I've ever seen, and his curly hair was so pretty I'd marry him if I were older."

Firy nearly choked, "What did he say?"

"Okay."

"What did he mean, okay?" Firy jerked the last button through its hole and spun Anna Marie around.

The little girl laughed, then scrambled under the covers. "I told him I was still a kid, so he could have you instead. That's when he said, 'Okay.'"

Firy grabbed a pillow, covered her face, and fell back on the bed.

EIGHTEEN

The sawmill's whistle blew. Bill Wall shut down his planer, untied the bandanna protecting his mouth and nose, used it to brush the sawdust from his clothes, and hustled down the beach. At midnight, the men coming on shift talked about a pitcher like no one had ever seen in Sitka.

This GI had pitched eighteen innings, and the first game was a no-hitter! Bill knew he'd get the whole story from Jake and Ade. And, of course, Ivan would present his opinions as fact.

Bill heard snippets about the game as he made his way through the street-side dining room to the round table in the back. Although the café was full, his chair waited for him. No one dared sit at the round table unless authorized. He barked his order to Mike. Before Bill finished his first cup of coffee, Mike placed a full plate before him, then sat down.

"That was fast," Bill said.

"All these years, you've never ordered anything different. Besides, I saw you running down the beach."

"You eat what Mike give," Ivan said.

"Suits me." Bill sawed at the large venison steak on his plate. "Now, fill me in."

"You mean our Firy and soldier?" Ivan blurted.

"What?" Bill slammed his fist on the table, jarring his coffee. He ignored the hot liquid sloshing over his fingers. Mike quietly wiped the table with the corner of his apron.

"I meant the pitcher," Bill frowned and found it was hard to swallow. "What's this about our Firy and a soldier?"

"It's the pitcher," Ade said.

"He had eyes for her," Jake added.

"Best pitcher," Ivan said.

Bill glared at Ivan. "Hang the pitcher. I want to know about our Firy and the soldier."

"Pitcher and solider. Same." Ivan grabbed the salt and pepper. "He save from GI."

"What?" Bill was half out of his chair, fists clenched.

"Settle down, Bill. This pitcher indeed stopped some GIs from making remarks," Ade said.

"He hit a home run for her."

"He stared into the stands after every pitch; he smiled and winked at her," Jake said.

"He walk her home. Not good." Ivan slammed the salt and pepper back on the table. He choked on his over-seasoned eggs.

The venison rebelled in Bill's stomach. He rubbed his belly and shoved the plate away, appetite gone. Mike reached over and pushed it back.

"Eat, Bill. You'll need your strength to deal with this GI."

After Bill pushed his plate away a second time, Mike shrugged and went back to his kitchen. Bill reached into his shirt pocket and pulled out a tobacco pouch and a packet of papers. He rolled four cigarettes, lining them up on the edge of the table like little soldiers. In silence, he smoked them, one after another. "I'm done, boys."

"What?"

"I've decided."

"What decide?" Ivan's wrinkled brow betrayed his confusion.

"I quit."

"Quit what?"

"Smoking."

Ivan nudged Bill. "There is soldier, with Sergeant GI at counter."

All the stools at the counter were occupied. The soldier waited patiently for Mike to notice him as he leaned over the end of the counter, talking to his Sergeant. Mike rushed by with his coffee pot, and the private asked him a question. Without stopping or speaking, Mike pointed to the big table.

Bill, who had half risen when Ivan nudged him, sat down, pulled his now cold plate toward him, and began to eat with a calmness he did not feel.

"Pardon me, gentlemen. I am looking for a Mr. Bill Wall."

Ivan's grin nearly obliterated his mustache as he clapped Bill on the back. "This, father of our Firy."

"Be quiet, Ivan," Jake commanded.

"What can I do for you?" Bill kept his eyes on his plate.

"Sir, my name is Bumps Baas, and I escorted your daughters home after the game." The private surveyed the men at the table.

"Best ballplayer."

"Be quiet." Ade brandished a table knife in Ivan's direction.

Bill frowned, leaned back in his chair, stuck his thumbs under his belt, and drawled, "That so?" He still refused to look at the GI directly.

"Yes, sir. I want to apologize for doing that without your permission, but I intend to do it again." He grinned and twirled his cap in his hands.

Jake gulped and almost choked. Ade froze, coffee cup midway between the table and his mouth. Ivan bit his lip. The entrance of

Sitka's Chief of Police cut the tension.

True to his name, Stormy Durand, plowed through the tables like bad weather, jostling one or two diners. The lawman, tall and thick as a Sitka Spruce, threw himself into a chair and glared at the GI, "You! This is your fault. I have a mind to lock you up."

Drama at the Sitka Café was sometimes the best entertainment in town. The old-timers licked their lips and leaned close. The half a dozen soldiers in the place looked confused but leaned in also. No one wanted to miss a word.

"Me, sir?" Bumps put his hat on and stood at attention.

"Is police," Ivan said, nodding in Stormy's direction.

"I don't understand." Private Baas looked toward the Chief.

"Tied in the seventh, and I had to leave, missed the rest of the doubleheader."

"We're in the middle of something, Chief," Ade said.

"You louts know I don't want to know what you're up to, me being the law and all. But this..."

"Easy Chief, no need to get riled up." Mike brought an empty mug and set it in front of the chief. Stormy snatched the coffee pot out of Mike's hand and poured himself a cup. He swallowed the too-hot coffee and nearly choked.

"It's okay, Chief. Nothing's going on here." Jake patted the lawman's shoulder.

Stormy shrugged it off and gave the baseball player a look of disgust. He jingled the handcuffs he always carried.

"Let the Chief talk." Bill hoped Stormy had something on the young soldier that would confine him to the base for the war's duration.

Stormy swallowed the last of his coffee and yelled for more. He leaned back in the chair and stared at the young soldier and began, "At the game, last night Frank Calvin, my clerk, almost a deputy, sold raffle tickets for the USO."

"Ten cents a ticket. Too much." Ivan said.

"Akervik donated 15 pounds of fruit. Bananas and oranges. And a pineapple, I think worth more than ten cents." Jake said.

An appreciative murmur went through the café. Fresh fruit didn't often appear in Sitka. When it did, it was expensive.

"My Yelena couldn't imagine getting an orange when it wasn't Christmas. Thank goodness for the American Legion, the Salvation Army, and the churches, or she'd never have any fresh fruit in winter," Ade said.

"My youngest think pineapple is apple in pine tree." Ivan scowled.

Stormy jangled his handcuffs again, and the conversation about oranges, pineapples, and bananas ceased. "You all know how Budnikov loves bleachers full of people, especially soldiers and sailors who always seem to have cash in their pocket. He began to grouse when Frank's raffle tickets cut into his profits. Budnikov crowded Frank to the end of the bleachers."

Most of the men had been at the game and saw the interaction between the two men, but they enjoyed the telling—several added comments and details. Stormy ignored them.

"Frank told me later he noticed shadowy movements below the bleachers, two men hunkered down and watching the game through slats in the wooden structure. Men I had put in jail the day before."

"Come on, Stormy, you know you always let everyone out for the day." A diner yelled across the room.

"Yeah, but it was past suppertime, and they should have turned themselves back in for the night," Stormy yelled right back.

"How could they when you weren't there?" An old miner asked.

"They ain't deputies. They couldn't put themselves in jail," another said, "they probably thought it was the next best thing, you being at the game and all." The crowd in the café nodded, and some laughed.

Chief Stormy Durand rubbed his thick eyebrows and faced the crowd. "We have a perfect system here in Sitka. Those fellows charged with minor infractions are sent to the Sitka Café for breakfast and are free to roam, as long as they return to their cells after dinner."

"Sure, Chief, that way you don't have to listen to their bellyaching." A diner said.

"And he doesn't have to fetch and carry their meals." another added.

The comments came from the other side of the room, and Stormy didn't recognize their voices. "The point is," he stood and scanned the room, "the law is the law, and they were supposed to be behind bars. I had to drag them back to jail."

"It was a cruel and unusual punishment to make them miss baseball."

"Crime has its consequences." If Stormy Durrand could have figured out a way to let the prisoners stay until the end of the game, he would have. He knew if he did, he'd have a real mess every time there's a ballgame.

The Chief glared at the young GI again. "By the time I locked up those two louts and got back to the game, it was over. You couldn't have waited before hitting that last home run?"

The men around the table looked from the soldier to the father to the lawman.

Bill, still grim-faced, laid a hand on Stormy's shoulder. "I have business with this young man."

"He break any laws?"

"Don't know yet." He turned and asked, "What kind of a name is Bumps, anyway? Kind of silly for a grown man."

"Yes, sir," the soldier grinned and twirled his hat in his hands, "Mam called me that when I crawled and bumped into things."

"Uh-huh!" Bill snorted.

Bumps straightened to his full stature, a mere five feet nine inches, but he stuck out his chest and said, "Sir, if it's good enough for Mam, it's good enough for me."

"And you want to see our Firy?"

"Yes, sir."

"I heard she didn't take to you."

"She'll warm up to me in time."

The men around the table stopped mid-chuckle when Bill glared at them.

"And how do I know you won't take advantage?"

Stormy rattled his handcuffs. Jake fingered his steak knife. Ade drew a picture of his gaff hook on a napkin. Ivan muttered he should have brought Katerina.

The private, still standing tall, his voice hard as steel, answered, "Mr. Wall, I have ten older sisters and brothers. Mam made sure her boys learned how to treat the female of the species. She'd take a stick to any of us that got out of line."

"The trouble is, I don't know this, 'Mam.' Your mother, I suppose?"

"Yes, sir. That's what we call them back home." The GI flicked his cap in the direction of the counter where Agrafena refilled the Sargent's coffee. "My Sargent will vouch for me, 'course, he's partial to me because of the way I play."

"Best in Sitka. Alaska, even."

"Shut up, Ivan," the men said in unison.

"Word around town is you're something with that arm. How do you handle a hammer?" Bill's eyes challenged the young man.

"Like John Henry." Bumps flexed his arm and grimaced.

"Looks like that haunch of venison hanging in Mike's cold storage."

"Feels like it. Doc says it'll be okay in a couple of days but cussed me out for pitching eighteen innings."

"The last two of which I missed." Stormy groused.

"Showing off?" Bill asked, ignoring the Chief.

"There's a pretty girl I tried to impress."

Bill snorted, reached for his tobacco pouch, then remembered he quit. He rubbed his unshaven face, scratched his belly again, and tried not to smile. *Cheeky cuss, I think I like that.*

Ade banged his spoon on the table. "Wait a minute. I think I have a right to put my two cents in about our Firy."

Bumps nodded to the man who had umpired the game.

"Young man, our Firy's my niece. The others here are, what we shall call, interested parties. We're committed to protecting her."

"You tell about Katerina," Ivan bellowed, rising from his chair.

"Is that your daughter, sir?" Bumps asked.

The men around the table laughed.

Ivan shook his finger in the soldier's face. "Do not speak of Katerina."

Ade glared at Ivan. "There's no need to bring Katerina into this.

Stop shouting and sit down."

Ivan glowered and said. "Always, she is ready."

Jake came around the table, pushed the hapless private into an empty chair, and growled, "Let me tell you something. Our Firy can kill a chicken with her bare hands, land a king salmon, club, gut, and clean it. She can shoot a deer, skin it, field dress it, and pack it out of the woods. She can chop firewood all day without breaking a sweat. Do you know what I'm saying?"

"She's helpful?" Bumps raised confused eyes to Jake.

"What I'm saying, boy," Jake poked his finger into the GI's chest with each word, "Our Firy's good with a knife, a club, an ax, and a gun."

The young soldier pushed Jake's hand away with a glower. He frowned, thought a minute, then his face lit up, and he laughed out loud. "Like my sisters, only it's hogs, not deer, catfish, not salmon, and they haul coal instead of split wood. Chickens are the same, I guess."

Out of arguments, Jake slumped in his chair and shoved a piece of toast in his mouth. Bill shot him a look of sympathy then told the young soldier to come to the house as soon as he could grip a hammer.

"Yes, sir." Bumps jammed his cap back on his head and whistled as he left.

"How long before you give that private permission to date our Firy?" Ade asked.

Bill took a long drink of coffee, set his mug down, looked at each man in the eye, and said, "I got a roof needs shingling and lots of other projects." He finished his biscuit. "I don't recall saying I'd give this Bumps permission to do anything."

The men's laughter turned to groans as Anna Marie dashed

into the café. "Papa, I just saw Bumps! Did he tell you he's going to marry our Firy? Oh, I wish it was me!"

Bill closed his eyes and reached for his tobacco pouch.

NINETEEN

Excitement and enthusiasm were at an all-time high at the ballpark, especially with Bumps on the mound. Everyone liked him, not just for his baseball expertise but for his willingness to share that knowledge.

To keep things fair, they attached him to every team in town. Budnikov carried the official record book of who Bumps played for last and which team was next. Budnikov's only interest was to keep the crowds flowing to his concession cart. Having Bumps rotate through the teams ensured that.

The GI's groused that Bumps needed to play for the army some of the time. Budnikov stood firm; their town, their field, their rules. When pressed, he pretended his English had deserted him, and the game began.

The army interfered with Bump's baseball schedule by insisting he attend to his military duties. When on leave and not playing ball, he could be found at Firy's. More often than not, he worked with Bill on various projects or teased Anna Marie as she played with Popeye.

Bumps remembered the first time he came to work at the white house with the green shutters. Bill had met him in the yard and handed him a hammer. They spent the afternoon repairing the roof. Firy hid in the house doing chores.

"Time for dinner," Bill said. "Let's wash up."

Bumps headed to the outhouse at the end of the garden.

"No need for that," Bill replied, slapping him on the back and turning him toward the house.

Conversation lagged at dinner. Bumps' signature grin ebbed. Firy glanced from Papa to Bumps. What had happened on the roof? Anna Marie peppered Bumps with baseball questions. He answered halfheartedly.

After dinner, the two girls cleared the table and washed the dishes. Bill motioned Bumps into the front room to listen to the radio.

When he had first arrived, Bumps gave his chocolate ration to Anna Marie. He now offered his cigarette ration to Bill, who decided not to tell the young man he'd quit. Those smokes would come in handy as barter for coffee or butter. Bill rocked in rhythm to the music. Bumps sat on the edge of the davenport.

After a few minutes, silently rocking and watching the young man look at the ceiling, the floor, and the walls, Bill couldn't stand it, "Out with it."

"Sir?" Bumps jerked his attention toward Bill.

"You're not the confident cuss I met at the café or the great ballplayer I saw on the mound. Heck, you're not even the hard worker on the roof this afternoon. What's going on?"

Bumps took a deep breath and let it out slowly. Then he gave a slight smile. "I might as well tell you the truth, Mr. Wall. I'll feel better when I've confessed. I'm embarrassed and ashamed." He took another deep breath, "That's it, then."

"What's it? You're ashamed of us?"

"No, sir, I'm just trying to picture you all at Mam's."

"And we embarrass you? Now listen here, young man, we are as good..." Bill quieted himself, lowered his voice, and said, "I think you'd better explain yourself."

Bumps pressed his hands together, "Well, sir, we have water pumped from a well but not indoor toilets. Mam uses kerosene lamps. You have electric lights, plus a radio, and a telephone. Back home, if anyone needs to make a call, we go down to Miller's barbershop." He shoved his hands in his pockets, leaned back, and stared at the ceiling.

Bill rocked in his chair, silent for several minutes. "We haven't had these luxuries for long. I heard you're in communications. Maybe when the war is over, you can wire your town for electricity and telephones."

"No, sir, I'm going to play baseball."

"You that good?" Bill raised his eyebrows.

Bumps took a business card from his wallet and handed it to Bill: **Mr. Ian McIntyre, Scout, Chicago Cubs.** Bill turned it over and saw the scrawled message: 'Come and see me when the war is over.'

"You had better take care of that arm. No more pitching eighteen innings, no matter how many pretty girls you see."

Bumps put the precious card back in his wallet. "I only have eyes for one."

Hands in hot soapy water, Firy leaned back and tried to hear their conversation. She knew she should tell Anna Marie to stop eavesdropping, but she was grateful for the reports. No need for him to be embarrassed about oil lamps and outhouses. They had used both for many years and still did when the power went out or the pipes froze.

"Firy, do you ever wonder how Bumps' mountain valley looks? He says the hills are round and rolling."

Firy looked out the window at the jagged, snow-covered peaks of Mount Verstovia and the Three Sisters and couldn't picture it. "Pennsylvania is too far away even to imagine."

"No oceans, just creeks and rivers, and catfish. I wonder if they taste like cats."

"Ach, don't be silly. No salmon, halibut, or clams. No briny tang in the air. It would be horrible." Firy said.

"I don't know. It would be an adventure to go to faraway places." Anna Marie said.

"We're perfectly fine right here in Sitka."

Anna Marie tiptoed back to the doorway to listen, and Firy thought about last Sunday when Bumps saw her near the entrance of St. Michael's. She still didn't know what possessed her to invite him to the service. She hadn't been there for years, not since before Mama was sick. Afterward, she let him take her across the street to the Sitka Café,

Since the war, Mike had chosen to ignore the blue laws, and Stormy had decided to ignore the café. Most of the townspeople forgot the café was even open on Sundays. Today there were only two other diners.

He bought her a soda. Mike wiped the counter in front of them again and again. Bumps picked up their glasses and took them to one of the small tables on the back deck. After pulling out a chair for Firy, he stuck his head back in and commanded, "Mike, stay." The diners laughed, and after a minute, so did Mike.

"So, what did you think?" Firy asked.

"About the church or God?"

"Both."

He laughed. "A three-hour service? In Russian? Standing the entire time? And that smoky, incense stuff? But why did you hustle us out of there so fast? I think the strange-looking minister wanted to talk to us."

"Father Alexi. He doesn't like me." Her face flamed.

He dismissed Father Alexi with a wave of his hand. "Our Firy," he put his arm around her shoulder, "my Firy, it was some kind of test. Did I pass?"

She nodded, and he squeezed her hand.

"As for the God part. Mam raised me to be a Bible-thumping, hand raising, hallelujah praising, foot washing kind of believer. We have more in common with Holy Rollers than we do with the Amish or Mennonite. Sometimes I think we're more hillbilly than Dutch, but I draw the line at snake handling."

"Snake handling?"

"Cousins on my Pappy's side way down in West Virginia believe you don't have real faith unless you dance with poisonous snakes."

"What if they bite you?"

"That's the point. They think the poison won't hurt them. My cousins say you won't go to heaven unless the snakes bite you."

"But there are no snakes in Alaska."

"God disapproves of a lot of things in this world. I think snake handling is one of them."

Firy listened to Bumps with part of her mind; with the other, she wondered what her girlfriends would think of this conversation.

"You won't go to dances or parties on the beach or long walks in Totem Park. You won't do anything fun." Mardel powdered her nose for the third time and snapped her compact closed. "I honestly don't know why he hangs around."

"You don't go anywhere except the ballpark, or he goes to your house and works for your Papa," Vivian said.

"Did you ever wonder how Bumps feels about it?" Mardel asked.

Bumps nudged her, and Firy focused on their conversation. "All I know is to love Bozhe and do what's right. That's what my mama taught me."

"In boot camp, we were given a little New Testament." He pulled it out of his pocket. "This is one of the verses I marked, 'For God so loved the world,' that's you and me. When you think that the God who made all this loves us, and when you feel it deep down in your soul, it changes you. It did me anyway."

"That's nice," Firy thought about Mama's Bible on the Beautiful Corner. It was Russian, and she couldn't read it. She must have said it out loud, for Bumps gave her the little testament and said he could get another.

Firy gazed at the water and thought about her girlfriends again. They regularly quizzed her about her feelings. How did she feel about him? Her heart lurched, and her hands started to fidget. She put them in her pockets.

She liked having him around and thought about him when he wasn't there. He made her feel comfortable; that was it. Safe. Everybody in town liked him. He fit here. That was good. But when she asked herself what she wanted or how she felt deep in her soul, confusion swirled, and anxiety raged.

TWENTY

The hinges protested as Stormy Durand crashed through the doors. "Cave-in on Chichagof."

Miners and regulars at the café pushed plates away, scraped chairs back, gulped down the last of their coffee, and shrugged into their jackets. The GIs watched with interest.

"I thought the government closed those mines," Ade said.

"Whole territory's closed to mining, no one's supposed to be there." Stormy tapped his foot.

"Government take miners for war. Not right." Ivan bellowed, "Not like Russia."

One of the miners yelled over Ivan. "Anyone hurt?"

"Got a radio message from Short Pants McGee. He's okay, but the other guy's trapped."

"How long?"

"Short Pants said it took him two days to clear the entrance, and then he had to hike to his boat to send a message."

Jake put on his watch cap and reached for the rest of his toast. "The Dorothy is still tied up at Conway's dock. I'll get her refueled and send you the bill."

Stormy cringed. The men crowded around the Chief of Police to get their orders. Ivan weaved between the tables, snagging the last of everyone's bacon and cigarette butts. His tobacco ration never lasted.

Mike's wife, Agrefena, used her wooden spoon to push her way through the men. The four-foot nine native woman bellowed up at the six-foot-four Chief of Police. "You know Chichagof is part of the Yacobi forest, nothing there but empty mines. You must take food, coffee, tools."

In his mind, Stormy was halfway to Klag Bay. He didn't want to spend the time or the money to get organized. His shoulders sagged as he thought about how long it would take to gather supplies, chug some fifty miles up the coast, and then go over to Chichagof Island.

Agrefena continued to bark out orders, "Mike, make more coffee. Ade, get Miss Ruth and her medicines, Doc's in Juneau. Ivan, get blankets. Soldier boys, tell your leader you'll be back tomorrow or the next day."

The GIs rose to their feet, and a freckle-faced corporal said, "But ma'am, all we have is a twelve-hour pass."

"You tell your chief you go to Chichagof, or the café is closed to the army for the rest of the war."

With a snappy salute, he ran to the telephone behind the counter. His buddies crowded close as he called the base.

"Finally, some action," one GI said.

"It's a rescue mission, not like the real war."

The corporal put his hand over the telephone's receiver and stared at his whiny buddy, "It's better than endless hours of drilling and training. Now quiet."

Agrefena banged her wooden spoon on the counter. "Line up."

The men shed their jackets and obeyed, avoiding Stormy's eyes. He shifted from one foot to the other, checked his watch, and looked for a place to spit his tobacco juice.

"Outside," Agrefena hollered.

Stormy aimed a stream of brown liquid in the gutter and

turned in the direction of the docks. His Spanish mastiff growled and nudged him back to the café. How that dog knew he wanted to retreat to his office irritated him, but he stepped up to the counter. Frowning, he hooked his fingers in his belt loops and rocked on his heels.

Agrefena put a loaf of bread and a knife in front of him. "Slice. I'll send you the bill." She winked, indicating the venison, cold halibut cheeks, pickles, and sea celery. Whatever she stacked on the counter was slapped between pieces of bread and wrapped in cloth napkins.

Bumps stood in the doorway and surveyed the organized chaos. Agrefena waved over the din, "Our Firy's baseball boy. Come."

He looked at his watch. "I'm supposed to meet our Firy here in half an hour."

"Mine accident. She will understand. In fact, if she gets here before you leave, she'll insist on going."

Bumps shook his head, "Too dangerous."

Agrefena laughed, "It would be more dangerous to tell her no."

Bumps agreed and followed the cook to her storeroom, where he found a stack of empty 100-pound salt sacks. Usually, Agrefena made them into napkins and dishtowels. Today they would hold sandwiches, smoked salmon, and canned peaches.

Mike poured the coffee into whatever thermoses the men had carried and the rest into glass jars. He folded an extra cup of grounds into waxed paper and stuffed it in his pocket. Agrefena slapped him with her spoon, "This is why I watch you like an eagle. Take the secret ingredient. Leave the coffee grounds."

"Dang fool war. Rationing everything," Mike growled, but he obeyed.

The Dorothy, one of four shore boats used to ferry passengers across the channel to Japonski, was open to the weather. Wooden benches were anchored port and starboard, and a double row bolted down the middle. She could accommodate up to thirty passengers, but today she held more than that as Jake piloted her north toward Klag Bay on Chichagof Island.

"I don't know that these old sourdoughs are going to be much help." Stormy leaned toward Jake, speaking over the noise of the engine.

"These mines are tricky. They'll provide the brains and the GIs, the muscle."

Stormy nodded, idly rubbing Bull's head. Miss Ruth organized her medical kit and prayed. Ade described every shoal and outcrop to the excited GIs on the way to the island. Ivan held his stomach. He built boats; he didn't ride in them. Bumps ate the fry bread Agrefena had tossed his way as he left the café.

Bumps recognized the determination on the faces of the silent sourdoughs. He had seen the same grit on people back home when the coal mines caved, or dynamite misfired. He prayed for a good outcome.

Short Pants McGee met them at the dock, "I told him there weren't no more gold. It weren't my fault. I ain't been down that shaft since Denver Dan met his Maker there some 30 years ago." The watery eyes of the old miner begged for understanding.

Stormy gestured to Ivan, nodded to Short Pants, and said, "Hurry, men." He trotted toward the mine's entrance.

McGee gulped a whole jar of coffee while Ivan tied several

salt sacks together and yoked them over his shoulders. The bags of coffee jars he carried in his arms. He glared at Short Pants, who had a sandwich in each hand, and whined between bites, "It weren't my fault."

Stooped under the weight of his heavy load, Ivan muttered in Russian through the woods all the way to the mine. Short Pants followed, not understanding a word.

Several of the men hovered outside the mine's entrance. Rusting equipment and animal droppings lay scattered about. One of the men had started a fire against the cold night.

Thirty feet into the shaft Sean Connor lay, ashen and barely breathing. His lower body was blanketed with rock and rubble. Miss Ruth fell to her knees, "Oh, Sean, what have you done now?"

A GI rushed to move some of the smaller stones.

"Hold it there, soldier boy. We need to shore up the shaft afore we do anything."

After listening to the old miners, Stormy barked orders, and the men rushed to obey.

Sean's eyelid's fluttered. "I found him for you, Ruthie."

"You're too old to be trudging through these woods, much less going into the mines, you old fool."

Sean tried to grin and failed, "I'll always be younger than you."

"Humph. Not by much." Miss Ruth, still worried, said, "What do you mean, you found him? My father?"

"Come, Miss Ruth. It's not safe." Stormy reached to help her up. She jerked her arm away and glared at him. Smoothing her face into a passive peace, she turned back to Sean.

"I put his... remains in there." Sean moaned and pointed a bony finger toward the entrance. She saw a crate labeled Dexter's Dynamite.

"How did you know it was him?" After half a century, Miss Ruth couldn't imagine Sean Connor had found her father.

Sean tried hard not to pass out. "Pocket, my poc..."

They heard a faint rumble, and dirt fell from the ceiling like rain.

"Hurry. Bring those beams."

"Found two, got some GIs chopping a couple of small trees," Ade said.

They shored up the area over Sean and removed the small rocks and debris. They freed his right leg, but the left remained imprisoned. Another discussion, another plan. The miners made a fulcrum using one of the tree trunks. After two hours and several attempts, they levered the boulder away. Sean screamed and passed out.

His leg was crushed, bones shattered, several large fragments pierced his flesh. His foot and lower leg, faded to a dull gray, was cold and numb. Sean burned with fever, and infection raged through his body.

Miss Ruth commanded the young GI standing next to Ade. "Bumps, find a saw. Ade, build up that fire. You know what to do."

She prayed Sean would not regain consciousness until they were back in Sitka.

She pulled a knife from her bag, doused it with alcohol, and cut a skin flap above the knee. It would cover the stump.

"Here, Miss Ruth. I sterilized the saw in the fire. Ade will keep the shovel in the fire until it's needed." Bumps said.

"I'm afraid I haven't the strength in these old hands." Miss Ruth looked at her gnarled hands and wished for the strength she had fifty years ago.

The men looked at one another. Sourdoughs as old as Miss Ruth shuffled out to the fire. Stormy stepped forward. As Chief of Police, he would take responsibility. He exhaled the breath he didn't know he held as Bumps knelt beside Miss Ruth. "My arm is strong. All those fastballs." Bumps' knuckles showed white as he gripped the saw. "Show me where."

Stormy and Mike held Sean tight to the earth. Jake and the others made a litter to carry the old sourdough to the Dorothy. Ivan stood at the edge of the activity eating halibut cheeks and tossing the bread aside. Bull enjoyed the unexpected offering.

Miss Ruth poured the rest of the alcohol on Sean's leg and showed Bumps where to start. He could feel the flesh rip and tear. "Give me the knife, Miss Ruth. It will make a cleaner cut. I'll use the saw for the bone." He blinked away the sweat that dripped into his eyes and clouded his vision. "Hold him tighter. He's coming to."

Stormy and Mike strained to keep Sean from moving. Miss Ruth held his face in her hands. Her whispered prayers calmed the men around her.

Ade retrieved the red-hot shovel and pressed it against the stump, sealing the wound. Miss Ruth held Sean in her arms and wept while Bumps leaned against a boulder, shut his eyes, and pitched a perfect game.

The shore boat was halfway to Sitka before Sean stirred. "Did you get it, Ruthie?"

"The crate, yes."

"Your father's watch." He motioned to his shirt pocket then passed out once more.

Miss Ruth turned the gold pocket watch over and over in her hands. "Except for the dents and the missing chain, it looks like Grandpa's."

Prying it open, she saw the words, 'Robert and Emma Merritt locked in holy matrimony.' She laid her hand on Sean's heart. "Bless you, Sean. You found my father, but at what cost?"

Bumps sat in the stern next to the dynamite crate. He felt the waves slap against the boat. He did not hear the men's snores or Sean's moans over the drone of the engine. Miss Ruth sat beside him.

"How is he?" Bumps asked.

"He'll live, thanks to you. And please, Bozhe, no more infection."

"I've never done anything like that. Made me queasy."

"I worried about the contents of my stomach the whole time too."

They shared a look.

"You know him, don't you?"

"Since I was a teenager in the west. He's part of what brought me to Alaska."

"What did he say about this box?"

Miss Ruth stared at the night sky. The Big Bear, brilliant, as it circled Polaris. She saw the question in Bump's eyes. She rested her hands on the crate and whispered, "I came to Alaska in 1890 to find my father. I looked for him for fifty years. According to Sean, that mine was his coffin."

"I'd like to hear about it." Bumps said.

Miss Ruth gave him a small smile, "I must admit it's quite a story. Perhaps, someday I'll share it with you."

"Fifty years, and you never found him? How sad." Bumps placed his hand atop hers on the dynamite crate.

"I traveled all over Alaska for decades following one clue or another. A lost dream."

"You may have lost your dream, but perhaps you found your destiny. You found a life here."

Miss Ruth brushed the tears from her eyes, and by the light of Alaska's night sky, she looked into his face. "You are wise, young Bumps."

"Just thinking about what I've found here in the North."

"Our Firy."

"Yes, my Firy."

Miss Ruth leaned against him and slept as the shore boat chugged toward Sitka.

Jake tied up the mooring lines as dawn warmed Sitka Sound. One by one, the men filed off the boat. Most avoided the injured man's eyes, even as they patted his shoulder and murmured, "Rotten luck, old man."

"Sorry, fella."

"Take care."

"Too bad, mate."

Sean moaned, "My leg hurts."

Last to leave the Dorothy, Ivan Mishkin pulled his cigar out of his mouth and tossed it overboard. "Leg not hurt, fella. I bury on Chichagof."

TWENTY-ONE

He stood on the mound and pitched his last game in Sitka. He'd tell her tonight. His orders had come. Germany. Although excited to get to the real war, he knew he'd miss this island. The northern air so crisp, it crackled. He could almost taste the pine and spruce from the forests and salmon from the sea. No coal dust blocked the sun or colored the sky. Here, at the top of the world, the heavens were touchable and the amber light, solid. Its golden sunsets warmed his soul. He took another deep breath and let the ball fly.

The townspeople cheered. He'd make this last game a good one.

Bumps saluted Firy and Anna Marie as he walked off the mound at the end of the game. He remembered his first time at this small-town ballpark when he noticed Firy and her kid sister. Skinny little thing, but she knew her baseball lingo. She had jumped around the players, pigtails flying, and babbling all kinds of statistics until the umpire banished her to the stands.

By the seventh-inning stretch, he knew he'd marry a girl called Firy.

That first game was the beginning, and he hoped this last one would begin something else. After the game, he and Firy walked on the beach, past St Peter's Church, then the Sheldon Jackson School. When they reached Totem Park, they turned back.

"You heard I'm shipping out?" He asked.

"Nothing happens in Sitka without everybody knowing."

They sat on the beach near the large rocks and driftwood logs, both worn smooth by the sea's nonstop action. The slow-moving tide crawled over rocks and kelp, and its foamy top buried the clamshells like dirty whipped cream. The familiar briny air and gull song comforted Firy.

The tide had rolled in, almost to the log where they sat. "What do you think?" Bumps asked.

"Huh?"

He sighed and took her hand. "About us. The future."

"I don't know. It's easy for you. Everybody loves you."

"Love is hard."

"What? How?"

"Firy, I watched each of my brothers quit school after eighth grade and go into the mines. Thirteen years old, they left home before dawn and came home after dark. The coal dust got into their skin, eyes, and lungs. It got into their souls." He stared at the incoming waves and smelled the salty seaweed.

"We were celebrating my eighth-grade graduation. Pap was partially paralyzed and couldn't speak because of a stroke. Mam fixed up a bed in the living room. I remember he took George's beer bottle, poured it on the floor, and stared at me. Mam mopped it up and gave him the evil eye." Bumps fell silent, lost in thought.

"Then what?" Firy asked.

"George told me he thought Pap wanted me to swear I would never drink, and I haven't. Pap stared at the baseball in my hand, then looked at the rest of my brothers," Bumps paused to wipe his eyes and looked out over the water.

"George put his arm around my shoulders. He faced Pap and said, 'Bumps will never go into the mines.' My sister Vera patted her round belly as if making the same promise to her unborn child.

George pledged my life would consist of high school, homework, and baseball."

Bumps cleared his throat and wiped his eyes. "The whole family made sure I graduated from high school and played baseball. Vera took in laundry. Annie babysat the principal's children. Mam sold her famous cinnamon rolls and pickled pig's feet."

He picked up a stick from the beach and scratched in the sand. "At times, it was a burden. I began to act out, but Mam sat me down on the porch swing and said love was freely given but expensive. It cost my brothers and sisters a lot, but they gave because they cared."

She patted his arm and agreed, "They loved you, so the cost didn't matter."

"It cost them a fortune just to keep me in baseball shoes, but it cost me something, too."

"What could it possibly cost you?"

"I had to let go of not feeling worth it and see myself through their eyes. You've heard it's more blessed to give than to receive?"

She nodded.

"Sometimes, it's a heck of a lot easier. It's humbling to be on the receiving end."

Firy dropped her head, "It's a beautiful story."

He took her hand, "Do you understand what I'm saying?"

She looked over the water then down to the sand. "Look, you've written your brothers' and sisters' names."

"I love them, too," he said, tossing the stick into the water. Bumps turned to her and said. "What do you think?"

"Your father was a good papa, a good man, I mean?" Firy's voice, thin and hesitant, was almost lost in the sound of the incoming tide.

"Of course, why would you even ask?"

"No reason," Firy shifted on the log, "Papa Bill's not my real father." She had not intended to speak.

"Tell me." His soft and gentle command almost convinced her she could tell him all the awful bits and pieces she remembered.

"I first saw Bill Wall on this very beach. In the middle of the night. Winter. I was barely four, I think." She looked at the log they sat on and the others that lined Crescent Bay. "We hid behind a huge log. Mama and Elizaveta cried. Henry clutched his slingshot."

She shivered. He scooted closer and put his arm around her. "What happened?"

Firy continued as if she hadn't heard him. "The midnight shift at the sawmill ended. We crouched lower behind the log as the men passed. Some trudged without speaking. Others laughed and kidded with each other. One had an old Ford pickup, and several men hopped in the back for a quick lift home. When they had all gone, Mama lifted us out of the wet sand and set us on the log. Elizaveta shivered and started crying again. A tall man, not skinny, well-muscled, asked if we were all right. His metal lunch pail glistened in the moonlight. Mama's eyes darted up and down the beach. Looking for a way of escape, I think."

"Do you need help?" he asked.

"No."

"I think you do."

"Why would you help me or my children?"

'Because you need it.' His voice was as soft as the moonlight filtered by the incoming fog, but there was steel in it." Firy's voice faded away. Lost in thought, she was unaware Bumps had taken hold of both her hands.

"Mama stood in front of us, shielded us. She lifted her head and faced this stranger and said, "Did you not notice I'm native."

"I noticed you were pretty."

Firy remembered the stars were unseen that night because of the fog. Clouds rolled over the moon. "When he said that, my heart pounded, and I couldn't breathe. That's how it always started."

"What started?"

She pulled her hands from his and put them up to her face. After a moment, she looked at the water again and said, "I don't remember. I was too little." But she did remember. She remembered all of it:

The memory played in Firy's mind like one of Budnikov's black and white newsreels. The awful day Mama had given them an empty salt sack wouldn't be colored. They looked at each other, confused. "Your clothes, children. Henry put in your little truck and your blocks. Elizaveta, don't forget your ragdoll and Firy your book. Hurry now; adventures don't wait."

Firy saw Mama's samovar and candlesticks bulging out of a salt sack. The Beautiful Corner was no longer attached to the wall. Firy trembled, and Mama hugged her tight. "It will be all right. We love Bozhe, but sometimes I don't know what to do."

"Do right, Mama."

Mama, her face drawn and pale, whispered. "Sometimes, I can't find the right."

Firy remembered how she held tight to Mama's hand as they walked to a small house at the end of Barracks street, up the hill near the Russian Cemetery. Once a bright yellow, peeling paint and a broken window repaired with cardboard, spoke of its neglect. Mama lifted her little ones over a missing step and went in without knocking. The children stayed on the porch. "Close the door. Were you born in a barn?" slurred a gravelly voice.

"Come in, children. This is your new home and your new papa," Mama tried to put some enthusiasm in her voice and failed.

The man, slouching in his chair, glared at Mama. "Get this place cleaned up and make me some food. And don't be telling your brats I'm their papa. They ain't mine."

"Yes, John." Mama hurried the children to the end of the room, "Mr. John isn't feeling well, children. You must be quiet."

"Hurry up," the slovenly man yelled.

Henry marched over and shook his fist in John's face. "Don't yell at my Mama!"

Mr. John gave him a shove. "You better learn your place real fast, boy. I got me a thick strap here." He raised himself as if to take off his belt. Henry scooted under the table.

Mama brought Mr. John a big bottle of what she called medicine. "Here, John, take this. He'll learn. He's a good boy."

"He better be."

Elizaveta and Firy joined Henry under the table. Mama gave them baloney sandwiches while she cooked Mr. John's dinner. At bedtime, Mama took their blankets and fixed them a place to sleep under that very table. She gave them each a long hug.

"Your new papa, I mean, Mr. John and I are going to sleep now. We will be right behind that curtain." She pointed to the end of the room where she had tacked up an old sheet. Mr. John argued it wasn't necessary, time her brats grew up and learned what life was all about. Mama insisted, so he got a hammer and let her hide the bed from the children's view.

"No matter what you hear, don't make a sound. You must stay

here until I get you in the morning."

Henry and Elizaveta scooted close to Firy. Henry shook his fist and whispered, "I'll get him! I will!"

Elizaveta clutched her baby doll. "I don't like Mr. John."

"Shh," Firy said. But she agreed.

The damp night air and the sound of the waves washed over Firy and brought her back to the present. She wondered if there had been any bad papas before Mr. John, but couldn't remember, didn't want to. There had been several after. Whenever fragments of those memories surfaced, she fought hard to repel them.

Bumps squeezed her shoulder, "Firy, are you okay? You've gone quiet."

Startled, she stared at him and knew she would never tell him that part of her past. She began to speak, her voice flat, bleak. "A man stumbled down the beach, drunk, yelling for Mama. It was Mr. John. We ducked behind the log again. He cursed and hollered for Mama to come back. No woman was going to leave him unless he kicked her out, especially a dirty, stinking siwash. Bill commanded us to stay where we were then he ran up to Mr. John. I don't know what he said or how he convinced that dirty old drunk to leave us alone, but he did."

She raised her head and looked into Bumps' stricken eyes, heard the pity in his voice, and resolved once again to keep her past a secret. She shivered and wished she could keep it a secret from herself. "Bill wanted to take us to the Russian Bishop's House, which was across the street from the beach. Mama wouldn't let him, wouldn't take charity. He argued with her a little, then fetched his horse and wagon. Mama told him to take us to Indiantown. The fishing season had just started, and she would find work. When Bill lifted me into the wagon, he said I was pretty like Mama."

"I've never seen your mother, but you are very pretty." Bumps said.

Firy turned away from him. Her heart pounded, and she hid her face. "You don't understand. It's better not to be pretty. That's when bad things happen." She pictured herself huddled in the bottom of the wagon all the way to Indiantown. The same fear threatened to choke her now.

Bumps took her chin in his fingers and tilted her head. It forced her to look into his eyes. "Your Papa Bill is a good man."

She wanted to tell Bumps she thought he was a good man, too, but she couldn't get the words out. "Mama thought so, and they must have gotten to know each other over the next couple of years. I was almost seven when he came for us. He changed, though, after Mama died."

Bumps rubbed his thumb over her knuckles and chose his words carefully. "Sometimes, when you love someone so fiercely and lose them, it alters you."

"Have you lost someone like that?"

"No, but I can imagine. What about us, Firy?"

Firy was silent for a moment, then pushed him off the log and ran down the beach. She looked over her shoulder. "That's what I think."

He was a patient man, but this was too much. Bumps ran after her, and before he could caution himself, he kissed her. He restrained his passion but let all the tenderness he felt for her flow out of him and, he hoped, into her.

The moon colored the waters of Sitka Sound in shades of platinum and silver. The sand on the beach sparkled like stars in the sky. Somehow, Bumps knew she carried deep hurt and pain. He wondered if she knew how wounded she was. He ached for her to be whole and happy. He loved her. Maybe it was enough.

TWENTY-TWO

Anna Marie rubbed her face in the pitcher's mitt Bumps had given her when he shipped out. It smelled of leather, oil, and sweat. She corrected herself; he had asked her to keep it until his return. As soon as the war ended, he'd go home to Pennsylvania, but then he'd come north to claim his mitt and his girl.

"Anna Marie, can you come in and help?" Firy called from the kitchen window. The house, hot and stinky from Firy's canning venison, did not appeal.

"The mail plane buzzed the town a little bit ago. Do you want me to see if there's a letter from Bumps?"

Firy stuck her head and shoulders out of the window and looked at her little sister. "Do you think there will be?"

Anna Marie laughed and threw the ball high in the air, almost falling over backward to catch it. "Before he left, Bumps told me he had a letter half-written, and he'd try to mail it when their ship reached Seattle."

"Alright, but hurry back. That buck Papa shot was big, and I have a lot of meat left to can. Aunt Ollyanna can't come until after supper, and I need help now."

Anna Marie pulled the rusty old bike from the shed. She remembered Firy's stories of how she'd pedaled through Totem Park to Great-Gram's with Anna Marie sitting on the crossbar. She could almost remember being rocked and sung to by the ancient woman.

Gone. Great-Gram, whose face had grown dim, and Mama whose face she couldn't remember. Sometimes there was an ache in Anna Marie's heart. When she missed her Mama, she ran to Firy for hugs and stories.

Papa often worked double shifts at the mill, and days would go by without her seeing him. When Henry joined the army, she wanted Papa to bring him home, but he said Henry was doing his duty. Masha lived with her husband's family in California. Elizaveta quit high school and ran off with her Coastie. Gone.

Anna Marie put her hand on her chest and rubbed that ache in her heart. Last night she woke with a terrifying loneliness. She crept into bed with Firy, who held her tight and promised never to leave her.

As she pedaled through town, almost everyone she saw had lost someone—Germany, Burma, North Africa, the South Pacific, Italy, or France. Lives had even been lost on Attu and Kiska. The boys and men of Sitka were spread across the globe, some never to return. Her loneliness sat on the bike with her.

An empty mailbox sent her back to the house. She spent the rest of the weekend in the kitchen with Firy, Aunt Ollyanna, and the remains of the buck. For the first time in her life, she looked forward to school.

Anna Marie chewed on the end of her pencil. The clock showed three minutes until freedom, but still, the teacher droned on about homework, quizzes, and other unimportant things.

She looked out the window. The beach, crowded with bare feet and buckets, beckoned. She saw Mardel, Vivian, Marie, and Firy clamming down the gently curved beach, mid-way between the sawmill and St. Peter's.

The bell rang, and the children bolted. More than half ran across the street to join their families. Anna Marie sat on a log, removed her shoes and socks, stuffed them in her school bag, and set it next to her empty lunch pail. She squished the sand between her toes.

Firy's buckets were almost full, so Anna Marie asked if she could help the Bravebirds.

The native families had silently segregated themselves farther down the beach. As Anna Marie bent over to pick up a starfish, she heard Mardel complain to Firy, "Why do you let her play with those native boys?"

"You forget, Mardel, Anna Marie, and I are Creole. Native."

Vivian stopped digging, "I never think of you that way."

"You better not let your Papa hear you say you're native," Marie said, "and besides, you pass for white."

"But why should I have to," Firy muttered as she concentrated on digging. The three girls looked away and said nothing. Firy picked up her bucket and shovel and told her little sister to be home by supper time.

Anna Marie tossed the starfish into the surf, stuck her tongue out at Firy's friends, and ran toward the Bravebirds. She wished Papa didn't insist they sit on the white side of the movie theater and baseball bleachers or attend the white church and school. Sometimes they got mean looks and whispers, but Firy said not to tell Papa. Most of the time, Anna Marie didn't think of such grown-up things. Today, all she thought about was the thing in her pocket.

Petrov Bravebird, as ancient a man as Anna Marie had ever seen, gave her a long, pointed stick to poke the sand. She liked harvesting the traditional way with a stick and a digging tool made from cedar bark. She and Paul worked quickly with much enthusiasm. Teenaged Joey plodded beside them, frustrated by the old ways.

"Did you ask him?"

"He says you must speak for yourself," the boy muttered, eyes down.

Anna Marie approached the Tlingit elder and pulled a raven's feather from her pocket. "Mr. Bravebird, will this raven feather protect my friend in the war?"

Ignoring her, the shriveled old man, skin like burnished leather, eyes black as obsidian, poked his stick into the wet sand. Joey nudged her and whispered in her ear. She tried again. "Grandfather, please tell of Raven."

He took the feather and held it to the sun, where its blue blackness glistened. His hair, tied in the back, was as black as the raven feather, not a trace of grey.

"Raven, the keeper of our people, is powerful. I tell the story as it was told by my grandfather, who was told by his grandfather. I must tell the whole, not the part. You are not Raven. You are not Tlingit. You are Yupik. Because I honor your mother's life and memory as Raven, I speak to you what my grandfather spoke to me."

Anna Marie put the feather back in her pocket and sat on the sand. All of Grandfather's family sat silent as he told the story. Long. Complex. Convoluted. She thanked him politely when he finished, although her question remained unanswered.

The native families gathered their clams and set off to Indiantown. Joey said their grandmother's grandmother believed natives and whites were not separated when Russia owned Alaska. Even one of the Russian Governors had a Creole wife, and no one thought it wrong. Anna Marie wished it was still that way. Joey said it changed when America bought Russia.

She pushed such weighty thoughts away as she watched the Bravebirds carry their buckets down the sand of Crescent Bay. She looked for glass floats as she turned and walked in the opposite direction, but her thoughts remained on the raven's feather.

Miss Ruth sat on the steps of St Peter's. She looked up from her book, "How are you, Anna Marie?" she called across the way.

"Kinda lonely, now the soldiers are gone. Even baseball's boring." Anna Marie crossed the gravel road.

"Not as exciting without Bumps and the other GI's?"

Anna Marie nodded then showed Miss Ruth the raven feather. "I'm going to send this to Bumps. Its power will protect him in the battles."

"Who told you that?" Miss Ruth frowned but kept her voice soft.

"Joey Bravebird's grandfather. Well, he didn't exactly say it would work, but Raven's powerful. Joey's not sure if the feather will lose its power by going through the mail. What do you think, Miss Ruth?"

Miss Ruth took the feather and ran her fingers through it. "Soft, isn't it?"

Before Anna Marie could agree, they heard birdsong. Above them, a flock of ravens danced across the sky. "Look at them, Anna Marie. Who made them?"

"Bozhe. He made everything."

"So, who has the power?"

"Bozhe! It took a lot of power to make all the birds and the sea and the sky and everything."

"Right. If you want Bozhe to protect Bumps, we can ask Him right now. He sees Bumps over in Germany and Henry in the Pacific."

"We don't even know where they are, exactly."

"Bozhe knows."

They bowed their heads, and Miss Ruth prayed. The young girl added a sweet amen. "But I wanted to send Bumps something to show I cared. Henry, too. I'll find another feather for him."

Miss Ruth picked up the book she had been reading and flipped through the pages. "Listen to this. It's from Psalm 91:

> *He shall cover thee with His feathers, and under His wings shalt thou trust: His truth shall be thy shield and buckler. Thou shalt not be afraid of the terror by night, nor the arrow that flieth by day; Nor for the pestilence that walketh in darkness; nor for the destruction that wasteth at noonday. A thousand shall fall at thy side, and ten thousand at thy right hand; but it shall not come nigh thee."*

"There's a lot of big words in there, Miss Ruth."

"Bumps will understand, sweetheart. It says don't be afraid, even if everybody is falling down near you. I'll copy these verses for you."

"But what shall I do with my feather?"

"God covers us with His feathers to protect us like a mama chicken covers her babies. Feathers are important."

Anna Marie breathed a sigh of relief. "I knew it. I just knew it."

"You could put it by your bed to remind you how important you are to Bozhe, or you can send it to Bumps and tell him what God says about feathers."

Anna Marie put it back in her pocket and read the verses Miss Ruth copied. She stumbled over the longest words. She looked at the bay, lost in thought, then asked, "What about the thousands?"

Miss Ruth hugged the girl and exclaimed, "You are like your sister; curious, questioning, yearning to understand."

"What about the thousands and ten thousands that fall, Miss Ruth? Doesn't Bozhe love them? Won't He take care of them?"

"I don't have everything figured out, Anna Marie. Nobody does. But I know Bozhe doesn't want anybody to fall and die without Him because they would be in hell. But He won't force anyone to love Him."

"I've chosen Him, Miss Ruth. I have Jesus here," she placed her hand over her heart.

"That makes me happy." Miss Ruth wiped her eyes, "Thousands will fall in this war, Anna Marie. The ones who have Jesus know that Bozhe will pick them up and carry them to heaven."

"Miss Ruth, when I fall, will you take care of Papa and our Firy? Popeye, too?"

"Why, Anna Marie, most girls your age don't think about such things."

The young girl sighed and looked at Miss Ruth with tears in her eyes. "There is a picture of Mama beside my bed, but I don't know her. When Bozhe carries me to heaven, I'll be with her forever." Anna Marie reached up and patted the spinster's wrinkled face. "Bozhe told me He would come soon. Sometimes, I want to stay with Bumps and our Firy, but heaven's the real 'happily ever after,' isn't it?"

Miss Ruth held her close.

"But what about our Firy?" Anna Marie's lip quivered, and she sniffed.

"Your sister would be very, very sad."

"She hurts inside, you know. All the time."

Miss Ruth silently marveled at the insight of this child.

Anna Marie continued. "Bumps wants to take care of her, but I don't know if he'll be back in time."

Miss Ruth took a deep breath and let it out slowly, "When the time comes, Anna Marie, I will take care of your family."

"Thank you, but it's almost suppertime." Anna Marie shrugged off her serious thoughts as she listened to her stomach growl.

"You better hurry." Miss Ruth sat on the steps of St Peter's and watched the waves. The smell of rotting seaweed in the salty air reflected her mood. She pondered the unfathomable and sometimes unsettling ways of her Lord.

She stood and shook out her long black skirt and wished she could shake out her dark thoughts as well. She asked herself if Anna Marie had genuinely heard from Bozhe or had an overactive imagination. What would the coming weeks and months bring to a world at war and this family in particular.

TWENTY-THREE

The big round table in the Sitka Café's backroom had been 'Opinion Central' for decades. Issues discussed, decisions hammered out, and opinions verified. Nothing did more to damage that process than the war. The men remained a band of brothers, willing to stand together and help one another, but they had not often reached a consensus about how the war should have been conducted. Nearly a year after the allies' victory, a consensus concerning peace-time policies was still elusive.

How to deal with Japan and Germany was a hot topic. What about the Jews, refugees, and other displaced persons? Mustering the men out of the various services was on-going, and GIs were still returning to civilian life. Where were the jobs and housing for thousands of returning veterans? What about those who needed extreme care? Many questions. Few answers.

"Do not speak such things," Ivan said. "We wait. Life will be same."

"The world has changed," Jake said.

"We top of world. Military go. All be same."

"Now we have the Al-Can Highway from the States through Canada and into the interior. People are going to travel that highway. We have military bases with airstrips. I bet they'll become civilian airports. Thousands of servicemen have been here. Do you think they'll forget?" Bill asked.

"Our backwoods way of life is over, boys. The war has pushed Alaska into the 20th century."

Mike slammed the coffee pot down. "Talk about something

else, will you?"

"I looked at a new boat engine in Juneau last week. The political types talked nothing but statehood," Ade said.

Ivan choked on his coffee, and another round of discussion began.

"I said talk about something else," Mike growled. He liked his customers to agree. It kept appetites intact and profits high. He sought another topic of conversation, one less volatile. "Say, Bill, has our Firy heard from Bumps?"

Bill pulled a letter out of his pocket, laid it on the table, and then lifted his mug. "It's not good, boys." The letter lay in the middle of the table; the men stared and drank their coffee.

Everyone knew Bumps promised to return after the war. Anna Marie, half in love with him, talked of it endlessly. Firy blushed when anyone asked about her GI.

Ivan blustered and chewed on his mustache. "Katerina is ready."

"Hold on. He still wants to come north, but things are bad in Pennsylvania. He lost two brothers in the war. His sister's husband is missing, and she moved home with her kids. His mother is beside herself with grief, and of course, they have money troubles. He's been working in the coal mines ever since he mustered out of the military. And he meets with that baseball scout in a few months."

"I think, not real," Ivan said.

"I thought he'd join me on the boat," Ade said. "He was a pretty good deckhand the few times I took him out."

"I wanted him to pilot a shore boat," Jake added. "Everybody liked him."

Each man at the table had thought about how Bumps could support a family here in Alaska. They loved watching him play baseball, but their imaginations couldn't picture him in the big leagues. Their world didn't extend beyond the north.

Bill set his empty coffee mug on the table. "He sent me a bank draft to purchase a ticket to Seattle with enough left over so our Firy could buy a train ticket going east."

"I don't like it," Jake said, "traveling across the country by herself. All kinds of soldiers and sailors on the trains."

"He did say he might be able to scrape the money together to meet her in Seattle if I didn't approve of her traveling alone."

"Unmarried? Not good." The others agreed with Ivan.

The men examined the pros and cons of each option. In the end, they decided, although they respected Bumps and considered him honorable, Firy was too tempting.

They discussed this for the better part of three days before Bill told them there was another option, "Elizaveta and her husband," Bill stressed the word, "live in a small fishing village north of Seattle. What if they meet her ship and see to it our Firy's married before she heads east with Bumps?"

The men agreed but spent the next two hours grilling Bill about how long he'd known Elizaveta's whereabouts. He ignored their questions and said, "There's another problem. Anna Marie."

"It will break her heart to lose her sister," Ade said.

"It's a double loss. If Bumps doesn't come back, she'll fall apart." Jake said.

"To tell you the truth, I spoiled Anna Marie. At her age, our Firy helped Masha with the cooking and housework and cleaned the schools."

"She hunted and fished with me," Ade said.

"I wanted Anna Marie to have a childhood." Bill sighed.

"Our Firy's never gone farther than Japonski," Mike said.

"She's been farther on hunting and fishing trips. And she spent that summer in Port Alexander with Miss Ruth." Bill reminded them.

"Still, she's never been more than a hundred miles from Sitka and never alone," Ade said.

"She's fearless," Jake said. "She'll go."

"I don't know about that," Ade said. "Ollyanna thinks our Firy hides herself and does what's expected no matter how she feels inside."

"In that case, she won't go. Bill needs her at home, and Anna Marie thinks of her as a mother. I think our baseball player's doomed to disappointment." Mike said.

Agrafena, Mike's wife, listened while she cleared the nearby tables. "She will put her Papa and sister first."

That night, Anna Marie had a Girl Scout meeting at St. Peter's by the Sea. Papa told her to come home right after. Popeye lay by the door and whined.

After she left, Bill showed Firy the letter.

"Why didn't he write to me?" Firy asked.

"I think he wanted my blessing. Maybe he thought it would be easier coming from me if you rejected him."

"I don't know what to do."

"You graduate on Friday. The Star of Alaska sails on Sunday."

"He's supposed to come here." Firy threw herself down on the davenport and hugged a pillow. Popeye came and sat at her feet.

"You must choose," Papa said.

"How will Anna Marie get on without me? I'm all she has left."

"There is me," Papa said with a half-smile.

"You're just her father. Why can't he come here? It's not fair."

"He's helping his family, and there's baseball."

"A dream. I thought he would fish or work at the mill."

Bill sank into the rocking chair. "He probably would if you asked him."

"I can't do that!" Firy, wide-eyed and miserable, stared at Papa.

"Okay, you figured that out. Now. Are you willing to go off-island and be a part of his dream?"

Firy hugged the pillow tighter, then threw it across the room. "I can't think."

Papa took her jacket off the hook by the back door and whistled for Popeye. "It's almost twilight. Take a walk on the beach."

Firy dragged her feet as she left the house, glad she didn't meet anyone on the short walk to Crescent Bay. Popeye sniffed and snorted, then ran down the rocky beach. When he returned, he laid a dead fish at her feet. "I'm not throwing that smelly thing. Get a stick."

He came back with a driftwood stick, and Firy threw it down the beach and occasionally into the water. After an hour, she sat on a log, and Popeye settled at her feet.

"What will I do, Popeye? Anna Marie's like my child. She's growing up fast. Who will she have if I go? What will my life be like if I stay? What about Elizaveta? I can't miss seeing her. And Bumps?"

Popeye continued to crunch his stick. Twilight shimmered the waters of the bay. She gazed at the tiny waves lapping the shore. Day not yet over. Night not ready to come.

She wished she could remember the Scottish poem she studied in school, something about the gloaming, that mystical time when the sun first dropped below the horizon.

She lifted her head to moonrise and the first star. What is it about this Peter Pan time? She looked into the sky and wondered what's on the other side of the deep navy blue?

Once, Firy asked Miss Ruth about the ache she felt when looking at the night sky, so beautiful it hurt. Miss Ruth told her that deep soul yearning was a longing for Bozhe.

Firy felt Mama's words in her heart. 'When the earth turns away from the sun and the angels peek through heaven's windows, look up. Think of how He loves you.'

"Oh, Mama," Firy whispered aloud, "what's the right thing to do?"

Firy shuddered, afraid of leaving Sitka, sailing the ocean, traveling across America, getting married, and especially leaving Anna Marie. She feared not doing it even more.

The sky darkened then turned bright with a million stars. Popeye kept pace with her as she walked the beach and talked to Bozhe.

She picked up several rocks and threw them with all her strength. Popeye chased them into the surf. The clouds covered the moon, and a diffused light came from the Milky Way. By the time Firy walked home knew she would cross America as her ancestors had crossed Russia and, by Bozhe's grace, fare better than Mama.

Tomorrow night she would graduate from high school, and Sunday, she'd leave Sitka. Time to pack.

Firy pulled Papa's suitcase from under the bed. Inside lay the Shirley Temple doll, as pristine as that long-ago Christmas Eve when she locked her in the case.

She tugged on one of Shirley's curls and thought of the countless Saturday nights she had wound Anna Marie's freshly washed hair into pin curls, always hoping for that Shirley Temple effect.

Firy reached for the drawing and read all that she had written that long-ago night. Fresh embarrassment warmed her cheeks, and she wondered how she had worked up the courage to ask Mr. Akervik if he was her father.

Courage? More like desperation and stupidity. She had put that memory out of her little girl mind and did not appreciate its return. It annoyed her that the memory returned every Christmas and birthday when a delivery boy came with a gift. Never a card or note.

Henry demanded to know where they came from. Papa Bill silenced him with a look. Elizaveta pouted for days because there was no gift for her. Papa told them both to knock it off. Firy was allowed her own life.

Henry shrugged. Masha patted her on the shoulder and said, "It's okay. I think I know."

Betty stuck out her tongue when Papa wasn't looking.

After several years with no acknowledgment that she was his daughter, Firy decided she didn't want Mr. Akervik's gifts. She quietly gave them to the Salvation Army. If he didn't love her enough to sign the card, she would treat him like any other shopkeeper in Sitka.

Hands shaking, Firy tore the drawing into bits and threw it away. "Anna Marie, come here. I have something for you."

"What's that?" Anna Marie stood in the doorway. Her eyes darted from the doll to the suitcase and back. Firy told her the story of Mr. Akervik and the Shirley Temple doll but left out that Mr. Akervik was her real father.

"I want you to have Shirley. She will comfort you when I'm gone."

Anna Marie put her hands behind her and backed up. Firy held the doll toward her little sister, "Go on, take her."

Anna Marie ran her finger down the doll's nose then across the painted lips. She snatched it and threw it across the room. "I don't want your stupid doll."

Shirley's porcelain head hit the wall and shattered. Firy fell to her knees and picked up the bits and pieces. Anna Marie ran to her sister. "I want you to stay at home. I want Bumps to come here."

Firy let the fragments fall from her hands and pulled her sister into her arms. "I know. I know."

The little girl hiccupped and wiped her sleeve across her eyes, "I'm sorry, Firy. I know you loved her."

"Oh, Dodo. When you wore your overalls and straw hat and weeded the garden with me, you were my Rebecca of Sunnybrook Farm. When we sat on the dock and watched Uncle Ade offload his fish, I pretended he was Captain January, and you were my Star. When you sang in the Christmas program, I clapped and imagined you were Little Miss Broadway. It's you I love."

They sat in silence for a moment, then Firy said, "You've always been my very own baby doll. Mama gave you to me before she, before..."

"Before she went to heaven." Anna Marie lay her head on Firy's shoulder. The sisters wept together. One for the mother she had loved so fiercely and lost. One for the only mother she had ever known and would soon lose.

The ceremony bored the eight graduating seniors with long, dull speeches.

Firy eyed her navy-blue serge suit. Masha had sent it from Los Angeles, California. True, it came from a thrift store, but one near Hollywood. Firy felt elegant and suspected a Hollywood glamour girl had worn it.

Sitka's shopping proved limited. There was Mr. Akervik's general store, of course, and the Sitka Bazaar. And both Sears and Roebuck and Montgomery Ward had catalog stores in town, basically a counter and a clerk. You selected your item, placed your order, and waited for its arrival.

Mardel preferred Wards. She claimed it more fashionable than Sears. Vivian wouldn't even look at the Sears catalog. It reminded her of too many visits to the outhouse when she was younger.

The clothing from both catalogs was new. In that sense, it was a step up from the Salvation Army Thrift Store or the Sitka Bazaar. However, from the first day the catalogs arrived, one of the most popular forms of entertainment for girls in Sitka was, "If you could choose one thing on this page, what would it be?"

When any female in Sitka wore a new item from either catalog, it was as familiar as if it had come from the thrift store. Firy looked over at Marie. Yes, she had on the dark brown rayon suit from page thirty-seven of the Spring and Summer Montgomery's.

Firy smoothed the lapel of her Hollywood suit. She felt the smoothness of the skirt and sat up straighter. No one in Sitka had seen it before. She would graduate, travel, and be married in it.

The ship's whistle blasted. Firy stood at the railing and waved. Mrs. Trent, the grammar school principal's wife, traveled with Firy.

Mrs. Trent's mother was scheduled for surgery and needed her daughter. Papa said it made sense to travel together.

The ship's schedule included stops at Juneau, Petersburg, Wrangell, Ketchikan, Prince Rupert, and Vancouver before docking in Seattle. Passengers would embark and depart.

Mrs. Trent leaned close to Firy and spoke above the noise. "Willard and I said our good-byes at home, dear. I am going to the cabin."

Firy nodded and kept her eyes on the pier. Anna Marie had not spoken all morning. Firy and Papa tried to make the girl look them in the eye as they began their trek to the docks. Papa carried Firy's small suitcase, and Anna Marie lagged behind. She dragged her feet and sniffed every third step.

A horn beeped at the trio. They thought it was the Single-O Taxi Papa called earlier. Tommy Herman, the driver, had several fares and said he would be there as soon as possible, but start without him.

Instead of the Single-O, they saw Mr. Akervik in his Studebaker Coupe. He rolled down the window. "Hop in."

Anna Marie sat in the back with Papa and stared out the window, biting her nails. Firy found herself stealing glances at the shopkeeper. She longed to hear him say he loved Mama and her more than anything and that she was his girl. His hands gripped the wheel until his knuckles were white, and he stared straight ahead, silent.

Mama was always polite and kind to Mr. Akervik. Firy imagined Mama saying, do the right thing, forgive him for his silence.

Papa lifted her suitcase out of the trunk and gave it to a ship's porter who stamped her ticket. Firy had so many things to say, but the words choked her. She longed to hear a farewell speech. Papa gave her the ticket and hugged her but did not speak.

Papa told Anna Marie to go home as soon as the ship sailed. She needed to get the chores done, both hers and Firy's, and make dinner. Anna Marie sniffed and held her tears at bay. Papa looked at Firy with sad eyes, said goodbye, and hurried to the mill.

Mr. Akervik reached into his coat pocket and pressed an envelope into Firy's hand. "A little something for the journey and a little something extra to buy flowers for your wedding. Yellow roses are my favorite, but you buy what you like."

He held out his hand for her to shake. She ignored it and hugged him tightly. "Mr. Akervik, yellow roses it is. I will think of you when I look at them." He stepped back with tears in his eyes. He patted her on the shoulder and said, "You are a good girl, Glaphira Larissa. Do not forget about us here in the north."

When she heard those words, Anna Marie let out a wail and grabbed Firy around the waist. Firy hugged her little sister as Anna Marie sobbed and cried, "Don't leave me! Don't leave me!"

"I have to, sweetheart, but we'll be back soon." The ship's whistle blew again, and Firy pried the young girl's hands from around her waist, thrust her toward Mr. Akervik, and hurried up the gangplank, the last passenger to board.

The crowd waved and hollered their good-byes, and Firy found a place at the rail. Deep within the ship, the engines began to rumble and vibrate. Firy shivered with the reality of what she'd done. She closed her eyes and gulped.

"Don't leave me!" Anna Marie fell to her knees at the edge of the dock. Tears streamed down her face, and with arms outstretched, she continued her frantic pleas. The crowd backed away. She pounded the pier. "Don't leave! Please, don't leave!"

Firy heard her sister's screams over the noise of the ship's engines. Anna Marie's pain mirrored in Firy's soul, and she screamed. The third blast from the ship's whistle covered her cry. "Oh, Dodo, you are my heart!" She pushed through the waving passengers.

Too late. The gangplank had retracted. The voyage had begun.

Firy gazed over the water long after the other passengers had gone to their staterooms, the salon, or the dining room. She had seen Uncle Ade and Mike at the far edge of the crowd, push their way to Anna Marie.

She looked at the watch Papa had given her that morning, a graduation, bon voyage, and wedding present rolled into one.

She stared as Baranof Island became a blur on the horizon. A steward asked if she was alright. She nodded. He gave her directions to the dining room. She nodded again, still staring at the water. He shrugged and continued on his way.

Firy imagined she could ride the ship's wake back to everything safe and familiar. She stared at it until night fell.

TWENTY-FOUR

Firy sat in the ship's lounge with her writing paper and the elegant fountain pen Mr. Akervik gave her for graduation. Her words streamed on paper like the sun through the porthole. She wrote bright, warm, and cheery things to avoid the overwhelming feelings within her.

Dearest Anna Marie,

I'll write to you a little at a time and try to mail this when the ship reaches Seattle. Mrs. Trent says she's seasick, but I don't think she's telling the truth. When I come into the cabin, she turns away and pulls the covers up to her chin. When she thinks I am asleep, she sneaks romance magazines out of her suitcase. I guess Mr. Trent isn't romantic enough for her.

Firy thought about those magazines and wondered why Mr. Akervik hid them under the counter and only sold them to married ladies. She chewed on the end of her pencil and continued with the letter.

The dining room on the ship looks glamorous with white linen tablecloths and napkins. I felt a little intimidated at first, but the room's filled with fishermen and miners, and my manners are as good as theirs. The few men in business suits with their wives in fancy dresses paid no attention to me. If they looked askance at anyone, it was the rough Alaska men, who I'm sure would be more comfortable in a bar or the café.

The first night, the waiter brought big bowls of tomato soup filled with rice and vegetables. I ate it all, and he replaced it with a big plate of salad with croutons. That's French for bread cubes. Who would have thought to fry stale bread in butter, cube it, and throw it on your salad?

By this time, the band of my skirt tightened, and my stomach bulged. Then came a plate of roast beef, green beans with mashed potatoes and gravy. I did my best and ate half of it. After that, the waiter presented us with a tall glass of tapioca pudding and shortbread cookies. I unbuttoned my skirt so I could finish.

My stomach rumbled, and I waddled to the cabin. Mrs. Trent had been there all afternoon with her love magazines. She thought I was seasick. Better than having her know I was a little piggy-piggy.

Every lunch and dinner challenged me, but I did my best to eat it all. Breakfast was mostly typical, flapjacks, oatmeal, eggs, and beefsteak, but none of Mike's venison or herring roe. Although, they did have something once that looked similar, called caviar. You know I can't stand fish eggs.

Oh, and they had the most beautiful fruit: A little dish of orange balls about the size of quail eggs. They were not at all like the orange we get in our Christmas stockings. I asked the older gentleman at my table if they grew on trees like pine nuts or bushes like blueberries.

He did the strangest thing, Anna Marie. He took a small notebook and pencil stub out of his vest pocket and wrote down what I said.

He said the fruit was called a cantaloupe, and it grew on vines like a pumpkin. "Awful small pumpkins," I said. He laughed and told me they were about half as big as a basketball, and there is a little tool called a melon baller to scoop out the fruit. Someday, you and I will eat cantaloupe together.

The gentleman's name is Mr. Aaronson, and he is Police Chief Stormy Durand's cousin. He's a reporter for the Seattle Times. I guess the Chief asked his cousin to see me safely delivered. Like I was a package or something.

It's bad enough having Mrs. Trent give me the third degree every time I come into the cabin. Do you know she told me I could not ask for more cantaloupe until I've eaten all my gluey, yucky oatmeal? And me, practically a married lady. Whenever I think about it, I get irritated all over again. I need to take a walk around the deck and calm down.

I feel better now. The businessmen and their wives went crazy watching a pod of orcas. Mr. Aaronson says they're political types who were in Juneau talking about Alaska's statehood. He asked me what I thought. "About whales or statehood?" I asked.

"Whales," he said. "Statehood is years away, and the opinions of young girls aren't going to matter."

I should have been insulted, but instead, I told him how you and I had been closer to whales when fishing with Uncle Ade and how once I helped rescue a beached calf. He wrote it all down and said I was a real human-interest story. Sometimes, though, he shakes his head and says, "I can't believe they let you off the island." I don't know what he means.

Anyway, sweet Dodo, we dock in Seattle tomorrow. Mr. Akervik included a roll of stamps with the money he gave, so I'll be writing often. Stop in and see him sometime, will you? Tell him no matter what, I will have yellow roses for my wedding.

Love from your big sister,

Firy

Dear Dodo,

The drive to the little town of La Conner took over two hours. Betty's husband, Ern, borrowed his boss's delivery truck. We bounced and bumped our way north.

La Conner's half as big as Sitka, and the distance to Fidalgo Island is closer than Japonski. Fidalgo Island blocks the view to Skagit Bay, which is part of Puget Sound, which joins the Pacific Ocean, which is adjacent to Sitka Sound and connects to you and home.

In LaConner, there's a bridge instead of shore boats, and they make all the natives live on Fidalgo, which is kind of like Indiantown.

La Conner nestles in a valley dotted with small towns. In between are dairy, strawberry, and flower farms. The mountains are towering, like at home, but are far away. Betty says it smells like home when the town's single fish cannery's running full blast.

Bumps will arrive sometime after midnight, and we'll be married in the morning. I'm a little worried about the yellow roses. The flower farms are all tulips and daffodils, and the only roses I've seen in the neighbors' yards are red and pink. Betty's mother-in-law, Anora, told me not to worry. She says a bride must have her wishes, and I will have yellow roses.

I wanted Papa to walk me down the aisle of St. Peter's with you as my bridesmaid. I wanted Miss Ruth to fix our hair and fuss over us. I can't think about that, or I will cry.

I'm glad tomorrow is supposed to be sunny. The wedding will be in Anora's backyard with Betty's little family present.

Thank you for the blue handkerchief. Betty gave me a locket. I put your picture in it, and Bumps is bringing his Great-Grandmother's gold ring. Something old, something blue, something new, and the borrowed backyard to fulfill the tradition.

Love from your almost married sister,

Firy

Dear Anna Marie,

My wedding day: sunny and bright. Bumps got in late last night, and I won't see him until the ceremony. I touch the locket around my neck and think of you.

Oh, Anna Marie, you'll never guess. Right before the ceremony, Anora thrust a bouquet of sweet peas into my hands. They are her favorite flower, and her yard is covered in them. They smelled glorious, but they're not yellow roses.

I felt myself begin to tear, but she patted my face and said: "Have faith, Firy, things are not always as they seem." I didn't know what she meant, but I nodded and took the flowers.

During the wedding, the sweet peas' scent and how blue my new husband's eyes caused happy tears, but also ones of sadness. The person I love most remains in Alaska.

I thought about how you'd have to tell Mr. Akervik his favorite flower didn't make an appearance and teared up again. Can you see me scrubbing my face with your poor hanky and giving myself a lecture? You know how I hate to cry.

Guess what? Anora covered her kitchen table with a white linen cloth and displayed the wedding cake in the center. Three layers, creamy white icing, and yellow frosting roses! Anora winked and handed me a knife, so Bumps and I could cut it.

We gobbled the cake because we had a train to catch. Ern borrowed the truck again, and the four of us squeezed into the front seat, groceries to be delivered in the back. Betty and I cried all the way. I'd just found her and don't know when I'll see her again. I wish we all lived in Sitka together.

I think about Henry in occupied Japan, Masha in California, Betty in Washington, and me on the way to Pennsylvania. I asked Bozhe why families can't stay together. If He answered, I didn't hear him.

At the train station, Bumps bought a copy of the Seattle Times, and sure enough, Mr. Aaronson had written a story about me. Stormy Durand must have gotten my graduation picture for him because I smiled from the pages of the paper. The article made me seem like an idiot from an igloo.

Bumps said I sounded sweet, fresh, and wholesome, and people needed that after all the war news.

Love, from your newly married and very embarrassed sister,

Mrs. Firy Baas

Dearest Anna Marie,

We've been on the train for three days and three nights. I thought the ocean big, but America is vast. The train chugs along. We stop to pick up more passengers and let others depart. Most are servicemen. Bumps says they're still being mustered out.

You know Bumps can talk to anybody, especially when it comes to his beloved baseball. I think all soldiers must love the game.

Mostly, I have been trying to sleep on these hard bench seats. We couldn't afford a cabin or even the curtained beds the stewards make up at night.

We finished the food Betty packed for us. I've brought a piece of our wedding cake for Bumps' mother. He says I am to call her Mam. It doesn't sound warm or gentle, not like mama. In a way, I'm glad. I don't think I could call anyone mama.

We've pulled into a station now and have ten minutes to stretch our legs. We ate the cake.

Tomorrow we'll have coffee and toast for breakfast and split a bowl of soup for lunch. We spent all of Mr. Akervik's money on food, even the yellow roses' money. Please don't tell him. I mustn't write any more about food, or I'll make myself hungrier than I already am.

By the way, dear, when that female thing we talked about happens, go to Miss Ruth. She will help you.

Love from your weary, traveling sister,

Firy Baas

She folded the letter, put it in the envelope, and tried to sleep. As she drifted off, she could hear Bumps still talking about baseball. Always baseball. She sighed and turned to the window. The clackety-clack lulled her into a fitful sleep.

Dear Anna Marie,

We've settled into Mam's house. I hope by now you've received my first letter. I miss you more than I can say. I remind myself to love Bozhe and do what is right. I don't know how in this strange place. There's food here, but I can't eat it.

They make cheese in the head of a pig, and what's worse, blood sausage! You know how careful Uncle Ade always was to hang a deer and let it bleed before he butchered it. Here they catch the blood in a basin and mix it with ground-up meat. I am afraid to ask what else they put in it. They even cut the feet off the pigs and pickle them.

I push the food around on my plate, and when nobody's looking, Bumps eats it. I'm losing weight; he's gaining, and we haven't fooled anyone. I'm sure they think I'm strange and ungrateful.

They make something called scrapple; it looks and smells like it sounds. Ugh! I think it's made with pig innards. Last night they served shoo-fly pie. I can't even imagine what's in it.

When everyone's busy, we sneak into the garden, grab the tomatoes or pull up some carrots. I long for fried halibut cheeks and Mike's clam chowder. Wasn't Bumps brave to try all the things he did, clams, crab, herring roe, mussels, sea celery, and such?

I hope you're spending time with Miss Ruth. She's been a good friend ever since Mama died. You can read the note I've enclosed for her if you want.

Bumps says he'll write soon and send you his baseball card collection. He says other than me; it's his most precious possession.

Love from your starving sister,

Firy Baas

Dearest Anna Marie,

I wish I were the little sister at home with Papa, and you were the married lady on her way to a fancy wedding at a swanky country club in Virginia. Yes, that's what I wrote.

I mean, it's so different here in the Appalachian hills of Dauphin County (I still can't call them mountains). What will it be like in the big city of Richmond, Virginia? I'm just a Creole from Alaska. Who do I think I am?

You, dear Dodo, are like Bumps and would love the adventure. I don't understand how you and he can be comfortable with so many kinds of people. Here's how it all came to be.

During the war, your wonderful brother-in-law saved the life of a GI named Richard, and now he wants Bumps to be his best man. Richard sent us train tickets and paid for a hotel. I'll pretend it's my honeymoon. That part's exciting, but going to a big society wedding is not.

Richard paid for my dear husband's tuxedo rental, but I don't think he thought about me. Why should he? I hope that Masha's California thrift shop suit will pass inspection, but I doubt it. Bumps hasn't thought about proper clothes for me either, and anyway, I can't picture myself in a fancy dress.

Be sure to tell Viv and the others about my adventures. I'm sure they'll think they're wasted on me, especially Mardel.

Love from your nervous sister,

Firy Baas

Dear Anna Marie,

The hoity-toity of this world are not for me. The wedding looked like something out of a Fred Astaire movie. All the ladies wore elegant flowing dresses, and the men, fancy tuxedos. Maude had seven bridesmaids. Seven!

The maid of honor batted her eyelashes at Bumps through the whole ceremony. I didn't like that at all. I'm not so naive I didn't see how they looked down on my thrift store suit and wild Alaska ways.

I'm going to give you some advice, little sister. Never go on a honeymoon with another couple. When Richard heard we had never had a proper honeymoon, he slapped Bumps on the back and said, "You're coming with us."

I assured him our stay at the hotel was a fantastic honeymoon for us, but he insisted we accompany them to the New Jersey coast for a week of sun, sand, and sea. I shook my head, no, but Bumps nodded.

Maude's face stiffened, and she said through clenched teeth, "Yes, do come."

Which even I know meant, 'Don't you dare.'

Richard and Bumps went off, arm in arm, making plans. Maude and I stared at each other and wondered how this happened. She scowled and stalked off to her bridesmaids. Soon they all glared. I wanted to crawl under a rock.

I slipped out the side door and sat on a little stone bench. A waiter walked through and shook a silver bell to signal the reception dinner was ready. Bumps found me but couldn't understand my silence. He was having such a good time, so I decided to do what's right. I slipped my hand in his and let him lead me to dinner.

A long table for the bridal party spanned one end of the room. Bumps helped me find my place, and it happened to be in the back near the kitchen doors. He kissed my cheek and then went and sat next to the batty-eyelash girl.

I picked up the little card with my name printed on it. The table setting was worse than on the ship. There were four forks, four spoons, two knives, several goblets, a cup and saucer, and two smaller plates next to the big one. One of the smaller plates had a knife on it, and above the dinner plate were a little spoon and fork facing each other. Afraid of making a mistake, I folded my hands in my lap.

"Welcome to the wilderness," a middle-aged man said as he raised his glass.

He turned out to be the disreputable uncle. He told me every family had one. Anyway, he talked all through dinner. Told wicked stories about each member of the bridal party as he drank steadily. I rather liked him. He saw me hesitate over the forks and winked, "It's just silverware, my dear. Follow my lead, except for the drinking."

I told him all about the head cheese and blood sausage and how I missed halibut cheeks. He laughed and asked questions about Alaska. He didn't see me as a fish-sliming, chicken killing, deer gutting gal from the uncivilized north.

I'm sure that's what Maude thought, and nothing during the week at the ocean changed her mind. I know I've made you curious, dear, and I'll have Bumps write and tell you about it. I'm still too upset.

I did enjoy getting up early to watch the sunrise. That great ball of light climbed out of the sea. Everything here is the opposite.

Love from your humiliated sister,

Firy Baas

TWENTY-FIVE

Firy bit the inside of her cheek and let the screen door slam behind her. She wanted to scream. *What's wrong with me? Why don't you like me?* She knew the answer, of course. She wasn't one of them. She didn't fit. They probably thought she lived in an igloo and ate whale blubber. She heard the whispers, "Indian. Eskimo. Some kind of mixed breed. Not like us."

She didn't fault them their ignorance, but the disdain and scorn that colored their stupidity cut her deeply.

Not only that, she couldn't breathe here. This valley, small and land-locked, squeezed the air out of her lungs. Bumps had not warned her about the hot, humid air. He did explain that the mountains were more like long ridges or rolling hills. Nothing substantial or majestic about them. She couldn't even picture the ocean or remember how the seabirds swooped and dived for her cast off crusts. She could hardly remember how their begging squawks sounded.

She longed for the breezes bringing salty sea air from Sitka Sound or even the rolling fog that often came with the tide. With its temperatures soaring into the 90s, this valley suffocated her as much as his family did. Firy shuddered and remembered Bumps warning about rattlesnakes. Last week, he killed one in the garden by hacking its head off with a shovel—nasty things.

She kicked a rock in the road and pictured herself confronting his family. Instead, she took daily walks and thought about what she'd say. The image of her husband's face and the hurt that would fill his blue eyes stopped her. She kicked another rock out of the dirt road. Chopping kindling, yanking weeds, wringing out laundry, flinging rocks into Sitka Sound, and hiking Harbor Mountain took the anger out of her when she fell into frustration in Alaska.

She thought of Popeye, always a loyal listener but stingy with his advice. She thought of the times they shared on the beach. There were no beaches here and no Miss Ruth. Ah, Miss Ruth, even when Firy couldn't get the words out, Miss Ruth soothed her soul. There was nothing and no one in this valley to do that for her.

Bumps knew something was wrong. Of course, he did. How could she tell him his mother wouldn't let her help with any of the housework or cooking? Mam's widowed daughter and her two children had moved back home. Day and night, they ignored her. Three of Mam's daughters arrived at the small farmhouse every morning with their children in tow. Blond hair, blue eyes, stocky build, she had trouble telling them apart. They stayed all day and ignored Firy.

The sons that had returned from the war had returned to the mines. She barely saw them, usually only on Sundays. These men were tired and depressed. Going back into the mines after seeing Europe and the South Pacific was difficult. They talked little and drank much. Sometimes Firy was awakened at night by their screams. Their nightmares would rouse the whole house. No one talked about it, but everyone was on edge.

When Bumps went off to Chicago, Firy took even longer walks. The townspeople waved and greeted her politely. After all, she was the wife of their baseball hope, even if she wasn't one of them.

When no grown-ups were around, Bump's nephews, Dippy and Dumpy, eight-year-old peas in a pod, became her solace and joy. After many hours and tales of Alaska, Firy earned their trust. She raised her right hand, pink swore, hoped to die, spit in your eye, and the boys told her how to tell them apart.

During Sunday dinner, Firy asked, "Dumpy, please pass the potatoes." Mam mashed them with fresh clotted cream and sauerkraut, but Firy choked them down.

"Sure," he said and reached for the bowl.

Silverware stopped clinking, and people stopped speaking. Karl said, "Tell her you're not Dump."

"But I am."

Peter said, "Tell her you're Dip."

"I'm not, am I, Ma?" The boy looked at his mother.

Her eyes flashed, but she agreed Firy was correct.

Firy knew she had crossed some kind of line but wasn't sure what she had done wrong. The boys accepted her, loved her even. Did the family resent that? Did it matter that she could tell the twins apart when most family members couldn't? Firy had hoped it would bring her closer to the family, make her a part of them, but they seemed to resent her even more.

More than once, Firy heard them wonder how this outsider could tell the twins apart. Did she think she was better than they were? She wasn't. She needed to stay away from the boys, from all of them. What was Bumps thinking, bringing her here? Marrying her?

Why couldn't he have married a nice Dutch girl from Dauphin County, Elizabethville, or Pottstown? Even a half-Dutch hillbilly would have been better than whatever she was. Alaska wasn't even a state. Maybe she wasn't an American. She certainly didn't look like one. Not like them.

"I wish Mama didn't tell us to keep away from Firy."

"I'm not going to do what Mama says. Not this time." Dumpy said.

"You hardly ever do what Mama says."

"Are you going to stay away from Firy?"

Dippy hung his head, pulled his sox up, then looked at his brother. "I wish we didn't have to go to school. I'd rather stay with Firy. She's better than a princess."

"Yeah," Dumpy said, "princesses can't hunt or fish or trap."

"Princesses are dumb. Alaskans are--what, Dump?"

With the wisdom of being four minutes older, Dumpy answered. "Alaskans sparkle and shine."

"Huh? I don't get it."

"It comes from living at the top of the world." He held one fist up to represent the earth and another, higher and off to the side. "See, Dippy, this is the sun, and it shines on the top. It never gets dark where Firy's from."

"Firy lives on top? How come you know such things, Dump?"

No breakfast sounds or smells came from Mam's kitchen. Firy peeked into the old woman's room and saw her fast asleep, then Firy headed to the kitchen, determined to produce as excellent a breakfast as she ever had back home.

She had learned from Great-Gram how to manipulate and control a wood cookstove. The cast-iron monster in Mam's kitchen looked similar, but Firy didn't know how much or what kind of coal to use. One bucket next to the stove contained large black rocks, and the other looked like pebbles made of charcoal. She dumped some of both into the stove and reached for the iron skillet.

Coffee boiled over and sizzled on the too hot stovetop. The grounds burned, and the eggs scorched. The biscuits in the oven blackened, and smoke filled the room.

Mam, in a long white nightgown, shrieked in Dutch, grabbed the frying pan, burned her hand, snatched the towel from Firy, and threw the whole mess out the back door, including the skillet and coffeepot.

The doorway to the kitchen filled with those offspring who still lived at home. They all spoke, but no one listened. Myrl put her arms around Mam, shot a look of pity at Firy, who fled to the front porch. Myrl guided Mam back to bed, and George barked at everyone to clean up the mess and get their own breakfasts for once in their lives.

Myrl brought two cups of tea to the porch. "Don't mind, Mam. She gets in a mood when she doesn't feel well."

"She seems to be in a mood whenever I'm around."

"You married her favorite, and she doesn't like to share."

"I don't understand," Firy said.

"Don't take it personally."

"How can I not?" Firy sighed, "Thanks for the tea, Myrl. I better clean up the mess."

Myrl put her hand on Firy's arm. "Don't. I promised Mam you'd stay out of her kitchen. The others took care of it. Hungry?"

"I couldn't eat a thing. I feel useless."

"You're probably just missing Bumps. He should be home from Chicago anytime."

"And then what?"

"You'll know if you're a baseball widow."

"What?"

Myrl gave her a long look. "What'd you think life would be like if Bumps played professional baseball?"

"He'd play, and I'd watch, like back home."

Myrl, the only one of Mam's offspring that pitied Firy, kept her voice calm as she told Firy about the months of spring training, farm teams, road trips, and the minors' grueling schedules. It could take years to get to the majors.

"I didn't know. Why didn't he explain?"

"He thought you knew. Your little sister did."

"How do you know that?"

"He mentioned it in one of his letters. They were full of you and Anna Marie."

"Poor Anna Marie." Firy's face dropped into her hands. "She must have thought I left her forever."

Myrl patted Firy on the shoulder and went inside so the girl could weep in private. Firy stared across the valley to the ridges beyond. She folded her arms around herself and leaned against the pillows on the porch swing. How far away the north felt.

No one looked at her that day or the next morning. Firy escaped to the sunny side yard. No shade meant she would be left alone. A slight breeze blew from the east near the pump dam. She flipped open her writing tablet.

Dearest little sister,

It's just you, Papa, and Popeye now. They're both getting older, but I know you'll take good care of them. Give yourself a big hug from me. I miss you all, even Popeye!

Bumps should be back from Chicago soon, and we'll find out about the future. I thought baseball was a pie in the sky thing, and we'd be back in Sitka in a few weeks.

People here talk about baseball constantly. Expectations run high, and the whole valley's counting on him. I can't even go for a walk without everyone asking about Bumps and baseball.

Bumps knows you like the White Sox better. "But they weren't smart enough to want me," he says. If he becomes a Cub, he'll send you a cap and hopes you'll be his biggest fan. I told him you already were.

I honestly had no idea that this baseball thing could take years. I'm ashamed to say I hope they reject him. If they do, we'll come right back home. We can all live in Papa's house, or maybe Bumps and I will buy a little house close by, and you can stay as often as you like.

I hate baseball. But then, how can I hate something you and Bumps love so much. I remember how the two of you sat at the kitchen table. I'd made popcorn, and if Papa gave permission, cocoa.

Bumps would say something about baseball, and you'd reply how it's like life:

He said, "There's a rule book."

You said, "That's the Bible."

"Life throws things at you."

"Like the pitcher."

"Do-overs."

You thought about that but then said. "Your next at-bat."

"The goal is to get to home plate."

You shouted. "Heaven."

Remember when Bumps said you're on a team, but they track your stats. That's the choices you make. Teammates help and encourage you.

That's your family and your friends. But you play the game and live your life.

Oh, how I miss my little girl. I took care of you like a mama. What kind of mother leaves her child? Can you ever forgive me?

I needed to write all this down, even if I never mail it. I keep asking Bozhe what I'm supposed to do.

It's twilight, dear Anna, what the Scots call the gloaming. It's magical, even here in this lonely place. I watch the stars come out and think of you.

Love, from your sister, mama, friend,

Firy Baas

La Conner, Washington — Present Day

Emma Lee sent her children to school, poured herself another cup of coffee, and sat at the kitchen table with Gramma's letters. She'd read them all more than once. What a glimpse it gave of a life lived in an unknown time and place.

The sun shining through the window did not cheer her. She felt as grey and dark as a winter day in the Pacific Northwest. The hints of Gramma's past abuse in the letters tore at her heart. What a burden Gramma had carried all her life. *I wonder if she ever told mom or anybody?*

Emma Lee never thought about Gramma losing her mother at such a young age and being a teenager in a world at war. And poor Grandpa, she had never heard about his baseball sacrifice. Another family secret. How many more could there be? It must have been heart-breaking, and she loved him even more.

She folded the horrific letter from Miss Ruth and stuffed it into the envelope. Tears floated in her eyes. How had Gramma survived?

Gramma shaped my childhood, but she never spoke of her tragic past. She made sure we had fun, tea parties, playing pretend, going to movies, goofing around, and laughing. And yet, all those sorrows were buried deep in her heart.

Sasha, her Russian Blue, jumped into her lap. Emma Lee wrapped her arms around the sweet feline. "I've discovered my grandmother, a girl called Firy." The tears fell on the cat's ears, and she rubbed her head against Emma Lee's chin. "Yes, Sasha. I'm going today. I hope she'll tell me more about Anna Marie."

Big band music echoed through the hallways. Emma Lee took her grandmother to the back of the sitting room. Some of the residents watched a Katherine Hepburn movie. Others napped in the comfortable chairs.

Emma Lee took the older woman's hand. "Tell me about Anna Marie."

"But you were there, Miss Ruth. You told me." Firy's chin quivered, and tears filled her eyes. "I've lost my hankie, and I hate these paper things."

Emma Lee sighed. "It's all right," she watched her grandmother's hands shred the tissue.

Firy blinked. "I wasn't there, you know. Oh, Emma Lee, if only I had been there," she grabbed the younger woman's arm, and the tissue fell like confetti.

The pain communicated itself to Emma Lee, who didn't know how to respond. "It's okay, Gramma. It happened a long time ago."

"Yesterday."

"What?" She couldn't keep pace with how Gramma's mind traveled through time, but she remembered the aide's advice to go along. "What happened yesterday?"

"The telegram." Firy's shoulders slumped, and tears ran down her plump cheeks. She leaned against Emma Lee and sobbed. They rocked together like mother and child. The motion and lullaby from Emma Lee seemed to soothe Firy.

TWENTY-SIX

Bumps tried to track the ballfields and parks as the bus ground eastward. Each tiny town and hamlet in middle America had at least one. He saw a few baseball diamonds in the Amish parts of Ohio and Pennsylvania. He assumed they belonged to the Mennonites rather than Old Order Amish. Baseball had patched itself into the crazy quilt of America, as it wove itself into the fabric of his soul.

Baseball belonged to everyone, even the Japanese. Henry had reenlisted and served in occupied Japan. His last letter said MacArthur had asked for Bibles and missionaries, but nameless bureaucrats at the State Department shipped him baseballs, bats, and mitts.

Bumps gazed at endless fields of corn. As much as he loved baseball, he knew it couldn't save anyone, and it wouldn't save Japan. He wondered if they'd ever play in the World Series, then laughed out loud. Crazy.

He patted his jacket pocket where the precious contract lay, a confirmation of his Big-League potential. He'd often doubted himself. Of course, he couldn't let anyone know that, not even Firy.

Sometimes, he talked to Bozhe about baseball, the lens through which he viewed and understood the world. He wished Firy reacted a bit more like Anna Marie. Little Dodo looked at the world through the prism of baseball, like he did. The game made them happy, simple as that.

As near as he could figure, Firy's childhood, displaced by grief and the things she locked away, gnawed at her soul. Firy had poured her heart into caring for sisters. She was like a mother to Anna Marie, and the little girl thrived in Firy's love. Elizaveta rebelled against it.

Bumps wanted to give his new wife excitement and adventure: new things, places, and people. Good things to exchange for the not so good things of her past. So far, it hadn't worked out the way he had planned.

Bumps stared out the window and listened to the thrumming of the bus's engine. He knew baseball wouldn't pay enough for them to be together. There would be years of farm teams, trying to claw his way to the minors, and possibly the Bigs. Possibly? He knew he was good enough, but plenty of guys couldn't hack the endless hours on the team bus, playing in every podunk scrub town and village across the several states. Eating in cheap diners and greasy spoons or packing peanut butter sandwiches.

At first, he'd make barely enough to pay for meals and a room at a sleazy boarding house near the training field. Even those in the major leagues had jobs during the off-season. If he wanted to make a decent living, he should just go into the mines. The unions were more assertive now, and the pay was good.

Baseball players played for the love of the game. He couldn't imagine doing anything else with his life. The problem was finding a place for Firy. If only she could fit in at Mam's. Why couldn't his mother's love extend to his wife?

He enjoyed the sound of the pages rustling as he patted his pocket again. Firy and baseball, what could be better? Anna Marie's face flashed before him. Wouldn't his hugest fan love to watch him play in the Bigs? Heck, she'd love to watch him in the minors or even the farm teams. She'd come to every practice, and the guys would adopt her as their mascot. He laughed out loud as he pictured the girl cheering at batting practice, hollering instructions and advice.

Would Firy be happier if he could somehow get Anna-Marie here? He tried to picture it but frowned, knowing Bill would never allow it, and besides, it would cost a fortune. He tossed his baseball from one hand to the other. He'd figure it out. He always figured it out.

A few more hours to Harrisburg, then a connecting bus through Indiantown Gap and Tower City. He'd hitch or walk the last three and a half miles to Williamstown. He leaned his head on the window, closed his eyes, and pitched a perfect game.

Every Saturday, Dippy and Dumpy perched in their treehouse. If they leaned and grasped an overhanging branch, they could pull themselves up on their toes to see Mam's house. When they saw Firy leave for one of her many walks, they intercepted her, usually at the ballpark. They sat on the bleachers and begged for stories of Alaska.

This Saturday was no exception. "Dip, fill these Mason jars with water from the hose while I see what I can find in the root cellar."

"Why can't we have lemonade?"

"If you go into the house to get it, Ma will want to know where we're going, and you can't keep your trap shut. She'll find out we've been meeting Firy and get cranky." Dumpy said in one long breath.

"You sure are smart, Dump."

"Yeah, that's why I'm the oldest."

As they passed Miller's barbershop, he motioned them in. Besides being the town's barbershop, Mr. Miller stocked penny candy, soda, tobacco, and notions. He sold newspapers and handled most of the village's communications, including the US mail and telegrams. Most gossip and rumors originated here as well.

This morning a red-faced Mr. Miller paced and muttered, "Sit down, boys. This is not good, not good at all. Better you should stand."

The confused boys obeyed his commands. Mr. Miller continued to pace. "I have news, and it's not good."

"What news?" Dippy asked.

"Better you should mind your own business."

"But Mr. Miller, you called us in here," Dumpy said.

"Yes, yes. This is a telegram, official from Alaska. For Firy. Bad news, boys. Terrible bad."

"What bad news?" Dippy asked again.

"I told you never mind. What to do is the problem."

"We can take it to Firy. Isn't that why you wanted to see us?"

"I changed my mind. Better Bumps should have it."

"He's not back from Chicago, you know, the Cubs," Dippy reminded him.

The barber glanced toward the sports pages scattered on his empty barber's chair. "Ah, yes, the Cubs." He paced some more, reread the telegram, and looked at the boys. He repeated this cycle several times, then dropped into his barber's chair. "Can you boys take this telegram to Mam Baas without reading it?"

"Uh, no," Dippy said, but Dumpy nudged him aside and held out his hand. He assured Mr. Miller they could, indeed, follow his directions.

The barber folded the telegram several times and handed it to Dump, who stuffed it into his trouser pocket. Once around the corner, Dumpy stopped and leaned against the building.

"Dumpy, you told Mr. Miller you'd give it to Mam without reading it."

"You dummy. Mr. Miller asked me if I could. He didn't ask me if I would, so I'm in the clear, see. Could and would aren't the same."

"What about should, Dumpy?"

"Aww, don't go getting all Sunday School on me. It's too late. It's already in my hands, right up here in front of my eyes, see?"

"Okay, Dump, you're the smart one."

His eyes scanned the paper, and the color fell out of his face. "This is not good."

"Read it to me, Dumpy."

"Not until we get to the treehouse, and you got to stuff your bandanna in your mouth."

"Why?"

"You'll find out."

They were out of breath when they reached their sanctuary. Dippy begged his brother to read the telegram. Dump shoved the paper at him and turned away. "C'mon Dump; you know reading's hard for me."

"Okay, but get your bandanna. I'm going to read it once, and I'm going to whisper:

ANNA MARIE KILLED. STOP. HOLDING F NER-AL PER YOUR ARRIVAL. STOP. WILL PHONE MONDAY 8:00 PM YOUR TIME. STOP. Miss R

"Kilt?" Dippy said, "like dead, kilt? What are v

"We ain't gonna do nuthin'. Mr. Miller's right.

"But he isn't here, and what about the phone call?"

"It's the day after tomorrow, and he might be back. In the meantime, we have to stay away from Firy."

"But I like her," Dippy whined.

"Don't you get it, you little rat? Firy's little sister is D-E-A-D."

Dippy, glad his brother made him get the bandanna, mopped his face with it. "You think I'll tell her, don't you? Well, don't you?"

Dumpy ignored his brother's question. "We're going to stay here and watch the road from Tower City. We'll take turns. I'll sneak out at night in case Bumps gets in late. But we have to act normal. We can't let Ma suspect anything."

"What about Mr. Miller. Won't he tell?"

"He can't. Telegraph people have to take an oath or something."

"Why?"

"Telegrams are holy. It would be like breaking a commandment. I think Old Man Miller has to wait until everybody knows before he talks."

Saturday and Sunday passed slowly. The confined space of the treehouse led to arguments over nothing. Dumpy decided to see Firy. By now, she must be wondering what happened to them. "Don't worry, Dip, I can act natural. I'll tell her you're sick or something. You keep an eye out for Bumps."

"What'll I do if he comes? What'll I say?"

"Tell him to go to the big maple tree by the pump dam."

"But Dumpy, he'll want to go home."

Dumpy sighed. Sometimes he thought he must have gotten all the brains, and Dippy got scrambled eggs. "They haven't narried long, and they still like to do the mushy-squishy.

Tell Bumps you'll bring Firy to the tree." Dumpy made loud, kissy noises.

"That's yucky," Dippy said.

"I know, but they like it."

Dippy watched the road like an Indian scout, like the Lone Ranger, or maybe Dick Tracy. His eyelids drooped, and he held them open with his fingers. He distracted himself by counting caterpillars and ladybugs, then remembered he had to watch the road. Sweat dripped into his eyes as he waited for his Uncle Bumps. The torture lasted until Dumpy returned.

On Monday, the boys climbed into their tree after saying goodbye to their Ma. Every week she wrestled the wringer-washer on the back porch and pinned the loads of laundry to a line in the backyard. "I don't feel right, Dump. What if Ma finds out we didn't go to school?"

"She won't if you keep your mouth shut."

"It's hard when we do wrong stuff. Makes me feel bad."

"Your teacher never told you about the greater good?"

Dippy hung his head in shame. Although twins, the brothers were in different grades. Dippy had flunked first grade twice. "Nope, they never did."

"It means you can do something bad if you figure something good will happen."

"But what's the greater good, Dump?"

Dumpy saw Bumps walking up the road and jumped out of the tree, glad he didn't have to answer.

Bumps waved to the boys and wondered why they v school. He almost shouted his news but wanted to tell F

They grabbed his hands and yanked him throug'

lot to the pump dam. Bumps' conversation and questions fell on deaf ears. The boys pushed him onto the stone bench, and Dumpy pulled the crumpled paper from his pocket. In silence, he handed it to his uncle.

The twins' eyes darted to the water, the maple, the bushes, anywhere but Bumps. Heads down, they shifted from one foot to the other and shoved their hands into their pockets. When they finally looked, they saw tears run down their uncle's face. Bumps cleared his throat and tried to speak.

Dumpy rushed in. "We got this day before yesterday. Mr. Miller told us to give it to Mam, but we didn't. We waited for you. Nobody knows."

"Mr. Miller told us not to read it, but he did." Dippy pointed an accusing finger at his brother.

Dumpy ignored his brother and said, "It said killed, that's worse than dead, isn't it, Uncle Bumps?"

"Why is kilt worse than dead, Dump?"

"Because, you moron, dead is when you live a long time then go to heaven when you're sleeping or rocking on the porch or something. Killed is when they gets you and does you in." He drew his finger across his throat and made gurgling noises.

"Oh, but dead is dead, right, Bumps?"

Bumps took his hands from his face and took a deep breath. "Quiet boys. Let me think."

"Did we do good, Bumps?" Dippy asked tearfully.

"You did well." Bumps replied and hugged the boy.

"Firy's on her walk now, Bumps. She always sits awhile at the ballpark; do you want us to get her?"

"Tell her to wait for me, but then you two hightail it out of there. I don't want you to let anything slip."

Dumpy clenched his fists. They hadn't let anything slip for the last two days. He almost gave voice to his indignation but kept quiet when he saw his Uncle's tears. He didn't know a man could have so many, and men weren't even supposed to cry, were they?

Bumps read the telegram three more times, then shoved it in his pocket next to the baseball contract. He wanted to warn the family before he told Firy. When he reached home, they crowded around him, excited and hopeful. When they saw his tear-stained face, they commiserated.

"There's other teams, Bumps, better ones."

"I never liked the Cubs anyway."

"The Pirates, maybe you should try Pittsburgh."

Bumps help up his hand then read the telegram aloud.

"The little sister?"

"Killed?"

"What?

"How?"

"What are you going to do? You can't afford to go to Alaska."

For once, all his siblings had no advice. One by one, they patted him on the shoulder, mumbled they were sorry, and left.

"You'll be going north," Mam said.

"As soon as I can beg, borrow, or earn the money."

"You won't be coming back. She doesn't fit."

Bumps looked into his mother's eyes. "I promise, Mam, someday I'll bring your grandchildren to see you."

"Just a minute, son."

She shuffled into her bedroom and pulled a box from the top dresser drawer. She held it in her hands and thought of the consequences if she showed it to Bumps. Would she lose him forever? No, he had promised to bring the grandchildren. She knew her son. He would keep his word.

She sat on the edge of the bed and opened the box. Nestled inside were bunches of envelopes bound with different colored ribbons, one from each son in the service. She held the letters from the two sons that had not returned. She held them to her heart and wept.

"Mam? You okay?" Bumps asked from the doorway.

She motioned him in. He sat next to her and put his arms around her. She leaned into him and sobbed. He recognized his own handwriting. "You saved our letters?"

"Yes, from all six of you. They're all I have left of…" she couldn't say their names.

Bumps pulled his handkerchief out and wiped his mother's eyes. She handed him his packet bound together with his military allotment checks.

"Mam?"

"I saved most of them. I can pinch a penny or two." She handed him the bundle.

Bumps fingered the allotment checks and hoped it was enough.

"I'm sorry about the baseball, son."

"I'll always have baseball."

"Not the Big Leagues."

"No, not the Bigs."

He watched as Mam dragged herself to the front porch. He

knew sitting in her glider and staring across the valley soothed her.

Alone in the kitchen, he lifted the cookstove's burner and saw the glowing red-orange coals. He took his future with the Chicago Cubs out of his pocket. It burned quickly.

TWENTY-SEVEN

Firy, vaguely aware that Bumps sat beside her on the porch swing, stared across the valley. The evening air, heavy with humidity, waited for the clouds to crawl over the hills and release their moisture. There was an unopened letter in her lap.

"It's from Miss Ruth. Shall I read it to you?" Bumps asked.

She continued to stare, silent, unmoving. Bumps tried to tilt her face to his, but she resisted. He leaned against the swing's cushions and rubbed his eyes, then plucked the letter from the envelope and read aloud:

My dearest Firy and Bumps, too, of course,

By the time you read this letter, we will have already talked on the phone, but long-distance calls are expensive, and I wouldn't have said all that's in my heart.

Robert Nelson has taken over the business from his father. He's a good pilot, and if you know when you will arrive in Seattle, Robbie says he'll meet you and fly you home. There'd be stops for fuel and food but much faster than a ship. The only charge would be the cost of gas.

Enclosed, you will find $42.00, the entire contents of the church's benevolent fund, and a collection Petrov Bravebird took at Indiantown.

Father Alexi came to see me, and we had tea. I chuckled, seeing his thick fingers wrapped around the tiny teacup. He didn't speak until I slipped some of Mike's secret ingredient into his tea.

"Is this some kind of Episcopalian vodka?" He asked.

My face flamed, but it seemed to break the ice. He pulled some bills from his wallet and said his people were too poor for him to take an official collec-

tion. He also offered to have Anna Marie buried at the Russian Cemetery. I asked how that was possible since she hadn't been baptized at St. Michael's. Father Alexi said, "For Firy and their Mama, I make it possible."

I asked him to make it a Russian funeral. He seemed surprised but pleased. Marie and Vivian have made little Russian crosses to hand out. Sam Mitchell donated some fancy paper he had at the Sentinel, and Father Alexi approved the design.

I tell you, Firy, underneath it all, he is a good man. I'm ashamed I never asked Bozhe to show me Father Alexi's heart.

Do you remember our springtime trips to the cemetery? We raked leaves, chopped weeds, then brushed the dirt from the wooden Russian cross on your Mama's grave. We gave it a fresh coat of white paint and planted forget-me-nots. You looked for others you knew, and we tidied their graves, too. Then you always said, "Miss Ruth, is it time for tea and cookies?"

That reminds me, Father Alexi commissioned a flat gravestone identical to your Mama's but smaller. Papa Bill would let no one else make the wooden cross. It's lying on Anna Marie's bed until the funeral.

A deep heaviness invades my heart, knowing next spring when the snow is gone and lilacs bloom, we'll have double sorrow as we visit the graves.

Elizaveta and family will arrive in the next few days, but Bill says he won't have the funeral without you, no matter how long it takes. Hopefully, you'll have the money soon. I can see a day when people will be flying across the country instead of taking the trains. I wish that day were now.

As you know, Firy, or perhaps you don't, Sitka has no coroner or medical examiner. Between the Doc and Chief Durand, whatever needs to be done, gets done. They talked to the owner of one of the fish canneries, and Anna Marie's there in cold storage.

After you left, we spent a lot of time together. I fear I neglected my other duties. Soon I will have to make visits to Haines, Kake, and Angoon. I will, of course, be here for her funeral.

One day Anna Marie and I walked as far as your Great Gram's old place and watched the new family. I felt we should introduce ourselves, but Anna Marie would have none of it. We were Russian fur traders who stumbled upon a Tlingit village. We must do reconnaissance and report to our Captain. So, we hid in the bushes and watched a mama and papa, four children, and an older gentleman, probably the grandpa. Goats, chickens, ducks, and a pregnant sow rounded out the population. A tired old hound, tethered to the porch, howled and tried to break free. I'm afraid our scent gave us away.

The mama screamed, 'Bear attack. Bear attack.' Her children yelled and ran in circles, which caused the dog to howl even more. The papa tried to calm the mama as she screamed at the kids to hide in the cabin. The grandpa continued to hoe and shook his head. Chickens cackled, goats bleated, and the pig squealed. I must admit I joined Anna Marie in her side-splitting laughter. It was better than going to the movies, why one time-

Forgive me, Firy. You want to know about your sister. First, let me say, the men at the mill made a beautiful coffin from a piece of Koa wood. The owner had it shipped from Hawaii for a dining table. He donated it and carved a life-sized relief of Popeye on the lid. Anna Marie would have loved it.

Poor Bill. He's been sitting in the house, rocking, and smoking. I go every day. He looks at me and says, "I quit, you know."

"That's good," I say, then open the windows to get rid of that nasty tobacco smoke.

As a newly married woman, Mardel took it upon herself to arrange for meals. The Frigidaire is full, and the food's piled everywhere. I didn't want to discourage her. She is doing this for the love of you.

The men from the café spent many mornings with Bill. I suspected Mike brought the secret ingredient. They ate the casseroles and meatloaves for breakfast, then finished it off with pie, upside-down pineapple cake, and mountains of cinnamon rolls and cookies. Bill didn't eat much, and the food kept coming.

Ivan takes Katerina whenever he escorts his daughters through town. Stormy questioned him about why he was packing a loaded rifle. Ivan looked the Chief straight in the eye, but before he could answer, Stormy tipped his hat and said, "Forget it. I know."

When you left, Popeye accompanied Anna Marie to school. She waved to him from the classroom window, and he wagged in response. All the kids played with him at recess.

Did you know Mr. Trent's wife has not returned to town? Rumors are, her mother wasn't sick, and there were other reasons she left, romantical ones. Did she say anything to you when you traveled together to Seattle? No, don't answer that. Oh dear, I didn't mean to gossip, but one wonders. Anyway, Mr. Trent didn't like Popeye at school.

I'm no doctor of the mind or heart, but I thought it natural for Anna Marie to pour all her loneliness into that dog. How wonderful of Bozhe to create dogs. They do all they can to share our burdens. Popeye was a tremendous help to Anna Marie. I imagine his mangy fur coat soaked up a lot of tears.

I explained all that to Mr. Trent, and he had no further objections. Several times, I saw him on the school's steps with his arms around Popeye. I hurried by, unwilling to disturb Popeye's ministry of giving comfort.

Forgive my rambling, dear Firy. I do not want to write what I know I must. My heart aches when I think of you reading this.

Remember when we sat on the backyard log when your dear mama died? I sit there now.

Miss Ruth set aside her writing paper, stretched, and went into the house for a drink of water. Bill sat in his rocker, motionless. She feared one day his soul would fly away and leave his tired body behind.

Her nose wrinkled as it filled with tobacco smoke. She raised the shades and opened the windows, then saw his lips twitch. Good, she thought, there's still some life there.

Her heart plunged into heaviness again as she sat on the log and picked up her writing tablet and pen.

One day Popeye disappeared, and Anna Marie could not be consoled. Bill borrowed a truck from the mill and explored the roads. Miners criss-crossed the foothills, and loggers scoured the woods. Ade and his fisherman friends sailed into near-by coves and surveyed the beaches.

Bill didn't have the heart to make Anna Marie go back to school. When he went to work, she pedaled to all the same places calling for Popeye. No-one stopped her, and then one day, she didn't come home.

Everyone joined this new search. Three days later, the bike leaned against the house, and Bill discovered Popeye's and Anna Marie's bodies under the front porch. Nobody knows how they got there. I will spare you the details for now. We will talk as much as you want when you come home.

Stormy Durand wanders through town with Bull. He curses and mutters to himself. I know he wants this solved but has few clues. I think he's worried it may happen again. Everyone is extra vigilant.

I believe your sister and Mama are together, happy and whole, in the arms of Bozhe. The tears we shed, dear one, are for ourselves. The more we love, the greater our loss, the deeper our pain.

I'm sorry this letter rambled and meandered. We can talk as long as you like when you arrive. Remind me to tell you about a conversation Anna Marie and I had last year.

Love,

Miss Ruth

P.S. Bill buried Popeye behind the woodshed, and I said a prayer.

Bumps folded the letter and turned to his wife. He searched her face and didn't like what he saw. "Firy?"

"Yes. Fine. Read the letter." She stared across the valley as a summer storm made its way over the hills. Hot, humid air thundered, and then the rain fell. He began to realize that as his soul knit itself to baseball, hers was knit to Anna Marie and the north.

"It's okay, dear one. I'll take you home." Bumps pulled his wife to him. She did not resist, but she did not respond either. "Did you hear me, Firy? We're going home."

"Go ahead. Read."

He looked at the letter crumpled in his fist. He smoothed the paper and began again.

Memory Care Center — Present Day

Emma Lee reached across the table and grabbed the gnarled hands. "I can't bear it, Gramma."

Firy's eyes filled with a compassion that came from years of pain, "It was a long time ago, dear one."

"How could you live with such losses? I couldn't imagine growing up without Mom." Tears threatened the young woman again. "The whole world at war when you're a teenager, and then you married grandpa and tried to be happy and then–"

Emma Lee's tears fell on their entwined hands. Firy looked at those hands, hers stiff with arthritis, wrinkled and weak with age. She squeezed her granddaughter's young, strong hands. "You have not had anyone close to you die. Soon."

"Don't leave me."

A pain stabbed Firy's heart as Anna Marie's anguished cry 'don't leave me' echoed through the decades. She shook it away. "Hush now, I spent most of my life wrapped in grief. Promise me you won't make that mistake."

Emma Lee shuddered again and stared out the window.

Firy patted her cheek. "My grief controlled me so much that I cost your grandfather his dreams."

"You would never do that, Gramma."

"After he died, I found a letter among his papers asking why he never came to spring training. The Cubs offered him another chance. He never took it."

"Why not?" Emma Lee pulled a handkerchief from her purse.

"I think your grandpa felt he had to take care of me. Perhaps, if we had talked about it," she sipped her tea. "My generation wasn't good at talking. You've got us beat there. All your generation does is talk."

Emma Lee ignored the comment. "But Gramma, I remember you as happy and peaceful. Content."

The old woman reached for her teacup and leaned back in her chair. She looked at Emma Lee with soft eyes, "I learned to love Bozhe and do what's right, but it didn't come easy."

TWENTY-EIGHT

Firy swept the wooden sidewalk and the back porch, hung her sweater by the door, and wondered why Anna Marie hadn't worn her jacket today. There was a definite chill in the air. She sagged against the familiar plaid and hugged the garment as fresh pain flooded her soul. The funeral, only three months ago, still filled her every thought as she went about her daily chores.

"Oh, Dodo, you're gone." She pushed her face into the fabric and breathed deeply. She could have screamed. Not a trace of Anna Marie's scent remained.

When Mama died, Papa said no one must touch her things. A year later, Aunt Ollyanna took Mama's scant wardrobe to the Salvation Army Thrift Store. Papa didn't speak to her for months.

After Anna Marie's funeral, Papa closed the door to her room. No one dared go in or touch her homework on the coffee table. The reminders of Anna Marie and Mama pierced Firy's heart.

Every day Papa looked at Firy and Elizaveta with red-rimmed eyes. Bags like bulging suitcases weighed him down. Feet shuffled instead of walked. He sat in the chair, rocking endlessly. Silent.

After several weeks Papa dragged himself to the mill, but in the evenings, he sat in the rocker and stared out the window.

Firy also had to force herself to get up and go through the motions of daily living. Make breakfast. Do the laundry. Take care of Bumps.

The image of the half-sized coffin being lowered into the ground etched itself into her mind. The beautiful carving of Popeye on the lid broke her heart. The shovelful of dirt that thudded on the burial box echoed through her soul.

Masha was in the final stages of her second pregnancy and was not allowed to fly. Henry had flown in from Japan on a military plane, attended the funeral, and left the next day for Washington DC. Firy wished he could have stayed longer. Papa Bill needed him. Maybe, she did, too.

She wiped her tears, opened the Frigidaire, and pulled out containers of left-overs, and dumped them in a pan. Her appetite had deserted her long ago, but Bumps would be home soon.

Even Miss Ruth had deserted her. Firy knew that wasn't true, but when they arrived in Sitka, Miss Ruth was in Kake. She managed to make it back for the funeral but had to leave several days later. Now she was in Haines with some crisis at the mission school. *I need you more than a bunch of stupid school kids. Can't you see that?*

Firy forced herself to walk to the post office every day. If there was no letter from Miss Ruth, disappointment kicked her in the stomach. She kept her head down and ignored well-meaning platitudes from everyone. Every day she detoured to the See House behind St. Peter's.

"No word yet, my dear."

"I'm sorry, Firy, she should return soon."

She'd heard those words all week. Today, she sat on the cold, stone steps of the church. Gray waves still slapped the shore, creation's soft applause. Seabirds and ravens still swooped and squawked. Off to her right, the sawmill belched dirty gray smoke, as it had for years.

How could Miss Ruth leave her? How could she have left Anna Marie?

The school bell clanged, and as Firy used to, most of the students ran across the street to play on the beach before heading home. She watched them from the steps of the stone church.

Angry clouds roamed over the islands in Sitka Sound. Firy sighed and wondered if she and Bumps should find their own little house, one without memories, but that would leave Papa Bill all alone. It wouldn't be right. Dark clouds formed in her soul, and she couldn't think.

"Firy! Firy!" Mardel jumped from her bike and let it fall. "The Star of Alaska arrived with Miss Ruth. She sent me to tell you she'll have supper with you tonight."

Firy managed a small smile as hope found a place near her heart. "Thanks, Mardel."

Mardel looked at her watch. "You better get home and start cooking. I've been looking for you for an hour. My side hurts, and my legs ache."

Firy hugged her slim and trim friend, "Good exercise."

"You know I hate that." Mardel grabbed the handlebars and shoved the bike at Firy. "I'll get it tomorrow or the next day. I might never ride it again. Not really dignified for us married ladies, is it?"

Firy leaned close to her friend and whispered, "The Sisters baked bread all day, and if I'm not mistaken, blueberry pie."

Mardel rubbed her flat stomach. "I'm glad that I can eat whatever I want and not gain weight, not like Marie."

Firy ignored the jibe at their mutual friend.

Mardel patted her stomach again, "I think I'll drop in and let them know about Miss Ruth."

Firy pedaled home and looked at the unforgiving sky. "Bozhe, can you please make Miss Ruth fix me?"

TWENTY-NINE

Miss Ruth had been back from Haines for a week, but her daily walks gave her no solace.

Today she headed to Indian River. The clerk from the Salvation Army Thrift Store hailed her as she passed. Miss Ruth waved and walked on. The natives on the beach wanted to share their clams and shellfish. She shook her head.

She passed Sheldon Jackson. It was her first place of employment nearly a half-century ago. What a chechako she had been. She smiled at the memory. She still visited the school often.

"Miss Ruth, come play."

"Miss Ruth, tell us a story."

"Miss Ruth sing to us in Tlingit."

"No. Yupik."

The children crowded close to the entrance of the schoolyard. A stern-faced teacher appeared in a doorway, grasped her handbell, and pumped her arm up and down. The children groaned and marched back to their classroom.

Miss Ruth waved and increased her prayers for the school. She neither slowed her pace nor her prayers until she reached her favorite beach at the river's mouth.

She sat on the damp sand and leaned against a large boulder. Miss Ruth pulled off her cowboy boots and heavy wool socks and wiggled her toes. Vanilla foam edged the incoming waves, and it enticed her to stand ankle-deep in the cold water. As the waves rolled out, they pulled the sand from under her feet. *Bozhe, I feel as gray as today's sky. You know Firy is the child of my heart. How can I ease her pain?*

Seabirds called to one another, and Miss Ruth strained to hear a voice beyond this world. Gulls argued over a dead crab, surf sang to sand, and heaven remained silent. Miss Ruth sagged against the boulder. She wept, then surrendered her will to the Almighty.

A sizeable gray gull emerged from the sea with a small fish in its beak. Other gulls followed. The smell of rotting seaweed clinging to the rocks was as familiar to her as the Earl Grey she brewed every morning.

The wind pulled wisps of gray hair from the braid falling down Miss Ruth's back. She stuffed them into her old hat. Made of leather, it had lost its shape years ago—another memory.

As she picked up the remains of her lunch, the Almighty asked Miss Ruth if she was willing to watch and pray, perhaps for years. She would not have the power or authority to change Firy's life.

She threw the crusts of her sandwiches near the water, and half a dozen ravens fought over them. "You're doing what's best, Bozhe, even though I can't see it. I will trust you."

Miss Ruth put her socks on and retrieved her cowboy boots. She rubbed the leather uppers that had softened over the years. "We've shared a lot of life, and you've taken me many places," she told the boots. She should order a new pair, but the idea of breaking them in prevented her. The soles had been repaired twice and the heels three times. She would ask Petrov Bravebird's advice. Perhaps, he could retool them the Salish way.

The ravens crept closer, and the seagulls squawked for more. Miss Ruth showed them her empty hands. High-pitched screeches echoed their disgust as they flew away.

She held her hands high and praised her Lord on the beach at Jamestown bay. *My hands are empty, Lord, but I will watch and pray. One thing I've learned, dear Bozhe, is You know the end from the beginning, and Your heart is kind.*

Through the decades, Miss Ruth had become acclimated to Alaska's weather. But today, the drizzle chilled her old bones. The biting wind and cold mist from the surf sprayed her face. She put her head down and turned toward town.

Bozhe had taught her to live above the cloud cover, where she could feel the warmth of the Son. She asked for that warmth now as she returned to the See House.

THIRTY

Firy jabbed the mop back into the bucket heedless as water sloshed over. She glared at her sister. "Don't. Just don't."

"Have a cup of coffee, Firy, and I'll explain."

"There's nothing to explain. You're leaving, and that's it."

"Firy, please." Betty guided her sister to a kitchen chair. She stood behind her and kneaded Firy's shoulders. "It's been three years since Anna Marie's funeral, and every day I've thought about returning to the Skagit Valley."

"How can you leave, take your babies away from me? They were born here. This is their home."

Betty sat down and took both of Firy's hands. "I stayed for you. But it's been hard on Ern working two dead-end part-time jobs. I never see him. He can get his old job back in La Conner, and he'll have time for us.

Firy's shoulders caved. She placed her hands over her stomach. Should she tell her? She looked over her shoulder and imagined Betty's reaction to her news. Yes, she would tell her about the baby. But, when she opened her mouth, she heard herself say, "When do you leave?"

"End of the month."

"So soon?"

"You love Sitka, don't you, Firy? The mountains, and the ocean, the Russian Church, the native traditions. You love it all."

"It's home."

"Not for me, and not only because of what happened when we

were kids. It's eighteen hours of darkness in winter."

"But there's all that light in summer."

"There's twice as much rain as in Washington. I hate rain," Betty said.

"It keeps everything green."

"I feel like the mountains are pushing me into the sea." Betty continued as if she hadn't heard Firy's comment, "There's no room on this island."

"It's safe."

"Safe?" Betty grabbed her sister by the shoulders, "Do you hear yourself? Safe? When were we ever safe? Was Anna Marie safe?"

"I can't leave her or Mama. I can't."

"They're dead, Firy. Gone."

"I tidy their graves, bring them flowers, talk to them. And besides, there's Papa and Miss Ruth."

"That old spinster missionary..." Betty lifted the chipped enamel coffee pot from the woodstove. She poured her words as slowly as the coffee. "Papa Bill tried, but he's not our real dad. We don't owe him anything."

"Betty! That's not right! How can you say that?" Firy's voice reached the ceiling and cracked. Of course, Papa Bill had been strict and reserved, especially after Mama died, but he was not a bad Papa. Firy had no words for how she felt about Miss Ruth.

"I have to get away from my memories," Betty whispered. She stirred sugar into her coffee and asked, "Why don't you use that electric percolator I bought for Papa's birthday?"

"We like things the way they are, the way they used to be." Firy looked out the window and saw another time. *Mama, the yellow flowers have budded. Mama, the fishing boats have come in.*

Mama, the mail plane buzzed the town. Firy saw herself innocent. Safe. Happy.

"I'm going to live my own life!" Betty gathered her things.

"Don't be so heartless."

"Don't be so stupid."

"Elizaveta!"

Hand on the doorknob, Betty looked at her sister, "I wish I could make you understand."

Firy clutched her belly again. She should tell her sister there would be a baby before autumn. But no, her sister chose to abandon her.

"Goodbye, Firy." Betty took a step toward her sister, but Firy stiffened.

Firy stood by the sheer white curtains she had loved since she first came to Papa's house and watched her sister walk away. Betty did not turn around.

Later, Firy wandered through the house, mop and bucket forgotten. She touched Mama's samovar and candlesticks and looked at the Beautiful Corner.

She twisted the doorknob of Anna Marie's room and rubbed her still flat stomach. They would need this room for the baby. Perhaps she should call Miss Ruth and ask her to clear out Anna Marie's things.

Firy chewed on the inside of her cheek and paced outside the room. She was a grown-up, married lady. She could handle this herself.

The clock said it was time to start dinner for Papa and Bumps. She'd tell them tonight. About the baby, not about Betty. Maybe her sister would change her mind.

Betty's little family left Sitka in a small floatplane. When it bumped across Sitka Sound and flew over Mount Edgecombe, Firy didn't wave. She felt Bumps put his arm around her and shrugged it off when he said, "I need to get back to work. Are you okay?"

Firy stood unmoving as the sound of the propellers faded, and the plane flew into the clouds. "I need to make lunch for Papa."

"Don't let him go back to the mill. I think he's ill."

Firy overlooked the concern on her husband's face. Consumed by her misery, she forgot his warning about Papa Bill.

No matter the season, the daily duties of Firy's life fell softly like winter's first snow. Year after year, they blanketed her heart without warmth. Spring breakup never came. The landscape never changed. Cold. Barren. Frozen, it was all Firy could do to breathe.

He stood at the wooden gate, his bat bag at his feet. Through the kitchen window, he saw Firy thrust her hands into a sink full of dirty dishes. Sharon, his little girl, poked her head under the sheer white curtain; it draped around her shoulders like a wedding veil. She pressed her nose on the glass and waved good-bye. Beyond her, his son sat in the high chair and smeared chocolate pudding everywhere.

He waved, adjusted his baseball cap, slung his bat bag over his shoulder, and headed to the ballpark. Firy hadn't attended any of his games since she was pregnant with Sharon. The other wives brought their toddlers and babies to the bleachers. Sometimes they rotated the kids through each of their houses and took turns babysitting so they could enjoy the games free of children.

Not Firy. She refused to join in even though her friends had pleaded with her. When he pressed her, she had snapped, "It was Anna Marie who loved baseball, not me."

If only she hadn't gone to Pennsylvania. If only he hadn't had an interview with the Chicago Cubs. If only. Breathe, she told herself, just breathe.

Bumps considered giving up the game but found he couldn't do it. His American Legion team was about to win the semi-finals, and then they'd go to Fairbanks for the Midnight Sun Tournament. Oh, how he'd like his team to win that championship game. Baseball still gave him joy, but without Firy, it was a lonely joy.

There was an invitation in his eyes and a hesitation whenever he left for the ballpark, but Firy never made eye contact.

He watched her in the morning as he shaved and she made the bed. He watched her after dinner as he cleared the table, and she did the dishes. He watched her as she twirled the radio dial looking for her soap opera, and he put the kids to bed. He longed to find the Firy he loved. The Firy he had lost.

"Breathe," he told himself as he entered the dugout. "Just breathe."

THIRTY-ONE

As a child, Firy had enjoyed the daily migration to the post office, but the loneliness of the last few years filled the trek with anxiety and concern. The massive Art Deco-style structure, built twenty years ago in the early thirties, sat across from the seawall. Townspeople still referred to it as the new post office and hailed it as a significant link to friends and family in the lower forty-eight.

Like his father before him, Robert Nelson buzzed the town every morning before landing his floatplane with the mail. Everyone knew precisely how long it took old Mr. Jack and his clerks to sort everything. Most bulk packages and freight still came by ship.

As a child, Firy pedaled down the sidewalk. She wove in and out of the Tlingit women who sat on their blankets selling trinkets. They swatted at Popeye as she yelled for him to keep up.

This daily ritual became a social event in her teen years. Firy gave up the bike to jabber with her girlfriends. Most of them collected and traded exotic-looking stamps from foreign pen-pals. Firy listened to their dreams of traveling to those places, but she had planned to stay right here in Sitka; letters from Franella Feddersen had been enough for her.

During the war, the post office became an even more vital link to those who had enlisted or been drafted. After Bumps shipped out, Firy's worried. Would there be a letter today? Was he getting enough to eat? Had he been in any battles? Was he safe?

The women clustered like a flock of ravens outside the post office and read their letters. On more than one occasion, a girlfriend, wife, or troubled mother stumbled away in tears, heartsick.

After Bumps left, Anna Marie often slipped out of school and met them on their trek. Firy hadn't the heart to force her back. Bless him, Bumps included the little girl in his letters and sometimes sent Anna Marie one of her own.

That was then. Today Firy forced a deep breath through cold lips. She pushed the buggy over the cracked sidewalk, and her memories walked with her. She glanced at the woods behind the Pioneer Home. The evergreen covered hillside was the home of the Russian cemetery. *Mama, can you see me? Are you and Anna Marie happy together?*

Firy thought about the 'what-ifs' and the 'if onlys.' Miss Ruth declared Firy must live life with what is, not what if. Firy bit the inside of her cheek. It would not do for Miss Ruth to find out how often Firy 'what if-ed' and 'if only-ed.'

Firy's son, Eddie, let out a yelp as the buggy clunked down the curb. "Sorry, baby, I was thinking. Nothing to worry you. I'll keep you safe."

The stark white post office squatted before her. Why didn't Betty write? Had something awful happened, or was she so happy she forgot all about her sister? Granted, she'd never been a good letter writer, but seven months had crept by since her last letter.

Firy parked the buggy at the bottom of the stairs and untied the rope she used to keep her son in the buggy. The chubby three-year-old was a climber and a runner. She really should think of him as a little boy but knew he would always be her baby. They found the post office lobby nearly empty.

Mr. Jack made faces at little Eddie, and the toddler laughed. Firy shifted him to her other hip and sighed.

"Come on, then, give us a smile. You have a letter from Betty, oops, I mean, Elizaveta." Mr. Jack's voice boomed through the lobby.

Firy grabbed the envelope and rushed away as Mr. Jack yelled, "Where's my smile?"

Next in line, Ivan Mishkin said, "I give smile. You give big letter."

"Nothing for you today, old man."

Ivan looked around. "You only old man here."

Mr. Jack yelled, "Next."

Firy sat on the seawall, held her letter in one hand, and rocked the buggy with the other. Ivan crossed the street, peeked at little Eddie, then sat a few feet from mother and child.

Firy scanned the paragraphs for bad news. Satisfied, she returned to the first page. A smile hovered and tried to break forth.

Ivan, who had been holding his breath, let it out in a whoosh and slid closer to read over her shoulder. He admitted to himself the strange English alphabet confused him. *Better I should talk. I expert at Russian and English talk, not so much Tlingit, except for swear.*

He kept one eye on Firy while he scanned the docks and post office, alert for news, gossip, or rumor. They always lurked on the streets of Sitka.

Jake emerged and waved a letter over his head. Ivan scratched his ear and pulled at his mustache. The hairy thing wiggled as he muttered under his breath. Startled, Firy looked up.

She patted the old Russian on the knee. "Go, Ivan. I'll send Papa or Bumps to the café with all the news."

His face fell, and his mustache drooped, "I was to be first. To tell, you see?" He twirled his watch cap in his hand.

"Come for coffee in an hour, and I'll read you Elizaveta's entire letter."

Ivan looked at his watch. "I come when school out. See little Sharon, yes?"

Firy nodded. "You're such a good extra grandpa to her."

Ivan's head bobbed up and down as he jammed his watch cap back in place. "Hold on, Jake. I come." He turned around and, with solemn eyes, said, "You are good girl, Glaphira. Like your mama."

Firy nodded as the color in her face sank to her feet and drained out. It had been twenty years since Mama died. When anyone mentioned her, the pain stabbed Firy's heart as it did when she was eight-years-old following the coffin through town. Firy shook her head to dispel the image. The pain remained as she stared into the murky water below the seawall. She stuffed her letter back in its envelope.

She looked across Sitka Sound to Mount Edgecombe. Its classic volcanic shape rose out of the water—the snow-covered peak, pristine. You've been here all my life. Solid. Stable. Nothing moves you.

Too often, her sorrow flowed like hot lava. When sadness and grief rumbled and erupted, it spewed anger and despair. She couldn't control the molten mass of fiery emotion. *Bozhe, make it go away. Please make it go away.*

"Firy! Firy!" Joey Bravebird pedaled as fast as he could. Cars honked as he circled her twice and skidded to a stop. Eddie woke with a cry. Firy waived the envelope in front of the baby's face, "Don't fuss, little one. Your auntie sends her love."

Joey shrieked again, "Firy!"

The panic in Joey's voice caused the volcano to rumble. "What's wrong?"

"It's your Papa Bill. Something's wrong. There are lots of people at your house. They sent grandfather for Doc and me to get you." He stared at his shoes, then lifted his face and whispered, "They said… hurry before it's too late."

Firy stood frozen. Joey pushed his bike into her hands. "Go. I'll follow with Eddie. You know he's safe with his Uncle Joey. I'll be right behind you."

Hot lava burned her, smoke and ash blinded her. Firy ran, and the letter fluttered away.

THIRTY-TWO

Firy twisted the sodden shirt, squeezed, then shook it, and fed it through the wringer. Betty had described her automatic washing machine in her last letter. Put clothes and detergent in, shut the lid, turn a few dials, and an hour later, the clothes were ready to hang.

Firy's arms always ached past her elbows by the time she pushed three loads through those hard rubber rollers. For safety's sake, she did the laundry when her daughter attended school, and her little boy slept.

Two weeks ago, Mardel's son had flattened his hand in the rollers, and Doc removed two fingers, the bones splintered. Last month in Haines, a toddler had his arm crushed, then amputated.

More than laundry caused concern. Axes slipped while chopping kindling. Chimney fires engulfed whole houses. Canning kettles overturned and scalded little ones. Oil stoves exploded.

Last fall, while hunting on Mt. Verstovia, a boy leaned his rifle against a fallen tree and scrambled over it. Somehow, he jostled the gun. His father carried him through the woods, but the boy bled out before they reached the edge of the forest. Another of Sitka's families was broken, forever.

Every year storms at sea swamped large and small fishing vessels or native canoes, and explosions in the mines took several lives. Hunters and hikers became lost in the forests and died of exposure or encounters with bears. Logging accidents were not uncommon. Even the cannery workers faced danger with all that heavy machinery. Once, a man, locked in a retort, died as temperatures soared to cook the cans of fish. Even in this day and age, Alaska endangered her people.

Firy hung the clothes out to dry and thought about her sister. Perhaps we should move to her valley. Strawberries, peas, cows, and tulips. The ocean and forests, out of the way. The automatic washing machines close. Perhaps, it's easier to keep children safe there. She glanced at Mama's Beautiful Corner and saw the pysanka that wasn't there. She pictured it in the grave with Mama.

Clutching her stomach, she ran to the bathroom and retched. The doctor said the baby would arrive in late fall. For now, she had a lot to do. The ground had thawed. The shovel and rake leaned against the back door — boots and gloves placed in a basket next to them. The cardboard box of forget-me-nots and a small can of white paint waited. She'd go to the cemetery tomorrow, and she'd take Sharon and little Eddie. It was time for them to get to know Mama. She wouldn't wait for Miss Ruth's return from Kodiak Island.

Months ago, when Papa collapsed, Doc sent him to the veteran's hospital in Seattle. She still needed to tell Mama and Anna Marie.

Saturday morning, Bumps told her to take as much time as she needed. He and Uncle Ade would take the kids fishing. Maybe that was best. Keep them away from the sadness. Firy dragged herself to the cemetery. She wanted Miss Ruth beside her.

Forest ferns grew over the paths and hid the graves in the Russian cemetery. Dead leaves, moss, weeds, and twigs covered the area. Firy and Miss Ruth had always started with Mama and Anna Marie, then worked their way around the entire cemetery. If the weather held, they made their way to the City Cemetery and then the National Cemetery at the other end of town. Today, Firy looked after her family. The others could wait.

She sank to her knees between the graves and pulled at the weeds and moss that encroached the flat gravestones. After a time, her words tumbled out one after the other. "Oh, Mama, I have the cleanest house in town. I make Sharon and little Eddie behave. I take them to Sunday school. You said love Bozhe and do what's right. Then what?"

Firy's words echoed through her soul, and she couldn't stand the hurt in them. She clamped her lips together. She scrubbed and cleaned. It was never enough; she was never enough.

She knelt next to the grave and spoke aloud. "Sometimes I see a sadness in Bumps' eyes. Does he resent me because we stayed here after Anna Marie died? Thank goodness the baseball people didn't want him. Perhaps he's mad at whatever it is that gnaws at me."

Firy pulled the weeds and planted the forget-me-nots. "I miss you, Mama. I write to Betty, Masha, and Papa Bill every week. I even write to Henry. All I do is write letters. It's the right thing to do, isn't it?"

The sun streamed through the evergreens and dappled the graves, some over two hundred years old. "Henry sent me a Christmas card and one for my birthday. Masha called on Christmas day but couldn't talk long because it's expensive. I reminded her stamps cost a few pennies, but she says life in California is different, exciting, and she doesn't have time to write. Betty only writes two or three times a year."

Firy, glad the cemetery was empty, didn't bother to lower her voice, "I'm hollow inside, Mama."

Firy sighed and wiped her nose on her sleeve. "Life goes on day after day, week after week. Sharon will be in first grade in the fall, and little Eddie is already three."

Firy had clawed at the same clump of grass for several minutes. She smoothed over the bare spot on the grave and tried to get the dirt out from under her fingernails.

"Oh, Mama," she cried, throwing herself across the grave. "I lost the baby."

Deep sobs wracked Firy. She pressed her hand to her chest. Breathe. "Forgive me, Mama, but we're going to Betty's peaceful valley. Miss Ruth will have to take care of you and Anna Marie. We'll be safe there, and I'll have an automatic washing machine."

"Good breakfast, dear." Bumps said and kissed her on the cheek, "Come on, Sharon. I'll walk you to school."

"Daddy. I'm big."

"I know you are, sweetie. May I walk you to school, little princess?" He bowed before his daughter.

She jumped into his arms, "And hold my hand?"

Firy wiped Eddie's sticky face and asked Bumps to drop him off at Mardel's, who would bring him home at naptime.

When the house emptied, Firy poured herself another coffee, put the dishes to soak, and made mental lists as she scurried around the kitchen.

She'd sell Papa's house to pay his ongoing medical bills. She tapped her cheek with the end of her pencil then chewed on the eraser. She needed to figure out how to present this move to Bumps. He liked his job and the teams he coached. He might not want to start over. No matter. This is going to happen. She gathered the lists and shoved them in the top drawer of the desk.

She pulled out the last of her special stationery. She took a swallow of coffee and nearly spat it out. Down the sink went the cold brew. This move demanded something better. She reached for the cocoa.

She thought about all the memories in the tins of cocoa; when Mama enjoyed a day without pain, when Uncle Ade caught the biggest halibut of the season, and Popeye's girlfriend, the mutt next door, had puppies. Henry's sparse war-time letters meant twice as much cocoa. And so did all of Bumps' home runs.

Tears waterfalled down her face. She sipped the cocoa through them.

Robert Nelson arrived at Kodiak with the mail. As usual, there was a large stack for Miss Ruth and a box containing many packets of lemon drops. He'd picked them up himself in Anchorage.

Before she opened even one of her letters, she'd grill him about everyone in Sitka. She'd also want to hear the news from all the villages he had stopped at along the way. He reviewed his information on the short walk to her cabin.

She welcomed him into the front room, and embers glowed in the fireplace. "Let me refill your wood box for you, Miss Ruth."

"Thank you, Robbie. I've made a chicken pot pie and cranberry muffins."

"Cranberries still in season? Or did you can them?"

"They aren't quite ripe yet. These are from last season. I fill a barrel in the basement with low bush berries from the Kenai every year. If you keep them in cold water without letting them freeze, they will last all winter and into spring."

It was a pleasant visit, but soon Robert had to go. He held up a bag. "Thanks for the muffins."

Miss Ruth gave him her outgoing mail and walked with him to the nearby beach he used as a runway, but only when the tide was out. At high tide, he had to switch to pontoons.

Miss Ruth opened her letters and sat by the fire as she read the news Robert had already told her. Lastly, she opened Firy's letter and gasped.

Dear Miss Ruth,

Exciting news. We're moving to Washington state. Mama's things have too many memories attached, so I'll give them away. I haven't told Bumps yet, but it shouldn't be too hard for him to find a job. I'll miss you terribly. But this is right. I'll make it right.

Love, Firy

Miss Ruth stared into the embers; she should put another log on. Her face dropped into her hands. "Oh Bozhe, Firy doesn't realize the past will go with her. Tell me how to pray."

Miss Ruth poked the dying embers with the fire iron then let it fall to the stone hearth. It sounded like the thwack of a fastball hitting a catcher's mitt. What will Bumps think? Oh, Lord, give him wisdom. She blew her nose, folded Firy's letter, and placed it in her Bible.

Bumps put the kids to bed most evenings, then left for batting practice. Firy listened to her soap operas on the radio and wondered about her life.

She had lived her whole life on this island, except for that brief period when they married. Before the war, he had spent his in that Appalachian mountain valley in Pennsylvania.

"C'mon, Bumps. That's your third wild pitch." Ade chased the ball to the backstop.

Bumps threw another.

"That one's low and outside. What's wrong with you tonight?"

Bumps shrugged. He did his best thinking on the mound. It didn't usually interfere with his pitching.

"Give me something to hit, will ya?" Jake yelled.

Bumps pulled his thoughts away from Firy and her crazy idea.

After batting practice, he went for a run on the beach, how he loved this island. He missed his family, of course, and he didn't allow himself to think about what kind of a life baseball might have given him. Here in the north, he found he had a heart for coaching and the skill set to go with it.

He loved the kids and their joy in the game. His American Legion team had played in the Midnight Championship in Fairbanks for the last several years. They had placed but not won. Maybe, next year.

He stopped running and leaned against one of the immense

boulders clustered in the curve of the bay. If he agreed with his wife and they moved, his team would be without a coach. And he would be without a team.

And the guys at the café? How he would miss them. Although a generation older, they had accepted him into their midst. He had baseball to thank for that. He had a good life here. This place. These people.

Anna Marie's death had killed something in Firy, and she couldn't settle. He knew a change in geography was not the answer. He knew Firy believed if she were near Betty and Papa Bill, everything would be okay. It hadn't solved anything before, and he didn't think it would now.

He pushed himself away from the rock and jogged back down the beach, already wondering what kind of baseball opportunities there were in Betty's valley.

THIRTY-THREE

Firy looked at the cardboard boxes Mr. Akervik had given her and thought about Mama's salt sacks.

"Sharon, you're old enough to take some responsibility."

"I'm big. Seven."

Little Eddie chimed in, "I can take sponsors billy. I can."

Firy laughed and ruffled his curls. "You are such a good boy. I want you to put all your favorite things in these boxes. Don't worry about your clothes. I'll pack them."

"Mama, are we going somewhere?" Sharon asked.

"We're going to live outside." Firy turned back to the stove and added more kindling.

Eddie's lower lip quivered, and he tugged on Sharon's sleeve. "I don't want to live outside. It's cold."

Sharon took the boxes and led him to the bedroom they shared. "We're not going to live outside..."

"But Mama said..."

"It means we're leaving."

"I don't want to..." He started toward the door. "Mama!"

Sharon blocked the way. "Don't say anything. It will make her sad, and when that happens, she gets cranky."

"What's canky?" Eddie wrinkled his nose.

"It's like mad."

"You said, sad. Are sad and mad the same?"

"Big people don't like the sad, so they get mad instead."

Eddie put his thumb in his mouth and nodded. "I don't like

Mama when she gets mad."

"Me either, so don't say anything?"

He gnawed on his thumb and nodded.

Firy put the coffee on and checked the cupboards and closet. She piled the kitchen table with household goods and all the bits and pieces of her past. As she waited for everyone to arrive, she peeked in on her children.

Eddie had put his Lincoln logs and a truck into the box, and Sharon added his Roy Rogers' double holster set, with the twin cap guns. He climbed on the bed, stuck his thumb in his mouth, hugged his teddy bear, and watched.

Sharon threw Raggedy Ann and Andy into her box, then the Tiny Tears doll. Firy wondered whatever happened to the Shirley Temple of her childhood, then blinked away the memory of Shirley's smashed face. Sharon dumped the toys out and emptied her bookshelf into the box.

Firy hurried to answer the loud knocking and 'Yoo hoo's from the front door. Soon cigarette smoke wafted through the house, accompanied by loud laughter. Sharon put a finger to her lips, crawled into the living room, and hid behind the davenport, followed closely by her little brother. From there, they looked into the kitchen and saw the table heaped with Gramma's things.

Eddie's eyes popped, and Sharon threw her hands across his mouth. She shook her head then pulled the little boy onto her lap, one of his favorite places. His thumb went back into his mouth.

Lipstick stained cigarettes nestled in ashtrays. Coffee cups rattled in saucers as they were filled and refilled.

"I still don't understand why you're leaving," Mardel said.

"I don't want to talk about it anymore," Firy held up a large samovar, "What will you give me for this old thing?" She yelled over the chattering women.

Vivian leaned over and whispered while the women bid on the samovar. "Betty's been gone for several years, and now that Bill's in the veteran's hospital, she has no family here."

"There's her Uncle Ade and Ollyanna."

"It's not the same." Vivian lit another cigarette.

"I bid one thousand dollars," Marie laughed, waving her Monopoly money.

The bidding caught Vivian's attention. She blew smoke rings through bright red lips and said, "A hundred thousand."

"Sold," Mama yelled.

It was great-great; Sharon didn't know how many greats, but she knew some grandpa had brought the samovar from Kaluga, Russia. It made its way down the table. Soon each woman had a pile in front of her. Then Mama tugged the battered steamer trunk into the kitchen. "Last of all, we have a 24-place setting of old china. One cup and saucer are missing, and there are three chipped plates."

"How old is it, Firy?" The lady who lived across the street asked.

"My great-great-grandfather had it shipped over from Russia when he married, so pretty old." The delicate dinnerware had traveled so far, so long ago. Firy wiped her clammy hands on her apron and pushed away from the ache in her heart. She refused to look at the hand-painted, "forget-me-nots."

She passed a cup and saucer around the table. Mardel rubbed her thumb over the tiny blue flowers, stood on her chair, and waved her cigarette wildly. "I've always loved those dishes, and I'm prepared to keep the bidding going all night. And I also want your Mama's candlesticks and the old Russian sewing machine."

Firy had planned on keeping those two things, but perhaps she should let them go. There were some glares and groans as Vivian nudged Marie and said, "I think Mardel brought extra Monopoly money from home."

"Not fair," one of the women muttered.

Vavara hissed, "I think she wants to be Russian."

"Why?" Vivian asked.

"She never knew her people," Marie said. "She was adopted from the orphanage."

"No! Why didn't you ever tell me?" Vivian asked.

"It happened before you came to Alaska. Old news."

"Tell me now."

Marie shrugged. "I think she never felt like she belonged, and that's why she's so... so..."

"So, Mardel-ish?"

All those who heard the whispered conversation laughed. Those sitting close to Mardel looked away. Mardel's face flamed. Firy patted her friend's shoulder and whispered, "You can have Mama's candlesticks and the other things. You're like family." Mardel nodded, eyes misty.

The women finished their coffee and snuffed out their cigarettes. They gathered their treasures and said their goodbyes. "Bring your husbands tomorrow night, and they can bid on the tools."

"And the furniture?"

"Yes, furniture, too." Firy put the dirty cups and ashtrays to soak. Behind the couch, Sharon continued to hold and rock her little brother.

"What will we sit on, and how can Daddy fix things?" Eddie's lip quivered.

Sharon hugged him tighter. "Let's pretend we're at Sandy Beach. Close your eyes."

A few days later, Firy taped the boxes shut and put them on the front porch next to several suitcases. She and Bumps walked through the rooms, pulled down shades, and closed the doors. A horn honked.

Eddie tugged Sharon's shirt. "What's happening?" he whispered.

Sharon swallowed the lump in her throat. "I think we're going away."

Eddie scrambled onto her lap and held her tight. "I don't want to go away. Are Mommy and Daddy going away, too?"

Bumps came into the room, scooped them up, and settled them in the back of Mr. Herman's taxicab. After several minutes, Bumps told him to sound the horn again.

Firy walked through the house one last time. The bare walls and curtainless windows mocked her. *You can leave us, but you will not forget.*

She knelt before the old dresser in Papa's bedroom, the one nobody wanted. She closed her eyes as her hands touched the stuffed manila envelope. The horn blasted again, and Firy thrust the packet inside her coat and slammed the drawer.

See, the house echoed. *You cannot leave us behind. We will follow you forever. Hurt. Pain. Loss. We invade you, own you.* Firy felt the packet through her coat; she needed to separate these photos, keep the few good ones. She determined to do the same with her memories.

Try, the floorboards squeaked. *You won't succeed*, hinges on the doors squealed. *You will remember,* hissed the walls. Firy slammed the door and stomped to the taxi. Bumps and the kids saw her red cheeks and wet eyelashes.

Firy sniffed and stared out the window. How could she be sad about leaving? It was her idea. The taxi eased into the road, and Firy almost regretted leaving the Beautiful Corner behind.

THIRTY-FOUR

And so, they moved to Betty's sweet valley. The neighborhood church was just a block from their small house. A different denomination, but what did it matter? The preacher talked about loving God and doing what was right. The children went to Sunday School and learned their memory verses. Bumps' played on the church's baseball team and soon became the coach. Firy attended the Women's Missionary Circle but quit after a couple of months. Sewing for the missionaries and pricking her fingers led Firy to believe the missionaries were better off without her.

She did get that automatic washer and loved it. Bumps bought the matching dryer, but Firy never used it. Nothing smelled as fresh and clean as laundry hung in the sunshine. Never mind that she often had to run and rescue those clothes when the rains began.

After five years in Washington, the kids were growing and doing well in school. Bumps had a good job and coached Babe Ruth baseball. But Firy, still not settled, lost herself in the repetitive mundane duties of life. Cooking, cleaning, laundry, errands.

Papa Bill's house in Sitka had been right. Painful memories stored deep within had followed her. When they pushed to the surface, she gritted her teeth and forced them back into the darkness. They might lie dormant for weeks or even months, but the fact that she never knew when they would erupt again kept her on edge.

Firy looked out the window, not a cloud in the sky. The first day of summer and Firy couldn't enjoy it. Just do the next thing, the right thing. Get through the day and the next and the one after that.

Father and son entered the house, laughing and talking about the game.

"You won, of course," Firy said.

Bumps nodded and described Eddie's every at-bat. Two doubles, a single, a walk, and no strike-outs. Firy turned to her son, "Take your bat bag to the garage, put your uniform in the laundry, and take a shower." She tossed him an apple.

Eddie's grin faded when he didn't hear praise from his mother for a game well played. Bumps frowned at Firy, ruffled Eddie's hair, and said, "We'll play catch after dinner."

Eddie nodded, but the frown remained.

"Where's Sharon?" Bumps asked.

"In her room trying out a new hairstyle."

Good, he thought. "I talked to Mr. Lynn after the game."

"About baseball, I suppose."

"No, he says if I come to the bank on Monday, he'll fill out the papers for a loan."

"I wish you hadn't done that."

"There will be enough for a plane ticket to Juneau and a little extra for whatever might come up."

"I'm not going." Firy opened cupboard doors then slammed them. Bumps crossed the kitchen. "Firy, look at me."

She stared at his shoes.

"Betty and I both think you need this trip."

"You talked to my sister! How could you?"

"You can't go on like this, letting whatever is eating away at you consume you. We want our Firy back. I want my Firy back." He tried to take her in his arms.

She pulled away. "I don't know what you're talking about."

"Yes, you do. It's guilt or grief or pain. I don't know, but you have to deal with it. You should have dealt with it years ago."

She pushed past him and jerked her sweater off its hook by the back door. "I'm going for a walk."

She walked through the neighborhood and then the downtown business area. She didn't even stop at the post office.

Mardel and Marie wrote often and filled their letters with bits and pieces of Sitka gossip. When Firy left, Vivian vowed she would never write since Firy was abandoning them. Still, the two Ms kept Firy informed about Viv's life. Yelena wasn't much of a letter writer, but she sent picture postcards several times a month. Firy treasured the images of Alaska. And Franella, what a dedicated penpal she had become after that long-ago summer in Port Alexander. Each letter brought a wave of homesickness, and Firy wondered if leaving Sitka had been the right thing.

Firy glared at the post office as if it was somehow to blame for her troubles. Her scowl prevented anyone from greeting her. An hour later, she found herself past the edge of town at the fish cannery. The smell reminded her of home, as did the dark water. It was only a channel that connected Skagit and Padilla Bays to Puget Sound. Firy imagined its link to the Pacific Ocean then north to Alaska.

And so, season followed season. Sharon's eighth and ninth years were difficult for Firy. She looked at her daughter and thought about her own childhood. Mama's illness and death. Grief. Loss.

When the girl turned eleven, the age Anna Marie was when she was murdered, it devastated Firy. Guilt. Loss.

More horrible than the grief was the guilt that anchored itself to her soul like barnacles. Like a cow chewing its cud, the guilt and grief ground at her soul like a dog gnawed a juicy bone. Day after day, Firy did the right thing. Of course, she did, but it wasn't enough. She clenched her teeth and locked her jaw and did the next thing, the right thing.

Were Betty and Bumps, right? Did she need to sit in a courtroom and see Anna Marie's murderer? She couldn't, not when she was the one that should be on trial. If she hadn't abandoned her little sister, Anna Marie would still be alive.

Firy sat on the cannery's dock and stared over the water with empty eyes. The briny air, the stink of fish heads and guts, the cry of the gulls; they all took her back to Sitka. She thought she could leave her guilt behind, but it clung to her bones like barnacles. The grief attached to her stony heart like lichens. Firy fisted her hands and beat the sides of her head. "Stop thinking. Stop feeling. Stop remembering."

"Are you alright, Miss?"

Firy jerked her head up, eyes red-rimmed, stricken. "I'm okay."

"You don't look it. Can I call someone?"

"I just need to sit awhile. I'm okay now."

"If you're sure," He flicked away his cigarette, pulled a watch cap from his pocket, and went back into the cannery.

Firy stared after him, then trudge toward home on leaden feet. No matter where she was, she couldn't escape. The fault, the blame, all of it was hers. She might as well have wielded the knife that killed Anna Marie.

She stumbled over a pothole in the road. Bumps and Betty were right, she couldn't go on like this, but she couldn't go to the trial either. They couldn't force her. Love Bozhe, do what's right. Sometimes she hated those words. Do the right thing. She repeated those words the last three blocks. By the time she reached her back door, she was numb again.

Bumps watched her from the window. He closed his eyes for a moment, then opened the door.

"I'll go." She said.

"You'll be glad you did."

"I said I'll go. Don't expect me to be happy about it."

He reached for her, but she turned away.

The two-hour drive to the airport gave Firy's anxieties time to build. Her son chattered all the way, but it didn't distract her. Bumps twisted the radio dial, 'Top of the eighth. Bases loaded. Two out. The count three and two.' The game didn't distract her either. She stared out the car window and frowned as they came to the airport's parking lot.

Sharon, now a teenager, dull haired and pimpled face, turned away from her mother's dutiful hug. Ten-year-old Eddie, freckle-faced and chubby, hugged her back and grinned. He said he wished he was going to the wilds of Alaska with her. Bumps kissed her, gave her a book she wouldn't read, and a Hershey bar she knew would be gone before the plane left the ground.

Going home for Anna Marie's funeral sixteen years ago had devastated her. This journey to Juneau pained her as much.

As she boarded the large Boeing jet, Firy remembered Robert Nelson's six-passenger floatplane. They island-hopped from Puget Sound to the Queen Charlotte's and then to the Alexander Archipelago. Today, she would be in Juneau in a few hours.

The engines rumbled, the jet taxied down the runway and lifted off. Firy watched Seattle's hills grow small. Soon all she could see was the waters of Puget Sound and the Olympic Mountains.

She took the letter out of her purse and rubbed her finger over the return address. The state seal of Alaska looked so official. Alaska had joined the union a few years ago. Firy wondered if it would feel different, then shrugged. What did it matter? What did any of it matter?

The chocolate bar lumped in her stomach. She wondered if Bumps would get the kids ready in the mornings. Of course, he would. They'd stay with Betty after school until he got home from work.

"We're almost teenagers. We can take care of ourselves." They were right, but safety first. If it irritated her husband and upset her children, so be it.

State of Alaska, Superior Court. Juneau. She fingered the corner of the envelope again. They had discovered the identity of Anna Marie's killer. It was the boy who lived next door. He was a man now.

Firy tried to imagine Anna Marie as a young woman but couldn't. A pain ripped through Firy's body. She doubled over. The passenger across the aisle buzzed the stewardess and pointed.

She whispered, "Are you alright? Can I get you anything?"

Firy shook her head. The stewardess hurried away, then returned with a paper bag and held it over Firy's mouth. "Breathe."

It took several minutes for Firy to follow the stewardess's directions. She looked around, grateful the other passengers had returned to their books and magazines. Firy leaned back and closed her eyes. The stewardess brought her a glass of water.

Grateful for a window seat, Firy leaned against the cold glass. The landmass below must be Vancouver Island. She hoped the thin clouds would dissipate over the Queen Charlottes and the islands of the Archipelago.

Alaska. Raw. Real. Painful. In the lower forty-eight, Firy strictly scheduled her housework and the children's lives. She vowed once again that her children would never know pain or loneliness. She had protected them from abuse, loss, and grief. Had she done enough?

A break in the clouds showed Firy the northern half of the Queen Charlottes. In a bit, they would fly over Prince of Wales Island and beyond that, Baranof and Chichagof. The forested islands reminded her how she hunted and fished in waters a bit closer to Sitka. There had been a time she'd rather skin a deer or gut a fish than do laundry or cook.

Firy gazed at the scenery below but saw the time she had talked Anna Marie into a fishing trip. They left on Uncle Ade's boat at four in the morning and wouldn't be home until the next night.

At dawn, Uncle Ade heard chatter over the radio that fish were biting off Little Biorka. Uncle Ade and Firy baited the lines and threw them over the side. Anna Marie turned purple and refused to pick up the baitfish, so they sent her to the galley to make toast and coffee.

Sometime that morning, Uncle Ade stabbed himself in the hand with one of the big gaff hooks. He wrapped it in a rag and kept on fishing. Within the hour, he threw up. A few minutes later, he fell to the deck, moaning. Anna Marie scrambled to the deck and saw her Uncle writhing in pain. She fled back to the galley.

His arm, neck, and face puffed up. Soon his eyes were mere slits in his bloated face. "Firy, you're going to have to pilot the boat back to Sitka. I need the Doc."

Firy swallowed. "I've never piloted through the straights. I don't know where the shoals are or where the currents change."

"I'll guide you as best I can. Get Anna Marie up here. She can help watch for the landmarks I describe."

Anna Marie cried all the way back to Sitka and could hardly hear Uncle Ade's instructions as he panted through his pain.

"Anna Marie stop crying," Firy commanded, "stand by Uncle Ade. If he closes his eyes, sing."

"I can't, Firy," the little girl cried.

"You must. We can't let him fall asleep," Firy barked. "He needs to tell me what hazards to avoid."

"Don't be mad."

Firy bit her lip and softened her tone. She was terrified. "I'm not mad, Dodo. I need you to be a big girl."

Anna Marie sniffed, "Okay."

"Good girl," Uncle Ade groaned.

Firy bit her lip and silently pleaded, "Help me, Bozhe."

When she docked the boat, Anna Marie scrambled onto the dock and screamed for help. Captain Frank came aboard and pried Firy's hands off the wheel. Her jaw had clenched so tight her teeth ached for days. The doctor gave Uncle Ade one of those new antibiotic wonder drugs, and he was back on his boat within the week.

The next time Uncle Ade invited her to fish, Firy accepted, as excited as ever. She pretended not to notice when Anna Marie and Popeye crawled under the kitchen table.

The islands below reminded Firy of Whale Island, although she was sure it was farther north. Memories flooded her soul, and she remembered when Uncle Ade and Aunt Ollyanna stuffed them all on the Olly-B and sailed off on an adventure. They didn't have any children yet, so doted on little Firy.

Uncle Ade secretly hooked a baitfish on the small fishing pole, and Firy thought she had caught the biggest salmon ever.

Then there was a hunting trip with Uncle Ade, Papa, and Henry. They had taken the boat to an island in the Chatham Strait.

Gifted with Papa Bill's old hunting rifle on his fourteenth birthday, Henry was anxious to get into the woods. Uncle Ade said he and Firy would set up camp while Bill and Henry went deep into the forest.

Uncle and niece had worked in comfortable silence until he cursed in both Russian and Tlingit. Firy bent over the campfire and hid her face. She didn't want Uncle Ade to see she understood every word. Henry always said if they didn't let on, they might learn new words. Firy listened, but there was nothing new to report.

"What's wrong?" Firy asked.

"I left the coffee on the Olly-B."

"What?" Firy shrieked. There was no way the men could go for a week without their coffee.

"It was right there on the table in the galley. I don't know how I could have left it behind."

"I'll get it. What about Mike's secret ingredient? Did you forget that too?"

"How'd you know about that?"

"Everybody knows."

Uncle Ade blushed. "It's in a brown paper bag next to the coffee."

"I'll get them,"

"It's at least three miles to the beach Firy, and then you'll have to row out to the Olly-B. Are you sure?"

"I've been around when you and Papa haven't had your coffee. Besides, you don't want him to make a big story out of it at the café, do you?"

Uncle Ade looked at the sun, "Run!"

For Firy, it had been an easy run out of the woods to the beach. The deer trails were worn, and it was mostly downhill. The return trip would be more demanding.

She had untied the dinghy from the large piece of driftwood that anchored it. Firy rowed hard and made good time out to the boat. She snatched coffee and the secret ingredient, stuffed them into a waterproof knapsack, and turned to go.

The bunk looked inviting, and Firy thought it wise to rest for ten minutes. It wasn't. She woke when the dingy knocked against the Olly-B with the incoming tide, the sun slanted across her face through the porthole. She heard Henry's rifle crack.

She scrambled to the deck and into the dingy. She rowed halfway to shore when she used some of Uncle Ade's words. She had left the knapsack aboard.

This time, she slung the pack over her shoulders. She hoped to make it back to camp before Henry and Papa.

This island, known for brown bears and Sitka deer, was dangerous during evening feeding time. Firy trotted along the deer trail, singing as she went. Autumn sun shadowed the forest, but she remained unafraid. She was an Alaska girl, after all. She used all the skills Uncle Ade had poured into her over the years.

She picked up a stick, beat the bushes, and sang, "Oh Mama bear, go back to your den. It's me, Firy, round the bend. I mean you no harm. You pay me no mind. I'm not your dinner, so be kind."

Her forehead rested on the jet's window. Another island. Another memory. Firy's little cousin Yelena decided she was old enough to go fishing with her father. Eight years younger than Firy, too young. Besides, she was such a girly girl.

The fish did not cooperate, so Uncle Ade steered to one of his secret hunting spots. He hunted for a couple of days with no luck and left Firy in charge of her bored and whiny cousin.

Firy cajoled and bribed Yelena to behave. When Uncle Ade returned empty-handed to camp, she used those same tactics to convince her uncle to let her hunt.

"Are you sure, Firy? You've always had Bill or me with you."

"I'm seventeen. I can handle it."

He handed her the rifle and told her to be back by dark.

Firy headed north following a well-worn deer trail. A few hours later, she fired two-shots and then a signal she'd made a kill. Uncle Ade would track her, his daughter in tow.

Oskolkoff family tradition demanded she skin and gut her first kill without help. Firy cut the meat and wrapped it in empty canvas salt sacks Uncle Ade used to short cure his fish. First, she'd have to pack them to the campsite, then the beach, then to the Olly-B.

She cut out the heart and liver and set them aside. She'd need energy for the labor to come. A thick venison steak would do the same, but tradition demanded she eat the liver and heart.

The animal's dead brown eyes gazed at her. She had looked into them a few moments ago and forced herself to pull the trigger. Hands bloodied, Firy wiped her eyes and wept.

Uncle Ade arrived and taught her the Tlingit prayer for slaying an animal. It sounded holy and made her feel better.

Yelena screamed, "Firy, your face is all bloody."

"It's not my blood. It's the deer's."

Yelena turned green and trailed them as Firy packed the salt sacks to camp. The young girl refused to accompany Firy to the beach.

Firy packed the first load down the mountain, heaved it into the dinghy, and rowed to the Olly-B.

Uncle Ade fried up more heart and liver, Firy choked it down and kept working. Close to midnight, she sank next to the campfire and poured herself some coffee, which she wasn't allowed to drink.

Uncle Ade took the cup from her and pointed to the animal's hide. She groaned. Bone weary, she looked at Uncle Ade. "Can't we bury it or throw it in the ocean?"

"It's your skin. You can do anything you want."

"You mean, I'd get the money for it."

"Your kill. Your hide. Clean shot, it should fetch a good price."

Re-energized, Firy thought of having her own money. In the past, she'd helped Uncle Ade scrape the bits and pieces of flesh off the hides. "Will you talk me through it?"

"Of course." He handed her an ulu. "Scrape as much flesh off as you can. We'll do the rest back home, soak the hair off, condition the skin, then stretch it over a wooden frame and store it in the attic with the others. Tie a bandanna around it, so you'll know it's yours."

Yelena annoyed her all the way back to Sitka with ideas of what she could buy, but Firy turned a deaf ear.

In the spring, she sold the hide and bought the biggest bottle of Evening in Paris toilet water she could find and a matching box of bath powder. It came with a fluffy white puff.

She'd had a long soak in the tub that day, dried, then used the puff to powder herself all over. She opened the sophisticated blue bottle and took a whiff.

So elegant, so glamorous. Firy usually didn't care about such things, but Evening in Paris made her think of movie stars and posh parties with Fred Astaire and Cary Grant.

Firy danced around her room. Popeye ran in to join her. She laughed at his attempts to dance, then shrieked as his tail knocked over her Evening in Paris. The box of powder fell to the floor, and high white clouds filled the room. Another wag and the blue bottle fell on its side, the contents pouring over the edge of the table.

Firy dashed across the room to grab the bottle. She fumbled it to the floor, where it mixed with the powder. Popeye rolled in the gooey mess and barked his delight. Firy yelled, and Popeye fled, taking the scent throughout the house, accompanied by clouds of powder.

Her sisters and Masha thought the house smelled wonderful, and Popeye, though a mess, was the most fragrant canine in Sitka. Papa opened the windows. "It smells like a house of ill-repute with floozies everywhere!"

Anna Marie followed. "Ill-repute Papa? Does that mean our house is sick? And what are floozies? Are they like fairies? I don't see any fairies? What are you talking about?"

Papa threw his hands into the air. "I need the company of men." He took himself off to the Sitka Café.

Henry threw his hands into the air, yelled, "Me too!" and ran after Papa.

Firy looked again at the bays and coves below. Fresh, salty, northern air. Dark, icy, Alaskan waters. Summer's golden light to pierce your soul. The chug of the boat's engine, the tug of a fish on the line, a winter's supply of venison. Good memories.

Firy shuddered as she remembered mink and marten. She ran traps with Uncle Ade and Jake twice, and then she told them she couldn't stomach it. "Please, Firy, we'll give you enough pelts to make a mink jacket."

"Their beady little eyes look right through me when the trap hasn't killed them. They know I'm going to club them to death. When wolverines get to them before us, it stinks so bad! I hate it."

"Okay, then," Jake sighed.

"I'll do it if you need me, but I never want a fur. If women had to trap, they'd never have mink coats."

"You're probably right about that. It's okay. We'll drag Sven Anderson or even your Papa along with us."

Firy leaned her head on the jet's window and saw the mountain tops come closer. The engines whined, and the plane began its descent. Firy pulled herself away from that memory, glad she had never run a trap line again. Fishing and hunting for food were entirely different, at least in her mind.

The letter fell from her lap, and she put it back in her purse — the trial. Firy didn't want to see the murderer or hear his defense.

Yelena met her at the airport. She'd lived in Juneau since her marriage many years ago. Her house overlooked the state capital, and the courthouse was within walking distance.

"I wish Betty had come with you."

"She said Anna Marie forced her back to Alaska once. She wasn't going to let her do it again." Firy's voice dulled, and Yelena gave her a quick hug.

"Henry?"

"West Point is giving MacArthur an award, and he wanted some of his old staff with him." Firy turned to her cousin, "It's an honor, but truthfully, I think Henry was glad for the excuse." They walked in silence for half a block, then Firy asked, "Are you sure you don't know when Miss Ruth's plane arrives?"

"You remember Robert Nelson, don't you?" Firy nodded. Yelena continued. "He went up to Nome a few days ago to fetch her. He said he'd have her here in time for the trial."

"It will be good to see him again. How is his dad?"

"Living out his old age in the Pioneer's Home in Sitka, telling tall tales to anyone who will listen," Yelena said.

"Someone should write them down."

"You don't think all those stories are true, do you?"

"Papa Bill always said Bob Nelson told it straight with never a wasted word or exaggeration."

"I wonder how many of those stories he passed on to his son

Robert?" Yelena murmured as she went to start dinner, refusing any help from Firy. "I remember how you felt about cooking."

Firy laughed and poured herself a cup of coffee. "Do you think Miss Ruth will look the same? She seemed so old when we were kids."

"I don't think her face has room for any more wrinkles. I'm surprised the Episcopalians haven't forced her to retire."

"Or the Lutherans," As she sipped her coffee, Firy wished she had the money to take Miss Ruth to Sitka after the trial so that they could tidy the graves. As determined as she had been to leave Sitka and forget everything, she now felt homesick for the little town or at least the gravesites.

THIRTY-FIVE

True to his word, Robert's floatplane landed in Juneau before the trial. Firy waited on the steps of the courthouse. Miss Ruth and Firy hurried in just as the bailiff cried. "All rise, the Superior Court of the State of Alaska is now in session this day, June 22, 1962. The Honorable Nathan Cooper presiding."

"Nathan?" Miss Ruth said aloud.

"Quiet in the courtroom," the bailiff thundered. Miss Ruth frowned, and they hurried to take their seats.

When the prosecutor asked the defendant details about the murder, Firy trembled. As they got more graphic, she grabbed Miss Ruth's hand. Miss Ruth jumped to her feet and shouted. "I object!"

Heads turned, gasps escaped astonished lips. Firy continued to shake.

Judge Cooper pounded his gavel. "You can't object."

"I most certainly can, and I do, Nathan Cooper, and don't go banging your little hammer again, or I'll tell all these people things I'm sure you'd rather they not know."

"I need to get a photographer over here to get a photo of that fiery old lady." A reporter from the Alaska Daily News whispered to himself.

"I can already feel my editor's love," a reporter from Anchorage said.

Heads swiveled back to the judge. He paled and peered over his glasses, "Is that you, Miss Ruth?"

"It is." Miss Ruth stood even straighter and stared at the judge.

"I thought you were dead," his Honor muttered.

"I'm not, and I still object."

Sam Mitchell, Jr. chewed on the end of his pencil. Miss Ruth had been a familiar sight in the Sitka of his childhood, but he hadn't paid much attention. His fingers tingled. He must interview her.

'Now, Miss Ruth, this is an official court of the United States of America and—"

Miss Ruth interrupted him, "I've been here longer than the United States...why I've been here almost since the Russians sold the place, which they had no legal right to do."

"She looks about a hundred years old," the stringer from the Seattle Times said.

Heads turned to Miss Ruth. The prosecutor glared, and Judge Cooper capitulated. He leaned over his bench and whispered, "Exactly what are you objecting to, Miss Ruth?"

"Why, Nathan, I wanted a warning before you allow these lawyers to get into all the horrid details of the..." here even Miss Ruth faltered, "of the event. This is Anna Marie's older sister, and she would appreciate some notice."

All eyes went to Firy, who squeezed Miss Ruth's hand even harder. Judge Cooper saw the bowed head of the young woman. He saw the reporters writing furiously, and he saw the fire in Miss Ruth's eyes.

Sam's eyes focused on the woman next to Miss Ruth. Firy Wall had been several years behind him in school. He remembered her and the best baseball player he had ever seen, who was interested in her. Whatever happened to him, anyway?

"Now, Miss Ruth. Perhaps she shouldn't have come."

"Nathan?" Miss Ruth's eyes glinted, and she folded her arms across her chest.

He banged his gavel. "The court apologizes for not being sensitive to those in the courtroom who might be disturbed by the proceedings. There will be silence in the courtroom while Miss Ruth and the sister of the victim exit while this testimony is given."

Firy would have fallen if Miss Ruth had not grasped her around the waist and half-carried her into the hallway. They sat on a bench in the corridor. Firy leaned on Miss Ruth's shoulder while the older woman murmured words of comfort. Miss Ruth prayed, and after a while, Firy stopped shaking. She gave Miss Ruth a weak smile.

"Excuse me, Miss Ruth. I have a few questions." The editor of the Sitka Sentinel had followed them.

"Hello, Sam. No, I don't think we will be answering any questions."

"Just tell me your story, then. Talk to me."

Miss Ruth put her index finger to her chin and cocked her head to the side. Her eyes focused somewhere above Sam's head. "Hmmm, Yes. Can I tell him?"

Sam glanced upward. Was she talking to herself?

"Sammy boy, someday you are going to be a great newspaperman, but not today."

"Now you sound like my old man."

Miss Ruth smiled and pinched Sam on the cheek as if he were eight years old. "Yes, I have it on excellent authority; that's what He said."

"Huh?"

"And Sam, be careful what you print."

"The people have a right to know."

"Ah Sam, your father knew when and how much the people had a right to know. He balanced that with the consequences of his reporting. He also knew when a story was complete. This one is not."

The bailiff came and announced His Honor said they could return. Firy rose and took a step toward the courtroom, but Miss Ruth stopped her.

"No, I don't think so," she said to the bailiff. "You tell Nathan that we will not return."

The bailiff paled and shook his head. He never talked to the judge if he could help it. Not his honor, Nathan Cooper.

"Would you rather I tell him?" Miss Ruth took two strides toward the courtroom.

The bailiff's face remained colorless as he stammered, "Perhaps you could write a note."

Miss Ruth stopped mid-stride, looked at the quaking man, and nodded. She dug into her old black pocketbook, found what she needed, and scribbled a note to the judge. She handed it to the bailiff. He fled.

"Come," she said to Firy, "I've had a word from the Lord. I must get back to Him to be sure of the details. I need more clarity. Goodbye, Sam. Don't look so disgruntled. You'll have your story one day."

"But Miss Ruth, Bumps and Betty said I need closure."

Miss Ruth dipped her head and looked over her wire-rimmed glasses. "It's not closure you need, dear one."

Sam watched them leave, crumpled the paper in his hand, closed his notepad, and thought about kicking it across the room. Instead, he shoved it back in his pocket and re-entered the courtroom.

Miss Ruth and Firy walked to Yelena's house in silence. It reminded Firy of the many walks she had taken with the old woman. She put her arm through Miss Ruth's.

Yelena worked at her beauty shop while her boys attended grammar school. Her husband was out fishing and wouldn't return for several days. The house was empty, and of course, no one in town locked their doors.

Miss Ruth put Firy to bed and brought her a cup of sweet tea. "You've had a shock, dear. Drink this and try to sleep. I'm going to walk the beach and talk to Bozhe. I sense He has much to say to me."

She placed her hand on Firy's cheek and pulled the covers up to the young woman's chin. "Even if you don't sleep, stay in bed until I return."

Firy escaped into a dreamless sleep, the cup of tea forgotten.

Miss Ruth walked the docks and beaches for hours. Others saw an old woman in clothes from a by-gone era, who paced and mumbled to herself. Angels in heaven and those swirling around her saw a great warrior preparing for battle. They sharpened their swords.

When Miss Ruth returned, Yelena, who had returned a few moments prior, said, "She's still asleep. Rough day?"

Miss Ruth told her the events of the day and the advice she had received from Bozhe.

"We'll move to the apartment over the shop. I've no renters right now, so no problem."

"What will the boys think?"

"They'll think it's great fun. I recently got my barber's license, and they love to hear those old sourdoughs gossip. I mean, tell stories about the old days, when Alaska was wild."

Miss Ruth kissed Yelena on the cheek. "Bozhe told me that was the plan. Still, I thank you for offering, so I didn't have to ask."

"As if anything would stop you from doing what He says."

Miss Ruth joined in Yelena's laughter. "I do enjoy it when He goes before and irons out the details."

Yelena took a casserole from the oven. "Are you sure you don't want any?"

"It smells good. But no, dear, Firy and I begin now."

Yelena packed the dinner, told Miss Ruth she and the boys would be praying, then hollered for them to come. They threw a few things in an overnight bag, ran down the stairs, and hugged Miss Ruth goodbye.

Miss Ruth left a note on the kitchen table for a still sleeping Firy and went to see Judge Cooper.

Appalled by her plan, Judge Cooper cited laws and precedents. She cited scripture. He quoted policies and procedures. She quoted chapter and verse. He threatened to call her Bishop. She threatened to call his mother. He blustered and bluffed. She remained adamant.

In the end, they compromised. Judge Cooper agreed to do what Miss Ruth proposed. They would meet each evening, and he would give her a copy of that day's transcripts and answer all her questions. He thought it highly illegal. She believed it right.

The fear that had been attached to her childhood memories attacked Firy. She shivered and quaked as she lay in the bed in a fetal position. All the unshed tears from childhood spilled onto the pillow. Miss Ruth returned to find Firy awake and crying, "I want my Mama."

She gathered Firy in her arms.

"I remember, Miss Ruth, everything. All the bad papas. I can't stop seeing them."

"Tell me."

Firy pulled away from Miss Ruth, "Betty was right. We were never safe."

Now that her memories had surfaced, Firy didn't think she would ever be able to forget again. She sobbed like a child, without restraint. With every shaking breath, her grief escaped.

"Pray for me, Miss Ruth. I have no words."

Miss Ruth's voice was like honey on Agrafena's fry bread. "The One who made you sees your heart. He gathers your tears, each one a prayer. He hears you, dear one."

Several days later, Miss Ruth sat down on the chintz-covered davenport. She patted the spot next to her, and Firy sat. "Bozhe gave me a picture of your soul; I saw you on the jet plane. You pressed your forehead on the window and gazed below. The islands were your hurts, abuses, grief, everything you lost. He also showed me your overwhelming guilt about Anna Marie."

Firy squeezed her eyes tight and put her hands over her ears. Miss Ruth gently tugged them away.

"That guilt is not yours. The sea represented the Holy Spirit. He desired to wash those islands away with a great tsunami of cleansing love. You resisted. You let Him into the harbors and even a few secret coves. But you feared to let Him flood you with His all-consuming love. You clutch your grief, Firy, and hoard your sorrows and hold your guilt tightly."

Firy shuddered. "Grief and sorrow are all I have left of Mama and Anna Marie. If I let go, I'll have nothing."

Miss Ruth bristled. "Stuff and nonsense. Honestly, Firy, have I taught you nothing over the years?"

Firy sniffed. Dear Miss Ruth, a tender, comforting saint one moment, formidable as a drill sergeant the next. "You've taught me everything."

Two women sat on a chintz-covered sofa in the young state of Alaska. Two ordinary women, one old, one young. Women unnoticed by the world, yet angels peeked through the windows of heaven, leaned as far as they dared into this realm, not wanting to miss a single syllable.

Firy whispered, "I try to love Bozhe and do what's right."

"I think you use all your energy to do what's right and have little strength left to love Him. And what's worse, you won't let Him love you."

The last several days of fasting had weakened Firy's body but sharpened her mind and given clarity to her spirit. Her understanding of herself was increasing. "Trying harder didn't make anything better, did it?"

Miss Ruth folded Firy in her arms as she had so long ago. "All we need to do is take the time to crawl onto Bozhe's lap, lean into Him until we can hear His very heartbeat. Learn to receive His love, and you will cease to fear."

"I knew something inside of me was off-kilter, but I couldn't figure it out. Do you think that's it?" She pressed her hand to her chest to stop her racing heart, "I want to feel His love. I really want to, Miss Ruth."

Miss Ruth tried to take the sting out of her words. "Decades ago, you lost the joy of life and wallowed in your grief and guilt. Despite your sorrows, Bozhe will bring joy in the morning. And Firy, your morning is long overdue."

Firy sobbed great, cleansing tears. "Oh, Miss Ruth, I feel like Jacob wrestling with Bozhe. Only He said, 'I will not let you go until you let Me bless you.'"

"Let Him bless you. Let Him love you." She rose and headed toward the door.

Firy panicked. "Where are you going?"

"It's time, dear one. You need to finish your wrestling match. It's the only way you will be able to love Him the way you want to."

Before leaving, Miss Ruth kissed Firy on the top of her head. "I'll be praying," she turned at the door and said. "Always remember, Firy, His heart is kind."

Miss Ruth sat on the back steps and prayed while heavenly business took place inside. When Bozhe released her, she peeked in.

Firy, exhausted, lay back on the faded chintz. "It hurts me that Anna Marie didn't get to live her life. It's my fault. If I hadn't left."

The old woman took Firy in her arms and said, "Tell Bozhe, Dear One. Tell Him how you feel."

So, our Firy talked to Bozhe deep in her heart. She felt His kindness well up within her until she thought she would explode. "Miss Ruth," she stammered, "I think Bozhe is telling me to walk the beach. What should I do?"

"I'll get your sweater."

"Come with me. You're everything to me."

Miss Ruth handed the sweater to Firy, "I can't be everything to you, nor should I try. Only God can tear down the walls you've built around your heart, higher and stronger than those of Jericho. I've marched around them for decades. Now, the angel of the Lord is blowing the trumpet, and those walls will come down."

Firy sat on the sand and leaned against a driftwood log. She looked through a gossamer mist. A young girl ran toward her but stopped as she approached the shimmering, silver curtain.

"Our Firy, grown up and a Mama, too. I'm happy for you. But I'm sad because of the guilt you feel." Anna Marie twirled around, arms outstretched, "Oh, if you could know how the colors sing, the air breathes, and the water is life. I know it's been years and years where you live, but here it's always NOW. I feel like I've been here forever, but also like I just arrived."

Anna Marie's eyes shined with brightness and joy that Firy had never seen. "I know my death torments you, but Jesus held me."

Firy stretched out her hand and touched the misty silver curtain. Anna Marie stretched out hers. Did the realms of heaven and earth merge? Did fingertips touch? The mist dissipated, the image of her sister faded, and Firy whispered, "I love you, Anna Marie."

"And I, you, our Firy. Always."

Firy stared over the water, thankful for her sister's visit. Whether it happened in her mind or right in front of her didn't matter.

"Thank you, Bozhe." Firy sighed as tears fell down her face. The water glistened and glowed as the waves applauded the shore, and Mama appeared.

Firy stayed in Mama's embrace until she saw a growing brightness over Mama's shoulder. "Is that radiance Michael the Archangel? He's brighter than the icons in the church."

"No, Firy, it's Him."

"Baby Jesus, all grown up?" Firy squeezed her eyes shut.

"Go to Him."

"I can't, Mama, the brightness hurts my eyes, and my heart is...I don't know..."

"Take a step, and you will be able to gaze into His wonderful face. When you do, you will see His heart is kind." Mama squeezed Firy's hand and watched her daughter take a tiny step nearer to the glorious brightness.

Firy held her breath as He came close. Mama bowed before Him, and He rested his palms on Mama's head.

Firy gasped as her mother faded from view. Jesus looked at her with eyes gentler and more tender than a doe. "It's all right, Firy. Your Mama and Anna Marie are eagerly waiting for you."

Firy nodded and felt the ache in her heart recede, although she would always miss them.

"I've brought someone else. Would you like to meet her?"

Tears veiled her vision, and she wiped them away and wondered who it could be. "Please."

A little girl, dirty and ragged, stepped out from behind Jesus. He held her hand. Firy's face crumpled. "That's me."

"What do you see when you look at her?"

For a long time, Firy could not speak. "Oh, Jesus, she's afraid." Firy folded her hands over her heart. "Her Mama's gone, and there is nobody to love her."

"Look deeper."

"She's dirty inside, abused, rejected, broken."

"Yes, terrible things have been done to her. I love her, and I can heal her if you let me."

Firy sank to the ground, wrapped her arms around herself, and dared to believe. Even with her eyes closed, she saw Jesus kneel before the little girl. He placed His cheek on hers and breathed.

When He stood, the little girl's dress was lacey and new. Her hair was brushed and tied with pink ribbons. Eyes ethereal, with a soft glow and a face, scrubbed clean. The little one looked up and said, "Hi, Glaphira, it's me. I mean, you. I mean, we're us." She looked at Jesus and giggled.

"Come, let Me unite you with this brand-new little girl." He held them both, and Firy felt the warmth as little Firy's soul joined hers.

Firy stared at Jesus, she gasped, but no words came. Jesus patted her shoulder. "No need for words. I hear your heart. There is another. Shall I take you to her?"

Firy, though afraid, nodded. Jesus lifted her chin with his nail-scarred hand. "I love you with my perfect love. Receive it, and there will be no room for fear. Can you trust Me?"

Jesus held out his hand. She put hers in his, and immediately they stood at Anna Marie's headstone. A 19-year-old Firy lay across the grave and wept. "I'll never forgive myself for living my life at the expense of yours."

Firy looked at the guilt that ate at her soul like leprosy. Shame ravaged her mind like cancer. She dropped Jesus' hands and covered her face.

"Murderer. My fault."

"You took guilt and responsibility that did not belong to you.

It shattered your already broken soul."

Firy stared at Him, then the girl at the grave, and then Him again.

"Do you believe I can heal even this?"

"I don't know." Her voice barely above a whisper, "I want to believe."

He held out his hand, pierced, scarred, holy. Feeling braver than she thought she had a right to, Firy put her hands in his. "I think so, Lord."

His eyes gentled her, she sniffed, raised her face, and said in a faint but firm voice, "Yes, Lord Jesus, I believe. Forgive me for owning that guilt for so long."

Jesus knelt by the still weeping woman. His light, cleansing breath washed over her as it had young Firy. After He united them, she cried, "I'm clean."

"My love for you will cleanse, heal, forgive, and comfort. Know this also, our Firy; I will never leave you."

Firy looked at her shoes, then slowly lifted her head, "There is one other thing." She looked down at her shoes again.

"Firy." The tenderness in his voice soothed her, and the love in His eyes engulfed her as He said, "I have given you strengths from both whites and natives but know this, dear one, it's not where you belong but whose you are. You are mine."

There at the water's edge, Firy fell on her face and worshiped.

As she walked back to her cousin's house, joy washed over her. She was strong, an Alaska girl once more. No, not Alaska, but a woman of another realm.

She let herself into the living room and saw Miss Ruth asleep. The older woman woke, looked up from the couch, and said, "You're healed."

"Yes!"

"Good. I'm hungry."

Firy laughed. They called Yelena and met at the local Chinese restaurant. Firy had never tried it before; something new always carried too many risks. She picked up the chopsticks and laughed along with the others at her awkward attempts to eat. Firy wondered what else she had missed over the years.

They talked for hours about their lives in Sitka. This, too, was part of our Firy's healing.

Memory Care Center — Present Day

The day, gray and grim, matched the wavering of Firy's eyes. She looked at Emma Lee and whispered, "Who are you? Why are you crying? I don't like crying."

"Gramma, it's me."

"I don't know you. Go away. I don't like crying."

Emma Lee stumbled to her car, tears streamed down her face, and her heart screamed. "Bozhe, don't take her from me, not yet. You healed her soul and her heart all those years ago. Won't you heal her mind now?"

"Very soon, Dear One, she will come home."

"That's not what I meant."

"Do not be afraid. Our Firy will be whole in every way. I have prepared a great celebration for her and her family."

"O Bozhe, I almost wish I could be there, and yet I beg you, don't take her."

"I arranged for our Firy to tell her story so you could grieve with hope and confidence. It will be a short separation. All is well."

Emma Lee wiped her nose and started the car. She hoped Bozhe's idea of soon was different from hers. She stopped and placed a standing order at the florist. When the time came, Gramma would have her yellow roses. And no matter what anybody said, they would have hot cocoa instead of coffee at her funeral reception. After all, it would be a special occasion.

The next time Emma Lee visited her grandmother, Firy asked the aide to bring the hatbox from her dresser's bottom drawer. "I had Miss Ruth write it down, but I've never read about her visit with Anna Marie's killer. When you're done reading Emma Lee, take this hatbox home with you."

"What's in it, Gramma?"

"Bits and pieces of my life, dear one."

Emma Lee forced herself to read the account but not out loud. Her eyes burned and often darted to Firy, who stared out the window.

THIRTY-SIX

At last, the trial ended. The jury had rendered a guilty verdict. Now they were in court to hear the sentence. The guards shuffled the prisoner to the massive oak doors, ankles shackled. "Guess you know where you're going to spend the rest of your life," one of them hissed.

"All rise."

Judge Cooper entered, fluffed his robes, and seated himself. He usually gave a lengthy review of the case, his personal opinions of the crime, admonishments to the prisoner, commendations to the jury, and so forth.

When he spotted Miss Ruth sitting behind the defense attorney, he began to sweat. Miss Ruth caught his eye and nodded.

Judge Cooper bellowed, "Life in prison, no parole." He banged his gavel, yelled, "Court adjourned!" and fled to his chambers.

Back in the courtroom, the spectators filed out. The prisoner awaited transport to the state prison. The lawyers shook hands and agreed to meet later for a drink. A newspaper reporter asked Miss Ruth for a statement when he couldn't get Firy to talk.

Miss Ruth preached, the reporter disappeared, and the crowd moved faster.

Firy had tossed and turned all night. The goodbyes the next day were bittersweet, promises to stay in touch, heartfelt. Miss Ruth and Yelena took Firy to the airport, "Try to sleep on the plane, dear one."

"Yes, Miss Ruth." They hugged, and Miss Ruth slipped a Hershey bar into Firy's pocket.

"How did you know?" Firy asked.

"I know a thing or two about you." Miss Ruth's eyes twinkled.

Yelena gave Firy another hug, "Miss Ruth knows everything about all of us."

The peaceful flight ended at Sea-Tac with a perfect landing. Firy gathered her things, impatient to leave the airplane. She wondered if Bumps and the kids would see the changes in her. How could they not?

Departures and arrivals caused people to scurry here and there in the massive terminal. Announcements over the sound system could not always be understood, and confused travelers looked at their tickets and scanned the area for anyone who looked official.

Bumps and his son stood at the window and watched the jets land and take off. Sharon sprawled on the bench with her nose stuck in a movie magazine.

Bumps pointed and said, "That's Mom's plane. She'll be here soon."

Eddie pressed his nose on the glass, "I'd like to fly. Go to Alaska. I barely remember it."

Bumps put his arm around the boy's shoulder, "Someday, son."

She laughed aloud as she scanned the crowds. Her soul danced and sang for her own little family. Precious. She knew now it was up to Bozhe to keep them safe, and His heart is kind. Her own heart pounded like a native drum.

As Firy left the jet, she pictured herself waving her arms above her head, coat, purse, and magazines flying. She saw herself screaming like a mama elephant trumpeting. "It's me! Bumps! Kids, it's me! I'm here!"

Years of silent stoicism held her back. Even so, she approached her family with an awareness she never felt before. She hugged her son, who grinned, then put his transistor radio back up to his ear while asking dozens of questions about Alaska. Her teenage daughter, like her in so many ways, suffered the hug in sullen silence, then pulled away and stuck her nose back in her magazine.

Firy bit her lip and shut her eyes, fighting shame and guilt. *I have so much to make up for, so many wasted years.* Bozhe's gentle voice pulsed through her. "Be anxious for nothing. I have forgiven all, healed all, and I will restore all."

Firy knew her encounter with Jesus had healed her and felt it had also softened her face and gentled her voice. She hoped her husband could see that.

Firy turned to Bumps and smiled, "It's me!"

The smile came from her eyes, and he felt her heart as well. She stood there, grinning, saying nothing. Something was different. She was different. Her eyes sparkled, and she giggled. He took a deep breath and saw his teenage daughter watching him. Sharon always watched.

Bumps knew Sharon sensed her mother hid behind walls as rugged as Alaska's wilderness. Firy often froze them out. He wished he knew how to help his daughter deal with that. He wished he had handled it better all those years.

Perhaps this new softness he saw in Firy could help them walk a different path, one that would include their daughter. His son was all comic books and magic tricks. At this point, he knew nothing about what was under the surface.

What was under the surface? Frustrated years of him loving her yet unable to help her. He rubbed the sweat off of his palms and pushed the frustration away, and asked Bozhe to help him love his Firy even more.

He took her into his arms. "Are you here, our Firy?"

She snuggled close and whispered, "Yes. For the first time, I believe I am."

"Well then, our Firy, my Firy, let's go home.

THIRTY-SEVEN

The phone rang in the middle of the night. Firy jerked awake and clambered downstairs, heart pounding. Its shrill tones of long-distance meant one thing. Someone was dead or dying—someone in Alaska or Pennsylvania.

She stepped on the hem of her robe, stumbled down the last stair, and grabbed the banister to steady herself. She gathered her nightgown into shaking hands and hiked it above her knees. She ran into the dining room, where the phone rested on a small table in the corner.

Firy snatched the offending handset from its cradle. "Hello?" she whispered. "Yelena?" Someone from Alaska then, the boys, Henry? Uncle Ade? Names and faces collided in Firy's mind. They came out of her mouth in a rapid-fire staccato burst that Yelena could not stop. She yelled into the phone, "Firy!"

Firy winced and pulled it away from her ear. "Who?"

"Firy, sit down," Yelena answered quietly. "I still can't believe it."

"Tell me."

"Miss Ruth."

Firy covered her mouth to stop the wails that would wake the entire household. She groped for the handset that fell when she slumped into a chair. A glass dish of lemon drops spilled across the floor.

She could hear Yelena's tinny voice coming through the earpiece. "Firy, are you there?"

Firy opened her mouth, but no sound came out. She heard Yelena ask if she was alright. She managed to croak, "No. I will never be alright again."

They cried together, one in Alaska, the other hundreds of miles to the south. Yelena shared what little she knew. Robert was still in Nome, and details scant.

"Yelena, long-distance is so expensive. Perhaps, we should hang up."

"Don't worry about that. I can always schedule a few extra haircuts and perms."

Firy could not think beyond the fact that Miss Ruth was gone. Her mother, mentor, friend, rock. An inner voice whispered, "I am your Rock, no other. Miss Ruth was, indeed, your friend and mentor. She mothered you when you had no mother. She is with me now. Do not begrudge her that."

Yelena's voice faded, and Firy responded to a gentle voice that was not her own. "Oh, Bozhe, she helped me so much. I still need her."

"Miss Ruth wore herself out for Me. She has yearned for heaven and home but stayed for your sake Firy, and I gave her extra years so she could watch and pray. She knelt before My throne daily for you. You filled her heart in a way no other did. And because of that and My great mercy, you are healed and will continue to be healed."

"But Lord, I miss her already. It hurts. Too much."

"I am familiar with hurt. I hurt all the years you would not receive My love."

Fresh tears poured from Firy's eyes and heart as this truth pierced her soul. The voice continued. "Hush now, Dear One. Miss Ruth is with Me and continues to be my Dear One, as are you."

Firy clung to His words. She pressed them to her soul. The endearment wrapped itself around her heart, and while it did not lessen her grief, it contained it. Somehow, amid her sorrow, she was comforted. She tried to picture Miss Ruth in heaven. She felt Bozhe put his arms around her. "Yes." He said, "Picture her with Me."

"When I do, Lord, I feel great joy, and my heart ribbons with praise and light, but all the same, I'm experiencing a great loss."

"Remember these words from one of the earth's greatest hymns, 'sorrow and love flow mingled down.' It tells how love and loss, grief and glory, jubilation and tribulation often live together in you. Do not try to corral or control them; let them be. But now, Dear One, focus on your cousin."

Firy found herself still slumped in the dining room chair, the phone in her lap, her hands full of lemon drops. Yelena's voice continued its mournful lament. She picked up the receiver.

Firy remembered how Miss Ruth often talked about being in the throne room of heaven and speaking to the King while mopping the floor or walking to the post office or even in the middle of conversations with friends.

Firy's smile became a full-fledged grin, and she almost laughed out loud. You're still letting Miss Ruth teach me, aren't you? Heaven smiled.

Firy and Yelena talked and wept until dawn. "Are you sure you can't come, Firy?"

Firy sighed, sad but somehow at peace. "We haven't paid back the money we borrowed for my ticket to the trial. It's okay, Lena."

"You haven't called me Lena since we were kids."

Firy laughed. "You said it didn't sound Russian enough."

"I tried so hard to be Russian instead of native even though Miss Ruth thought Aleut and Yupik were wonderful."

"She taught me to be proud of our Alaskan heritage."

"I may have to go back to that old nickname.

"Lena, did Robert mention a memorial?"

"Next week in Nome. Too expensive for me to make it, but if they have another one in Sitka, I'll go."

"They have to," said Firy, "It's her real home."

"I'll let you know," said Yelena, "I'll be your eyes and ears."

"Thank you, Lena. I know you will, and I love you for it."

Yelena laughed again at the use of her childhood nickname. "Firy, do you know where Miss Ruth was from or when she came to Alaska?"

"We talked about it once, but I can't remember. She always focused on me. I feel so selfish."

"She wouldn't want you to feel that way."

Firy agreed but wished she knew about Miss Ruth's early life. She knew Miss Ruth had come to Alaska many years ago, but from where? And why? Somehow, it seemed important to find out as much as she could about Miss Ruth.

"I will keep my eyes open for an obituary, Dear One, and send a copy as soon as possible."

"What did you call me?" Firy demanded.

"What? Nothing. What do you mean?"

"You called me, Dear One."

"Okay?" Lena's voice held a question mark, so Firy told her cousin about the conversation she just had with Bozhe. Silence.

"Lena?"

"Oh, Firy, I feel like Miss Ruth is right here."

"Not Miss Ruth. Bozhe.

Memory Care Center — Present Day

"I'm sorry my story upset you. I should've kept it to myself."

"No, Gramma. I want you to tell me everything." Emma Lee's lashes tipped with tears, and she tried to blink them away. Firy pulled a cloth hanky from her sweater pocket and handed it to her granddaughter.

"You're always prepared, Gramma."

"No honey, that was Miss Ruth."

Emma Lee took the hanky and scrubbed at her eyes. "I don't understand why I'm feeling so sad. It's not as if I knew her or anything."

"That's the kind of person she was. Now wipe your eyes and give me back my hanky. I need it too."

"Yes, Gramma."

Firy shook her head. "It was a sad day when women gave up their pocket-handkerchiefs."

"Yes, Gramma."

Firy tucked the hanky back in her pocket. "Next time, I will tell you happy stories. I promise."

"Okay, Gramma. I'll be back soon." Emma Lee kissed her Gramma's cheek.

She sat behind the wheel and wondered how she could grieve for a woman she'd never met. Miss Ruth lived in the stack of letters she wrote to Gramma. And she lived in Gramma's heart.

Emma Lee brushed her hands across her eyes and under her nose and wished she had that hanky. She searched the glove compartment for tissues. Nothing. In the backseat, she found a couple of used napkins from the last time she took the kids for fast food. Gross. They would have to do.

She blew her nose and threw the ketchup stained napkins into the car's tiny trash bag, but her mind and heart remained in the Care Center with Gramma. So much happened to you. So much hardship and heartache, but you survived. You tried to love Bozhe and do what's right. Oh, Gramma.

She leaned back against the seat and watched the clouds through the sunroof. A few moments later, she sniffed and told herself to get a grip. *Here I am, Gramma. Alone but talking out loud to you, like you used to do to Miss Ruth.* She remembered Gramma said, "People will think you are talking on that Bluetooth thingy. Back in the day, they thought I was strange."

As she drove home, Emma Lee was sure the other drivers saw her talking to herself, "You're right, Gramma, they probably think I'm on my Bluetooth. I'm glad God sent Miss Ruth to you. In many ways, Gramma, you are my very own Miss Ruth.

She opened all the windows and sang *I Love Humpback Salmon* at the top of her voice.

THIRTY-NINE

Firy took her coffee and writing tablet to the back yard where sunlight warmed the white metal table and chairs. Today, she would write her letter to the editor.

No more wadded up papers or failed attempts. She would write to the Sitka Sentinel and explain what Miss Ruth meant to her. Firy sipped her coffee, then chewed on the end of her pencil. She spat out the eraser and wrote: "Dear Editor."

She thought Sam Mitchell, Jr. was a lot like his father, crusty but sweet on the inside, much like a toasted marshmallow. That's how she had Sam Sr. figured and assumed his son was the same. She understood his plea to know everything about Miss Ruth.

She listened to a robin on the branch above her and glared at the cheerful bird. "You're not helping."

Firy looked back at her mother's funeral. On that day of death, the black-clad missionary woman had become life to her.

Nine-year-old Firy ran to the See House behind St Peter's every day after school. Tea and graham crackers with Miss Ruth. Several times a week, Miss Ruth walked her home and shooed teenaged Masha out, and told her to go and find her friends. Whenever Masha protested, Miss Ruth looked over her spectacles and said. "I've had a word from the Lord about this. You don't want to argue with Him, do you?"

Masha didn't. Then Miss Ruth spent the afternoon teaching the others how to prepare simple meals.

"It's stupid girl stuff," Henry slammed the frying pan on the stove.

Miss Ruth ruffled his hair, kissed the top of his head, and said, "Someday, your wife is going to be a delighted woman."

"I ain't cooking when I get married. That's woman's work." Firy had to smile. Henry was now the executive chef of Anchorage's most exclusive restaurant. Thank you, Miss Ruth.

"How do I put all of that down on paper?" Firy asked the robin. He kept his eye on the oatmeal-raisin-dried cranberry cookies on the saucer next to Firy's coffee. Miss Ruth's recipe, of course.

"Are you hungry?" Firy asked the bird as she crumpled half a cookie and tossed it onto the grass. The bird sang his thanks.

She sipped her coffee and pressed the tip of her fountain pen onto the paper once more. She hadn't used the treasured graduation gift from Mr. Akervik in years. Her letter still only said:

Dear Editor.

Miss Ruth deserved better. Write something. Tell how Miss Ruth held you together when Anna Marie died. Tell how she mothered you when you stumbled through the valley of the shadow. Firy shed sweet tears for Miss Ruth, who always shared Bozhe's heart.

She threw down her pen, went in, and put a load of laundry in the washing machine. She remembered scrubbing clothes with Miss Ruth. They had often used an old washtub and scrubbing board, even though Papa had bought a new wringer-washer when Mama got sick. Miss Ruth was not in favor of them. She preferred doing laundry the old-fashioned way.

As she threw Bumps' dirty baseball clothes into her automatic washer, she wondered how he could get them so filthy coaching Babe Ruth and Little League. She grinned and thought about the day Bumps had challenged Miss Ruth and the Sisters of the See House to a game of baseball.

"There's not enough of you, Miss Ruth." Anna Marie's voice rose an octave, "You need nine players."

"You're right. Go and ask the Lutheran minister's wife, then the Baptist's, and the Methodist's."

"I'll ask Petrov Bravebird's niece. She's not a preacher's wife, but she's Orthodox, and she can swing a bat. We've got to have somebody that knows baseball."

Miss Ruth ruffled Anna Marie's hair. "You're the manager. Do what you think best."

On game day Miss Ruth's team wore baseball uniforms from a women's college in Ohio. Somehow, those uniforms ended up in the missionary barrels the Lutheran church received from their mother church.

Before the game started, Bumps said, "Perhaps Addie May should be the umpire."

"Oh no, we need her. She's our pitcher." Miss Ruth said.

"She pitches? From a wheelchair?"

"She's in her forties and strong as an ox," Miss Ruth pulled her baseball cap low on her forehead then lifted her eyes to Bumps. "Wait until you see her knuckleball."

"What about batting?"

"Ivan's oldest, Ivana, is Addie's designated hitter. His youngest daughter is her runner."

Bumps shook his head and headed to the dugout. Because they

played old women, the men on the American Legion team said they'd pitch and bat left-handed.

The crowd went wild as the ladies lined up and curtsied. Addie May's knuckleball kept them in the game. The men had won 3-1.

Firy lifted her face to the sun's warmth as she remembered Miss Ruth's home run in the ninth. She stopped to rest on second base. Budnikov ran a soda out to her and charged half-price. Miss Ruth had no money on her. The crowd booed when Budnikov made her sign an IOU.

"Run! Run!" The crowd screamed.

The umpire said the rule book did not list a minimum time to round the bases, and the game would not be over until Miss Ruth touched home plate. He shook his face mask at the crowd and told them not to leave.

Miss Ruth finished her soda, ran to third, and then walked her seven-decades-old bones to home plate. She whispered to Firy, "Thank Bumps for that fastball right down the middle."

The memory faded, along with her smile. Firy gulped her now-cold coffee then bowed her head. "Bozhe, I miss her. Thank You for bringing us together one last time, even though it was during that horrible trial. You healed my hurt, and as usual, Miss Ruth was a big part of it."

Firy got the old pasteboard hatbox out of the hall closet., a gift from Miss Ruth. The hat was long gone, but Firy kept letters from her dear friend in the box.

She sat in the sun and reread letters filled with advice, prayers, hope, and encouragement. Firy held this last letter to her nose and breathed deeply. A faint essence of lavender comforted her.

She reached under the letters for her journal. She flipped

through the pages but didn't need to read the entry. Firy leaned back on the warm metal chair and closed her eyes.

She sensed the robin hop to the edge of the table. Firy remained still as the robin tiptoed to the saucer and pecked at her last cookie. "Enjoy the cookie, little one. I am going on a fey adventure with Miss Ruth."

The sun, a lemon drop in the sky. The air, warm with the scent of a hundred thousand wildflowers. Miss Ruth knocked on the front door and tapped her foot. She grabbed Firy by both hands and danced her around the room. Miss Ruth dropped to her knees and whispered in Firy's ear.

The girl's eyes grew big, and she shrieked, "Papa, can I spend the day with Miss Ruth?"

Bill leaned against the door frame, coffee cup in hand. "Chores done?"

Firy cupped her hands around her mouth and whispered, "No, Papa, but Miss Ruth is feeling fey."

Papa Bill looked over the top of Firy's head to Miss Ruth, who pretended she had not heard the girl's whisper.

"Is she now?" Papa gave them both a long look, then asked Miss Ruth, "And what exactly does that mean?"

"Wonders and whimsy, fantasies and fancies, adventures of the heart and soul. Want to come along?"

Bill downed the rest of his coffee and shook his head. "Will you have her home before dark?"

"Let's see, it's eight in the morning, and twilight will come in another fourteen and a half hours. I think my feyness will have worn off by then."

Papa nodded his agreement. Firy clapped her hands.

"Come, Anna Marie, give Miss Ruth a love." The three-year-old peeked out from behind Papa Bill's legs and ran to Miss Ruth.

Miss Ruth called to the teen-ager washing the breakfast dishes. "Don't forget our girl date tomorrow night, Masha, my darlin."

"Yes, Miss Ruth."

"Where's Elizaveta?"

"In bed, not feeling well." Papa Bill said and poured himself another cup of coffee.

"She needs a fey story of fairies and flowers and handsome princes and evil witches. Firy, you help Masha for a few minutes while I sprinkle some feyness on your sister. It's the best medicine."

"Papa, is that what fey is? Fairies and handsome princes and sprinkled medicine?"

"Danged if I can figure it. Ain't no handsome princes in Sitka, fairies, neither. Still, with Miss Ruth, you never know."

Firy pranced as she and Miss Ruth headed downtown. She had heard stories about Miss Ruth when that fey thing came over her, but she had not believed them. And now she was off on a fey adventure.

"Where're we going, Miss Ruth?"

"We are going to the Alaska Steamship Company. There are some significant people on the ship. We are going to be the welcoming committee and tour guides."

"That doesn't sound very fey."

"It will be, my dear."

"Who are these people, anyway?"

"They are stuffy, starchy people who are going to invest in

Sitka. By the end of the day, we're going to free the little children locked inside of them."

"What's invest?"

"They are going to spend a lot of money, maybe build a fish cannery or two."

"But my teacher says we're depressed, and nobody has any money."

"Some people will always have money. They're the very ones who have a hard time being fey, poor things."

"Okay, if you say so." Firy put her hand in Miss Ruth's and willed herself to believe.

Miss Ruth squeezed Firy's hand and said, "Let's run."

Across the ballpark's outfield, down the little hill, and onto Lincoln street, past St. Michael's and Akervik's store, the fey companions skipped and sang.

Firy wanted to stop at Wellerton's for an ice cream cone, but Miss Ruth said it was better to be fey on an empty stomach. Firy's stomach didn't think so, but since she wasn't sure what FEY meant, she had to trust Miss Ruth.

The Star of Alaska, the Alaska Steamship Company's premier ship, was moored beyond the floatplane's dock.

Miss Ruth opened her satchel and produced a long black cape for Firy. She placed little pretend spectacles on the girl's nose. Firy, covered in black from head to toe, looked like a miniature Miss Ruth.

Firy laughed out loud, "I believe I feel the fey-ness."

"Good girl," Miss Ruth turned and hailed the captain, "Good morning, Commodore."

"Good morning. How are you?"

"Feeling a bit fey. Permission to come aboard?"

"Feeling fey, you say?" He shook his head, took off his captain's cap, put it back on, and stuttered, "Permission granted, but keep your feyness away from me."

"You know, Commodore, it's difficult to control."

He hailed the first mate. "I have important paperwork in my office and am not to be disturbed."

The first mate saluted and heard his captain mutter as he passed, "Get her off the ship as quickly as you can. She's feeling fey."

The first mate blanched and called to the steward. "I have important business in the wheelhouse. Take care of Miss Ruth. She's feeling fey."

The steward hailed Miss Ruth. "Can I help you?"

"I need a list of the passengers, but I must warn you, I'm feeling a bit fey."

He whipped off his cap and bowed, "I have a bit of the Celtic in me. Mind if I watch.?"

Miss Ruth curtsied, Firy laughed and held tight to Miss Ruth's hand.

The Alaska Steamship Company, primarily a cargo company, had one class of berths for a dozen or so passengers on all its ships. With its frequent and swift schedules from Seattle, it was the preferred mode of travel for many from the states.

Miss Ruth hailed the half dozen businessmen as they prepared to disembark. "I am Miss Ruth, and this is my assistant, Firy. Welcome to Sitka. We're your official tour guides."

The men looked upset. One, in particular, groused, "I don't have time for any tours. We're here on business."

"Your luggage has been taken to the hotel. All of your meetings have been rescheduled for tomorrow and the day after. Mr..," she looked at her list, "...Jonas? You have all the time in the world. We planned the day with you in mind."

Mr. Jonas looked disgruntled, "Be still, Eric," his wife laid her hand on his arm. He shrugged it off and scowled.

"Before we disembark, I will teach you a typical greeting in Russian, Tlingit, Haida, and Yupik Eskimo. You must master at least one of these greetings before we leave the ship."

Firy followed behind as Miss Ruth instructed them one by one. She took their hands in hers and stared into their eyes, "Repeat after -"

Amazed these grownups could not get their tongues to follow directions, Firy laughed out loud at their attempts. Soon everyone chuckled at themselves, except Mr. Jonas, who refused even to try a native greeting.

"Now see here. I have important business."

Miss Ruth answered in Tlingit.

"Speak English."

She answered in Yupik, which even Firy couldn't pronounce.

"I've had enough of this..."

Miss Ruth handed him a lemon drop. "It will sweeten you up."

Mrs. Jonas hid her smile behind her hand and winked at Miss Ruth. "Eric, you are a warrior in the boardroom, everyone knows that, but perhaps you've met your match."

His investors, would-be partners, and employees pretended they had not heard.

Miss Ruth continued as if nothing was amiss. "Sitka has fourteen miles of roads, some of them paved. We're going to travel all of them before the day is over. But first, I will escort you to Sitka's very own castle."

Miss Ruth pointed in the direction of Castle Hill with the

enormous Victorian mansion on the top. Not the Russian one, of course; it had burned down years ago. This large building housed government offices, but everyone still called it the castle.

"The last Russian governor was a prince, so handsome. Ladies, you would have loved him and his wife, Princess Maria Maksutova. She presided over a small imperial court in the style of the Russian aristocracy. The balls and receptions, ornate and exclusive. The gowns, the jewels, the bowing, and the kissing of hands. No wonder they called Sitka the Paris of the Pacific," Miss Ruth said, "it was all so elegant."

Miss Ruth curtsied deeply in front of Mr. Jonas. Firy did the same. The ruthless businessman, embarrassed, swallowed his lemon drop and choked. His wife pounded him on the back. The others twittered and tried to hold back their uncomfortable laughter. Miss Ruth remained in her deep curtsy while Firy lost her balance and thudded to the deck. Mrs. Jonas helped her up.

After a moment, Mr. Jonas whispered to Miss Ruth, "Will you get up?"

"I can't, not until you bow to me. Court etiquette, you know."

"We're not at court," he growled and backed up a step.

"Can you not see the aristocracy watching? Mind your manners, my lord."

Mrs. Jonas came and curtsied to Miss Ruth, then stood and pushed her husband and forced him into a tiny bow.

Miss Ruth rose and held out her hand. Mr. Jonas had an idea of what was expected and balked. She stared, and he stared back.

Miss Ruth moved close and whispered in his ear, "I can stand here all day with my hand held out. Sometimes, my dear Mr. Jonas, the best offense is a tactical retreat."

He threw back his head and laughed, "I would love to have you on my board!"

"Better allies than enemies."

The stern businessman reached for Miss Ruth. He twirled her around. "Let's get this party started!"

He must have a bit of the Celtic in him, or else my fey-ness is more contagious than I thought, she mused as they all climbed the knoll to the castle.

Miss Ruth told stories of the Governor and his Princess, how, when the United States took possession of Alaska, it broke Princess Maria's heart. When the Russian soldiers lowered their flag, and the US Marines raised the Stars and Stripes, she fainted.

Miss Ruth described everything as if she was there. Firy counted on her fingers. She tugged on Miss Ruth's skirt," You aren't that old. I mean, you're old, but..."

Firy floundered, and Miss Ruth hugged her. "Let them think what they will. It's a fey day."

Firy led the way through town to St. Michael, the Archangel, Russian Orthodox Church. Father Mikhail showed them the tapestry on the south wall and said Firy's mother repaired the ancient cloth with gold thread and great love for Bozhe. He also showed them the Sitka Madonna, an old and priceless icon.

The women wondered why there were no pews or chairs. Father Mikhail explained that all the people stood for the entire service.

"It's long," said Firy.

"Yes," Father Mikhail said. "About three hours." The women groaned. The men shuddered. Father Mikhail winked at Firy, "I heard lemon drops help."

Miss Ruth escorted her little flock to Crescent Beach. Petrov

Bravebird and his grandsons had built a fire and boiled several kettles of water.

Miss Ruth conducted introductions between natives and businessmen. The Tlingit natives remained passive as the Americans tried to say hello in Tlingit and Haida. Mr. Jonas shook Bravebird's hand and said, "Thank you for not laughing. I'm sure English was as difficult for you to learn as Tlingit is for us. You should be laughing on the inside. I am."

Bravebird's eyes twinkled; he nodded and prepared the cedar plank salmon with sea asparagus and Indian Fry Bread. Jonas hunkered down to watch.

"No time for that, if you want to eat, dig," Miss Ruth handed him a shovel and a bucket and pointed to the sand. The others already scoured the sand for little bubbles, indicating where the clams hid. Shoes and socks discarded, pant legs rolled up, ties askew.

Jonas breathed deeply. "Miss Ruth, I didn't realize how much I needed to get away from my office and endless meetings. Thank you."

"You'll learn to play today, Mr. Eric Jonas, and you'll learn to hold things loosely. After we eat, we potlatch."

"What's that?"

"You will see," she said, eyeing his expensive watch and cuff links. She looked into his eyes and liked what she saw. She knew he would end the day without the links or the timepiece.

"Jonas, take off your shoes and socks and let the sand get between your toes."

He looked at her and tried to sound gruff, "Is that an order?"

"Everyone has already discarded their footwear. It's time for you to join in."

Miss Ruth watched with satisfaction as he obeyed. She sat on an overturned bucket and took off her cowboy boots. "Come, Firy, we'll dance as they dig for their lunch."

One man and his wife chased each other in the surf. She squealed when a clam squirted her. Others caught unaware by an incoming wave were drenched past their knees.

"See, Firy, the imprisoned children are beginning to feel free." Firy didn't hear her. She chased old Petrov Bravebird around the fire.

The men waded into the surf with their buckets, and when they had washed their clams, took them to the old Tlingit. The Bravebird boys placed driftwood logs in a circle around the fire. Everyone sat and ate.

Mr. Jonas stuffed himself and declared, "Clams, salmon, sea asparagus, and even the black seaweed was more enjoyable than dining at that expensive restaurant in Seattle last week."

Miss Ruth leaned over to Firy, "Look at their faces. Rosy cheeks, bright eyes, happy smiles. They are children. Fey."

Firy stuffed more fry bread in her mouth; happy herring eggs were not in season. "Now what?" she asked.

"We'll take them to Totem Park and tell the stories that live in the totems. They'll pick wild blueberries, and then we'll take our little flock to the Russian Cemetery. While I tell them tales of the folk buried there, you have a little visit with your Mama. Then we'll come back to the See house for tea and blueberry scones."

"And after that?" Firy asked.

Miss Ruth laughed. "After that, Bob Nelson is going to take them on a tour of Baranof and the surrounding islands. There are six passenger seats, so he'll make two trips."

"There's no room for me?" Firy asked in a tiny voice.

"There's no room for you in the passengers' seats."

Firy nodded. Her shoulders sagged, and she bit her lip.

"Firy, did I not tell you. It's a fey day."

"Yes, Miss Ruth."

"You'll have to sit in the co-pilot seat next to Bob." Firy squealed and hugged her old friend. Her first ride in an airplane! It was a fey day, indeed.

Buckets of blueberries were picked in the park while Miss Ruth and Petrov Bravebird told the Totems' stories.

Mrs. Jonas decided to stay at the See House and help bake the scones. She wanted to ask the sisters about their programs and ministries to the community.

They left the See house and walked past the church. Miss Ruth pointed to the round stained-glass window above the door. "About 1900, the church commissioned that window from an artist on the East Coast. They requested two things, lilies and a Christian symbol in the center."

The little group craned their necks. "I don't believe it."

"What?"

"Look."

"What do you see?"

"Oh, my goodness, it's a Star of David."

"When church members pulled that window out of the packing crate, you could have heard their shouts as far as the Denali. A Jewish symbol in a Christian church, unthinkable. Yet it would cost a fortune and take too long to send it back and have it redone."

"Well, it's obvious they decided to keep it." Eric Jonas said.

"After endless meetings and debate, they decided nothing could be better than the Star of David? After all, Christianity is Jewish."

She saw the puzzled looks on their faces. It would do them

good to ponder that a bit.

Miss Ruth sat on a bench on the seawall near the floatplane dock while Bob loaded his passengers for the first trip. Firy waved out the window and blew kisses to Miss Ruth. For those left behind, she answered questions about Sitka and her life in Alaska.

"You impress me, Miss Ruth, with your knowledge of Alaska politics and the territory's laws, rules, and regulations," Jonas said.

"I've been here since 1890, and I've learned a thing or two. I love this land."

"Decades!"

"Yes, Jonas, all of my adult life. This is a good land, don't ruin it."

"There is so much here. I don't think the sea will ever run out of salmon, or the forest, its timber."

Miss Ruth shook her head but remained silent, glad she came to Alaska when she did.

The sun wandered to the west, and twilight approached. On the way to the hotel, the excited passengers chattered about the islands, forests, and sea life. Firy told about a mama bear and her twin cubs on the beach. Bob had flown low so the men could take pictures.

Firy closed her journal, held it to her heart, and breathed a prayer of thanks that Bozhe had sent Miss Ruth into her life. She carefully replaced everything in the old hatbox and put it on the closet's top-shelf. She poured herself another cup of coffee, picked up her pencil, and wrote:

Dear Editor:

Thank you for making subscriptions to the paper available to us who are so far away from Sitka. It's a little bit of home in my mailbox every week.

Now, about Miss Ruth. I'm sure you've received many letters that revealed her love for people. It would take a score of books to record her adventures and service to others.

That would horrify her. Miss Ruth believed all glory and honor belonged to the High King of Heaven.

She had her feet firmly planted on the ground, but her soul lived in heaven. Love Bozhe and do what's right is something my Mama told me, but Miss Ruth showed me.

And so, dear editor, although I have many stories about Miss Ruth, they are written in the annals of Heaven and my heart. And there they will stay.

Sincerely,

Firy Baas

Memory Care Center — Present Day

The parking lot at the care center was nearly empty. Not many visitors today. Sad. As Emma Lee walked toward the entrance, she saw pewter pigeons soar under a slate sky. Above them, trumpeter swans and Canada geese, who wintered in the valley, squawked and honked. The pigeons looked for quiet in the branches of a friendly tree. She envied their freedom of flight. If you don't like your situation, fly away.

She popped a lemon drop in her mouth then stared at the bag in wonder. How many generations of her family had been popping lemon drops as if they were antidepressants? Mom, Gramma, and her Mama, and before them, Miss Ruth.

She should have bought stock in a lemon drop company years ago. She could've made a fortune from her family alone. She signed the visitor's log.

Please let Gramma be herself today. She sniffed, scrubbed at her face, fished her lipstick out of her purse, and attempted a smile. I love her because she's Gramma, but I also love a girl called Firy. Please, God.

Firy shuffled across the common room. Her slippers made sandpaper noises against the bare floor. She wobbled and staggered, and the aide rushed to get the wheelchair. Firy slapped at legs that often didn't work.

"Hi, Gramma." It was going to be a day of blank stares. The knot around Emma Lee's heart constricted. She ached for all the people in this room. Every person a life. Every life, a story. So many, untold and forgotten, no one here to turn the pages.

Gramma hated the wheelchair, so Emma Lee helped her settle in the loveseat. Firy pushed at the hated wheelchair. She then batted at Emma Lee.

"It's okay, Gramma. It's me."

There was no recognition in Firy's eyes, only confusion, frustration, fear. They both looked away. Tears fell down the young woman's face.

Firy's eyes pooled but did not spill over. Her lips quivered, her mouth moved, but the words would not form. She shrank into herself, where the fear grew and spiraled.

Emma Lee took Firy's face in her hands, "Gramma?"

Again, Firy tried to pull away. It made the younger woman cry all the more.

The aide came and placed two cups of cocoa on the coffee table. She took Emma Lee's hands in her own. "Try to calm yourself, my dear. You're scaring her."

"I'm sorry. I'm so sorry, Gramma," she whispered. Firy tried to get up from the loveseat, then fell against the cushions. Emma Lee asked the aide, "What can I do to help her?"

"Nothing, I'm afraid. Her times of lucidity will become less and may disappear altogether as this pestilence progresses. She could even lose the ability to speak."

"I can't bear it." Emma Lee grabbed a handkerchief out of her pocket. She felt the bag of lemon drops. They couldn't help her now. She held them in her lap anyway.

Emma Lee turned her tear-stained face to the aide and said, "Gramma always said a woman should carry a real handkerchief."

"I know," said the aide, pulling a lacy thing from under her sleeve. "She gave me this."

Emma Lee laughed. "I bet she never gave you one of her big red bandannas. She kept those for herself, said if she were ever going to have a cry, it would be a monster." Emma Lee used her hanky then continued, "Mom isn't doing well, either."

"I know, dear. We talk every time she comes, and she's so grateful for all your visits."

Emma Lee shrugged.

"It's hard on everyone, especially our Firy. She's one of my favorites, you know."

"She is pretty special." Emma Lee gazed at her grandmother, huddled in the corner of the loveseat.

"We're not supposed to have favorites, but, of course, we do. Sometimes, in the night, I lay down beside her, another violation, but I don't care. I'll rub her back. She used to sing the Humpback Salmon song to me. Now I sing it to her."

"Thank you. I hadn't thought about Gramma alone and awake in the night." Emma Lee took a deep breath and tried to push the image away. Poor Gramma.

"She's not alone when I'm on the night shift, and I truly believe, somewhere deep in her soul, she knows her Bozhe is with her."

Emma Lee squeezed the aide's hands and thanked her again.

"I tried to hover nearby when she told you her stories."

Emma Lee blushed, "I didn't notice, and I'm embarrassed to say I don't even know your name."

"I never said. It's Anna Marie."

"I don't believe it!"

"It's true, just the same."

"I'm sorry. I didn't mean to say that out loud."

"I never told our Firy, in case it would upset her."

Firy had grabbed a pillow and held it to her chest.

"You said 'our Firy,' that's what the family always called her. Thank you." Emma Lee hugged the aide, "She might like to know Anna Marie is here."

"In that case, if the opportunity presents itself, I'll tell her."

The wonderful aide named Anna Marie leaned toward Firy and whispered, "Drink up. It's a special occasion." She kissed Firy on the top of her head, mouthed goodbye to Emma Lee, and continued with her duties.

Firy wiped the spittle collected at the corner of her mouth. Her lip quivered as it often did before she disappeared. Her body tensed as she commanded her mind to stay. Sometimes it allowed her to struggle against the fog, and sometimes the confusion rolled over her so fast she wasn't aware she was leaving. Who knew time and space were so important, so comforting?

When she didn't know who she was or when she was, the fear held her captive. The strangers in this place seemed nice, but she didn't know them, didn't trust them. This creeping inability to remember was visiting her more often, and she couldn't stop it.

She gazed out the window. The sun had dropped just beyond the mountains. Its feeble rays climbed over the peaks as if yearning to stay with her. Twilight lingered, holding back the darkness. Her heart reached for the light and what lay beyond the mountain.

Today, Firy won the battle. She looked at the others in the room, her companions on this desperate final journey. A journey none of them wanted or planned for. Firy squeezed her eyes tight and clenched her fists. I'm here. I'm here, and I know who I am.

She saw the young woman across the table pouring the hot chocolate. She knew her; of course, she did.

"Hi Gramma," Emma Lee said softly.

Of course, it was Emma Lee come to visit. Firy watched Anna Marie walk away, then turned to Emma Lee, "I remember my little sister, and I remember you. I even remember the hot cocoa." Firy cradled her granddaughter's face in her hands.

Emma Lee's tears rested in the folds of her grandmother's wrinkled knuckles.

"Don't cry, dear one, soon Bozhe will come and take me to the land of endless summer and no snow."

Emma Lee's shoulders shook, and the bag of lemon drops fell.

"No lemon drops today," Firy said, "This is not a sad thing. Look at me."

Emma Lee raised her eyes to Firy as her grandmother whispered, "He knows me, even when I do not know myself. I am eager to be with Him. Take care of your Mama when my time comes."

Emma Lee wept, and the older woman held her close. "Pooshkay. Do you remember pooshkay?"

"Yes, Gramma, it will be what it will be. But I am going to miss you so."

"You will tell my stories to your children and their children, yes?"

"Oh yes, Gramma. I wrote them down, so I'll always have them."

"You have them here." Firy placed her hand on her granddaughter's heart.

Her touch seemed to lighten the grief in Emma Lee. The pain that had been encroaching on her soul for months. She knew now, Gramma was there, even when she wasn't.

Firy leaned over and sniffed at the cocoa. She dipped her finger in, then licked it. Her hands shook, but she lifted the mug and sniffed again.

"It's cocoa, Gramma." Emma Lee said and lifted her own mug.

Firy sipped, then gulped the now warm drink. The awareness in her eyes faded. "Is this from the good Papa?"

Emma Lee patted her grandmother's knee, "Yes, our Firy, this is from your own good Papa."

Firy set her empty mug on the table and licked at her chocolate mustache. She shivered and pulled her sweater closer around her and said, "Mama, I'm scared."

A heart pierced by tenderness but one that raged against this disease, Emma Lee folded her grandmother in her arms. "It's okay, our Firy. Mama's here. Mama's here."

The frail, old woman snuggled close as her granddaughter sang about the humpback salmon that splashed in Sitka Sound.

The arms of Bozhe encircle them both.

Coming Soon

ABOUT MISS RUTH

Book Two

ONE

The Sitka Café 1962

Sam Mitchell, Jr., the editor of the town's only newspaper, leaned his head on the doorpost of the Sitka Café and closed his eyes. He had seen her yesterday in Juneau and asked her to come back, and she said she'd visit in a few weeks. Now, this. He couldn't grasp the news, although he shouldn't be surprised. She had been doing it for over thirty years and in worse conditions. Whatever the cause, he believed Rob Nelson was not at fault. He tapped his head on the doorpost, sniffed, and forced himself to open the door.

The sights and sounds of the café were familiar and dear to Sam. He scanned the area and focused his gaze through the archway to the back room. As usual, Agrafena banged pots and pans in the kitchen. Sam half-smiled despite himself.

The café, crowded and noisy as always, bustled. The owner, Mike Evans, had died several years back. Everyone in town knew that Agrefena had sent their son Mick off to college to study medicine. Unbeknownst to her, he had taken financial and marketing courses instead. When Mike died, Mick came home and took over Capitalize Café. Soon, he was behind the counter, coffee pot in hand. Agrafena, disgusted at first, soon came to rely on her son just as she had her husband.

The old-timers in the back room gave him a hard time at first, but Mick gave as good as he got, and soon folks had a hard time remembering he was not his father.

Cruise ships anchored in the sound and the café was overcrowded. The men at the round table talked louder and embellished their stories of the old days—the café's unofficial entertainment for the tourist trade. Sam's heart pounded as he remembered how often she had taken center stage in those stories.

Mick delivered breakfasts to the overflow in the front dining room. "What's wrong, Sam? You look like heck!"

When Sam explained, Mick took a step back and covered his mouth. His eyes darted to the kitchen door and back to Sam, "You sure?"

Sam nodded.

Mick paled, then called his mother and whispered the news. She howled. All conversations in the café stopped. Agrafena leaned on Mick, and he led her to the center of the backroom. "I can do it, Mom. You should go home."

She shoved him away and climbed on a chair. With tears streaming, she choked out the words, "Our dear Miss Ruth is gone. She and Rob Nelson fell out of the sky. He is alive. She is not." Agrafena fled to the kitchen. The silence was deafening and disturbing.

Ivan leaned toward the others and whispered, "Miss Ruth not fall from sky."

"I feel like the sky itself is falling," Jake cradled his coffee mug and stared into the brown liquid.

"Rob's a great pilot. I wonder what happened?"

The diners slumped in their chairs. Food grew cold, and cigarettes burned themselves out. Heads bowed. Grief and silence settled on everyone except for a small group of tourists who wolfed down their food, chatted about their vacations, and complained about Sitka's miserable weather.

"No respect," Ivan growled.

"Leave it alone, Ivan. They didn't know her," Ade said.

"What are you talking about, old man?" A leather-jacketed young teen, among the tourists, smoothed back the hair flopping over his forehead.

"Respect," Ivan said.

"Be cool, man. It's not like a big jet plane crashed."

Ivan's chair fell to the floor as he bolted out of it. He shook his fist in the boy's face, "Evil boy. Miss Ruth is, you." His speech descended into Russian curse words, which some of the older Alaskans understood, and the tourists did not, but all could see his rage.

Jake picked up the chair, and Ade guided a still cursing Ivan back to it.

The boy brushed his hand over his Byrlcreemed hair and straightened his jacket, "Ignorant, old man."

"Paulie, be nice." His mother patted his arm.

Paul shrugged it off and grabbed another piece of toast. "I'm cool."

Mick slid back the opening of the secret compartment and pulled out a bottle of amber liquid. "Finish your coffee, everyone. We will drink a toast of the secret ingredient to Miss Ruth."

Paul laughed and said, "Don't you hicks know Prohibition was over a long time ago, before I was born, even."

The diners overlooked his rudeness and held their mugs high. "To Miss Ruth."

Ade put his mug to his mouth and pretended to drink. He couldn't swallow past the lump in his throat. Jake let his napkin fall to the floor and wiped his eyes with it as he bent to pick it up.

"To Miss Ruth," the teen mimicked. He stood and held up his mug. "That's all we've heard about in this town. Miss Ruth this, and Miss Ruth that."

"Paulie, please." His mother, red-faced, looked at the diners, who raised their eyebrows and stared back.

"Son," His father whispered.

"I'm only trying to figure out why everybody thinks that old lady was God's gift to Alaska."

"She was that," Ade said.

"I bet she was just a religious old meddler." The boy tipped his chair back and glowered at the round table.

The men rose as one and stood in front of him. Across the table, Paul's father averted his eyes. His mother glanced at the men, picked up her coffee cup, and set it down again. She chewed on the end of her thumb.

Paul scowled at his parents, then lifted his chin and tried to stare down the men. Ivan, Jake, and Ade stared back. Stormy Durand and Mick joined them. Others at the café moved in their direction, but Stormy motioned them back to their seats.

The retired Chief of Police commanded respect, so they obeyed but kept their eyes on the good-looking but arrogant and disrespectful teen.

"I'll take you on one at the time," Paul fisted his hands, and his veins bulged. "I'm not afraid," but his voice cracked.

Agrafena raced out of the kitchen and pushed her way through the men. Her face blotched from weeping, her eyes swollen, but she smiled and said, "Thank you for visiting Alaska and my café. Enjoy your breakfast. Young man, help me in the kitchen."

Paul sneered, "Look, lady, I'm not the hired help."

Agrafena stood tall, all four feet, nine inches of her, "I said I need help."

It was only then that Paul and the others noticed the large

butcher knife in her hand. Paul's father tried to stand, Jake and Ade pushed down on each of his shoulders. Agrefena caught his eye, wiggled the knife, and winked. Defeated and confused, he shrugged his shoulders and nodded slightly.

"Go." Agrafena stabbed at the boy. Every few steps, he felt the prod of her weapon in his back and whimpered, "Mom, help me."

"Oh, Paulie."

Ade handed the nearly hysterical mother his handkerchief.

Agrafena pushed the boy through the kitchen door, then turned and raised a large wooden spoon above her head. Mick chuckled and held up the butcher knife. No one had noticed the exchange.

Paul's mother continued to wipe her eyes and moan, his father blew out his breath and rubbed his chest. The tourists sat open-mouthed, and everyone listened to the sounds coming from the kitchen. A pot dropped.

"Pick it up."

Pans smashed together.

"You hear me?"

Muffled cries came through the door. "Your mother must feel shame, despair; I don't know."

A yelp, then another. "Do not disgrace your father."

A silence descended, so loud it hurt Paul's parents' ears.

"Poor Paulie." His mother kicked her husband under the table. "Go on," she said and glanced toward the men at the round table.

"Excuse me, gentlemen, but I would like to apologize for my son," the man said.

Ivan slammed his mug down. "No!"

"What?"

"What Ivan means to say is your boy is old enough to apologize for himself."

The man's shoulders slumped, "He never has."

A loud crash came from the kitchen. Agrafena yelled at the boy in several languages.

"What? Speak English."

More yells and bangs.

"Please! Please!"

"My poor Paulie!"

Mick came around the counter and put his hand on the father's shoulder. "Your son has been in the kitchen alone with my mother for over an hour. I figure he's ready."

"Ready for what? To be respectful? Polite? I hope so." Paul's father shook his head and reached for his coffee. He frowned at his wife and put his finger to his lips, but she kept complaining and whining.

"She won't hurt him, will she? He's such a sensitive boy," the mother wrung her hands.

Ade rolled his eyes, Jake choked on his coffee, and Ivan muttered his favorite curse.

"Is good he hurt," Ivan said.

Paul's mother scrunched the handkerchief, "I knew we should've gone to Hawaii. I told you Alaska was too wild for my little boy."

This time the diners joined in the eye rolls. Most had finished their breakfast; none had left. All wanted to see the boy's condition once Agrafena finished with him.

"They come," Ivan said.

Agrafena carried a large platter, and the boy followed head down. He brought small pots of butter and jam. She set the tray on the table and said, "Paul has made this fry bread for you." She motioned to the teen.

"Excuse me, Sirs." He swallowed, bit his lip, and swallowed again, "I, uh, sorry." His voice faded away. He set the jam and butter down, stepped back, and stared at his shoes.

"What are you apologizing for, son?" Ade asked.

The boy's head jerked up, "Well, that is, I..."

"You want to say you're sorry for bad-mouthing Miss Ruth," Agrafena tapped him with her wooden spoon.

"Insulting her," Jake added.

"Slandering someone who has lived here for over three-quarters of a century," Stormy said.

"A friend to natives and whites, alike," someone yelled.

There were nods and affirmations about Miss Ruth throughout the café. The boy's eyes darted about the room. "Yes, that's it," he said.

"You knew nothing about her," Mick said, "She wasn't religious."

"But she knew God better than anyone," Agrafena said.

"She shared her God with anyone interested," Jake added.

"And plenty who weren't," one of the diners at the back complained. Sam caught his eye, and they shared a look.

"Shh," several others cautioned.

"She would have liked you, boy," Ade said.

"And found out everything about you," Jake said.

"Everything?" He glanced at his parents.

Jake slapped him on the back, "Miss Ruth knows everything, that is," he choked and wiped his eyes, "she knew everything about all of us."

"How did she find out?" Paul asked.

"We told her," one of the Alaskans shouted.

"Despite ourselves, we told her," Stormy Durand sighed.

"I'm sorry I didn't meet her. Maybe she'd have made me say stuff," Paul whispered with a slight glance toward his parents.

"That's right. Shake." Jake said.

"Yes, sir." The boy shook hands around the table but faltered when he came to Ivan, who sat with his arms folded across his chest.

"Sir?" Paul extended his hand.

Ivan shook his head, and Agrafena thumped him with her wooden spoon. He peered at her, then stood. "I go to Olga, tell of Miss Ruth."

Paul shoved his outstretched hand in his pocket, backed up, and slumped into his chair. He couldn't look at his parents. Agrafena brought them a platter of fry bread. "Paul made this by himself."

Paul's mother beamed. His father leaned back in his chair and closed his eyes, "I wonder if we could leave him here for a year or two."

He didn't realize he had spoken aloud until Agrafena whispered, "Miss Ruth would say yes, so I say it, also."

Now that the drama had subsided, the tour guide hustled his little group out of the café. Mick poured another round, and the Alaskans quietly talked about Miss Ruth. Sam tried to hear and take notes. He set his mug down, none too gently, and rubbed his burning stomach. Better slow down on the caffeine, Sammy boy.

"What do you know, Sam?" someone called.

"Alaska Air will do an investigation. There'll be a death notice in this week's Sentinel. She'll be buried in the native cemetery in Nome."

"Why, Nome?"

"There don't have facilities there to store the body. They've got to get it in the ground."

Agrafena, who had retired to her haven, now burst through the kitchen door, and her staccato voice issued orders. "We must bring her home. Sam talk to the Fathers, the Episcopalian one, and the Russian; they will make an official request. Jake, call Alaska Air; they can fly her here. We will take up a collection to pay for transport," she choked on the word. "Ade, tell Ollyanna she and I will plan the funeral." Her shoulders slumped, and she sank into the nearest chair.

The diners' sad applause covered her weeping. Paul's father reached for his wallet. After setting a generous donation in front of Jake, he gulped the last of his coffee and hustled his wife and son to catch up with their tour group.

"I must get home before Ollyanna hears about Miss Ruth from someone else," Ade nodded to the others and reached for the money, "You know I'm always the treasurer."

Paul rushed in, dropped a handful of change into Ade's hand, then ran out without a word.

Sam settled in an empty chair at the roundtable, "Well, guys?"

Stormy Durrand shook his head and left, "Later, Sam."

Jake lifted red-rimmed eyes to Sam, "I need to get on the water."

"It's your day off."

"I'll take my skiff out, go to the places Miss Ruth and I fished and clammed." Jake stared through the café's windows. Sitka sound was calm today, peaceful.

Sam watched him shuffle out of the café. Why he's getting to be an old man. In Sam's mind, the men at the round table were like Miss Ruth. Fixtures in this town, in his life. Their mortality shook Sam. Like Jake, he needed to be alone. He spent the day hiking on Mount Verstovia.

Sam had questions, and as always happened when he didn't find the answers quickly, his sleep was disturbed. He dreamt of his father, Miss Ruth, and Katherine Hepburn. Why her?

The next morning Sam woke early, skipped breakfast, and walked the sidewalks of Sitka. He stopped at the sea wall and gazed at the horizon.

"Get it together, Sammy boy," he could hear his father's voice, "there's a story out there. Go and get it."

"I can't find the angle, Dad."

"It's right in front of you, Son."

"The department of vital statistics in Juneau has no record of her birth or a Social Security number, not even a driver's license. She's not listed in the census records or on the payroll of any of the churches or missions. How had she lived?"

Sam turned toward his office, lit his cigar, and watched the people of Sitka go about their business. Most of them or their parents knew Miss Ruth. Sam tossed his match into the gutter and hurried to the Sentinel.

"That's the story, Sammy boy. People gravitated toward Miss Ruth, find out why. What drove her to Alaska, and when? And what the heck did Katherine Hepburn have to do with it?"